KEEPER OF THE King

NIGEL BENNETT

KEEPER OF THE KING

P.N. ELROD

KEEPER OF THE KING

A Baen Books Original

Baen Publishing Enterprises
P.O. Box 1403
Riverdale, NY 10471

ISBN: 0-671-87759-3

Cover art by David Mattingly

First printing, January 1997

Starline is an imprint of Baen Books
Distributed by Simon & Schuster
1230 Avenue of the Americas
New York, NY 10020

Library of Congress Cataloging-in-Publication Data

Bennett, Nigel, 1949–
        Keeper of the king : a novel / by Nigel Bennett and P. N. Elrod.
            p.   cm.
        "A Baen Books original"—T.p. verso.
        ISBN 0-671-87759-3
        I. Elrod, P. N. (Patricia Nead)   II. Title.
PR9199.3.B3782K44   1997   96-36663
813'.54—dc20   CIP

Typeset by Windhaven Press, Auburn, NH
Printed in the United States of America

This book is dedicated to

CERRIDWEN,

Goddess of the Arts, Creativity, and Magic.

For Lou.

(With a special thanks to Bill,
for bringing it all together.)

Chapter One

Orleans, Normandy, the Beginning

An old man, and he was only thirty-five.

His arms felt like lead, his back ached, and sweat streamed into his eyes, creating false tears. He'd fought the whole morning and well into the afternoon and felt every harsh moment, but he couldn't show any weakness. Not to this crowd, not with so much at risk.

A hundred men had started the great tourney and now the numbers were whittled down, as they always were, to the final two. Himself, Richard, third son of Montague, the Duc d'Orleans, seasoned, hard . . . and that damned boy.

Richard had managed by a series of strategies, alliances, and pure skill to defeat some seventeen men. They had been strong, yet he had been stronger or smarter or both. But now, as he faced his final opponent across the shattered turf, now he was tired. More tired than he could remember. Every inch of him was bruised and his helmet, grown heavy from the constant battle, chafed around his neck.

Richard looked across to the galleries of the old Roman-built arena taken over for the contest. They had been nearly empty for most of the morning, but as the day's climax neared, they fluttered with the movement of the onlookers. Even the duke his father had deigned to show his face at last along with his

1

fat firstborn, swollen even now with the expectation of his inheritance. No such joy for the third son of most houses. For him was the bitterness of a few thin gold coins and the polite request to leave. Richard would go, eventually, but on his own terms and with honor. He would make a show for them they'd never forget.

It had been his only real misfortune, Richard d'Orleans, to be third born. Nothing other than that accident of timing could have marred him. He was tall, over six feet, and handsome. He had inherited his mother's eyes, so he was told, of icy blue. He'd never seen her, for she had died bearing him, bleeding her life away as he was rushed to the wet nurse, screaming. He had cried for three days, whether from hunger or from grief no one ever knew. His fair hair came from his father, as did his size and strength. Montague d'Orleans had gained his place brutally over the bodies of many an enemy and not a few friends. His third child came by his streak of cold determination honestly. If you knew the father, you knew the son.

Richard's childhood had been no better and no worse than anyone else's of his station. A wry grin crossed his face as he thought of it. His station! The third son had no station. The first born inherited, the second went to the clergy, and the third? The third simply went, the farther away the better, unless he could earn his keeping.

Thank God for the tourneys. Early in his youth he had shown the unmistakable signs of being a natural warrior. In play as children, his older brothers were easy prey for one of his precocious strength and skill. In the course of his years of training he went on to ever older, larger opponents, and beat them all. Never once had he lost. When his body flagged, his brain saved him. He possessed a tenacity and intelligence that, coupled with his size, made him a natural champion. Pray God these qualities would not forsake him now. So long as he could continue as the favored champion of Orleans, bringing glory and honor to his family name, then his parsimonious father had good reason to allow him to remain home. Anything less and he would be shown the door quickly enough. Neither his father or oldest brother had said as much in so many words, but it was clearly understood. The outcome of this tourney would decide many things for them all for some time to come.

Richard d'Orleans looked to his callow opponent, studying him. The youth could have been no more than sixteen, the age of a squire, but was tall, muscled beyond his years, and heavy-boned in broken and ill-fitting mail. His breathing was labored as he leaned for a brief moment of respite on his sword. *A bastard,* thought Richard, *and all the more dangerous for that. Longing for honor. Longing to make a name.*

Because of his youth, he shouldn't have been allowed in the tourney, though there were always exceptions. If the boy had had the good luck to capture a noble of some rank on the battlefield, rather than submit himself to be ransomed by an inferior, the noble would have knighted his captor on the spot, saving his name from the humiliation. Richard didn't know or really care about this adversary's past, his own future was all that mattered. The boy was nothing more than an obstacle to overcome.

The trumpets sounded their strident calls. The defeated had been carried from the field, either to be bandaged or buried, depending on their luck. Now it was the time of champions. The crowd would be silent, awed by strength and savagery, by the heat and the rush of blood and hope, until, as one of the champions fell, a great roar would go up in exultation of the victor. Richard stood straight as silence descended, facing his quarry, quiet as a statue. In past contests, so simple a ploy had often been enough to unman even the boldest fighter. Soon he would find out if this stripling was in that number.

The herald called their names out to the crowd, shouting what was already known, that the victor of this single combat would win not only the tourney purse, but all the arms and armor of the loser. Richard had little use for the boy's shoddy equipment, but he wanted—needed—that purse of gold and all the important honors that went with it. Then would he have the freedom he craved, to make the *choice* to stay in his father's court or to move on to serve in another, better house.

Despite his secure position as the firstborn with a son of his own to carry on the title, his oldest brother had made no secret of his jealousy for Richard's abilities. The teasing rivalry they'd once shared as children had grown spiteful over the years, at least on his brother's part. All too aware of his dependence on the good will of their father, Richard had grimly done his Christian duty and turned the other cheek to keep peace in the house, but it was damned difficult at times. More and more often his whispered confessions to the priests included his great temptation to pound Dear Brother to a jelly. Even after a day such as this he could do so without much effort, and oh, but didn't Dear Brother know *that* well enough? The priests, of course, cautioned him against so grave a sin, and he reverently submitted to the penance without a murmur. No one could accuse him of disdaining the knightly virtues.

But enough of that. Memories of the past and fair

dreams for the future could wait. All thought, all attention must be fixed upon what was to come. That purse of gold wasn't yet tied to his belt; he had to first earn it. This new opponent had unquestionably fought well, defeating more than a dozen veteran fighters to get this far; it would be foolish to underestimate him just because he was a boy.

I was that young once, that desperate to prove myself. Why should he be any different?

Richard continued to hold still, letting his cold gaze pound against the boy's scratched and dented helmet. He was distant enough to not be able to see the boy's eyes, but still . . . *Can you feel* that, *young pup?*

The boy held still in turn, perhaps wise to Richard's game and attempting to play as well. The stillness seemed to spread out from them, encompassing the field, the crowd, until the least murmur was stifled to silence. For the tiniest moment Richard thought he could hear their very breath in their throats.

Then in the stands, the kerchief fell. Battle was joined.

Those who watched would tell later that this was the greatest struggle they had ever witnessed. It was a struggle between man and boy, between experience and youth, confidence and desperation.

At first, little happened. The two adversaries circled each other warily, searching for weakness or fear. Then quick as lightning, they fell to it. For over an hour, the clanging of sword on shield, of metal against metal rang out across the damp Normandy countryside. For over an hour, it was the only sound to be heard, as if not merely this crowd of watchers but the whole world held its breath. No bird sang, no animal called, no infant cried. All was rapt attention, centered on the contest.

Initially, the young boy clearly had the upper hand.

He'd used his moment of respite well, and was full of energy and spirit. He attacked with all the confidence of being sixteen and immortal. His sword arced through the air time and again, driving Richard back. It looked to all that the older man had finally, brutally met his match.

Richard, however, felt only serenity in his soul. He'd faced this many times before. Indeed, it was often a tactic of his to allow a brash opponent the upper hand in the early going to tire him out. Then he would come on full strength and finish off the unfortunate. He'd convinced himself that this was the case now, and sure enough, the boy was slowing, and the force behind his wild blows had faded. Richard chose to forget the fact that he had been truly shocked by the sheer ferocity of the boy's initial rush.

Now it was his turn. He hefted his great sword and swung it into smooth, practiced motion, this time for attack, not defense. The boy staggered well back under the onslaught, and for the first time, a collective murmur arose from the crowd. Richard basked in their gift of approval, all but feasted on it in the brief pause as the boy fought to recover himself. Time now to undermine his confidence while he was yet vulnerable.

"I will have all you possess, all you desire. You are mine, boy."

"Not yet, I'm not," the younger man gasped. "I will *not* be beaten by an old man such as you."

The words stung Richard. Unexpected, that, but easily returned. "Age, my lovely youth, is in the eye of the beholder." And he struck again, down once to jar, then hard to the side and up, driving the boy's sword from his grasp to send it flying through the air, a flash of silver in the fading sunlight.

It was nearly over. An unarmed boy against

Orleans's greatest champion —all that remained to be decided was how much injury to give before Richard chose to stop. He should cripple the jumped-up bastard, for no champion wanted such a dangerous opponent to ever challenge him again. But as he prepared to deliver the blow the boy suddenly charged him, fast as the wind, faster than he could bring his sword around, arms wide to wrestle him to the ground. An old trick, was his fleeting thought, tried often and doomed to fail.

The boy crashed against him with a grunt, the shock of impact passing hard through his mail and padding beneath. More bruises for later. He felt burly arms wrapping around his waist, trying to lift him, to topple him. He twisted to break the boy's hold. Just for an instant he saw their long shadows black against the churned, blood-soaked grass, saw their shapeless forms struggling, striving, one against the other. He lifted his sword high, the blade catching the lowering sun behind him. Sparks of light reflected off its polished surface, blinding him, but he didn't need to see to accurately bring the thick pommel down on the back of the boy's neck just below his helmet. It wouldn't kill, but it would give Richard the moment he needed to tear free and finish the job. No mercy for this one, not after this humiliating trick. He could hear the hooting from the galleries already.

Just as he'd raised his arm high enough, the inexplicable happened. Not that he had time to work out exactly what caused it, all he understood was that an invisible hand seemed to seize the sword from his grip and send it flying through the air.

"Slipped away from him, by St. George!" someone crowed.

Thunderstruck, Richard's mind howled a silent

denial at this even as he tried to recover from the setback. Not slipped! He *knew* better. Something had . . . had *taken* it, plucked it right away from him when he needed it most.

Then his feet left the damp grass, he lost all purchase, all balance, and the world spun crazily beyond the confines of his helm. The earth came up and slammed him in the back, then another weight threw itself upon his laboring chest. He was down with the boy on top of him.

Even now, with his surprise about the sword necessarily fading against changing circumstance, he wasn't worried. He'd been in this situation more than a few times before, wrestling in the mud before pinning his opponent and rising first to claim victory. But this time, he found it more difficult. The youth was heavy and fighting with all the ferocious recklessness of one who truly needed the victory. He wrested out of Richard's grasp, quickly pushing himself to his knees. Richard clawed at his legs to drag him back, but the boy pulled out his dagger and slashed down at the older man's hand, driving the thin blade between the protective rings of his mail glove like a hammer. Richard roared with equal parts of pain and outrage. Blood spurted, mingling with the mud as the boy yanked the blade free then twisted Richard's helmet off. The sudden air was freezing against his sweat-soaked face and hair. Richard brought a now clumsy arm up and over, barely managing to block the next fall of the knife. He tried to strike the boy's face, but that poor fit of a helmet was sufficient protection. Not so for Richard. The boy's own mailed fist connected like the club it was against the side of Richard's now vulnerable skull. The sun whirled and flamed behind his eyes leaving behind a shuddering darkness.

The next thing he felt was a hand roughly grab his

hair, pulling his head back, exposing his throat. For an awful, bottomless second he was utterly certain of his death. His time had finally come. All the victories of the years past meant nothing. He was lost. Everything he had was lost.

The boy's leering face swam into view. *"Yield, old man!"*

His heaving breath stank, and the sweat dripped from his forehead onto Richard's own streaming face. He pressed the dagger hard against Richard's throat, cutting him. A thick trickle of blood slid hot over his cold skin.

"Your life, your possessions are mine no matter what. Yield to me and I will spare you. *Old man.*"

He spat the words out, and Richard knew he had no choice. He became aware of the clamoring crowd, the blaring trumpets, the screams, the laughter.

"I yield."

The words came with no effort. Those words that he had fought so hard over the years never to have to say. They simply fell from his lips. Contemptuous, the boy released him and threw his arms skyward in victory and staggered like a drunk away to the welcoming shouts of his supporters.

Richard's strength was quite gone. He could only lie in the grass and reddened mud, staring at an empty sky. His lungs labored painfully, his heart pounded far too hard and fast for comfort, but gradually both eased their breakneck pace, allowing him the single clear realization that he'd finally met defeat.

So it had happened at last, and strangely, very strangely, he felt free, released.

But God's mercy, how he *hurt*.

Dusk fell as Richard squatted alone in his tent by the

lake. His servants weren't there when he'd returned from the field, nor had he expected to see them after his failure. They were, after all, attached to his father's household, not to him. However, the boy's new page and squire, grinning like fools, had most timely come to remove everything. His good chain mail, every trapping and weapon that he'd used in the tourney, all his best possessions were forfeit. Even his great broadsword, his soul as a fighter, disappeared, taken from him as he had taken it from his first victim. The spoils ever went to the victor in this kind of contest. It was a lesson Richard had learned long ago and benefited well from. Now, as though a great wheel had turned, it was his time to suffer.

"Our master will have your horse in the morning. He has no need of it tonight. Do not try to remove it," the squire had sniffed as he went, "or he will surely remove your head."

Richard said nothing. His left hand hurt like the devil. When he'd removed his mail glove to give to the page, his severed ring finger had fallen right out to the beaten earth. The smirking child doubled over, whooping with laughter at Richard's surprise. The squire bent and picked up the finger to offer it back with mocking politeness. Richard stared at him until the youth shrugged, tossing it onto the old blanket that served as a bed. The two of them finally finished their scavenging and hurried away in the growing darkness, laden with their master's booty, anxious to deliver it and pass along their tale. They'd left him the tent, too tattered to bother claiming, his clothing, a bed, such as it was, and an oil lamp. After fourteen years of service to his father's house, this was all he had left, but he'd be damned before he begged for aught else.

And now Richard squatted by the lamp's feeble light looking at the lifeless bit of flesh that had once been a part of him. The blood was all gone from it; it felt absurdly light and small.

What to do, he thought, *what to do?* The idea of taking his horse and riding like the wind for the coast and a ship to Britain or even Wales had, indeed, crossed his mind, but he dismissed it. Bad enough that he'd lost; he would not run away like a beaten dog. No honor in that, more's the pity.

Ah, yes. Pity. The most favorable response he could anticipate for his defeat . . . and the least tolerable to his temperament. God's death, but it was easy enough to pity others, but for himself—better to be scorned as the defeated champion than to suffer charitable sympathy. The other response would certainly be contempt—especially from Father and Dear Brother—for what had happened.

And what *had* happened? How could he have lost his sword so easily, so damned carelessly? At the time he'd have sworn on the church altar that it had been solidly *plucked* away, and so it still seemed to him now, but that was ridiculous. It had to be. No one had been close enough to them to . . .

Had the young bastard had magical help? Had someone been working witchery in his favor? Richard was aware of such things, but in all his long years of fighting had yet to see any for himself. No, that couldn't be it. That very morning he'd made his confession with all the others who were to fight, been absolved, prayed at mass, taken Communion, and worn his blessed cross all through the tourney. Surely no sorcery, no matter how strong, could have touched him. No, despite his strong impression of the incident, he must have mistaken things, somehow muddled them. The deed was done, anyway, over forever and the bleak consequences from the resulting loss were only just beginning to take root in his weary heart.

What to do?

He knew the fate of men in similar straits, having seen it often enough. He'd always thought them pathetic and somehow deserving of their ignominy, that they must have brought it upon themselves in some manner. He was well on the way to revising that belief, for it looked to be his future, too, wandering from court to court in hope that some lord would decide he was worth the keeping. If lucky, Richard might attach himself to a wealthy liege and train other men to fight. If not, then dead on a muddy road because . . . because he was an old man now and an easy kill. The bastard had been all too right.

Old man.

He could still hear the boy's taunt in his mind, still feel the surprising pain of it. Thirty-five and an old man, at least as a fighter. News of this would spread far and wide, of how the great champion of Orleans was defeated by . . . what court would even have him after this?

Now who is raining pity upon you?

He looked up, sure someone had spoken aloud to him, but the tent was empty. He listened, hearing nothing except the distant noise of the revelers starting their celebrations, a feast he had no stomach to endure. The voice had been a fancy only. Perhaps he was getting a fever from the battering he'd taken, or from the lost finger. That would make a perfect end to the worst day of his life.

What to do?

Of course, if he really got desperate he could enter into God's service. It would mean dawn to dusk toil, broken by an endless series of prayers and masses, but he was used to heavy work and at least he'd be fed regularly. Without money he could never hope to rise very far in the church hierarchy, nor did he have influence to make up for the lack. His second-born brother, who had taken orders, bore as little love for him as the firstborn, scorning him for his success in the sinful vanity of tournaments. Perhaps if his younger sibling was sufficiently repentant might he be persuaded to have a change of heart.

But no, the cloistered walls of an abbey or monastery were not for Richard, not with his appetite for life's fleshy joys. For once, his most recent confession had had nothing to do with his oldest brother's slights and everything to do with the comely wench whose company Richard had so thoroughly enjoyed the night before. He'd gotten a weary penance for that sport, but she'd been worth it. Where was she? Helping to celebrate the new champion's victory no doubt. Not that he could afford her favors now. Sweet Jesu, but he didn't even have enough money to get decently drunk.

It was an effort to drag his mind back to the unhappy cares of the moment, but back it came, encouraged by a legion of aches. A full day of hard combat was difficult enough to bear when victory came at the end of it. Now with the bitter gall of defeat, the pain of his body was almost unbearable.

You stink, Richard, he thought to himself. *Go and bathe. Then have your wounds treated. Off to the good sisters with you.*

It was his custom after any trial of arms to visit the Priory of Our Lady the Virgin, give generously to the sisters, and take advantage of their skills in healing if he needed it. Perhaps tonight they would remember his past generosities and treat him for nothing. He hoped so, for he was in grievous need of their help. His left hand throbbed as he tore a strip from the blanket and wrapped it clumsily over the still seeping wound. He'd have to find some hot

wax to cauterize it, then have it properly seen to; unless
carefully treated he could lose his whole arm to rot,
perhaps even die from it.

There's a comforting thought.

With an immense effort of body and will, he slowly
stood and turned to leave, every separate stiffening
muscle shrieking protest at the movement. It was
then that he saw her, heard her soft voice drifting
to him across the dim tent like a gentle summer
breeze tousling the heads of wheat in a field.

"Bathing is an excellent idea, but if the good
sisters possess any sense, they will have nothing to
do with you."

She stood just in the doorway of his tent, and
for the first of many, many times, the Lady Sabra
took his breath away. He wasn't sure if she had
spoken the words he'd heard, for he hadn't seen her
lips move. Certainly he didn't know what to say in
reply, particularly since she had commented upon his
very thoughts. He stood like a dumbstruck fool for
what seemed an age, drinking her in with his eyes
like a pilgrim at the feet of a saint's statue. Such
was the feeling her presence inspired in him, as
though he were in church, but instead of a bit of
painted wood or stone this statue was alive, regarding
him with ancient eyes, eyes that had seen all and
could forgive anything. For an instant he wanted to
fall to his knees before their terrifying beauty.

"Lady, you mistake your place," he whispered,
finally mastering himself enough to speak. "If you
have lost your way . . ."

"I am not lost." Her voice was as cool and smooth
as the lake water, and she continued with her steady
regard of him. Smiling.

No lady of any rank—and her clothing proclaimed
her to be very high and wealthy, indeed—would have

been alone as she seemed to be, but here she stood, looking at him as though nothing at all was amiss. He found it difficult to believe, but perhaps this angelic beauty was a camp follower dressing well beyond her station. Only one of that number would travel about after dark with no escort and boldly come to a man's tent.

"You have no business here. I have nothing for you . . ." There, an inoffensive dismissal, an easy way for her to take her leave no matter who she might be.

"You are half correct," she said. "You have nothing for me, good Lord Richard, but I do have business here." And she smiled that devastating smile again.

What kind of creature is she? he wondered. She was built like a girl, small, tiny compared to him, and yet there was a strange wisdom in her face. Her eyes were of the darkest brown, so dark that the black center was indistinguishable. Her skin was clear and milky white, and her ready smile showed strong, white, even teeth. But there was something else about her that he could not readily describe. She was confident, yes, and there was royalty in her bearing for sure, and at the same time, something disturbing. Then it came to him. It was a sense of *power* so vast and great that for an instant the hairs on the back of his neck began to rise, and he felt an almost overwhelming urge to run away as far and as fast as he could.

"I am the Lady Sabra. You may have heard of me."

He tried his memory, but so unusual a name as hers meant nothing to him, and had he ever met her before he'd certainly have remembered. Had she been in the galleries? No, for he'd have surely noticed her there sparkling like a jewel amid the gold.

"No, Lady Sabra, I have not. Forgive me." How

abashed he felt, like an inexperienced lad with his first
woman.

"It does not matter."

"You are kind." Why was she here, a lady of her
rank? What could she want with him? A base idea
crossed his mind, one of many possibilities, but he
was reluctant to explore it too far. He'd learned long
ago that the pursuit of carnal pleasures with noble-
women was often of far greater danger than any
battlefield. Best to find out her business, then get rid
of her as fast as politeness allowed.

"I would ask you to sit, but as you can see, there
is nothing to sit on." He gestured with his right hand,
holding his left close to his body.

"I do not need to sit." She continued to smile at him
as she spoke, her gaze holding briefly on his injured
hand before shifting back to his face; an unspoken
challenge flashed from her remarkable eyes. "I watched
you today at the tourney. You did well . . . for an old
man."

God's mercy, but he did not need this now, no
matter how beautiful she was. His lips tightened in
an effort not to grimace. "I thank you, lady, your
compliment is appreciated, though the 'old' is
irksome. I have done better many times in the past.
Perhaps Your Ladyship should have seen me then."
There, he'd almost sounded civil, even to his own
ears.

"I saw all that I needed to see today," she said
evenly. Her gaze now swept over him from top to
bottom, obviously judging, assessing, noting everything. He was more than aware of his ragged appearance, the muddy filth, blood and bruises. It was of
no matter to him, if she wanted to talk to a gaudy
peacock there were plenty to choose from in Father's
court. "I saw," she continued, "a boy defeat a man.

I saw a man humbled before a great throng. I saw youth bring pride low."

God's death, but he did *not* need this. Had a man voiced such things to him Richard would have given in to temper and challenged him on the spot. Instead, for the sake of her sex he must endure her insults. *But she speaks the truth, so how is that an insult?* Still, his jaw ached for holding back a sharp retort to her. A woman such as she would surely have a champion. However tempting it was, he didn't want to offend her and get into another fight. At least not for a day or two. He took a deep, steadying breath before replying. "Indeed, lady. Forgive me, but I am not at my best, and truly do not need to be reminded of my defeat. Perhaps you should leave and allow an 'old man'" —despite his wish for control his anger and voice rose as he spoke— "to be alone with the ends of his overweening pride, and to treat his hurts as best he can."

"Forgive me Lord Richard." Her demeanor abruptly softened and she seemed truly repentant. "I did not mean to add to your misery. I've not come here to gloat."

How could she have known he was thinking that?

"I simply tell as I see. There is no judgment there. In truth, that boy will gain little from his victory. I see a short life for him . . ."

She stopped, as if uncertain whether to go on, then stepped toward him and looked up earnestly into his eyes.

"*You* are all my concern, Richard of Orleans." She cocked her head to one side, for all the world, like a curious bird. "What will you do now?"

His temper melted away. First he wanted to forgive her, then he wanted to be angry all over again for plying him with the one question for which he had no answer. A few quick meaningless responses crossed his mind, but before that searching gaze, that gloriously beautiful gaze, he could only confess the unhappy truth.

"I do not know. I cannot stay here. I was only tolerated by my father because I was, it seemed, invincible. Now that there is a new champion they've no place for me." *Why am I telling her this?* he thought as the words spilled from him. "I will move on. There is always need for those who train others." He felt a great sadness creeping over him. "Other than that, I do not know. . . ."

And he could not go on. Had he tried, his voice would have cracked and all the tears of his life, of his unspoken hurts, his loneliness, would have run uncontrollably down his bruised cheeks and betrayed his manhood, reducing him to being that little boy who had cried alone in the hayloft, longing for a mother's gentle caress that would never come.

She reached up her hand and placed it against his cheek. Her pale skin was cool and soft and delicately scented. His heart leaped so hard he felt an instant of dizziness from her touch.

"You will never be alone again, this much I promise," she told him with complete certainty. "Come to my pavilion tonight and we will talk further." She moved away toward the door. "You will find it easily. It is nearest your father's castle wall, on the west side. And Lord Richard . . . ?" She arched one eyebrow.

"My lady?"

"Bathe first." And as silently as she had come, she was gone.

"Yes, my lady," he said to the darkness.

For a long time Richard stood looking at the opening of his tent, trying to decide what to do. He

concluded that it was as before when the boy held
the knife to his throat: he had no real choice. He
needed work, a station to call his own, something
honorable to do, and she'd offered to help him. But
worldly practicalities aside, she was the most unsettling woman he'd ever encountered, bringing forth
a multitude of feelings and reactions from him such
as he'd never before experienced. His instincts
screamed warnings to his mind that she was uncanny,
and therefore dangerous, but his heart quietly assured
him that he of all people would suffer no harm from
her. With the back of his hand he touched again where
her fingers had brushed his face. Had she said and
done nothing else, that gesture alone would have sent
him hurtling after her, unable to resist her invitation.

Then he lowered his hand, grunted, and headed out
to the lake. She was right. He did stink.

The water was freezing cold. His open wounds
stung like wasps—especially his hand—his bruises
were stiffening and like to remain so for days, but
at least he was clean. As he stood naked at the edge
of the shore, drying himself with handfuls of sweet-
smelling grasses, he idly perused his body. For an
old man he was yet well muscled and as hard as iron.
There were scars aplenty, but none so bad as to be
ugly, except maybe for the one on his shoulder from
the sword blow that nearly took his arm a few years
ago. The sisters had done well with their healing on
that one. Not that his looks mattered. If Sabra had
an interest in him, it would not be for the unblemished perfection of his hide. He was a soldier, not
a reciter of poetry.

He pulled on his tunic and tied up his hose, slipped
his feet into soft boots, and looped a belt loosely
round his waist. These and a few other clothes were

about all that he had left. Perhaps he could find a rich wife somewhere, a girl with a wealthy father anxious to have a share in the d'Orleans name even if it meant a penniless son-in-law. Oh, but did he want to be saddled with *that* kind of trouble? He couldn't see himself ever getting quite that desperate, but it had happened to others. He shuddered at their lot as he walked from the lake.

The full moon had risen slowly, sluggishly above the trees and now hung heavy in the topmost branches like a huge yellow-gold ball. He could see his breath on the air in the chill of a late spring frost as he worked his way back toward the castle and the town. How he loved this time of year. He had ever since he was a boy. The new leaves, the damp smell of fresh-turned earth, and the wood smoke never failed to excite him. It was a time of breeding and of promise, trees heavy with blossom as the fallow deer was heavy with her fawn. It was also, it seemed to him, a time of magic and the unending mystery of life. As he looked past the trees, he saw the light of bonfires springing up far away across the fields, and the sounds of music and laughter carried to him on the gentle wind. Despite everything, all the calamities of the day, even despite himself and his failure, he smiled. Life could yet be good.

Soon the sounds of the castle came to him, and as he approached he could see busy servants running, shouting orders, making sure that all went well at his father's celebration banquet. A banquet he had not been invited to, but that was only to be expected. He purposely avoided the light from the flaming torches, and made his way around to the west face of the castle. Here, all was much quieter, for here the great west wall stood in defiance of all who might try to force entry, windowless, doorless, solid. He strained his eyes into the darkness, and for a moment was sure he'd been cruelly duped, for he could see no tent, no lights to signify habitation. He turned, about to leave in disgust, when a voice disturbed the quiet.

"You are in the right place, Lord Richard. Come, my lady awaits."

He turned again to the darkness, and became aware of a darker shape within it. A servant, no doubt. And sure enough, beyond the beckoning arm of the servant, there was the pavilion, torches lit, flags stirring in the gentle evening breeze.

The hair on the back of his neck rose again.

Magic? he thought, hesitating, feeling the cold air keen upon his flesh.

"Be so good as to follow me, Lord Richard," the man patiently requested.

There was something strange about this servant as well. Something about his voice, though for the life of him, Richard couldn't immediately fathom what it might be. It was neither high nor low, but of a disturbing middle tone, like that of a boy. Yet Richard was sure that this was no boy. Indeed, as they came into the light cast from one of the torches set in the ground near the front of the pavilion, he could see that the man was old, fat, and shiny-faced. Then it came to him: the man was no man at all, but a eunuch. Richard had once seen a dozen younger versions of such singing to God's glory in a church. He'd also seen less fortunate ones working in some of the larger brothels of towns he'd visited.

"My lady waits within," said the eunuch, gesturing politely.

Richard saw the pavilion door, invitingly open.

"I thank you . . ." and his voice trailed off, for the servant was nowhere to be seen. The man moved swiftly for one so large, and quietly. Richard swallowed his confusion, pushed away a last wave of trepidation, and went through the open door.

Even in the dim candlelight, he could see the luxury of the pavilion. A great pile of cushions lay atop a thick rug directly before him. A table stood to one side, laden with food, and on a smaller table near the cushions stood a gold pitcher of wine and jewel-encrusted goblets, also of gold. Brass braziers with smoldering charcoal warmed the air. This was a lady of some very high station, indeed. From somewhere he could hear muted music, the strains of a viol as sweet and plaintive as he had ever enjoyed. He stood waiting for some time, then crossed to the smaller table and poured himself some wine. It had a fine taste—deep red and full-bodied. He savored it and the rush of warmth it brought to his empty belly.

"I hope that it's to your liking, Lord Richard."

Her voice was as soft and sweet as it had been before. He turned, and there stood the Lady Sabra, breathtaking again in a gown of white with gold needlework, her long chestnut hair loose about her shoulders. Surrounded by candles, it seemed to Richard that she shone out like a beacon of hope for him in his misfortune. That feeling of reverence stole over him again and he stood rooted, goblet halfway to his mouth, unable to speak or move.

"My lady," he finally managed to say by way of an inadequate greeting. He fell to one knee, head bowed, suddenly and utterly certain that he was in the presence of *something* more beautiful and powerful than any person, place, or thing he had ever known. The silence was broken only by the rustling of her dress as she moved toward him. Then he became aware of her outstretched hand. It was so small, so delicate, that it almost vanished within his as he took it to press to his mouth. Her scent drifted to him, sweeter than any bloom.

"Rise, Lord Richard. Come, sit with me, for there is much to talk about."

He felt her hand pulling him upright and was surprised at the strength in one so small. Then she was sitting amid the cushions and beckoning him to join her, close by her side.

He hesitated. "My lady, it is not my place. I mistook you before. I did not know you to be one of such rank. Forgive me, but I have no right here."

"My good Lord Richard, I have chosen you to be here. That gives you the right. Do not question my decision, for like it or no, I will have my way."

He could see that behind her amused demeanor she would brook no argument, and it would be futile to try, not to mention bad-mannered. He obediently sat at her side, uncomfortable despite the soft cushions. He felt he should still be on his knees before her.

Her skin was clear and white and contrasted starkly with her hair and eyes. He hardly dared to look on her, lest he stare. Instead he tried to keep his gaze moving, taking in more details of her belongings, but not too much of that, either. He knew about the trappings of wealth, had lived with them all his life, but nothing like this. He abruptly felt like a swineherd in a palace.

What could she possibly want of me? She obviously had so much and he had nothing. Now. He was champion no more.

"You wonder why I asked you to come here," she said suddenly.

Now he could permit himself to look at her, for as long as he liked, for as long as she spoke to him. "How did you know?"

"I know many things. I have the Gift, as you may have guessed."

At once, Richard was all attention. He'd heard of such women before, women with the Gift of Sight: an uncanny, unholy ability, and linked to the Old Ways. His upbringing in the Church had taught him well the danger of the old magics. The priests who had tutored him told ghastly tales of unclean worship and bloody human sacrifice. He did not understand such things, nor ever wanted to, and so they frightened him, though he would never admit as much aloud. Finally comprehending the source of his earlier fears, he made to rise.

But she caught his hand, arresting him in midmovement. Her dark gaze held him as firmly as an iron chain. "Do not leave, Richard. Neither I nor she whom I worship will harm you. You should beware of believing all things that some of those of the Church would tell you of us. No one god monopolizes all the truth of the world." She drew him back to sit by her again. "All holy ones possess a portion of it. It's only their mortal servants who presume so much for them."

He had no reply to that, having once heard it from a past tutor. The man had cautiously whispered it, fearful of being overheard by his more dogmatic brothers. It gave Richard the reassurance he needed to stay a little longer with her. Her talk of the Old Ways was perilous, but was mere talk all the same. If she tried any of the old magic on him he knew his own faith and the blessed cross he wore would protect him, though he could not imagine what she might do to him or why.

Sabra placed her hand lightly upon his injury and felt the rough bandages covering his wound. "A mean blow. And it hurts still."

"Indeed it does, my lady," he said, glad for the change of subject.

"I can make you whole again, restore it."

His face fell, and he pulled his arm back. "The wound will heal, God willing, but my finger is lost, lady, nothing can restore it."

She smiled. "That, we will see."

She's so sure of herself. Why?

Sabra stood and took the goblet that he had by now drained and went to the small table to refill it. This time she poured a clear, straw-colored draught from a different pitcher. "You'll find this will give ease to the pains of your body."

Mead, he thought, carefully sniffing it before taking the smallest of sips. It tasted of herbs and other elusive flavorings. The good sisters at the abbey had given him similar refreshment for past ills; this could be little different. More warmth flushed through him when he drank the rest, leaving him lightheaded. *Drink without food—most unwise, Richard.*

The Gift must have served her again. Without a word, she went to the large table and brought back a tray laden with a fresh-baked loaf, a thick round of cheese, and several perfectly roasted squabs glistening with a glaze of honey.

"Please do not disappoint my cook," she instructed him. She spoke most somberly, but with her head tilted to one side and a light of mischief in her eyes.

He felt a faint twinge of laughter trying to emerge in response, but was yet uncertain of her or of himself, so all he presented in return was a brief, shy smile. "Won't you have a share as well?" he asked.

"Later. Take your fill. After the day you've had you must be quite starved."

Indeed. The needs of his body had roared to full life at the sight of such provender, and he wasted no more time in satisfying the demands of a great hunger. She said nothing else until he'd finished. Only then did he think it strange that she should not speak the whole time. It hadn't been an uneasy silence, at least not for him, which—given the oddity of his situation—was in itself strange. Perhaps there'd been more in the mead than simple healing herbs. Having reminded himself of it, he realized he was feeling much improved physically. Even the weary throbbing of his hand had lessened. If she was weaving a magical spell around him, then it was a benevolent one.

Through the open door, the fires that he had noticed earlier seemed to have become more numerous and brighter. Sabra, too, noticed them and stood by the door, looking, listening.

"Come here, Lord Richard."

He stood and crossed to her, standing as close as he dared, nearly touching her. She was so small her head barely reached his shoulder. That flower-sweet scent of hers was in her very hair.

"Do you know what day this is?" she asked.

"I know it is a day of defeat and bitterness, but other than that I have no idea."

"This is the feast of Beltane. Yonder are the Beltane fires. The people who light them are followers of the Old Way. They are my followers. They worship the Goddess as you worship your God."

She unnerved him with her simple stating of such dangerous things. "I know nothing of these matters, lady." He wanted to leave. "If my lady would permit . . ."

"Your lady does not permit. You will leave when I tell you and no sooner. Do you understand?"

He could feel the palpable power coming from her as strongly as though it had been a hand gripping his throat. He had no option, this he knew, and strangely the knowledge did not frighten him. Not too very much.

"I understand."

"Stand by me and I will tell you of Beltane and then you will understand all and know no fear."

God, he hoped so. As quick and as harsh as it had come, the power faded. No, that wasn't right . . . she'd pulled it into herself. It was held in check. For how long? Until he displeased her and she let it free once again, only this time to crush him? She could do so, could do so without even moving. His heart hammered at that possibility, but he stood by her to look outside, their faces lit by the dancing flames of the fires, and the Lady Sabra spoke.

"Beltane is the holiest of days. It is the day of creation. It is the day on which the Goddess, through her priestesses, takes a man to her so as to create life. Only the Goddess can do that, Richard. Only the Earth can create new life. No man can create in that way. Most men only destroy. Watch the animals, Richard, their behavior tells us all. Only when the hind is ready can the stag go to her to breed, and only the stag that she chooses will be allowed. That is the natural way. Whenever a new worship perverts that natural order, chaos follows. Men fight wars, slaughter the innocents, destroy the sacred places of the Earth in the name of their gods, when it has ever really been because of their own selfishness. Even your holy Jesus was killed by such men. Ah, his poor mother."

Sabra turned to Richard now, again unnervingly close to him, and as she looked up into his eyes he saw tears like clear gems upon her face and felt a great rush of pity for her. Perhaps he was in too much haste to condemn her beliefs, especially when she had spoken with unfeigned sorrow for his own Lord and His mother. Except for that one tutor he'd had, the priests had never been as charitable in their views of the Old Ways. Without thinking, Richard raised his uninjured hand to brush at her tears.

"Please do not weep, lady."

"Yes, Richard, I must weep. I weep for the Earth that it is destroyed by men. I weep for the womb that is ravaged by men. I weep for our loss."

She took his hand in hers.

"Once the whole world was of the Old Way. The whole world believed in the power and goodness of the Goddess, and now all that remains intact of it is that ancient isle known as Avalon."

Avalon. The name had ever and only been a tale recited by poets to speed the hours of a winter night. How could she possibly be from a place that had no real existence?

"The world is wider than you can ever dream, Richard, and full with many wondrous things. What is legend in one place is the truth of life in another."

The Gift again, hearing my thoughts.

"Open your mind to it; your heart already understands or you would not be here."

"It is no easy thing you ask of me."

"Yet you are capable. You have but to listen without judgment."

A small enough request. "I shall try."

When he said this such a light sparked in her eyes as to make his heart leap. He'd stay here all night and listen if she but looked at him like that again.

She'd held his hand this whole time, but now released it, turning slightly to better face him. "Know then, Richard, that I am one of the nine sisters of Avalon, a priestess of the Goddess, though not the highest. I have been sent from my home on a quest. *You* are the end of that quest, I feel it as strongly as anything I have ever felt. I have been searching and know now that you have been my goal. Listen to me well, for Avalon is in danger."

"In what way?"

"Hundreds of years past the ways of goodness and the earth were trampled by the Romans. There was no creation in them, Richard. They had their gods and goddesses, but the great Goddess was nowhere in their eyes or their souls. They sought to convert by force. They destroyed the sacred groves, defiled our altars, burned the priestesses and priests, deprived the people of the wisdom of the way, plundered, and took captives away as slaves."

"That was long ago," he said.

"Not so long," she whispered. "Not long at all. A mere moment of time as the stars make their wheel in the sky."

She returned to the cushioned floor. He let fall the curtained door of the pavilion and unbidden sat by her side. He sat closer now, his unease lessened, feeling somehow a part of her, at one with her and her grief for things long perished.

"There is a king in Britain now who is blessed by Avalon," she said, "one who is sworn to protect Avalon and the Old Way. He is to be the bridge between the old and the new, but he is threatened every day by the forces of chaos. He must be protected. You are the chosen protector. You are to be the keeper of the king."

She was so certain, so damnably certain, and doomed to disappointment. After some thought on the best way to tell her Richard at last spoke. "My lady, you saw today that I am champion no more. I would be no great protector for your king. I am very sensible of the honor that you propose me, yet I know that I cannot fulfill it."

"Not as you are, good Richard, but if you will allow, you will not be as you are. I have gifts, powers to give you that will make you the greatest champion that the world has ever known. I could force you to accept, yet I will not. You must make your choice freely."

Choices. Gifts and powers. Of course she could promise much to him, since such promises were little more than air. But that certainty of hers—he'd seen its like before on the faces of believers in church— that certainty was enough to make him pause.

"What if I refuse?"

"If you choose to say no, all will be the same. Your life as it is will be yours to live out as you wish."

As I wish. I did not wish for the day to have ended in defeat.

"If you choose to say yes, all will be beyond your dreams."

"That could be perilous."

"Indeed it could, but you've just been wise enough to see it. The Goddess has chosen well. Will you choose her?"

"To worship?"

"To serve as I serve. Anything more is a matter for your own heart to decide."

Richard stood and crossed to the food-laden table, needing time to think. Idly, he picked up some fine exotic fruit, the like of which he had never seen before. Its taste was strange, but wholesome. Was its presence an example of her power, perhaps? Or was he enspelled by her already and only imagining he had a choice? He turned back to the Lady Sabra and was not surprised to find her gone and himself alone. She'd known he wanted privacy. The music of the viol had faded now, as had the noise of celebration outside, and silence lay heavy in the pavilion like a blanket.

Gnawing at the fruit, he mulled over the proposition

that she had made. The greatest champion in all the world. That certainly attracted him. To be the protector of a king would be an honor indeed. And yet something stirred uneasily in his vitals as a warning. She had mentioned great powers, and he'd felt the hard touch of them during her one instant of impatience; that he could not deny to be real. Who was this Goddess? How dangerous was she? Why should she have chosen *him* of all men?

Or was it Sabra who had made the real choice, guided not by a goddess but by something more fundamental? He had enough experience of women to recognize when one had a specific interest in him. But if Sabra wanted but to sate her appetite for his body, there were less involved ways of going about it. She'd have found him more than willing and thankful for the privilege. No, all that she said about the Goddess was true, at least to her. He wasn't so ready to believe himself, yet.

Could it be witchcraft? But he had met too many in the contests full of the confidence of some crone's promised immortality and had defeated them as easily as any other opponent to give it much credence. This was a different kind of power, then. And the power of the Old Ways was ever strong in the hearts of the simple folk. The tutor had once told him that when enough people believe in a thing, no matter how impossible, their belief makes it real. Did enough of Sabra's followers believe to make a legend like Avalon real? Apparently so.

Then he thought of what faced him if he refused the offer. In truth, it was an empty prospect. Why should he not accept the challenge? His future with the Lady Sabra, whatever the risks posed by her Goddess and her magic, could be no worse than his future without. But still . . .

He dropped the remains of the fruit on a tray, scowling. Sabra had not told him everything, and *that* was why he was uneasy. And suddenly something made a great deal of sense to him, but he had to be sure; he had to get an answer from her on it.

"Then ask me what you will."

He managed not to start at the sound of her voice. She'd returned unseen and was seated once more among the cushions. She smiled slightly, encouragingly against his frown.

"My last contest today . . . was it this power of yours that took away my sword when I most needed it?"

"Yes."

He'd expected a denial or some convoluted explanation or excuse, but not this simple admittance of guilt.

"Not guilt," she said.

Now it was his time to show his anger, his power. "Saints damn you, woman, *stop doing that!*"

She flinched at his tone and her eyes flashed with temper, then subsided. "Forgive me, Lord Richard. You are quite right. I should respect the privacy of your thoughts."

And not beforetime.

She made no response.

That annoyance settled, he asked, "*Why* did you do it? If you've been watching me as you say, then you knew how badly I needed to win. You cost me everything with your witchery."

"Not so. Because of it you were spared."

"Or did you want me to lose so as to more easily tempt me with this proposal?"

"Were that the truth, then I would have answered no."

"But you caused me to lose, placing me in a position where I'd eagerly snap up the first bone tossed at me. Perhaps your Gift failed to show you

that had I won I'd have left this place anyway. You'd
have had a better chance persuading me into service
then than you do now—"

"No, I would not, *for you would not then be alive!*"
Her voice rang harsh in the confines of the tent,
followed by an equally harsh silence.

"What is your meaning?" he demanded.

"The Gift told me—"

"The Gift!"

"—the outcome of your fight with the boy—and that
he would defeat and kill you."

Richard's flesh prickled from a sudden chill from
within. "You're making this up."

"Am I?" She stood, facing him squarely, her face
white with suppressed fury. He felt the heat of it
beating at him. "Then see for yourself, Richard
d'Orleans."

And Sabra, the pavilion, and all the world he saw
ceased to be, and he was breathless on the tourney
field again fighting for his life. The boy charged him,
and as he'd done before Richard raised his sword
high, but this time he held on to it and brought the
knob of the hilt down hard as he'd intended. The
boy's forward motion faltered, but his weight still
carried them to the ground to roll in the bloodied
mud. The blow had stunned the boy somewhat, but
not enough; he fought as one in a frenzy. Richard
tried to bring his sword around but it was too long
for close-in work.

Then the boy rammed a hard fist into Richard's belly.
Twice, thrice, knocking the breath from him. God, how
it burned. Then he caught a glimpse of the knife in the
boy's hand, its thin blade liberally stained with blood.

My blood . . .

The boy stabbed him again and again—

No!

—each wounding a burning trail of fire searing all the way through his flesh to Richard's very spine—

Oh, God, no!

—until he lay still, mouth sagging wide, eyes open but sightless—

Noooo . . .

—dead. His last awareness was of sound, of the moan of disappointment from the crowd, the only mourning he would ever—

He could see again. Sabra, the richly furnished tent—all was as he'd left it, only now he was on his knees, blinking hard, arms wrapped tight around his belly to hold everything in, and a sheen of sweat coating his skin like hoarfrost. Shivering, he slowly, cautiously straightened, glancing fearfully down. No blood gushed from him; he was untouched.

The Gift of Sight. It's true then.

"The Gift," she repeated. "You saw the day as it would have happened. If I had not taken the sword from you in that moment, you would have surely died, and if you had not chosen to yield when bested, you again would have died. The power of the Goddess saved you, then you saved yourself. It is because of *that* inner wisdom you were chosen. It is not enough to have a man who knows only victory, but one who understands when defeat is also necessary."

Sabra stood before him, arrow straight, arms at her side, her face alight with the power, almost too beautiful to look upon. The memory of his pain and fear faded, replaced by shame. How could he have doubted her? How could he have dared to be angry? Here in front of him was holiness, was something greater than any . . .

She touched his upturned face. "Dear Richard, worship me not. I am *not* the Goddess, only her servant."

"Then shall I be your slave."

"No, never that. Never." Her fingers were warm and soft and real, made of flesh, not moonlight. He caught them in his good hand and kissed them. "Then your answer is yes." It was a statement, not a question.

As before on the tourney field, the words came with no effort and this time with no shred of repentance to follow. "My answer is yes."

She half laughed, half sighed. "I am glad." Now she leaned down and kissed his lips, and his heart began to pound near to bursting. His breath quickened from desire for her. Did he dare do this? Would she?

That smile again, appraising and amused. Servant of something divine or no, she was a woman after all; her next words giving him all the invitation he needed. "For the Goddess, such fleshy wants are considered sacred so long as both are pleased to share them. Come to me, good Richard, for you are chosen of the Goddess . . . and I would have you."

He smiled in turn. *Does this mean the hind is ready for her stag?*

In answer, she lay back among the cushions, her hair spilling over them, lips parted. Her eyes shone, almost glowed in the gathering darkness, for some of the candles had gone out. He crossed and knelt beside her. She reached up her hand to him, gently entwining her fingers in his hair, then suddenly, roughly pulled his mouth down onto hers. Her tongue forced its way between his lips, tasting him deep. They locked together in a long, long embrace. And in the embrace, it seemed to him that he heard her voice, echoing soft in his ears.

"I am yours, Richard, and you are mine. For tonight, and for evermore. For after tonight, there will only be forevermore. Come, the Goddess stirs within me and will not be refused."

She stood, undid her dress, and let it slip to the floor. She was naked in the dim light, her breasts firm and full, hard tipped with desire, her belly flat and smooth, her wondrous hair cascading down over her shoulders. She smiled and moved to lie down once more, her body all light and shadow and full of promise. Richard hurriedly stripped from his clothes and all but fell next to her. His hand moved down to the gentle swell of her breasts. He winced as pain shot up his arm from the wound, then determinedly ignored it.

Once again, their mouths locked, wet, hot, tongues deeply exploring. Richard's hands moved over her body, feeling its strength, its softness. He held her breasts, squeezing the hard nipples, bringing whimpers of pleasure from her sweet lips. Slowly, he moved his mouth down over her body, sucking, tasting her fullness. He could smell the muskiness of her womanhood, and as he touched her wetness, her back arched and a cry escaped her. Her hips moved against him, and her hands pushed his head down, down toward the darkness between her legs. As he tasted her, drank of her, she pulled him deep onto her and cried out yet again.

Then with unexpected strength she rolled him onto his back, and knelt astride him. He was hard, harder than he could ever remember, and a huge shudder seized him as she took him in her hands and engulfed him with the warmth of her mouth. His hands held her head rising and falling on him until she pulled away and, looking all the while into his eyes, lifted herself up above him and slid down, down, swallowing his great manhood inside her.

Their bodies moved together now, slowly at first, then faster and more urgent, uncontrollable, unstoppable. The sweat dripped down from her face onto his chest and there mingled with his own. He felt an intense heat growing deep within her most intimate embrace of him. It was nearly unbearable until, throwing her head back, convulsing in fulfillment, an almost inhuman cry escaped her. She hung on to him, nearly spent as he thrust himself deeper and deeper into her, his own need becoming more and more urgent. Then he too cried out as he pulsed inside her, pumping out his seed in that glorious moment of creation. Then his movements slowed, and still joined, she slumped against him to be cradled in his arms.

All was stillness as they slept.

He awoke to her hand caressing his chest with the touch of an angel. She lay next to him now, her fingers lingering upon his blessed cross. The night must be old for the candles had guttered, the darkness nearly complete. From within the darkness came her soft voice. Soft and sad.

"I will not bear your child, Richard. I cannot. You will know why. Yet I will have a child. You will be my child, my son, my lover, my best of all friends."

He tried to speak, but could not find the words. Perhaps at times all women looked on their men in such a varied manner. Sabra could think of him in any way she willed, for he was pleased to be all things to her. Soon now he would be pleased to fulfill his place as her lover again. He shifted, turning to kiss her.

"Anything my lady wishes," he murmured. His desire was as intense as the first time, but he moved slowly, savoring her, exploring her, finding out what she best liked, best wanted from him.

"This will pleasure you more than you can imagine," she promised. "And do not fear."

But there was no danger here, his inner knowledge told him that. All was well and as it should be. He was safe.

"Yes, Richard, you are safe. No mortal will ever be able to harm you again, for the Goddess protects you, and wills me to give you the gift of life."

He wanted to say that he already had the gift of life and did not need it to be given again, but could not. Instead, he looked intently into the gloom. He was sure he could see her eyes shining there despite the dimness of the night. He felt both her hands now, reaching out to him once more, caressing his body in earnest. Her lips brushed his thighs, her tongue licking. Once more he hardened. The beating of his heart thundered in his ears, and once more, she sank onto him, engulfing him. But this was different. This was *more*. His whole body was sharply alive, his skin sensitive like a new-healed wound, his every pore tingling in the cool night air. Riding him, her mouth swiftly came to his, and again their tongues entwined, drinking of each other until she drew slightly away.

"Now, my Richard," her voice was husky, low, "now I will give my life's vigor to you as you gave yours to me. Now you will become my son."

With a low growl she bit deep into his neck.

The abrupt pain of her sharp teeth tearing through his flesh made him cry out. He tried to push her away and could not. She held fast and would not be moved. He felt his life blood spurt into her mouth and her greedy forceful sucking at the wound she'd made. His heart thundered; without warning, he spasmed inside her, his seed gushing forth. He cried out again, this time in pleasure, in pleasure and pain together. It tore through him like a fire.

She lifted her head from her feeding. "See how we give life to each other in the name of the Goddess," she whispered, rocking against him. "Circle and encircle . . . like the sun and the moon."

He could just see her face, her stained lips, her

eyes glowing from the unleashed power within. Her top corner teeth were unnaturally long, wolflike. She had promised he would understand everything. Now he did, all too clearly.

She bit down. It did not hurt this time, quite the contrary. Richard ceased struggling against her. What would be the point? He lay unmoving as the vampire fed on his living body. Every few moments a long shudder of ecstasy took him, each raising him a little higher than the one before, like an ocean's tide. If this was to be his death, then he was a man to be envied, as his time of rapture continued on and on, surpassing anything he'd ever known.

Her quick breath hot on his skin, her body encompassing his writhed and trembled in such a way as to tell him her enjoyment was equal to his own. They moaned together, and he tilted his head farther aside, pressing the back of hers that her mouth settled more firmly against his throat.

Drain me to the dregs, my good lady. Take all that I have.

She drank until his arms had no strength to hold her. They slipped down and he could not raise them again. His hands and feet were like ice. Filling his lungs became a matter of conscious action, for the air had grown almost too thick to breathe. It was easier to take it in short, shallow gasps. His heart thumped and thudded at first, now it was reduced to a swift pattering.

Sabra drew back at last, her movements sluggish. She held his hand to her breasts, bowing her head once to kiss it. He could no longer feel her touching him.

"Do not fear, this will soon pass."

He could *hear* his heart, could feel its frantic flutter against his breastbone, dying. He shook as though with burning fever, but in all his life he'd never felt such terrible cold.

"It will pass," she promised him.

He listened as his heartbeat become weaker and weaker until, inevitably, it stopped. Her voice came to him, clear but as though from a vast and ever increasing distance.

"Sleep, my love, my child, my friend. Sleep. All will be well."

When he awoke, Richard's first thought was of Sabra, their lovemaking, their long night of passion, but as his eyes drifted open he found himself sprawled alone upon the cushions. There was no sign of the Lady Sabra anywhere. He was not worried. She would return. He knew it.

He stretched mightily, breathing deep. The air was warm for a morning—if it was morning. He glanced at the curtained doorway. Thin slivers of sunlight peered through the cracks. The door faced west. By God, but he'd slept the whole day through. Not that he minded and certainly he had good enough reason to do so. She'd fairly worn him out, but he felt better, younger, more robust than he had in many a day. He'd heard other fighters swear that enjoying a woman after a battle was the best way to ease one's wounds; perhaps there was something to that after all.

He sat up and looked about the pavilion, hungry. The food-laden table was untouched and waiting. He pulled his tunic on and padded over to investigate. Strangely, nothing there seemed at all appetizing to him, but nonetheless he broke apart a loaf of bread, dipped it into a dish of cold beef jelly, and took a healthy bite. At the first taste of it a heavy wave of choking nausea came over him, and he immediately spat the food out, retching until the last crumb was gone. Ugh. It must have gone bad during the night, or the wine had left his stomach too fragile for use just now. Such illness would soon pass, though; he'd suffered the like too many times before after a night of celebration to trouble much over it. Perhaps Sabra was also feeling the same and had retired elsewhere to physic herself.

He wondered just where his sweet lady had gone. The pavilion door was tied well shut, time he opened it and saw what was left of the day. The cords securing it came undone readily, and with an easy motion he threw it open.

The pavilion was on top of a rise with a fine view over the lake. The sun was close to the horizon; its red glow seemed to set the water aflame. He stretched again, embracing its heat.

Perhaps a little too hot, he thought, *but so beautiful*. A cooling swim in the lake would not be amiss. Sabra liked him clean, and if this evening held the same joys as the last, he wanted to do his best by her. Without further thought of it, he made his way barefoot down the slope, glancing back once at the pavilion and the castle behind it.

He was free and safe; he was to be the champion for a king in Britain and had the love of the most perfect woman in the world. His father and Dear Brother could go to the devil for all he cared.

His skin itched from the heat, but it wasn't so bad once he'd made it to the shady cover of the woods below. It looked to be a very hot summer ahead.

He found a tree-sheltered place on the lake and, stripping from his tunic, waded out into the water. By all the saints, it was *cold*. Much colder than before, like midwinter. Worst than winter, so cold it burned. Puffing, he could only briefly splash himself before it was too much to bear and he had to rush back to the shore.

As he used the tunic to dry off he saw his skin had turned red as a cherry, and the itch was much worse, stinging like ant bites. He could hardly stand to cover himself again. Was there some sort of contagion in the lake? He'd once heard of people throwing poisoned snakes into wells to foul the water . . .

He'd work it out later. Now all he wanted was to get back to the cool repose of Sabra's pavilion. He'd have more of that healing mead of hers again; that would take care of things.

As he emerged from the long tree shadows, the last of the sun struck him, as sudden and forceful as hammer to anvil. He fell back under the protective trees, cursing. What was wrong? Not half an hour past he'd felt superb, but now he was weak as a sickly babe. He faltered, caught himself, and gasping from the effort, sprinted up the hill for all he was worth.

The tent door was suddenly pulled open from within to receive him and closed just as quickly once he was inside. He stood panting from the pain and effort, face stinging, arms out from his body, not daring to move lest he further outrage his burned skin.

Sabra had been the one to hold the door. Despite his pain Richard had to pause a moment and drink in her unearthly beauty once again. Bands of gold-and-blue embroidery trimmed her gown, which was a rich brown, the same chestnut color as her hair. On her breast she wore a gold chain holding a gold and enamel medallion bearing the signs of the sun and moon with a cup between them. She'd braided her hair, the braid spilling over her right shoulder.

"What is wrong with me?" he finally asked, holding his red, now swollen arms out to her.

"It will quickly pass now that you are inside. From now forward, whenever direct sunlight strikes you,

you will feel this way. It is a warning, if you like, that the sun is no longer your friend."

"Why is that so?"

"Because of the new life you have from me. I hadn't thought you would wake so soon, or I would have been here for you. Where did you go?"

"Just down to the lake to bathe."

Her hand went to her mouth. "Oh, no."

"What? Was that wrong?"

"No, but very dangerous. Like the sun, free flowing water is bad for you. Too much of either will kill you."

"Kill me? The sun? How am I to be a champion for this king of yours if I cannot face the light of day?

"The same way I do. I will teach you all you need to know. Was the water very cold?"

"Like a witch's breath . . . that is . . . I mean—"

She made a calming gesture at him, smiling. "I'm not a witch as well you know. I should have been here but had to oversee something with my servants. I'm only glad you're all right. Is the burn easing?"

He examined his arms. The redness had faded to an angry pink. His face no longer felt as stretched and tight. "Yes, a bit."

"The sun's nearly down. Once it is gone you will be healed."

That was interesting. "Is this more of your Goddess's power?"

"The power dwells within you now and is healing you. It takes a little time, but is far faster than it would be for other men. Have you not noticed your wounds and bruising are no more?"

Another look. Yesterday he'd had enough battering to leave him black and blue for a month. Now his flesh was whole, marred only by his old scars, and one blemish in particular: his maimed hand. The bandagings on it were soaked through by the water, but that was all right. Now he'd be able to change them without worrying about the fabric being glued to his skin by dried blood.

She came close. "Let me see your poor hand."

He held out his injured limb and watched as she undid the rough dressing. Soon the bloodstained rags were gone and four good fingers and an ugly, scabrous stump were revealed. The wound had clotted over somewhat but would need stitching to properly heal.

"Is it a bad hurt?"

"Indeed it is, but I've lived with worse."

"No more." She glanced at the doorway. The light behind it had faded. "Good. The sun is gone, I can do something about this at last." And then to his astonishment she produced his severed ring finger.

"What do you with that? How did . . . ?"

"I sent my servants over to your tent to look. They were afraid you'd thrown it away or buried it."

"But why? Of what use is it to you?"

"See the power that we have together. See the power the Goddess bestows."

She took his hand, making him spread his fingers wide. Before he could ask what the devil she thought she was doing, she pressed the shriveled thing against his wound. He tried to pull back in disgust, but she held it firmly in place.

"Sabra . . ." he began impatiently. Then his breath deserted him as a shattering bolt of pain shot through his arm. He cried out, jerking away from her. His hand was afire, or so it seemed for much too long a moment . . . then, just as suddenly, the pain vanished.

Sabra smiled as she spread her arms, palms out. "See?"

Richard looked and gasped, for there was his ring

finger attached again—for all the world as if it had never been touched. Only a white scar remained encircling the base where the flesh and bone had been rejoined. He gazed in bald-faced wonderment, unable to speak. He stared at her, a dozen questions hovering on his lips . . . then forgot them.

She was radiant. A strange hunger washed over him. For her.

"How is this possible?" he whispered, holding up his hand.

"Dear Richard, do not ask. Simply accept the bounties that are yours."

"But I must know!"

"You will in time. Do you not remember last night? The last thing that we did?"

"I remember the lovemaking . . ." God, he'd never forget it. But then when she'd . . . his hand went to his throat. The skin was whole, smooth, but still . . . something hovered wraithlike beyond the edge of memory, and it was important. "There was more, I know somehow that there's more."

"Indeed, sweet Richard, there is more. I will tell you, but first you must feed."

Distracted by so much he'd nearly forgotten his empty belly. Reminded, he felt hollow to the core as if he'd never before eaten in his life. He went to the table again, but the sight, the smell of its food repelled him.

"What is wrong with me?" he again demanded of her. "I hunger, but I cannot touch any of this."

"You will be fed, do not fear."

Without being called, her eunuch servant appeared, but he bore no tray of edibles. Richard's hunger increased at this frustration, was becoming unbearable.

"Give me food!"

"My sweet, I have." She gestured at her servant.

This was no time for games. Richard looked around him in desperation. The greatest, most incessant gnawing that he had ever felt was growing inside him and yet Sabra and the eunuch continued to stand unmoved.

"My love," she said, "take what you will. Take what your soul desires and needs."

The eunuch stepped forward, a beatific light on his face, the elated light of a believer. He looked at Sabra. "Thank you, lady, for giving me this honor."

"Go to the Goddess with love and in peace," she told him. "You will ever be remembered in this world. I swear it."

He smiled and knelt with his back to her. Eyes shut, he raised his chin high, exposing his throat. She stood close behind him, bending over him, low enough now as though to whisper in his ear, then lower still until her mouth touched his neck. The old man trembled, smiling.

Richard watched with horrified fascination. She could not mean this. Then in a flood, the memories of the night came back to him—all of them—and Richard knew that, indeed, she did mean this, that *this* was the satiation for the terrible hunger inside him.

Sabra lifted away from her servant. Blood streamed from the man's neck where she had bitten him. Her eyes were glowing; her lips parted, revealing the sharp wolflike fangs, the exultant expression on her face.

Unclean worship . . . bloody human sacrifice . . . was *this* what the priests of his youth had meant? Why they hated the Old Ways?

He caught the scent of the blood. Breathed in a great draught of it.

The eunuch opened his eyes, looked up at him.

"Come, my Lord Richard. You are the chosen of the Goddess. Let me honor her. Please."

"You wish to die?"

"To be with the Goddess forever. Yes." Closing his eyes, he continued to kneel, waiting.

Richard felt a snarl of impatience rise in his throat. He looked to Sabra.

"It is his dearest wish," she said. "Deliver it to him. Feed!"

I cannot.

"You must."

He could not tear his gaze from the blood. He licked his lips, felt the change of his teeth. *I must look like her now, red of eye, wolfish, terrifying.*

And then there was the hunger. Inescapable. Growing. He felt a cramp start deep in his vitals like the stab of a knife.

"Wait no more, Richard," she urged. "Madness could take you if you wait too long. Feed now."

Trembling from head to foot, he moved toward the eunuch until he stood close behind him. Blood still flowed from Sabra's wounding of him.

Perhaps if I take only a little of it . . .

No, once begun he knew he would not stop. His need was that great.

"Sabra." His voice was thick. He hardly knew the sound of it.

"Speak."

"Will he become like us?"

"No, he has chosen to go to the Goddess."

"And there is no other way?"

She gave no answer.

The pain wanted to take him again. He fought against it. A moment longer was all he wanted. He willed his hands not to shake as he reached out.

"Stand," he told the eunuch. "No one should have to die on their knees."

He drew the old man upright, gently tilted his head to make taut the furrowed skin of his throat.

"With peace and in love," Sabra whispered.

Richard reared his head back above the eunuch, then battened hard upon him, sank his teeth into the exposed willing neck, and for the first of so many times, felt the warm gush of blood coursing down his throat, the life of another flowing into him.

How *good* it was.

Afterwards Richard lay with Sabra on the cushions, gazing at the ceiling of the pavilion but not really seeing it. His malignant hunger was gone, but at such a price. What sort of Goddess demanded the death of her worshipers? But the old man had been willing, so joyfully willing to die that Richard might live, and unselfish sacrifice was central to all he had ever been taught in his own church.

Other servants came to bear away the eunuch's drained body. She wept a little at this.

"Was this not for the glory of your Goddess?" Richard asked. He studied his arms; all sign of the burning had quite faded from his skin, as she'd promised.

"It was, and all is well with him. I weep because I shall not see him again. He was ever faithful and true. I will miss him."

"I am sorry." He leaned back, feeling heavy as though his bones were made of lead. *The feeding's done this to me.* "Must we always kill to live ourselves?"

"All things must kill to live, but we need not. I took much from you and that blood had to be replaced. The next time you feed you won't need a tenth of that quantity."

"The next time? When will that be?"

"In a few nights. You will know it when it happens."

"And who will I feed from?"

"I have many servants. We will teach you how not to bring permanent harm to the one you choose."

That was good. "Will animal's blood not do just as well?"

"Only if you've no other choice. Animals are for humans to feast on, but we are somewhat more than human—and like calls to like."

"What we've . . . what I've done, the priests of my church would condemn me, drive me away."

"Given the chance most people would kill you. There are those who hunt our kind and seek to return us to the Earth by driving a stake of yew through our hearts, but even that doesn't kill right away. It freezes us, pins us in place so we cannot move and feed. Those caught in this way die slowly, a lingering death of starvation. The lucky ones are beheaded."

He had heard stories in his travels of how best to deal with certain night-living demons who fed on the blood of men. He'd dismissed them as fancies. No more.

"We are of the Earth, my love," she said. "As immutable as the mountains, and as long living. This is the Goddess's greatest gift. Left alone, we will never die."

"And are we the first of our kind?"

"There are others in the world, but I know them not. I was the firstborn of the Goddess. I will tell you how I came to be and about the Goddess if you wish."

"I would like that, yes."

"There is a goddess named Cerridwen, who has two sons, Gwynn and Gwythyr, and they fight eternally for her favor. Each year they fight. At Beltane, Gwythyr triumphs and Gwynn is banished to his home in the underworld, and we have springtime and bountiful summer. But at Samhain in the darkening of the year, they fight again, and this time, Gwynn is the victor, and then the gates of Annwyn are opened, and the wild hunt of winter begins. The great white hounds of Annwyn, eyes as red as blood, come forth and search out human souls to take back to Annwyn where they will await rebirth. We are the children of this eternal conflict, for we are descended of the Hounds of Annwyn."

She stood and moved to the pavilion door to look out at the night. He followed her. The moon, just past its full, cast a brilliant cold light over the land. He could see every detail as though it were day.

"Cerridwen gave me eternal life so as to ensure that the ways of the Goddess would never be forgotten. She summoned Gwynn and instructed him to have his greatest hound feed on me, on my blood, and in the feeding, my mortal body was changed, immortality given in its stead. This is why the bright sun will destroy us, for the Hounds of Annwyn are creatures of darkness and the storm."

It sounded like a tale to him, something for the poets to recite.

"You may believe or not," she said. "Though here we are, proof of what I say."

He gave a quiet laugh. "Will I be able to hear the thoughts of others as you do?"

"No. The Sight has ever been with me. If it had not been for the Goddess's protection I'd have been killed for it by those who fear its truth. Your Gift is your strength, spirit, and mind. Soon you will put them all to good use. My people are even now preparing for the journey. Tomorrow we will leave for Britain."

"For your king who has been chosen as a bridge between the old and the new."

"As you are also in the same way a bridge." She touched her medallion and then his cross. "He is and will be a great king, blessed of Cerridwen, the once and future king of all Britain. His name is Arthur, and you, my love, will be his strong right arm in all things. You are the Goddess's gift to him, my gift to him."

"I shall do my best." He felt a familiar stirring within and put his arms around her, pulling her close. "In all things."

After a long, quickening kiss, he easily scooped her up to carry back to their nest in the cushions. There he sought to undo the laces on the back of her gown.

She leaned forward so he could better work, and her hand strayed down between his legs. "Indeed, you will be his greatest champion. I do not need the Sight to tell me that."

"Only touch," he murmured, delighted with what she was doing. If she kept on like that he'd have to abandon the laces and simply raise her skirts.

"I am Sabra of the Lake, you know."

"And very pleased I am to make my lady's acquaintance." There, the knot was loose and he could pull the cords freely.

"You are now my best weapon against Arthur's enemies." She gave him a firm squeeze that left him panting. "My lance. My lance of the lake . . ."

She laughed, until he covered her mouth with his own.

Chapter Two

Toronto, Canada, Present Day

Richard Dun idly rubbed the white scar that ran all the way around the base of his left ring finger and looked over the RCMP driver sent to pick him up. God, but they were getting them young, though he'd seen still younger ones in his time.

Apparently no one had briefed the driver on what to expect; he openly goggled at the luxurious accouterments of Richard's combination office and home. It had every modern electronic convenience, and a few unexpected old-fashioned touches, like the Botticelli on the wall next to Richard's desk. It was something of a risk having it here, but he liked to look at it and he could well afford the insurance and alarm systems.

While getting ready to leave, Richard Dun caught a quick glimpse of puzzlement on the young man's face before it dampened to poker-playing mode. Richard thought of giving out his usual innocuous reason for pulling on a trenchcoat, wide-brimmed hat, and gloves on a warm May morning, but decided not to bother. Let the fellow show a little initiative and find out for himself the reason behind the eccentricity if it held any interest for him.

The driver proceeded him out the front entry to wait at the foot of the steps, standing at much too obvious attention while Richard set the systems and locked the door. At least the man wasn't in his red uniform. As they went down the walk to the street Richard pulled up his coat collar to cover the back of his neck and put on some very dark wrap-around sunglasses. The man's face twitched.

Probably thinks I look like a leftover from a 1960s spy film, Richard thought as he hurried to the unmarked car.

"That's parked illegally," he commented in a mild tone, noting the thing's placement by the painted curb.

"I've got the flag up," said the driver, pointing to a placard on the dashboard that declared this vehicle was on official government business. He opened the rear passenger door and held it for Richard.

"Indeed, and in a place where everyone can see it. I thought this was to be low profile."

Another twitch. Annoyance this time. And embarrassment, to judge by the sudden pink tint of his ears.

"No need to use the siren, I hope?" he added and watched the man's ears deepen to a nice ripe red. So he *had* wanted to use it. Such a pity to spoil his fun. Richard got into the car, won a minor struggle with the inconveniently placed safety belt, and settled himself, prepared to spend the rest of the trip saying nothing at all to the back of the man's head. He had plenty of questions, but they could wait until he met someone with rank enough to answer them.

Wonder what the flap's on about this time?

Philip Bourland, a friend and one of his chief contacts in the vast government bureaucracy, had made the call early that morning to Richard's unlisted home number.

"Can't be specific over the lines," he'd drawled. "But it's important."

"There are degrees of importance," Richard countered, and waited for a reply.

Bourland answered with silence.

"So . . . it's *that* important. Very well, set a space aside for my car."

"We'll send a driver to your office. Lower profile, y'know." He rang off before Richard could fish for more information.

Now and then Richard would get a job from the Canadian government; the pay wasn't huge, but he did it not for his bank account, but for the contacts it brought him, like Bourland. They'd never before been in such a stir as to send a special driver to fetch him, though. Something interesting was up; perhaps it had to do with the impending trade conference. Lots of VIPs would be there, lots of room for trouble to happen. If they were in a sweat about security, they should have made an appointment two months ago, not at virtually the last minute. As it stood they'd quite thoroughly interrupted Richard's morning, causing him to reschedule three potentially lucrative consultations, and unless the meeting he was about to attend moved faster than the traffic his afternoon would be equally lost.

Ah, well, if it's in service to the Monarch, one must abide by their whim and thus the whims of their other servants.

The driver negotiated the crowded streets efficiently enough, going north from Richard's East York home to Danforth Avenue, then west until it mysteriously turned into Bloor Street. Then the driver went south again to Queen's Park. On their right were the extensive grounds and myriad structures of the University of Toronto, on the left, the restful green expanse of Queen's Park itself. Too bad they had to spoil it by placing the Ontario Parliament Buildings smack in the middle of things.

Instead of hunting for a parking space, the driver took them around to a side entry, paused the car, then got out to hold the door. At attention again. Why didn't he just launch a few fireworks with a bagpipe parade and have done with it? Richard considered miming a limp on the way inside as justification for this extra attention and decided it wasn't worth the bother. At least he was close in and spared a potentially painful hike in the sun.

"I'll find my own way, thank you," he told the man, praying he wouldn't get a salute in return. He got a sensible nod instead, then levered out of the car, walking briskly to the shelter of the building. Once within its shade he could comfortably pocket his sunglasses and gloves, and politely remove his hat. A young woman standing in the wide hall, apparently waiting for someone, approached him. Though he'd never seen her before, a look of recognition registered on her face.

"Mr. Dun?" She spoke only just above a murmur. No one around them appeared to have heard her.

He nodded. "I'm here to see—"

"Yes, sir. I'll take you right in." She gestured and walked just half a step ahead of him. No nervous turning around to see if he followed and no other names mentioned; things were looking up. Bourland must have briefed her himself on the basics of discretion.

Instead of a quick lift trip up to Bourland's office, she led Richard to a service stair going down. The drab halls here were more utilitarian than historical, but he didn't mind. Work was work no matter how humble the setting; besides, it was most definitely out of the sun.

She knocked twice by way of announcement then opened one of the many identical doors in this part of the rat's maze. It bore no descriptive legend; for all he knew she could be ushering him into a broom closet.

"Sir, Mr. Dun has arrived." She stood back so Richard could pass through. Smooth-mannered and attractive enough to gain his attention, he briefly gave in to temptation and locked his gaze on her, smiling. Her eyes went big for an instant, then she flashed him a dazzling smile in return, strictly nonprofessional. Artificially induced, yes, but still so good for the ego. He really must try to quit doing that sometime. He'd cut back quite a bit in the last few decades, but still, if the woman looked interesting . . .

"Richard." Bourland's voice brought him back to business. His fascinated escort, too. Continuing to smile, but with the voltage dimmed somewhat, she softly shut the door on them. Bourland, a fit six-footer with an amiable face and deceptively lazy blue eyes, stood up from what appeared to be a makeshift desk and crossed the bare floor to shake hands with him. "Really, now, what is it that you do to them?"

"Just my native charm," was his innocent reply.

"So long as you don't run into any harassment suits."

"Philip, you know I'm a gentleman through and through."

Bourland let one corner of his mouth twist. "You're one of the very few people I know who can make that statement and be believed. Come have a seat, but don't bother to get comfortable; we're going to a meeting in a minute." He glanced at a wall clock. It read almost a quarter past the hour. "Coffee? I have a thermos of decaf here."

"Thanks, but I prefer my vices as they were meant to be, uncorrupted by any hint of virtue." Richard shrugged free of the coat, dropping it on a spare chair and put his hat on a clear space at the edge of the desk. The papers there had the look of police reports. Some large color photos were in the scatter; the central subject of one on top indicated they were from a crime scene. A messy one.

"Allergy still a problem?" Bourland inquired, indicating the trenchcoat.

"Under control, especially when I'm not being yanked out of my office on a minute's notice. Now what's all this about? And what's this place? You've not been demoted, have you?" Richard waved one hand at the dingy room and its continuation of the hallway's utilitarian theme.

"No, but my head's close to the block for mentioning your name to the PM."

"I thought he liked me."

"He does, it's the other people on this that resent his calling in a security consultant from the outside. You'll be meeting them shortly."

"That old story. Nothing to worry about."

"Just thought I'd prepare you."

"For what?"

Someone knocked at the door, then opened it. The woman again. "Sir? Ms. Selby's arrived and is waiting."

"Damn. All right, we're coming. Sorry, Richard, no time to go into things, but you know the drills. Just try not to let Demarest annoy you. A personal favor."

"Of course." No need to ask why, Richard knew Bourland would have a good reason. Who the hell was Demarest, anyway?

"Leave your gear here, it'll be fine."

Richard followed Bourland to another, larger room furnished with a long, unadorned meeting table lined with mismatched chairs. The dozen people occupying the chairs were of a type similar to Bourland, middle-aged, long of face, well fed, and garbed in the standard dark suit and tie uniform of the species *bureaucratus conservatius* so popular in this century. They looked far too important for their plain surroundings.

Oh, yes, something's definitely up to drag this lot into the cellar.

He was introduced to them all, including a Chief Inspector Etienne Demarest of the Royal Canadian Mounted Police and a Ms. Dayna Selby, special assistant to the Prime Minister. Selby, a formidable looking woman of perhaps forty years, wore the feminine version of the uniform, brightened only by a gold pin of abstract design on one lapel. Everyone was civil in their greetings, guardedly curious, and unmistakably ill at ease.

Dear me, and I've only just arrived.

Selby began things as soon as Richard and Bourland were seated. "I want to remind all of you that what is said in this room is to stay here. No confidences to your spouses, best friends, lovers, or even your dog. The reason for this is that one of our people working undercover has died already, and we want no more casualties. If any *one* of you breathes a word, I will personally see to it your lungs are surgically removed with a dull knife."

Her gaze traveled over each of them in turn, causing them to shift a little. No one cracked a smile. Apparently Ms. Selby was known as a woman of her word. She sat and nodded once to Bourland, who launched into things with no preamble.

"The operative who was killed had infiltrated an IRA cell here in the city. He was not highly placed, but was occasionally able to pass along useful information to us. His last report had to do with a plan to assassinate the Prime Minister."

"Hardly news to anyone, Philip," said one of them.

"They've been known to try that sort of thing all the time."

"Agreed, but the agent's death, along with a few other details, have led our analysts to conclude that this report should be taken rather more seriously than usual. We think the group he infiltrated has a good chance of succeeding."

"Then we round up the leaders and—"

"Not this time. Indications are that this sterling idea is from a splinter cell operating separately from the ones known to us. We don't have a lot in the files about them except they are willing to take more chances than their fellows, and they've found money enough to hire an outsider to do the job."

"That's ridiculous. Whyever should they do that?"

"Because without the support of the main group they need someone with the skills and reputation to deliver the goods."

"But an outsider? I've never heard of them taking such a risk."

"Which is why we're taking this threat very seriously. The man we believe them to have contacted for the job is known in the trade by the name of Charon, after the Styx ferryman." Bourland glanced at Richard, who raised one eyebrow. "He is distinguished from his fellows by his reputation of never once failing to take down a target. Mr. Dun is a security specialist here at the PM's request because he knows more about Charon than anyone else, how he works, even how he thinks. Mr. Dun has also been known not to fail."

"There's a first for everything," said Chief Inspector Demarest. He was lean and dark, with a narrow hard-set jaw and an ingrained expression of annoyance. He fixed a glare on Richard that was obviously meant to reduce newcomers to jelly. Richard smiled back with just enough sunny sincerity to irritate, but not provoke a direct response. It worked. Demarest pointedly turned back to Selby. "My department is perfectly capable of protecting the PM, especially since we have a forewarning of an assassination attempt."

"Thank you for that reassurance," said Selby. "Since the safety of the PM is rightfully uppermost in your mind, then I'm sure you will extend every courtesy to Mr. Dun to see that his part of this investigation runs smoothly."

Demarest blinked once, his lips thin with distaste. Not a bad recovery for a man who's just been chopped off at the knees, Richard thought. He was vaguely reminded of Mordred at the old council meetings, that way he had of holding in all the destructive resentment—only Mordred had been able to hide it better. Demarest didn't look quite as smart. His next words confirmed it.

"Of course, Ms. Selby, but the calling in of an outside consultant is extremely irregular and certainly unwise. For security reasons."

Selby fastened a sub-zero, no-further-arguments gaze on him. "You will find that Mr. Dun has been granted a blanket clearance in regard to this situation by direct order of the PM himself. That should fully cover his free access to all the reports in the files, and he is to have people to help him if he needs them." Her gaze now traveled to the others, who were all department heads of one type or another, to let them know they were also included.

Richard was pleased. He'd made more contacts here in the last few minutes than in the last five years. Some of them might prove to be useful, but only some of them. Demarest, for instance, had gone quite red about the collar, directing another piercing glare at Richard.

Yes, my son, this means you have to share your toys. If you know what's good for you, you'll shut up before she hauls out that dull knife for some carving practice.

Thankfully, Demarest subsided. For the moment. Richard knew it would last only as long as the meeting. Bourland answered a few more questions on the assassination topic, but broke things up when it started to turn into a discussion group. He reminded them all one more time on the need for secrecy, then Ms. Selby excused herself, saying she had appointments elsewhere to keep before taking a return flight to Ottawa. Her next meeting turned out to be in the room where Richard left his coat. She was waiting there when he and Bourland returned.

"Philip," she said, not rising from her chair by the paper strewn table. She was studying the top photograph. "Mr. Dun."

"Yes, Ms. Selby?"

She looked him over, taking in the expensive suit, designer tie, handmade shoes, and finally the face that went with them. Her expression was polite, but on the cool side. "I have been instructed by the PM to give you every cooperation. That does not mean I welcome your presence any more than Chief Inspector Demarest."

Richard made no reply, as one did not seem to be required.

"If you decide against taking part in this investigation, you will still be paid for your time this morning."

"At this moment, my time is still my own, but it is at the disposal of Her Majesty's representatives."

One of her eyebrows went up. "Does this mean you'll do this job for nothing?"

"No, but if you're planning to give me a dressing-down vote of no confidence, I can still answer you back without worrying about getting sacked."

The right corner of her mouth twitched and her eyes sparked.

Great, she likes me. "As things stand no one has even asked, officially or otherwise, if I do wish to participate." He directed this at Bourland.

Bourland examined his nails. "Sorry, must have been an oversight on my part."

"Right."

"Very well. I say, Richard, how would you like to go on a little assassin hunt for fame and fortune? Or at least fame?"

"I'll have to look everything over first. I might not be able to help, and if not, then there's no point in my saying yes and wasting your time and mine."

"The preliminaries are all right there." Bourland indicated the table.

"And one other thing—" Richard turned to Selby. "Why the farce in there about security? You know that sooner or later someone's going to talk."

"Oh, yes," she said. "We know all about the 'two can keep a secret if one of them is dead' thing. That was all very much on purpose."

"You think there's a leak?"

"We're always wary of that possibility. This seemed as good a time as any to test them."

"Consequently putting my life on the line if one of them fails on purpose or by sheer stupidity."

"Possibly. But Philip has assured me that you are indestructible."

More than you think, good lady. "Do please write that sentiment on my gravestone should this have a disappointing outcome."

"As you wish."

She took her leave, and Bourland went with her. "When you decide yea or nay, ring me up. You know the extension," he said in parting.

The bloody hypocrite knows I'll say yes. But Richard held his peace until they were gone, then sat at the table to sort through things. Despite the appalling pile of paper there was little enough real information. McQuin, the dead operative, had been found only yesterday, and the post mortem was yet to come, though the preliminary report spoke guardedly about excessive violent trauma to his whole body. Probably beaten and stabbed to death, poor lad. The photos showed a gory mess indeed. They'd fairly gutted him. Richard hadn't seen death like that since the last lot of Germans bombed London.

The data they had on Charon was most discouraging for its limits. McQuin's final report stated that he'd heard the rumor that "the ferryman" was coming to take the PM across, but there was no hint of a time or place. One of the many annotations to the report raised the possibility that "ferryman" referred to Charon. This was followed by two more annotations attached to the first, one discrediting, the other supporting it. Both signed by the same person. Someone was being very careful on this.

How did this IRA cell get in contact with someone like Charon? How did they even know of him at all? He was known as a very high-priced specialist and didn't exactly advertise his services in *The Times*. Even in the intelligence community he was more often than not considered to be only a story, mostly because anyone making a project out of him wound up dead. Richard knew of three investigators killed for certain and two other possibles. Was he to be number six by picking up where they had left off? If so, then Charon was in for one hell of a shock.

Richard patiently read through all the reports, idly rubbing his white scar.

✦　　　✦　　　✦

"I'm glad to hear it," said Bourland when he answered Richard's call. "I'll get the paperwork started so we can put you on the clock."

"Wrong, you give me my standard deposit fee, then I'll send you a bill afterwards. Do the paperwork for that instead."

"Whatever you want. Oh, there's one thing, Richard, has to do with the chain of command. You're to make your reports to Demarest. His card is in the file you have, along with your special ID and authorization papers. Sign all four copies and—"

"Why not to you?"

"Because he's in charge of the case."

Damn, but it was only to be expected. "Why is that?"

"Because, as the Yanks say, he has his head up a lot of asses, including mine."

"How did you let that happen?"

"It's a long story, no need to burden you with it."

He'd get it out of Bourland later. "I'd rather report to you. You know he's going to be trouble. I'm familiar with the type, he'll make himself annoying."

"I know, but it can't be helped. Just close your eyes and think of Canada."

"Do you still want to know what's going on?"

"Of course, but only in an unofficial way. Protocol requires that I be more or less out of the loop . . . but if you should happen to run into me now and then, or accidently dial my number, I'm more than willing to lend an interested ear. I'd appreciate it, Richard."

"So long as it doesn't place your head up my ass."

"Perish the thought."

Richard rang off and started pulling the papers and photos together into neat piles and found folders for them in a drawer. Just as he finished the job a double knock sounded at the door. Bourland's pretty assistant came in.

"Your drive back is waiting, sir."

"Thank you."

At least she didn't puzzle about the business with the coat as he put it on. Perhaps Bourland had briefed her on it as well.

Richard pressed his gaze on her again, to be rewarded by another encouraging smile that turned rather blank the longer she held it. He stood close before her, taking in her scent, listening to her heart. He closed his eyes, letting it wash over him. So many, many years and he'd never, *never* yet tired of the sound.

She was tempting . . . and he was hungry.

He took one of her hands and lifted it to his lips. Very soft. Trace of cologne on the pulse point. He opened his mouth to kiss her there, tasting, savoring. He felt his corner teeth emerging in response, enjoyed the familiar sweep of fire and ice rushing through him—something else he never tired of, even after all this time. Indeed, over the years it had gotten more intense, more delightful.

He ran his tongue over her skin, heard her sharp sigh in return. Her eyes were closed, lips parted, breath shallow. God, but life could be good.

On the other hand, he had to be careful. The door was not the kind one could lock from the inside without a key. Bad luck for him if somebody walked in on them while he was . . . and then there was Bourland's joke about harassment suits . . . no, thank you.

With a great deal of difficulty, Richard pushed away from this particular temptation, putting his back to her. His own breathing was rather too ragged for comfort. Once the gate was open, the hungry beast within was always prepared to run free until he fed it. He managed to beat it back into its cage for the time being. *It's too risky now, but I'll tend to you soon. I promise.* Perhaps he was being overly cautious, but he'd never once had cause to regret such a policy in his long past.

When he turned around his teeth and eyes were quite normal again, and she appeared to have recovered from his control as well. The effect of it was such that she'd have no memory of the last few minutes, for which he was thankful. He didn't want to trust himself into imposing additional hypnosis on her, for then might he break down and indulge his appetite regardless of the risk.

No, better to wait until nightfall and go to one of his usual haunts.

There was no problem taking the files out of the building, and the young RCMP driver delivered him safely home. Richard fled inside, for it was bright noon, and despite his coverings his skin began to itch in reaction to too much exposure. Why couldn't Bourland have called for him on a nice rainy day?

Once in the house he removed his protections. The special room-darkening steel window blinds he'd had custom made for the place were never opened except on very dull days or during the dark of winter. As this not one of those times he turned on the lights. He could have done just as well without, enough sun came through the cracks to serve his sensitive eyes, but it always put the customers off.

Customers. Damn. He checked his appointments. Just one in the later afternoon. He had lots of time to play, then. Suiting action to thought, he parked before one of his computers and cruised through a dozen files before locating the one he'd built up on

Charon. The trouble with abbreviated titles and passwords was that he sometimes forgot them. It took a few tries before he could open it.

The data there was remarkably slim, all of it gleaned from reports of people in the business who had tried to investigate Charon in the past. The first man had died six years earlier in an auto wreck, another was an apparent suicide off a tall building, but the remaining three had been taken out from a distance by a long gun. Head shots except for the last, who'd gotten it in the neck. The bullet must have dropped slightly as it traveled.

According to them, Charon's talents were apparently not in the service of any one political group. Speculation linked him with several kills that served opposing ideologies and even rival organizations. *Nothing personal, just business.* Of those assassinations in the last two decades that were positively linked to Charon, a dozen were also with long guns. Snipers needed regular practice to keep their eye. He could put someone to looking into local shooting ranges, though he didn't expect anything from that; it was Richard's cast iron habit of covering every detail. He made a note and scrolled on until a name came up that caught his eye.

Arlie Webb. Well, well. The last investigator had noticed that Webb had been in the area just prior to three of the assassinations. Webb's name was also on the list of people McQuin had had contact with before his final report. Where was it? He dug through the paper file and compared it to the one on his screen. No photo for either, but the descriptions matched. A former Le Mans driver and part-time alcoholic striving for full-time status, Webb had no visible means of support, yet did a lot of traveling. Speculation ran that he was a smuggler and a good one. His last known location was some motel on the Canadian side of Niagara. Fortunate, that. Richard doubted his carte blanche from the Prime Minister extended over the border into the States.

A few phone calls to get the local RCMP to confirm things for him ascertained that Webb was still checked into the place. Almost as soon as he rang off Demarest called him.

"What's this business in Niagara?" he demanded without giving greeting.

"Chief Inspector Demarest? How good to hear from you." Richard winced; he sounded far too sincere to be believed.

"Niagara, Mr. Dun. Why did you have my people calling there?"

"Just a minor lead I wanted run down. Nothing to it."

"You do understand that you are to report to me."

"Most clearly, Chief Inspector, and I will be happy do so the instant I have anything to report. I've only just started, so give me a little time. Have a nice day." He dropped the phone in its cradle and turned off the ringer. Ten seconds later his answering machine went to work, Demarest again, according to the caller identification device. He didn't bother to leave a message. Richard hated when people did that.

The afternoon appointment netted him a very nice consulting fee and another satisfied customer to add to the roster. By sunset he'd gotten his preparations all sorted and was driving toward the lake and the rental boat waiting for him. Faced with fighting the evening traffic going around Lake Ontario or taking a boat trip across, he opted for the water journey, however hazardous. He detested water, at least when it came to huge free-flowing quantities of the stuff, but in this instance it was a calm night, and he had a nice, sturdy fiberglass shell between himself and disaster. Of course, he could have simply chartered a plane, but he detested flying even more.

One boat trip and taxi ride later Richard stood in the parking lot of a place calling itself Moonlight Court, an ambitious name if ever he heard one. It was a motel of the older type with individual bungalows intended as an attempt to give honeymooning couples a bit of privacy. He estimated that its heyday had been in the thirties when such rustic delights had proved a novelty to a less sophisticated society. Now its once cozy rooms would raise only a sneer from a generation used to the sprawling comfort of luxury hotels with their spas and king-sized beds. Whatever quaint charm Moonlight Court once possessed was now thoroughly debauched by age and the decidedly downwardly mobile neighborhood surrounding it. Why didn't the owner just post hourly rates and have done with it?

Tempus fugit, he thought with an inner sigh as he strode up to the office. He'd instinctively dressed below par for the occasion with faded jeans, a less than new shirt, an old leather jacket, and a comfortable pair of highly scuffed western boots on the verge of retirement. The ensemble suited the local scenery; the bored man behind the counter glanced up once to see that the new customer wasn't intent on armed robbery then went back to the cop show rerun blaring at rock concert level on his TV.

"I'm here to see Arlie Webb," Richard shouted. "Which one is he in?"

The man shook his head, not bothering to adjust the sound. "If he was expecting you then he'd have told you which one. What is it? A drug bust? Waste of time, he only does booze. What the hell, try cabin twelve at the far end."

"Thanks. Who's winning?" He nodded at the TV, where the blue-clad cop hero crouched behind some shiny new trash cans that were miraculously deflecting Uzi bullets.

"Captain Kirk, of course."

"Good for him." Richard started out, but the man called him back.

"Webb might be busy," he added.

"How so busy?"

"Has a girl in there. Nice redhead, legs up to here. Too pricey for me, or I'd flag her myself when she comes out."

"Redhead? She look Irish?" Perhaps she was an IRA contact.

"She looked female and plenty of it."

"Well, maybe Arlie will share." He winked once and went out to pay off the taxi.

"Sure you wanna do this?" asked the driver. "Not much chance of getting a ride back from here."

"You're willing to wait?"

"I got fares waiting, sorry." He did a fast U-turn and was gone, not so fast as to miss his tip, but gone all the same.

Richard walked slowly over broken, pitted concrete, the TV noise gradually fading behind him. He listened to the faint traffic sounds beyond the dark court. Busy night out there, lots of ladies doing business. When he finished with Webb, he'd take a walk in their direction and hire one to feed from. The girl would be ahead a hundred dollars, have a pleasurable, if rather vague dream, and Richard's hungry beast could retire comfortably to its cage for a few more evenings until the next time.

Richard paused before the twelfth bungalow on the row. Lights showed behind its red curtains.

He scanned the rest of the shadowed lot. The cars

looked on a level with the run-down area: an aging Pinto, oversized gas guzzlers that had seen better days, and a new Sentra with a rental sticker. He noted its plate numbers, in case it belonged to Webb, before going up to the door.

He listened before knocking, not that he had any compunctions against breaking in on a couple *en flagrante*—sometimes such occasions could be quite amusing. No action tonight, though, they were talking.

"Five grand," said the woman in a firm tone.

Good God, what on earth did she do that was worth *that* much?

"Get out," said the man, presumably Webb.

"All right, six."

"No."

So, she was buying not selling. As it was not likely Webb himself was worth that much then she was after something else.

"Ten, and that's final. It's more than you'd be getting from anyone else." She had a decided Irish accent. Well, well.

"I don't know what you're talking about."

"Oh, but you do. I'll not be goin' to the police on this one, an' that's a promise. I just want the item back and in good condition."

"Lady, you're crazy, you got the wrong man, and now you're gonna leave. Don't come back."

Richard quick-stepped away from the door and nipped around the corner of the building. Peering past it with one eye he saw a leggy redhead indeed, being pushed out by a much larger man. She wasn't dressed like the other self-employed women of this neighborhood; that, and the fragment of what he'd heard gave him to wonder just what her business was that she could be willing to drop ten thousand dollars on someone like Webb.

She whirled around, and Richard ducked so she wouldn't spot him.

"You'll never get the full worth of it from anyone, that's a given, so why not deal with me?"

"Because I've got nothing for you."

"What, you've passed it on already? Who has it? I'll pay you—"

"Go fuck yourself!" Webb slammed the door in her face.

"You first, you've had more practice!" she bellowed in return.

When no reply came back, Richard heard her footsteps stalking over the pavement, followed by the opening and shutting of a car door. The Nissan rental belonged to her. She gunned it to life, then roared out of the lot.

That was interesting, but he'd check on her later. Now it was his turn with Mr. Charming. Richard stepped up and forcefully knocked. Webb yanked open the door.

"Goddammit, bitch, I told you—" The shock of seeing Richard there instead of the woman added to the bleary surprise in Webb's bloodshot eyes. His mouth hung open, an unfortunate effect, especially coupled with the booze on his breath.

"Was that my little sister you were just molesting?" Richard inquired in his best Irish accent.

"Who the hell are you?"

"Someone a damned sight more careful than you are to be sure." Richard pushed past him. "What d'ye want to go puttin' on a show like that for? Y'know how important this job is."

"Job? What do you mean? My part in it's over."

"Ah, but the boss wasn't happy with your part of it." Richard kicked the door shut.

"I delivered on time and didn't get caught, what more does he want?"

"Your balls in a box unless you say where you put it."

"Right where it's supposed to be—wait, who are you? What the—"

But by then Richard had grabbed Webb's arm, twisted him around, and shoved him hard over the back of an armchair. It was surprising this place even had an armchair. The rest of the room consisted of a sagging bed, night stand, phone, liquor bottles full and empty, a twenty-year-old TV sitting on an even older bureau, and a faint sewage smell. Webb, poor fellow, suited the surroundings perfectly, being unshaven and shirtless in filthy jeans. His last bath was no more than a fond memory.

Richard bent low and whispered reasonably in his ear. "The fact is I need information from you or you could end up like young McQuin did, with his guts spread out all over creation."

Webb stopped struggling. "How you know about that? You're a fucking cop!"

"Oh, I'm much worse than that, my lad. Cops have rules and regs, but I don't bother with the silly things, so don't you forget it for one minute, I never do." He pulled Webb's wrist up high, making the man gasp. "Now why don't you tell me the story of your life? Skip over the dull bits, just give me the last week or so."

"You can't treat me like this, I'm an American!"

"They have my full sympathy. Come on."

Webb told him, in remarkably coarse language, to go someplace and do something rather painful to himself once he arrived, compelling Richard to push the chair forward until Webb crashed headfirst to the floor. He gasped and groaned until Richard hauled him up for a short lug over to the unmade bed, where he threw him onto it with spring-cracking force. Webb bounced once, then slithered to the floor again, legs everywhere, his back against the mattress edge.

"Can't keep your feet? You should get off this stuff." Richard plucked an empty bottle of vodka from the night stand. Grasping its base, he smashed it against the stand. What remained was a truly terrifying weapon, especially up close. He seized Webb's throat with one hand and brought the broken bottle between them at eye level.

"You've got two chances to tell me what you know, Arlie. Your left eye and your right."

"Wh-whatever you say." Webb raised his hands high, palms out, making nervous, placatory motions.

"Good lad. Now what did you smuggle?"

"Just some booze, that's all."

"Wrong answer." Richard nicked Webb's cheek with the bottle. "Oops! Oh, what a shame, my hand slipped! It could slip again if—"

"Awright, it was a gun!"

"What kind of gun?"

"Dunno, it was in a case, a big one, hell of a job getting it over here."

"And where did you take it?"

"A drop point. My car, their car. We pass each other. I hand it through the window and drive away."

"And they didn't pay you?"

"I get paid by—" Webb blanched and swallowed. "Someone will bring the money later."

"You're so trusting. You really think that will happen?"

"Always has, he—" He cut off again.

"Who are you expecting? Who's paying you? Charon?"

"Who?" But the whites flashed all around his pupils at the mention of the name.

"You heard me. Such a lousy pit for you to wait in—what's the matter, doesn't Charon pay you enough for a nicer place? Or maybe you drink it away, is that it?"

Webb shut up again. He was slick with sweat and trembling. Richard locked his gaze on him, concentrating.

"You're to tell me everything, in detail. Tell me about Charon."

"Charon?" Webb's voice thickened, but his resistance was better than most. The drink in his blood would make things more difficult, but Richard could be patient.

"When is the hit on the Prime Minister scheduled? Where is Charon?"

Webb blinked, his head dropped. "No . . . can't . . ."

Richard shook him. "Look at me! You can. You want to tell me everything!"

"Fuck you," rasped Webb, bringing his right hand around. Richard caught the movement with the corner of his eye and started to react. Too late. The revolver now in Webb's fist roared and flashed. Once, twice . . . Richard dropped heavily on his side with a grunt of pain. Another shot. His body spasmed. He felt hot blood spill over his hands as he clutched at the wounds in his chest and belly.

"Fuck you," Webb said again in a much fainter voice, like an echo. Still on the floor, he backed away, staring at Richard the whole time.

Richard groaned, paralyzed by the agony from the three distinct fires that blazed deep in his flesh. He dared not move, not until the worst shock of it had passed and the healing began. Betrayed again by his damned overconfidence. He should have looked for a gun; he knew better. Of course a man like Webb would always have one ready at hand. Where was the bastard? There, across the room now, slowly finding his feet.

Oh, God, don't let him shoot me again.

Webb brought the gun up. Fired.

The bullet hammered Richard square in the chest. He flopped on his back, his skull knocking hard against the bare floor, leaving him dizzy and too breathless to scream. Shattered breastbone, shattered heart. He could feel its frantic flutter as it continued to pump on despite the damage. Any other man would be dead by now. All Richard could do was wait it through until it knitted up again.

And endure the pain. Bad now, but it would gradually fade.

Just wait it out. Won't be long.

But the pain was *not* going away. It just kept on and on. Abruptly, a wave of sickness such as he'd never felt before washed over him like ice water, left him shivering. After a moment, it got worse, not better. He'd been shot before, knew what to expect, but it wasn't happening. Something was wrong.

"Jeez," came Webb's voice. There was relief mixed with disgust in his tone. "Now what the hell am I supposed to do?" He loomed into view, looking down at Richard, then moved unsteadily past him to get to the night stand. Webb fumbled for one of the vodka bottles there and got it open. Two good jolts later and he was dialing the phone.

Richard's shivering increased. Cold. Colder than anything he'd ever known before, right down to the soul. What was wrong? He should have been recovering by now.

Webb, receiver to his ear, stared at him. "Jeez, you take a lot of dying, don't you?" He aimed the gun at Richard's face, sighting down the barrel. "*Pow,*" he whispered, then grinned. "Take your time, you son of a bitch. All the friggin' time you need."

What was wrong with him? Cramp. A bad one.

With a strangled cry, Richard twisted on his side, doubling up like a fetus as a vise clamped down tight around his gut as though to squeeze him in two. God, what was *wrong*?

Webb got an answer to his call. "Sean? It's me . . . yeah, I know I'm not supposed to, but I've got a situation here, I need some help."

Sweat soaked Richard like a bath, and his breath came in little sobs like a panting animal. His corner teeth were out. All that lost blood. It would need replacing. Soon.

Now, whispered a familiar growling voice within.

"I can't talk over the phone about it, you have to come here."

His hunger . . . like that of the newly born. Excruciating. The beast was emerging, clawing free of its cave. He tried to push it back. Another cramp took him. His cry of pain was deeper, rougher than the last.

"No I can't, you have to come to me, this is *where* the situation is, goddammit!"

Clawing . . .

"You just come and bring a couple of your boys."

. . . free!

"I'll be right here at—*oh, Christ!*"

Webb's last coherent cry was for his long abandoned savior. His next was an appalling shriek because Richard was up and on him like a wolf, teeth bared, eyes blazing. Richard lifted him bodily, slamming him against the wall hard enough to shake the whole cabin. Webb feebly tried to bring his gun up, but Richard swatted at the weapon, knocking it across the room. Webb tried his fists next, to no effect; Richard was past noticing. He pushed Webb's head away to one side and, biting hard and deep, tore into his throat.

A gagging scream. A twitching, struggling body.

Richard ignored both as the first rush of blood filled his mouth. Not enough. Not nearly enough. He worried at the tough flesh. The beast wanted not just the surface vein, but the big artery, the real treasure hidden beneath the skin and muscle.

He clamped his jaws together and pulled, ripping away half of Webb's throat. The body shuddered, its bare heels cracking against the wall. The screaming abruptly stopped. A hot red fountain of glorious life jetted over Richard, blinding him. Too quick to swallow, then too slow. He couldn't feed fast enough to keep up with the hunger, with the sheer desperate fury engulfing him.

Mindless, he slashed and rent, drinking, greedily drinking all he could of the red nectar, all, until there was nothing left but the drained and mangled remnants of the pitiful shell that once held it.

The bathtub was only half full of cold water. It would have to do.

Richard plunged his head and hands into it. Scrubbing.

When he came up for air the water was dark with blood. Dark. He yanked the plug and watched it drain out. As the last of it swirled away he thought of the old Hitchcock film and had to fight an hysterical giggle trying to escape.

Not now. Later. Panic later.

He ran more water, got the shower working at full force, and stepped into it fully clothed. The shock from the cold went all the way down his spine as the stuff soaked through to his skin. He endured it. Had to.

He rinsed his face, his hands, turned and turned again in the freezing spray, rubbing at his clothes, washing away more and still more blood. There seemed an unending supply of it; just when he thought he was clean another fold of cloth would yield another stain, and he had to begin all over again. He shrugged off the leather jacket, hanging the sodden thing over the shower rod. Threads of red-tinged water streamed from it, half into the tub and half to the floor. He peeled off his shirt, wringing it, washing, then wringing, and put it next to the jacket, then did the same with his jeans. He threw his socks and boots in the sink.

Then he scrubbed himself down all over again.

His raw skin pinched from the gooseflesh when he stepped dripping from the tub; the nearly healed bullet wounds tingling right to the edge of fresh pain. He found a towel, used it, staring all the while at the slaughterhouse beyond the bathroom door. The heartsinking fear he'd been holding at bay threatened to paralyze him. He didn't want to go out there.

But I have to.

He took a breath. It didn't help. The place reeked of blood. Every corner, every wall. Filling his lungs, nearly choking him with its thick smell.

He edged into the room, but there was no way he could avoid contact. Parts of the floor were merely dotted by the spray, but others were slick with it.

What had he touched here?

Outside doorknob? He couldn't remember for sure.

He stepped carefully around the ghastly *thing* on the floor. He listened, hearing nothing before gently opening the door. He swabbed the knob down with the wet towel, shut himself in again, and wiped the inside knob.

The vodka bottle. Yes, for certain. He found it in the wreckage and polished it.

What else?

Webb. They could lift prints from bodies now. Hell, he had to think about DNA tests and God knows what else. Something like this would have a major forensics team poring over every inch of the room with their damned microscopes. There'd be his hair, skin, clothing fibers, even his own blood.

And Demarest would remember the calls his people had made to Niagara on Richard's behalf. He wouldn't let that go. He'd talk to the boat rental place, to the taxi driver, to the man in the office. Possibly Richard could get to them all first, persuade them to think they'd never seen him before and . . .

No. That was useless. He needed a better cover-up, something plausible to fit the situation.

Another look at the room and he had to forcibly quell the giggling again. Then the sob of fear that followed. He didn't have time for it. Maybe someone in this hellhole of a neighborhood had heard the shots and screams and called the police. Not likely, or they most certainly would have been here by now, but he couldn't take the risk. At least the office man had apparently missed everything, thanks to his TV addiction.

Richard went back to the bath, washed his feet clean, then put on all of his cold, wet clothes. Nasty. But necessary.

He wiped down everything in the room, the taps, the shower walls, edge of the tub, and checked the dimensions of the window. Small, but not too small. He rinsed the towel clean then dropped it in the tub.

In the outer room he went to Webb's cache of booze. Two full bottles of vodka, another of Scotch half gone. It would have to do. He opened the lot and poured the contents all around the room, particularly the body, bed clothes, and curtains. With his pocket knife he cut open the thinly padded arm chair. As he'd hoped, the padding was some kind of cheap foam stuffing. Almost as good as petrol. He spread it around where it would do the most good. He slashed at the mattress, making a thorough job of it. Accellerant and fuel. Only one more thing to complete the circle . . .

Matches. There, on the bureau. Obviously not a nonsmoking suite.

He smothered the giggle.

Blood on the matchbook. Sticky against his fingers. Had it soaked through? The heavy paper cover was soft. The matches inside were, too. He struck one. Nothing.

No, this wasn't the time to get the shakes.

Struck a second and a third. The fourth caught, then went out.

Calm. Deep breath. Bringing with it the smell of blood and the stink of booze.

And death. Don't forget death. It's hovering just over there waiting to see if I botch things.

Calm.

The next match stayed alight just long enough for him to drop it onto a patch of bedspread soaked with vodka. Hot blue flames leaped up, grew steady, grew fast, ran over the floor, up the walls, hopped impossibly from one side of the room to the other. He fell back from the sudden heat, the swelling sound.

The damned thing's alive.

He retreated to the bath just in time, the fire licking at him, wanting a taste.

He turned on the cold water for the shower again, then picked up the heavy ceramic lid from the toilet's tank and began smashing it against the wire-reinforced window over the tub. A few shards of glass flew. The aluminum frame bent outward. He felt fresh night air streaming in; behind him the fire roared to greater life.

Sweating now. He could tell even through the wet clothes and the running shower. His movements became mechanical as he beat at the window. Soon the glass was nearly gone, just the twisted bar across the middle remained, and one more hit would—there. Broken. He shoved it outward to clear the opening, dropped the tank lid, and pushed himself through the window. Tight squeeze. He was a big man even for this time.

The leather jacket spared him from the worst cuts, but not the jolt when he tumbled out to the pavement six feet below. He lay still a moment and took stock: scraped hands and a few bruises—nothing he couldn't live with.

This time the sobbing laughter wouldn't stop.

The rest of the night went as he'd hoped. Someone finally noticed the fire and called it in. The other bungalows were spared, but number twelve was thoroughly gutted, a total shambles by the time the firefighters had finished with it.

Richard allowed himself to be discovered, apparently groggy from a hit on the head, in the alley behind the place. He let the paramedics look him over and faked waking up fully when they gave him some oxygen. He produced his ID, mentioned Demarest's name, and let the bureaucracy trundle forward to work in his favor.

He reported everything that happened, veering from the truth only when he got to the part when Webb shot him. Instead, Richard stated that he must have been hit from behind by a third party already in the room when he'd entered. When he woke up Webb was dead and the place on fire.

Richard told his spellbound audience he couldn't get to the front door or larger window, but did just manage to break out through the bath. He was told in return that he was a lucky bastard, that his guardian angel had been doing some overtime, that they were glad he made it free. Draped in a blanket stamped with the logo "Property of Niagara County," he let himself be congratulated for his narrow escape while pretending to sip their vile coffee. He did not have to pretend to be shaken to the core by what had happened.

Loss of control. Complete and total. Such as he'd never had before.

That was what had happened.

The beast, as he'd come to affectionately call it over the years, the beast, responsible for so much pleasure in his long life, responsible for allowing him that long life to begin with, had slipped its tether and not come back. Not until it had fully indulged its vicious appetite.

He'd had *no* power over it, had just been along for the ride. While this rabid *thing* had torn a man to shreds and fed on the blood, the part of his mind that still knew itself to be Richard had simply watched. Done nothing.

But that son of a bitch Webb had shot him, he could tell himself in his own defense. Certainly he could be expected to have a reaction, a bad one. But Richard had been shot in the past, many times, and he'd never reacted this way before, not with such mindless rage.

Loss of control. Anyone's nightmare. But for him, for someone like *him,* it was worse than any sleeping terror.

"You see it?" One of the paramedics asked her partner. She must have thought they were out of range of Richard's hearing.

"The body? No way, I smelled it cooking, that was enough for me. How bad?"

"Bad. It's so messed up only the bones let you know it was human. I don't envy the med examiners on this one—not that I ever do," she added.

"Try not to think about it."

"Yeah, tell me another one. You know what it's like."

Richard's heart juttered once, then beat faster as the memory of what he'd done to Webb surged over him. His hands trembled so that he had to put the coffee cup down.

His mouth twitched. Not from fear or disgust now, but from remembered excitement.

Because . . . because . . . God help him, he'd *enjoyed* it.

Chapter Three

What was the point, Richard thought, of having an efficient highway system if it was always made inefficient by constant construction? It seemed to him that there were two seasons in Toronto: winter and rehabilitation. That was the new word for it, coined by other frustrated victims of progress, usually with a few choice descriptive epithets added in. Whatever the word the result was the same, lines of angry motorists sitting in slowly overheating cars, slowly getting angrier, glaring at apparently empty construction zones where no one appeared to be doing anything.

His E-Type Jaguar shuddered slightly as it ticked over in the late afternoon line up of homeward-bound commuters; he shifted to neutral and fed it some petrol. The carburetor was out of balance again. He'd have to get that fixed. This was a thoroughbred machine that needed lots of patient attention and frequent feedings at the premium pump, but he thought the benefits were well worth the trouble.

Richard had fallen in love with this long, sleek monster as soon as he'd seen it back in the sixties. There'd been a breaking-in period of course, where the vehicle's many mechanical and electrical faults turned up. He'd made a special project of finding the best repair shop in the area and set them loose on his beautiful wheeled pet to disprove the general opinion that it was merely a status symbol to be seen basking in one's driveway, but not for actual use. His car was now impeccably behaved: smooth acceleration, amazing power, and a degree of luxury conspicuously absent in other sports models.

All the defects worked out, he then bought six more identical models. Money was no object, so why not? He shipped one to Los Angeles for his frequent visits there, another to Vancouver, and the other four were in Europe: London, Paris, Rome, and Geneva. He would have had one stored in Moscow were it not for the lack of good service facilities and the city's yet uncertain situation of the present. Poor Russia. He'd spent many wonderful times there and was saddened by this century's varied upheavals. Perhaps one day, it would return to its former prerevolution glory, but without the attendant crime and tyranny— hopefully with a better economy to prevent additional rebellions. He thought it might. He'd seen enough changes in his long unlifetime to hope so. He smiled to himself at that word. "Unlifetime." What an accurate description of the gift that Sabra and her Goddess had given him.

But has it betrayed me?

Damned traffic. It gave him too much time to think. He'd had a surfeit of that in the last few days. The aftermath of what he had come to privately refer to as the "Niagara Horror" had required he do a great deal of thinking about it. And lying. It had been easy enough to lie to Demarest and later Bourland about it, holding to his story of being knocked out and waking in time to escape the fire. So far, forensic evidence to contradict him had not yet surfaced, neither had any of the investigators raised so much as an eyebrow at his accounting, so they believed him. So far.

The forensics team had scraped under his nails and

taken a blood sample. Bit of a risk, the latter, but it couldn't be helped; it would have aroused suspicion if he'd refused to cooperate. So long as they didn't subject it to a truly in-depth analysis it would pass as being within normal parameters. Only just, but tests down to the DNA level took time and cost money and most police departments had little of either to spare. He chose not to worry about it, having more important concerns.

His sodden clothes had also been taken away as evidence, but the department lent him some old sneakers, mismatched socks, and a florescent orange track suit. Richard didn't mind the vile color; the stuff was dry and didn't smell of Webb's death.

Demarest was not amused by any of the sordid business. He'd come down to Niagara himself when the police there called Toronto to inform him of the incident and to confirm Richard's special ID. Demarest heard the preliminary report from the senior officer on the scene, talked with a few other people, then eventually turned up at the local station house where Richard had been escorted after the paramedics were done with him.

Richard, seated in the dense quiet of an anonymous office, loathed having to speak with the tiresome man, but thought it best to get the ordeal out of the way as he had with all the others.

Demarest strode forcefully in and glowered at Richard. To no effect. "When I called you about your Niagara inquiry this morning you said it was a minor thing. I don't appreciate being misled, Mr. Dun."

"At that time it was only minor. I had no idea it would blow up in my face," he replied truthfully.

"Then perhaps you should leave such investigations to professionals."

Richard could have pointed out that he was

certainly himself a professional—with several lifetimes of experience—but disdained rising to Demarest's easy bait. "I'll keep that in mind, Chief Inspector. Until then I shall exercise more caution."

"All this is going into my report to the PM."

"I'm glad to hear it."

"Now why don't you tell me who S. Geary is?"

"Who?"

"The person who rented the Nissan. They traced the plate number."

"That's her name? What's the 'S' stand for?"

"You tell me."

Richard, tired beyond patience, wanting only peace, looked up to hypnotize him. He'd gotten far enough to lock gazes and about to go just a little deeper and tell him to leave, when the beast suddenly stirred.

No!

He shut things down and turned away. Fast.

Demarest shook instantly awake and seized upon a whole different meaning to Richard's reaction. "You know her! Who is she?"

It took him a moment to find his voice. "I don't know her, and I've no stomach to play your games. You have my report, and that's all you need."

"It's not nearly enough. You haven't told me everything."

"Yes, I left out the part about having a splitter of a headache and a need for air that doesn't stink of burned meat. If that's what you want, I'll be glad to add it in tomorrow. In the meantime, I'm getting out of here." He picked up the envelope holding his wallet and keys and suited action to word, shutting the door against Demarest's protests. A uniformed officer gave Richard a ride to the nearest large hotel and left him there. One of his platinum cards did the rest.

Locked in his room, he stripped and went straight in the shower. Hot water this time, but still soaping and scrubbing every inch of his skin.

For two hours.

He couldn't sleep. Paced instead. Then stared out the window at the cold lights of the city. Whenever his eyes closed he saw the bungalow again, Webb's pathetic remains, and the cheap, prosaic furniture coated with blood like a field after battle. No battle this, but savage butchery such as he'd never done before in all his time. What vivid pleasure the beast had taken in that feeding. He could not deny his enjoyment of it then, no more than his abhorrence of it now.

But that wasn't the worst. The worst was the difficulty he'd experienced attempting to push the beast back, of trying to return to his human self. For a hideous time it felt like he would never return, not because he didn't want to, but because he couldn't. And when, with a massive effort of will he did return, it was to squat cowering and shaking in a corner of the room for all the world like a rabid dog.

Very apt, that, for a descendent of a Hound of Annwyn.

And soon, much too soon, he *would* grow hungry again.

He could kill again and not be lucky enough to get away with it.

There were ways around the risk. With his money and contacts he could buy blood, as much as he needed. That would spare him the necessity of letting go, of letting the beast free, but it would not solve his central problem. No, he had to deal with it before his next feeding, and his heart told him who best to help him.

Sabra would know what was wrong. She always did.

He wanted to call her, but a few years ago she'd moved to a very isolated part of Vancouver and hadn't bothered putting in a phone line.

"When you want to talk, come see me," she'd said, what she always told him when the necessities of living caused them to separate for any length of time. Whenever he'd been troubled during his centuries of existence he had invariably gone to her, and she, with sublime wisdom, had always calmed him and explained all. How he loved her still and needed her. How he wanted to be with her now.

Do you hear my troubled heart, Lady?

Probably so. Her Gift had always been very finely focused on him no matter how many miles lay between them. Perhaps when he arrived in her private corner of the world she'd be right there to greet him and lift away his burden of fear with her smile alone. Just the thought of her was enough to give him hope and comfort. And finally, when the night was nearly over and the eastern sky paled from black to deep blue he drew the light-proof drapes and fell into restless sleep.

Two long days. Two, before the forces of law and order finally let him go.

He arranged to read the other official reports of the incident, overheard the gossip, the speculations; all that mattered was that they did believe his story. No one stopped him when he canceled his many business appointments and booked a first-class seat on the next flight to Vancouver. He'd narrowly escaped a horrible death, after all, who could blame him for wanting to take some time off?

Now, if he could just get through the damned traffic.

He eased the Jaguar into gear as the line began

to move and marveled as whatever obstruction ahead suddenly vanished, and all vehicles immediately went into high gear in their breakneck race to see who would reach the next line up first. He slipped into the passing lane and pushed gently through the gears until the car purred along at an effortless seventy-five miles an hour, leaving everything else in its wake. He had less than an hour to make the flight and no intention of missing it.

Fifteen minutes later he slid the Jaguar into a parking space at Pearson, got out, took his carry-on from the trunk, locked everything, and made his way to the terminal. He had forty minutes before takeoff.

His boarding pass was in order, now came the anticlimax of waiting to be called. He wandered to the passenger's lounge and sat in an armchair facing the window. Thick clouds today, thank goodness. One less thing to worry about, though his gloves and hat were along if he wanted them, as was a bottle of maximum strength sunblock lotion. His success with the stuff was limited, but it was better than nothing at all.

Richard watched the great jets lumbering down the runway before—magically, it seemed, defying all the laws of nature—they slowly took leave of the earth and soared into the sky. He understood the general scientific principles behind powered flight, but it still held more than a hint of the miraculous for him to see one of the heavy silver birds actually make it into the sky and stay there.

A voice cut into his reverie, announcing it was time for first-class passengers to board. He collected his bag and left for the gate.

A window seat. He could close the shade down if the light got too much for him. Once settled in, he concentrated his attention on something, anything, outside the window so he wouldn't have to look at the passengers heading back to the economy section. He always felt a twinge of guilt about traveling first class, and actually catching the eye of anyone not also enjoying his level of luxury added to it, so he looked away. Then the hatch was sealed and suddenly they were moving from the terminal building on the first faltering steps of their journey. His sweating hands tightened on the padded chair arms.

He *hated* flying.

The plane taxied out, dipping rhythmically like a bus with bad springs, and was soon at the end of the main runway, turning, ready for takeoff. This was the worst moment of all for Richard, being poised and waiting, he was never sure what for. Perhaps it was all show for the tourists to give them a bit of suspense, that or the airlines had a hidden streak of masochism for pale-faced passengers like himself. Then he heard the rise in pitch of the engines and felt the growing pressure against his chest as the plane lumbered forward and began its terrifying struggle for freedom from the ground. It bounced and swung, centering, gathering speed.

God, how I hate flying.

He reminded himself that airplanes were after all, made to fly, not travel at high speed along the ground, so the bumping and swaying, unnerving as it was, meant nothing.

Really, really hate *it.*

He had from the very first time he'd tried it ninety years ago. Once up it was all right, but the effort of getting there and back again never failed to terrify, though he well knew nothing permanent could happen to him if anything went wrong.

That still did little to ease his fears, especially a few decades later when he'd gone down in an air crash. Sometimes in dreams he could still hear the screams and prayers of the doomed passengers as the stricken plane plunged toward the ground. What stayed with him, stark cold in his memory, were the faces, the panicked eyes of the stewardesses as they tried to calmly put the quite ineffective crash drill into effect. One, he remembered, had been silently crying the whole time.

Richard himself had sat frozen, gripping the arms of his seat, white-knuckled, waiting for the pain. He discovered long ago that his agelessness came with a price. Every injury he suffered hurt him as much as if he'd been a normal man. The first time a sword blade ran him through after his change had been surprising agony. He could not then imagine what the aftermath of a plane crash was going to be until seconds later it hit the ground and utterly obliterated the lives and hopes and dreams of every person on board save one. He'd lain, body smashed, for what seemed an eternity of agony, wishing that he could die, until his body finally mended itself enough to move, and he was able to stagger away into the darkness before the arriving search parties found him feeding, by necessity, off the dead. Not something he was proud of, but better them than some hapless rescuer.

He'd tried his best to avoid air travel ever since. However, as the century progressed and aircraft became more and more indispensable in this speeded up, impatient age, he was often forced to use them.

But the fear never left him. And never would.

Faster and faster the plane went, and just as Richard had decided this was it, they weren't going to make it this time, the nose lifted and the ground swooped away. Trying to control his breathing, Richard went through his usual takeoff routine, counting slowly up to sixty. Someone had once told him during a stopover that if something happened within sixty seconds of leaving the ground, there was no chance of doing anything to avoid the catastrophe. So every takeoff he counted the requisite number and then felt marginally better.

Ritual complete. They hadn't crashed.

He gradually allowed himself to become convinced that they were safe after all. For the moment. Until they landed.

He pulled down the window shade, accepted the attendant's offer of pillow and blanket, and told her that he would not need the in-flight meal or any other refreshment. Then he turned to the window and closed his eyes, but not to sleep. He'd already had a bad dream about Webb; he didn't want to tempt his inner mind to more. Instead, he did his best to think about Sabra, and that cache of sweet memory helped as it always did.

Several hours later, in the gathering dusk, the majestic bird dipped its wings to begin a stately descent into Vancouver. Richard cautiously pulled up the shade and looked at the scene below. The seemingly infinite mountain ranges had finally ended and the plane had unerringly found its way to the Fraser River valley, following its sweep toward the Pacific. The lights of the city twinkled below him, and towering in the distance to the south was Mount Baker, flushed pink by the last rays of the setting sun. As the plane turned northward on its final descent the sun slipped below the horizon, picking out the Gulf Islands and the comfortable rectangularity of Point Roberts in a final act of defiance. Then the plane sank into the gathering night, and amid the screech of tires and the roar of reverse thrust, landed, managing to stop before the runway gave out, turning gracefully for the terminal.

Safe again. He'd cheated the odds again.

He surreptitiously dried his damp hands on the blanket.

God, how he *hated* flying.

His travel arrangements necessitated an overnight stay. It couldn't be helped; the smaller airline he'd booked with had not been interested in changing its regular running schedule no matter how much extra he was willing to pay. There were no other flights to the area. Tomorrow evening he would be hungry again and with it was the potential of losing control once more. The worry chafed him all the way out of the terminal.

He collected his second Jaguar from the long-term parking garage and headed for downtown and his favorite hotel. A large and modern structure, Richard liked it not so much because of its facilities, of which there were many, but because no one ever asked any questions of the reclusive guest who preferred his curtains shut all day and never called for room service. Discretion was the staff's watchword, and this endeared the hotel to him; in turn, he was endeared to the staff by the immense tips he left. All in all it was a very satisfactory situation.

He checked in, had someone take his carry-on up to the room, but remained in the lobby, knowing himself to be too restless to settle in for the night. Unlike the ephemeral people around him, he could not simply take a sleeping pill and wait for its chemicals to knock him out. If he could, he would, and save himself a few more hours of useless vexation.

Not to mention hunger.

It was there, the faint beginnings of it, anyway. The beast stirring in its cage.

He left the hotel for a walk around the block. He needed distraction and the exercise. The damp night air, even tainted with the day's exhaust fumes, felt good on his skin and in his lungs. At least it was alive and free, not that recycled stuff aboard the plane.

Perhaps . . . if he fed the beast *before* it fully wakened.

He'd already taken the measure of the area in one glance and judged it safe enough for hunting. After all this time such assessments were automatic to him. There were people about, but not too many, and convenient unlighted alleys for the few minutes it would take to accomplish. But did he dare make the attempt?

He remembered the slamming spray of blood from the severed artery striking his face, again felt the last futile struggles of Webb's body trying to hold onto life as Richard tore into him far worse than any animal. Worse, for animals know when to stop. The one dwelling within him had not, and its wanton brutality appalled him—now. He was sane—now. In control of himself. But for how long?

Richard watched several women going past, released from their downtown jobs, some hurrying to their car or bus ride home, others walking more slowly, catching his eye. It would be easy enough to find someone. . . .

The old cautions and practicalities, the sensible warnings against undue danger flooded his mind. Yes, he might be able to retain control as before; he wasn't in dire need just yet, perhaps not nearly to the point of putting the life of a stranger at hazard.

But you can't afford another Niagara Horror here, my lad, he told himself.

He would wait. Had to wait.

Firmly turning away from the temptations passing

him, all unaware of the presence of a predator, he went back to the hotel, this time going straight up to his room.

He awoke just before checkout at noon, left his customary gratuity on the night table and left, then it was a quick drive across the Burrard Street Bridge, onto Oak, and west to the airport. The day was one typical to the West Coast; good solid clouds and the threat of rain. Richard was glad, for it meant that he did not have to worry overmuch about cover. No wonder Sabra loved it here.

He'd dressed for the wilderness, jeans and sturdy walking boots, a flannel shirt, sheepskin coat, and a black western-style hat. Sabra had very much liked the hat the last time he'd seen her and teased him about being a cowboy. He'd promptly asked if she might enjoy having a ride and then they'd—

Someone honked when he started to stray into the next lane. Well, as pleasant as *those* particular thoughts were, he'd have to think about them later or risk crashing the car. He parked his Jag once more in its regular spot and went to claim his ticket for Port Hardy.

He'd already long ascertained it was impossible to drive to Kingcome. Typical of Sabra, he thought; when she decided that she wanted to get away from it all, she got. She'd written to him about it in full, giving him detailed instructions on how to get to her cabin. Kingcome was a small native community on the coast north of Vancouver, and only accessible by boat from Vancouver Island. Consequently, he had to fly yet again, this time in a petite prop job. He was sure it would prove even more harrowing than the flight from Toronto, but was wrong, however. This time there was no sweaty conviction that the plane would never take off; instead, he was amazed at how easily this light bird flew and how surprisingly pleasant it was to be so close to the ground for the whole trip. Things had changed much for small craft in the last nine decades. Compared to his very first flight, and especially compared to the larger plane of the previous day, this was more like a carnival ride than anything else. He almost found himself enjoying it. But only almost. They landed without mishap at Port Hardy, and Richard found himself at a tiny airstrip, suddenly quite alone.

Afternoon was beginning its slow descent into evening as Richard strode along the dirt road toward Black Point where the local mail-cum-ferry boat sat. As soon as he left all sign of habitation behind, he gradually increased his pace until he was little more than a blur. This was one of the advantages of his vampire state that he truly loved; the ability to move at incredible speed.

Like flying, he thought. The way people *should* fly.

This was not flight, but it came a close and much better second as far as Richard was concerned. The rush of wind in his face and the pure effortless speed always gave him a deep and genuine pleasure. Rarely these days did he have the chance to stretch himself like this. He was quite disappointed when the first houses of the tiny settlement came quickly into view. Their presence forced him to slow to a regular human pace, but slow he must until fully out of their sight. Sabra's training and his own past experience had taught him well. Discovery was not an option.

He'd arrived only just in time. The large silver-gray aluminum boat that carried the mail and various other supplies to the island was ready to cast off from the dock. He hurried forward—not too fast—calling for them to wait. One of the men paused at his work with a rope and waved him to come aboard. Richard leaped on, steadied himself and found a place to sit and put down his bag. Someone came by to collect the fare, but after that he had nothing to do but wonder how deep the water was.

Planes he hated, but boats he merely detested, and only because of their proximity to free-flowing water. He concentrated on that unpleasantness for a moment, instead of his empty belly, for the hunger was growing. He would have to deal with it tonight, but barring additional delays, he would soon be safe with Sabra. The power of her Goddess that had granted him this kind of life and had ever protected him would now help him again. It *had* to.

From his carry-on he drew out the letter Sabra had sent when she'd first moved to this place. She'd needed isolation, she said. She wanted time away from modern life so as to touch the land again, to be closer to her beloved Goddess. Apparently she'd found it here. He leafed through the fragile pages covered with the strong flow of her handwriting.

"The mountains hover around me in never ending shades of gray in the morning light, and clouds mingle with river mist around them, like laurel wreaths about the crowns of champions. The river teems with fish, and the forest that presses in on all sides is full of game; black tail deer, moose, the mighty grizzly, and soaring above, watchful guardian over all, the bald eagle rides the air currents effort-lessly, seemingly eternal.

"Kingcome Inlet itself is a tiny speck on the face of the world. It gained its strange name from a rash lie told by the government agent who first persuaded the local native band to give up their ancestral lands and move to the unfriendly strip along the river. He assured the chief that if they moved, the English king

would surely come and visit them to thank them, such was their importance. The poor natives believed the lie and moved without complaint and wait still for the visit of the king."

Not unlike Britain waiting for Arthur's return in the time of her greatest need. There was a better chance of that happening than for the current monarch to drop in here. As the boat brought Richard closer into the river estuary, he could well believe that only a lie of such magnitude could persuade anyone to live in such a desperate hole.

"Though surrounded by beauty, the settlement itself is an awful spot. Ramshackle wooden cabins in a variety of odd colors line the river. There is no doctor, no store, nothing. Strings of raggedy laundry flutter in the damp breeze, children run along the bank, chasing homemade toy boats, and men putter with aged outboards, convinced that the right degree of persistency will solve any problem."

That the actions of a supposedly benevolent government could reduce such a proud people to this squalor disgusted Richard. He huddled closer into his coat as he stepped off the boat onto the dock. He paused, unsure of his direction. Sabra told him to take the path into the woods from the settlement's lodge house, but he didn't know where it was. No one looked at him, or spoke, which he thought odd. In such isolation the presence of a stranger should have inspired some germ of curiosity. *Same country, different culture*, he thought. Finally, he approached a man hunched over some nondescript piece of rusty machinery.

"Excuse me."

The man neither looked up nor stopped whatever task it was that involved him.

"Excuse me, my friend," Richard reached down and touched him on the shoulder. "Can you help me?"

The man stopped dead still, then slowly looked up. Even as he saw Richard dark against the sky, his eyes widened with . . . what? Surprise, fear, expectation? All three perhaps? He began to tremble violently and mumbled something in his native tongue. He repeated it again, loud enough for others around them to hear.

His reaction startled Richard. Like certain animals, some people were sensitive to him, to what he was, but he'd not seen anything like this for a very long time. He decided to bluff it out and ignore it. "I am looking for a woman named Sabra."

Immediately the man lurched to his feet, wrested free of Richard's hand, and ran, disappearing between the houses. Alarmed, Richard looked around, but everyone else had also apparently vanished. Damnation, what was going on?

Having no better course to take, he followed where the man had gone, taking a well-worn path leading away from the village into the trees. He soon came to a clearing, in the center of which was the lodge. It was in good repair and decorated with native signs he did not recognize. More attention had been lavished on this building than the others, the result of community rather than individual effort. Boldly carved totem poles stood about like guardians, reminding him of the ancient standing stones of England with their hidden meanings and innate power. Sabra had described it all in her letter and had written also of the old shaman who resided over the spiritual needs of the people from this place. He and his daughter had quite impressed her, it seemed.

Richard started to cross the clearing—the path to Sabra's cabin lay somewhere beyond it—and stopped midway. Out of the lodge stepped an old man, upright, resplendent in buckskin, carrying an ornately carved staff, and wearing a headdress of eagle feathers. Richard knew this must be Black Eagle, the shaman of the village. The man paused for a long moment, staring across the clearing at Richard, then purposefully marched forward until they were only a pace or two apart.

"We welcome you, dark spirit," the old man finally said.

Nonplused by this greeting, Richard recovered and smiled at him. "I am no spirit, simply a man come to find a friend of mine."

"We *know* who you are, dark spirit, and why you are here. Your coming has been known to us for many months."

Richard was about to lie to cover himself, when it came to him that these people did indeed know about him—everything about him. "You know what I am?"

The shaman nodded. That explained the first fellow's startled reaction. Good God, had Sabra brought them *all* into her circle?

"And the woman I seek?"

"The great mother of the night who lives alone. Yes, we know that you are the dark mother's honored consort and the son of her blood. Come." Black Eagle turned and headed back toward the lodge.

Richard had lived long enough and seen enough to know that to question the wishes of a shaman was an invitation to trouble. Besides, the dim interior of the lodge would provide him with a welcome respite from the light. Though the day had been cloudy it still pressed hard upon him, bright enough to be uncomfortable and exhausting.

Inside the lodge, all was cool semi-shadow and quiet. A fire, bounded by rocks, smoldered gently in the center of the dirt floor, its smoke drifting up to a hole in the roof. The pungent, wholesome smell of burning sage and sweetgrass hung heavy in the air. The shaman sat cross-legged on a blanket on the floor near the fire and Richard accepted the unspoken invitation to sit across from him. Black Eagle lit a pipe from a glowing taper and for the longest time nothing was said. All that could be heard was the gentle crackle of burning wood, and the dry sucking sound of the old man smoking.

Richard wanted to speak, to ask questions, but quelled the impulse. There was magic here, he sensed that much, and it would not be rushed.

Black Eagle's mouth thinned slightly. Perhaps that was his version of an approving smile, for he offered the pipe to Richard. He accepted it with reverence and drew on it deeply, inhaling the heady, sweet-smelling smoke. It was not ordinary tobacco; Richard could not tell what else it was, only that it did him no harm and was offered in peace and friendship.

He inhaled again and understood at least one of the meanings behind the shaman's actions. Richard had just come from an age of rushing speed and disquietude, of cruelty and indifference. Now he'd suddenly stepped into a pocket of serenity from another century and needed to get used to the change. The flow of life ran differently here where the shortest unit to measure time was the length of a day.

The shade, the silence, and the smoke granted an unexpected ease to the burdens on his soul. He closed his eyes, content to feel the heat of the fire upon his face and gradually came to realize that for now, in this place, his hunger slept.

Some while later Black Eagle held a braid of sweetgrass over the fire. It caught briefly, then went out, being unable to burn. He held the smoking braid in one hand and chanted for awhile in his own language. The words were meaningless to Richard, but their rhythm was as soothing as a lullaby.

"I have asked the clouds to shelter you for the last steps of your journey," Black Eagle told him when he'd finished.

Richard wasn't sure what reply to make to him and settled on a polite one. "Thank you. That is very kind."

"The mother who lives alone came to us years ago. She needed rest from her good work and honored us with her presence. We have protected her and respected her wishes ever since."

The old man paused, looking deep into Richard's eyes. "I had a vision of her that told me her consort-son would come soon to find her. The vision told me to help him, and I will obey the dark mother."

"I thank you," said Richard, "I have not spoken to her for many years, and now my need to see her is great."

The old man looked into the fire. "Yes, she can help you. Maybe. But for her, help is too late. She is returning to the earth."

A fist closed over Richard's heart and squeezed. "What do you mean?"

But the old man stood abruptly and went to the door. "Someone waits outside now to guide you to the mother's house. You will be safe. The sun is hiding his face."

"What do you mean she's returning to the earth?"

"It is her place to tell you, spirit, not mine. Come."

Richard remained sitting, staring after him. Returning to the earth? Had Sabra been injured in some way? He knew well that vampires could not simply die.

Could they?

He went to the door. Black Eagle stood in the clearing at the center of the totem poles, looking down the trail into the woods. Silhouetted gray against the black of the trees was a shapeless figure shrouded in a long blanket. His guide, Richard thought. He shouldered his bag, walked over to Black Eagle, and they waited for the guide to join them.

A woman, he discovered when she got close enough. Black hair and eyes, dusky skin, native features strong in the fine bones of her face. The shaman said something to her in their language. She briefly lowered her head and pulled the blanket more tightly about her body.

"This is She-Who-Walks, my daughter. She will guide you, help you in any way she can."

"Very pleased to meet you," said Richard.

She made no reply.

Black Eagle turned to leave, but paused, his lips drawn thin again. "Good-looking woman, huh?" He raised an arm and with his fist lightly thumped Richard's shoulder twice in a friendly manner, then continued back to the lodge. He could not be sure because of the rustle of the wind, but the old man seemed to be softly chuckling to himself.

Then She-Who-Walks stepped forward and claimed Richard's complete attention. She looked calmly up into his eyes. Her midnight gaze seemed to burn right through him, seeing deep into the darkest recesses of his soul. He could not turn from her scrutiny, did not want to; was this what it was like when he pressed his own power upon others? He finally could stand no more and looked away. He felt suddenly naked and ashamed of his nakedness.

Until she reached out and took his hand.

She radiated peace and power in a way that he hadn't felt since his first meeting all those hundreds of years past with Sabra. He felt a sudden warm stirring in his blood and in his groin.

"Come." She released his hand, walking quickly, and was at the edge of the clearing before he could think to react.

She moved through the forest effortlessly, threading between the trees like a cat's shadow. He followed a respectful distance behind and wondered that a person not of the Goddess's blood could be so at one with the earth. He was sure that she was close to Sabra, closer than any except himself.

"Yes, I am," She-Who-Walks suddenly said, glancing at him. "I am her bridge with the world outside. She has told me many things of her life, of you."

So she has the Gift of Sight as well. No wonder Sabra chose her. "Is it much farther?"

She paused, a smile playing around her mouth. "Why? Are you tired?" She didn't wait for his answer, but slipped on through the woods.

No, he wasn't remotely tired yet, but growing restive again. The shelter and solace he'd found in the lodge were beginning to fall away, to be replaced by impatience . . . and the hunger. He hoped he could last it out. In all likelihood, he would have to feed upon She-Who-Walks. The prospect both aroused and alarmed him.

The pale light was visibly fading, both from the pending sunset and the thickening sky. Wind gusted about them like stray spirits and the temperature dropped. Perhaps Black Eagle might have overdone things when he'd asked for cloud cover. They were in for a hell of a storm to tell by the signs.

Then he felt *her*. Sabra. His mother was near. His lover was near. Just ahead of them. His heart quickened, the breath catching in his throat. With a surge of unnatural strength he sped swiftly past She-Who-Walks and burst into a clearing. There stood a small cabin, still and dark. No smoke rose from the chimney, no welcoming face appeared at the window.

"Sabra! Sabra!" His voice echoed from the cathedral pines surrounding them and was thrown back a thousand times over. But there was no other reply. She was not there. And yet, she was. He *knew* it. And then the sense of her faded and was gone like a mist in the woods, and he felt suddenly, desperately alone.

"The dark mother is not here now, but she will be. We will wait until she is ready." She-Who-Walks moved past him and into the cabin. As he followed under the symbols of the sun and the moon carved above the door and the cup sign of the Goddess, he heard Sabra's voice as clearly as if she stood next to him.

Feed, my Richard, feed. See what I have given you.

He looked back to the pressing forest. Yes, she was there, somewhere, but *why* was she hiding?

"Richard!"

She-Who-Walks's voice called to him from the dark interior. He hesitated for ten long seconds, then licked his lips and followed her inside.

It was so dark that it took a moment even for Richard's eyes to adjust. There was little there to see; a bed close to the fireplace where She-Who-Walks was now preparing and lighting a blaze, a small table, and a rocking chair were all the furniture. There were bunches of herbs hanging from the ceiling to dry, and books, many, many books lined in neat rows along the walls. They were old, wonderful books, the pick of the ones that Sabra had collected over her long, long time on earth, bound in leather and cloth, and some few tooled in gold, carefully preserved and loved.

The fire caught, and the flames threw wanton shadows everywhere. Richard picked up the text lying open on the table. It was an old reprint, a collection of Chrètien de Troyes' wildly fanciful romances. He hadn't thought of the fellow in decades. Not one of his favorite people, not after that ridiculous business de Troyes had put into his *Lancelot*. None of it was true nor even much his own work; the silly bugger had stolen from past writers or made it all up to flatter his current patron, and no amount of argument could persuade him to change things.

Richard recognized other books about Arthur and the Grail Quest, as it was now called, on the table: the Vulgate Cycle, Robert de Baron's *Joseph d' Arimathie*, von Eschenbach's version of de Troyes' *Perceval*, and a scattering of others, including that latecomer, Malory. Despite its many inaccuracies it was Sabra's favorite account of what had been living experience for them and mere legend to all others since.

"She loves that book," said She-Who-Walks. "I've seen her reading it many times, though she says that it is all wrong. I don't know why." Richard knew.

The fire smelled sweetly of apple wood and quickly warmed the cabin. She-Who-Walks now took the blanket from around herself and put it on the bed. He fairly gaped at the exquisite buckskin dress she wore. Covered with beads and fringe, he grasped that something such as this was meant only for very special ceremonial occasions.

"The mother told me what you would need," said She-Who-Walks, standing unnervingly close. He could smell the scent of crushed flowers in her shining hair. "I know what must be done, and I am here for you."

Richard felt the hunger's gnawing at his insides. It had been a full three days since he last fed, and its keen edge was painful; he'd not felt it so sharply since the very first time it had taken him. If he did not attend it, the cramps would take him, drive him mad again. "Most people would run from me now. Run for their lives and their souls."

"My soul is safe," she replied with disarming conviction. "I am loved by the mother and her Goddess. She will let no harm befall me."

Well, that was some reassurance. "Then I will take only what I need from you."

You must do more than that, my Richard.

He shivered at Sabra's touch in his mind. So close, so far. "Did you hear?"

She nodded. "Do what she asks of you."

"And what is it she asks?"

"Don't you know?"

"I haven't the Gift of Sight. Tell me."

Her dark eyes glittered. "You are to make me like you. Take all that I have and make me as you are, as she is."

Richard couldn't speak for a moment. He'd bedded countless women, nearly always feeding from them while at the height of passion, but never in all his time had he made another like himself. The idea disturbed, even frightened him. "Why?" he whispered, hardly loud enough to be heard.

"Because it is her wish. Is that not reason enough?"

"I don't understand."

"You will. She will tell you."

"She's not asked this of me ever before. Why now?"

"Because it is the right time. Do you know what day this is?"

He thought a moment before the right answer came. "Good God. It's Beltane, isn't it?"

"The holiest of days. The day of creation. The time has at last come for *you* to create. This is what the dark mother has told me. Are you going to grant her wish, or should we walk back to the village?"

Richard . . . please.

He'd never once refused Sabra in the past. He wouldn't begin now, but he had to at least warn this young woman. "There's a danger from me you don't know of—"

"Is it about the man you killed?" She-Who-Walks smiled at his discomfiture. "I saw it on your soul earlier. There is no danger for me. You will be all right with me if you really want to be. What happened to you then was brought on by your anger and pain. Such things are not in you tonight. Are they?"

Richard lifted his hand to touch her face then let his fingers comb through the thick black hair that fell over her shoulders. "No, they're not," he murmured. He bent and kissed her, lightly. Her mouth was soft, warm and giving. "You're utterly certain of this? In your own heart, you're sure?"

She smiled again. There was a familiar fire deep in her eyes, daring him, even mocking him. He'd seen it before in Sabra.

Answer enough.

This time he kissed She-Who-Walks hard and long and felt her firm strength melt into his, her body take the shape of his, almost become his. She pulled away after a moment, smiling, gently biting her lower lip. Standing by the bed, she undid the buckskin cord that served as a belt around her dress, and in a swift movement pulled it over her head. Naked in the firelight, she let it slip to the floor. The flames seemed to caress the velvet smooth contours of her brown body, deepening its shadows with their shifting light. She raised her arms high.

"See, see what the Goddess has prepared for you." And she lay back atop the blanket, waiting for him.

For a moment, he stood motionless, as if to test how long he could resist his nature and his need. He could feel the uncontrollable building within, could feel himself changing from the inside out. The wind howled beyond the cabin's thick walls, and rain pounded on the roof. His own heartbeat thundered in his ears as if to match the drumming in the sky.

He stood over her, finally reaching down to touch her, to rest his hand on the silken flesh of her inner thighs. His fingers moved upward in a slow caress as far as they could go. She was, indeed, ready for him. More than ready. As he was himself.

Unable to resist further, he surrendered fully to her. He was with her, on her, her hands and his tearing at his clothes, mouths open, kissing, biting, tasting, both in a fever of need. She reached down and grasped his hardness in her hands, then took it quickly within herself, gasping at his entry, moaning, hanging on to him with legs and hands and nails. And he was pushing, thrusting, beyond control, fully immersed in his true form. Fangs enlarged, eyes red, a great roar escaped him as he raised his head to strike. She turned her face to one side, crying out in her own ecstasy, and he took her, fangs buried deep in her neck, sucking hard, greedy in his want, spurting his seed into her as he drank. Her blood gushed into him, giving him life, nourishment, satiation in every sense. She held his head against her as he fed.

"I have done as you asked, dark mother," she whispered.

And Richard was suddenly aware, through the passion and the bloodlust, that *Sabra* was there, watching as he fed. He lifted away, blood dripping from his mouth onto the naked woman's belly, onto her breasts, and there through the window, outside in the shrieking wind and rain, he saw his mother's eyes, his lover's eyes, glowing bright from their own inner flame. That was all he recognized, though. The rest . . . her face . . . her body . . .

It's a distortion made by water on the window. It must be.

Lightning flashed close by, blinding him, leaving behind a nightmare afterimage of a small figure, vaguely human in shape, but there the similarity stopped.

It has to be . . .

He stared hard, trying to see detail, but caught only a blur of movement against the trees. A great howling scream rent the air, overwhelming the ferocity of nature itself, and the gleam of her eyes disappeared into the darkness of the storm.

Richard pushed himself up from She-Who-Walks and stumbled to the door.

"You cannot leave yet, your task is not complete," she cried weakly from the bed. "You *must* complete the making. The mother told me. *I* am to be the new mother. She has prepared me in all the ways. All that is left is to make me as you. You must, for her sake."

"What has happened to her?" He opened the door. Icy rain slapped him, as though to force him back. He could see nothing. "Tell me!"

"She is returning to the earth. It is the way, there is nothing to be done. Yet the work of the Goddess must go on."

"That's ridiculous. We cannot die. We're immortal."

"The mother knows, and she told me. It will happen. It is happening. There is no other way."

He slammed the door against the wild night and fumbled for his clothes. "I'm going to her."

"You won't find her. She has willed it to be this way." She-Who-Walks reached out, her featherlight touch enough to stay him. Her fingers were as chill and fragile as glass. "After the making, she will come to you. Only *after* the making."

Looking at her, Richard knew in his soul that what she said was true. Something was very wrong here, wrong with Sabra, but there was nothing he could do about it, not until the time was right. The fist tightened around his heart again, as unyielding as iron.

"Do not fear for her, Richard."

"I can't help it." He reluctantly went back to the bed, climbing in next to her. He started to look out the window, but she pulled his head down and kissed him, licking her own still wet blood from his lips.

"Take me. Make me. Give me your life."

He held her close, feeling more sad than he could ever recall.

"You must finish the making."

If this was what Sabra wanted, then this was what he would do even if he did not know why. He was sworn to her.

He tried to resume what they'd begun, but felt cold, dazed. She-Who-Walks rolled on top of him, taking the lead in things. Her movements were slower, less frenzied than before, but she continued to kiss and caress him until desire came to take the place of fear. She pulled him upright, pressing his face against her bloodstained breasts, coaxing him to kiss them clean.

It took a little time, but mutual need gradually overtook them. She sank onto him, sighing as he entered her, and wrapped her legs tight around his back.

Once more, Richard buried his fangs in her sweet neck, more softly this time, feeding steadily, intent now to take all her life into himself as he rocked her back and forth. She moaned and shuddered as each wave of pleasure he gave rolled through her body.

Her arms went slack, eventually falling away, and he had to completely support her.

Her breaths came short and shallow. She had to fight for them.

And still he fed. He had to.

Her heart fluttered, straining hard to pump what little remained.

He worked his teeth, cutting deep into her flesh. She made a last faint sighing moan as a final burst of crimson flooded his mouth, then the flow ceased.

When he eased her body gently down, it was not her blood that dripped onto her face, but his tears.

Richard spent the night squatted in a corner of the cabin, listening to every sound, watching. He watched She-Who-Walks in her deathly sleep, and he watched, too, for Sabra, but she did not come. The Beltane fire died to feathery gray ash, and the blackness, both without and within his soul, was complete.

Morning crept slowly into the cabin. Richard stretched and stood, rubbing his gritty eyes, and opened the door for one last look. If Sabra had not come by now, she would not for the duration of the day. Soon he would lie next to She-Who-Walks again and sleep himself until her awakening at dusk.

The sky seemed washed clean. The wind and rain had died with the dawn, and a great stillness held the forest. In the trees a deer stepped gently across the deadening carpet of pine needles, utterly silent on its meanderings. The sun shone this day, though it made little difference this deep in the trees.

Sabra was in trouble. His original reason for coming was unimportant next to that fact. He needed to see her, to help her, but how could he if she would not show herself? He studied the surrounding forest, no longer comfortable with its closeness and depth, seeing it now as a threat and obstacle.

What to do?

"Richard."

The deer bolted suddenly, tail flicking upright in alarm, and Richard turned to the voice, the voice that he knew so well. Only she could have come this near without his hearing.

"Sabra."

Though barefoot and wrapped in a old blanket she was as beautiful and elegant as on that first night in his tent at Orleans, smiling, radiant.

I knew you would come.

"How could I do otherwise?"

She all but flew to him and his waiting embrace. He held her hard and tight, wanting to hold her forever. Impossible, of course, but he did make it last until the knot in his throat softened and he could speak again.

"Tell me what is going on. I must know."

"Yes, my love. But inside. The sun."

He lifted her, sweeping her into the cabin and closing the door against the light. She clung to him a moment, then he reluctantly set her down. The blanket had pulled away from her and he saw with no small shock that she was naked beneath its tattered cover.

"Sabra, what is this about? Why are you—"

But she held one hand up to hush him, for all her attention was on She-Who-Walks. "She is beautiful, is she not? Did you complete it?"

"When she awakens, she will be like us. You aren't angry, are you?"

"It is as I wished."

"Why do I feel shame, then, as if I have betrayed you in some way?"

"Do not feel so, sweet Richard. She was my gift to you, given out of love."

"But I saw you at the window, looking at us."

"I watched out of love, not anger or jealousy." She looked at him, face glowing with a smile of pure childlike joy. "I had to see the birth of my grand-daughter." Sabra laughed, but the laughter suddenly turned to a gasp, and she doubled over.

Richard was beside her in an instant. "What is wrong? What's happening to you?"

She pushed him roughly away, her face pinched with pain, and fell to her knees. The blanket dropped. Richard reached out, but the snarl that came from her stopped him in midmovement.

"Sabra?" he whispered. Understanding flooded him. Cold and hollow. *Oh, dear God, not you!*

Her voice came to him, thick and heavy. "Do not come near me."

She stayed there on all fours, panting for breath, her back rising and falling, contracting in time to the spasms of pain spiking through her. Her hair had become dull and matted, and her nails thickened and curved long against the plank floor, scarring and splintering the wood. Another snarl came from her, followed by an anguished cry. Then she was upright, or at least as upright as she could be, and lunging for the door. But Richard was as quick and caught her before she made the threshold.

"What is happening, Sabra? *What is wrong?*"

He held her fast as she fought to leave, fought him with a strength near to his own, tearing, scratching, biting like a wild beast. Finally, exhausted, she went slack and that was when he saw her face for the first time. Gone was the beauty, gone the elegance. The thing he held so tenderly was neither human nor animal: face coated with hair, eyes wild and red, fangs extended. Then with a shudder that racked the whole of her small body she changed, and the Sabra that he knew, that he loved, was once more in his arms.

Fingers trembling, he brushed a dark strand from her face and kissed her brow. "I'm right here. I'll always be here for you. Everything will be all right . . ."

All the sadness in the world was in her eyes as she looked at him.

"You must let me go, dear Richard, there is nothing you can do for me. This is my end, my natural end."

"No, you said we were ageless, that nothing could ever—"

"I never told you, my love, for I dared to hope it would not be true. Yet true it is."

"Then tell me!"

"You know it now for yourself already."

"The man I—"

"I felt your delight when you killed him, the exultation, then heard the cry of your soul when it returned and you realized what you'd done. Felt your terror. My poor love."

Of course she would. But what—?

"We're old, Richard, and often have we called on the power within us. Each time we do, it becomes a little more difficult to take ourselves back to a human state. It's subtle, and takes a very long, long time, centuries before we ever begin to notice. Then we reach a point where the strength needed to overcome the beast within becomes greater and greater until in the end, we cannot match it. We become a beast of Annwyn and finally return to the earth. I can only maintain human form for a very little time before the beast takes me again. It's worse at the full of the moon, and this turning was the hardest yet. I'm getting weaker, soon I will not be able to fight it anymore." She stopped, exhausted with the effort of speech.

Richard continued to hold her, frozen to the point of panic. This was *Sabra*, his lover, his eternal friend, the mother of all he was, of all his world, speaking to him of death. Her death. He could not dream of an existence without her. But if what she said was true, then he would himself have no better future.

"There must be something I can do for you. Some way to help."

"Perhaps, but I don't know if it—" She began to writhe once more in his arms, moaning in pain as the change began to seize her.

"Tell me!"

"I—I must drink of the great Cauldron of Cerridwen. What the Christ-worshippers call the Grail. They searched for it to keep for themselves, to try to smother the power of the Goddess. But I hid it from them all."

"Yes, but will it help you?"

"I don't know, but I know not what else to do. I cannot travel to it. You must bring it to me and quickly. I don't think I shall survive the next turn of the moon."

"Where is it?"

"I hid it at the home of the nine sisters, the place around which the whole world revolves, the entrance to Annwyn, Ynis Witrin . . . Avalon."

Her body shuddered from a vicious spasm, and she changed once more, crying pitifully like a trapped animal and struggling to get away. This time he let her go.

She clawed the door open and rushed naked out into the deadly sunlight. It seemed to have no effect on her, or she was beyond noticing. He had to stay inside, shielding his eyes against the glare with one hand.

She paused at the edge of the trees, turning once to look back at him.

Find it for me, my Richard. Find it and release me from this agony.

She disappeared into the covering darkness of the forest.

His normal daylight sleep would not come. He had far too much to think about, to worry over, to fear.

The stacks of books about the Grail made sense now. He flipped through each of them, hoping to add to his knowledge, hoping to refresh his memory of a long-vanished age. Often he stopped to look out the windows or open the door, but Sabra was quite gone.

Where does she sleep? How does she feed? Has she killed as well?

His desire was to immediately leave. Sun or no sun, he wanted to drop everything and get started, but he could do nothing until She-Who-Walks awakened. Had circumstances been different he might have otherwise enjoyed the wait, the anticipation, but now he fretted over the delay.

At long last you've produced an heir and yet feel only vexation. 'Tis unworthy of you, Richard d'Orleans.

He scowled to himself and spent a little more of the endless day putting the place in order and read from several of the books. When the evening shade crept across a rain barrel next to the house, he ventured out to fetch water. He found a towel, wet it, and gently cleansed the stains of his feeding from the young woman's body, noting half in satisfaction and half in wonder that the savage wounds he'd made on her throat in their passion were completely healed.

She stirred as he bathed her face. Her lips parted

and she took her first breath of the night, holding it, then slowly releasing it with a sigh. Her eyes opened.

He caressed her, smiling. "What do you remember?"

A pause as she thought, then her hand closed over his and she smiled in return. "Everything." Now she ran her hand up his arm and to the back of his neck, pulling. He bent to kiss her. "Everything. You were good."

And he thought his ability to blush had long deserted him. "Well, thank you. So were you."

"Maybe we can do it again later."

"I should like that very much. Do you hunger yet?"

"A little."

"You should have a period of grace before it gets really bad. Half an hour, perhaps."

"Then we'll have time to get back to the lodge. Black Eagle said he would wait there for us."

Richard sobered. "Is he to be the one to . . ."

She must have heard the rest of his thought in her mind. "Our way is different from the time of your change. Instead of one making a great sacrifice of blood, many will each make a little sacrifice to share in the honor."

"Your hunger may be too strong to stop once you begin. It was so for me."

"That's why you need to be there. Black Eagle is my father in life and you are now my father in death. Between the two of you, you are to make sure I bring harm to no one until I've had my fill. The dark mother said I'd be all right after that."

"And so you shall."

She got up and slipped the buckskin dress over her head, retied the cord, and reached for the blanket, but it was liberally stained with red. She left it.

Richard put on his coat and donned his hat.

She-Who-Walks went to the mantel, opening an

old metal candy box that served as a bookend. "This is for you. She said it might help."

A slip of paper, folded once. He opened and read it.

"In case your recollection falters, remember that I wrote everything down in the Abbey Book. *The last I'd heard it was still safe in that museum in Ireland. It's all in the old tongue, of course—and in verse. I was never very good with verse, but was mad for it for a time, so please forgive my faltering efforts at poetry. Speed well, but take care, and try not to worry about me. I am in good hands.*

May the Goddess protect and guide you, my love, my child, my best of all friends."

She-Who-Walks read it when he passed it to her. "Soon she will not be able to come back. She will be one with the earth."

"Not if I have anything to do with it," he said, once more shouldering his bag.

She crossed ahead of him to the door, but hesitated on the threshold. "It feels . . . strange."

"It will for a time. You'll need to feed."

"Yes, I know. Do as she asks and try not to worry. I will care for her until she is no longer in need of care. I needed to be like you to have the strength for it. The work of the Goddess will go on."

She stepped through and walked briskly across the open space into the forest. Richard looked around at the inside of the cabin one last time, drinking in as best he could the lingering essence of the Sabra he'd known for so long. He picked up the copy of Malory's *Morte d'Arthur*, tucking it in the bag, then closed the door, the simple latch catching and holding. There was no lock. None necessary out here.

She-Who-Walks waited for him just under the trees, her hand out to take his. "Come . . . Father."

And he followed.

Chapter Four

Another full night gone and most of another day, just to get back to Vancouver.

On their return from the forest, She-Who-Walks went straight to the clearing before the lodge house where Black Eagle and what appeared to be the whole population of Kingcome waited in silence. She spoke briefly with her father in their own language, then he raised his staff as a sign to the others. In twos and threes they followed her into the lodge. Black Eagle looked at Richard, who had kept a respectful distance just outside the totem circle.

"You, too, dark father."

The new appellation pleased Richard.

"Our daughter grows impatient."

He waited for Richard, then they entered the lodge together.

I suppose this also makes me Black Eagle's son in a way, since his blood now flows in me through her, he thought. Richard now had a daughter, a lover, and, he hoped, a friend in She-Who-Walks, though what a modern psychologist would have made of the quasi-incestuous implications of their new relationship he dared not speculate. He smiled to himself, imagining trying to explain it all to Freud. *Well, Sigmund, it was one of those things where you just had to have been there.*

The ceremony they'd all obviously prepared for did

not take long. His daughter's awakened hunger would not allow for delay. Richard stood on her left, Black Eagle on her right, with one of the young men of the village before her. He was shirtless, but the lodge was warm from the blazing fire and the press of bodies, the air dense with the rough smell of humanity, burning sage, and curls of sweetgrass smoke.

She-Who-Walks's eyes were flushed red with anticipation, and when her lips parted Richard could see her sharp corner teeth budding to their full length. None of this was lost on the others. They said nothing, but glances were exchanged. Richard felt a moment's unease about so many people being witness to what was to come, then pushed it to one side. This was the Goddess's work, and he would trust there would be no trouble.

The young man held his arm out, a hint of apprehension in his eyes. Black Eagle touched his shoulder in a reassuring gesture. She-Who-Walks bent over the man's arm, the sheet of her raven-dark hair obscuring Richard's view of her face, but a moment later he caught the tantalizing scent of fresh blood. Sabra must have told her what to do; his new daughter fed as he usually did himself, taking from the vein inside the elbow. It was much less visible than a throat wound.

After a few long minutes, Black Eagle interrupted her, or tried to, for she did not relinquish her hold until he and Richard physically pulled her away. She tried to fight them, driven by desperate hunger to blindly continue feeding, but Richard's strength and Black Eagle's soothing words were enough to calm her until the next person came forward, a young woman this time.

The next instance she resisted them less as her hunger diminished, and the next was easier still.

The pattern repeated until Richard lost count of how

many shared their blood with She-Who-Walks. The thick air, his own lassitude from feeding so heavily the previous night, and the sheer emotional exhaustion brought on by worry for Sabra were having their way with him. Not until Black Eagle shook him from his standing doze did he realize that it was over.

"You need rest," the shaman told him and led him outside.

Cold fresh night air, tinged with the clean smell of fir trees and the damp earth of spring . . . Richard breathed it in with pleasure, rubbing the grit from his eyes. "I'll rest while I travel. Can one of your men take me across to Black Point right now?"

"Yes, he can, but don't you want to stay? It's gonna be a hell of a party tonight." Inside the lodge a drum and a mellow-voiced flute started up, and several voices began to chant to them.

God, but it was like the old times, the ancient times, when he'd celebrated with Sabra the various festivals of her Goddess in the forests of Wales or Ireland or on the plain of the Giant's Dance or in sacred Ynis Wytrin itself. A hopeless longing for those lost days rose in him, hard and fast, trying to choke him. He pushed it back.

"I want to, I really do, but Sabra—my dark mother is in great pain from the beast inside her. Every delay brings her more pain as the beast grows stronger."

Black Eagle nodded. "Pain is a part of living, but no one says we have to like it. I'll find someone to take you across, dark father."

"You can call me Richard."

"I know." The corners of Black Eagle's eyes crinkled with deep mischief. "But the tourists expect that kind of stuff. I like to stay in practice." He went back to the lodge. A moment later She-Who-Walks emerged.

"Will you return soon?" she asked, standing close before him.

"Well before the next change of the moon, I hope."

"With the Goddess's cup?"

"When I find it."

"I thought you knew where it was."

"Not the exact spot. There were some secrets Sabra did not share even with me." The Goddess was jealous of bestowing too much knowledge upon the guardians of her relics. In the past it had been enough for Richard to play the soldier and defend without question, leaving the inner mysteries to Sabra and her mortal sisters. That had all changed, now. "I will find it, though."

"Watch your back." He felt the power of her gaze caressing him, those dark, intense eyes, so much like Sabra's, and yet different.

"I always do."

"But more than usual. There's something waiting ahead in your path. . . ."

Her gift of Sight. "What can you tell me?"

"It is—it's dark and resents and fears your presence. The darkness keeps me from seeing anything but where its shadow has been. Where it walks it leaves a trail of blood . . . it thinks long thoughts and cold."

"Does it walk in this world or the one of the Goddess?"

"This one," she said decisively.

"Then I've little to worry about."

"Don't be too sure of that."

He knew better than to take a warning born of the Gift lightly. "All right, I won't. I promise." He saw Black Eagle coming, accompanied by another man. Time to go. Richard kissed her forehead, then drew her tight to him for a farewell embrace, wrapping his arms bearlike around her. How many times had he and Sabra parted in this manner over the centuries? Beyond count.

And it still hadn't gotten any easier.

The boat crossing was wretched; the wind had risen and an unpleasant chop nearly forced them to turn back, but soon Black Point hove into view, and he was on dry land again. Well, not really dry, for a torrential downpour began, and even with his inhuman speed he was soaked by the time he got to the airfield at Port Hardy. No planes would fly from there until morning, though, or at least until the weather cleared. He couldn't find a pilot foolish or greedy enough to make the attempt. After a few phone calls he learned that the earliest Vancouver/Toronto flight was over-booked anyway. He arranged for a standby on the next and tried not to grind his teeth at the delay.

I should have stayed for the party, he thought glumly while changing into dry clothes in the men's room. He debated having a quick shave, then decided against it. Why bother until it was necessary?

Instead, he took a seat in what served as a pas-senger lounge, watching and listening to the rain, and trying not to think about Sabra and failing miserably. Was she out in this stuff? Was she cold? Hungry? Afraid?

For distraction from the tormenting unknowns, he pulled out Sabra's book. He'd read it long ago when it first saw print, and recalled how odd it had felt to see a story written about himself and the men and women that he had known, loved and hated. Sabra was right, much of Malory's account was completely wrong, and yet the timeless tale was there, true in its essentials, and magnificently written. He remembered it all so well, the heady days of his immortal youth, that time of stretching his new powers, of testing them, and, on occasion, abusing them, such as he had done with Guinevere.

Dear Guinevere. Theirs had been a passion to conquer worlds, or so he'd thought at the time. She'd been beautiful and willing, but what a risk it had been, to dare to be the queen's lover. He knew why he'd taken it, having long ago worked it out. He'd done it simply because he *could*. The gifts the Goddess had bestowed upon him had made it possible, even easy.

Sabra hadn't been at all pleased, not because of his making love to another woman, but for the adverse political repercussions in Arthur's court. It was only Sabra's reminder of his oath to protect Arthur that ended things, but by then it was too late, and the scandal was already abroad like a fire, fanned by that damned sneak Mordred. If not for him then Richard might have been able to hypnotize them all, even Guinevere, into forgetting the whole thing.

I suppose they'd call it a learning experience now.

And then came the Grail.

The quest for it was Sabra's attempt to pull them all back together again, to give them a single goal to distract the leaders from the disaster of a civil war. With the power of her Goddess glowing within her, she had created the vision of the Grail Cup in the minds of Christian and Pagan warrior alike and the inspiration for them to go forth and search for it. And Richard—Lancelot—had been in their number. As Arthur's greatest champion they expected no less of him and certainly considerably more.

It had been a strange pursuit, looking for something that was not lost. Yet Sabra had insisted that he look, and longer than any of the others. A weary penance it was to be sure, but the idea had worked, at first, and peace continued in the land. It didn't last, of course, peace being such a fragile thing, but during that age a whole generation had grown up, bred, and died without knowing the terrors of foreign invasion except by hearing of it from their parents. That was the beginning of Arthur's legend, and ever after all of Britain's monarchs had tried to ally themselves with it, for they knew the hold the story had on the hearts of their subjects.

If Richard had known at the time he was helping to create a legend, he'd have taken more care than the singers and poets had done to preserve an accurate account of it. Once they'd finished, the truth was twisted almost beyond recognition and details were blown all out of proportion—like that business with Elaine and her son Galahad. What an embarrassment. Sabra had nearly laughed herself sick when, hot with outrage and exasperation, he'd confessed this latest calamity to her.

Richard himself was not fertile because of his changed state, but he had been close at hand when Elaine's belly started to show, and they demanded she name the father. Who better to choose than Arthur's own right hand? Not only did she avoid any serious reproach—for who could blame a maiden for falling in love with so gallant a fighter?—but she managed to get a favorable marriage out of it for herself, the scheming little bitch. She never did say who the real father was, either. Galahad turned out to be a decent boy, though, Richard saw to that, so the whole thing wasn't a complete disaster.

They were gone now.

Nothing left but their pale shades lingering in his memory.

Tears filled his eyes and unbidden fell in great drops down his face and into his lap. Had he been asked, he would have been quite unable to describe the depth of his sadness, for he did not have such words. It was beyond telling.

The weight of the years and their many griefs sometimes piled overwhelmingly upon him, but through everything Sabra had always been there. *Always*. She was his reason for life, his reason to continue ever forward, no matter how great the losses of the past. To face a future without her, however brief it might be . . .

Sabra. Oh, my poor lady. I will find it for you. I swear it by your Goddess and my God.

"Mr. Dun?"

He snapped awake, wincing against the harsh morning light beating upon the windows. A sleepy-eyed airport employee informed him the pilot he'd hired was ready to leave for Vancouver.

Toronto. His home for this particular life. He felt like he'd been away for years, not days, and sought to shrug off the feeling as he walked quickly along the drab tunnel joining the plane to the building and emerged into the afternoon brightness of the terminal. He longed for the dim sanctuary of his own house. Problems awaited him there, he knew. He still had to deal with the aftermath of the Niagara Horror, and help Bourland with his damned assassin hunt, but surely it could be put off for a few days while he—

Then perhaps not. He spotted the two plainclothes RCMP officers right away, one hunter recognizing others of his kind. No one smiled at the encounter, not even to show their teeth. The officers pulled out their badges, displaying them too fast for him to get any names or to see if the photos matched the originals.

"Are you Mr. Richard Dun? Please come with us, sir. It's a matter of security."

Oh, so polite, but they bracketed him, making enough of a disturbance to attract the brief notice of passersby. One or two stopped, staring at the two cleancut, suited men hustling a sinister, stubble-faced third off the concourse.

Perhaps I should have had that shave after all, was his first sour thought about the business.

A hand gripped his elbow just a little too firmly for comfort, and they steered him through a doorway marked EMPLOYEES ONLY into a too-brightly lit room and face-to-face with Etienne Demarest. They released Richard and backed off.

"Mr. Dun, how good to see you again," he said with a striking lack of sincerity.

Demarest was smiling, or at least Richard assumed that the strange look on the man's face was meant to be a smile. One could also feel the electric edge of excitement hovering around him, like a little boy about to play a trick on his teacher. Obviously, he knew something, or had something to say. Good God, had they turned up a bit of telling evidence at Niagara? Richard wished once again that he'd paid more attention to Sabra when she'd tried to develop an ability in him to read thoughts. She did it effortlessly, had always done so. The best that Richard had ever achieved was to read general feelings, and the feeling he picked up now was anything but good. He could easily sense dislike, suspicion, and . . . what was it . . . ? Ah, yes, smug satisfaction for a clean capture. Richard carefully preserved a bland expression.

"We thought you'd cut and run," Demarest continued.

We. Who did he think he was, some sort of monarch or a doctor? "Why on earth should I do that?"

Demarest didn't bother to answer, only gestured at one of the plastic chairs in the room. It was a dull, impersonal chamber, useful for most any purpose, from spare storage space to private interrogations. Demarest was likely intent on the latter, the way he stared. Richard supposed that this was for the purpose of discomfiting him. He was also expected to sit so that Demarest could have the psychological advantage of height. *Balls to that, my lad. I learned to do this sort of thing with the big boys.* He remained on his feet, forcing Demarest to do the same.

Richard broke the silence. "What's this about?"

"You tell me."

"I'm a busy man, Chief Inspector, I don't have time for these games. If you have something to say, then say it. Otherwise I'm going." He waited a moment, got no reply, then turned and found the larger of the plainclothes men blocking the door. The other one must be on watch outside. "And if you think he can stop me, you've another think coming."

The officer remained front of him. They were about the same height, though the man was rather more bulky. As Richard started past, the fellow reached to grapple him in the best training manual style. With a swift, almost casual movement, Richard spun and slammed him facefirst against the wall, immobilizing his arms in a surprisingly easy locking hold. Richard put on a little pressure, gently, and the man became very still.

"All right, Dun, that's enough," Demarest snarled behind him. "Leave my constable alone."

"Then cut the crap and tell me why I was dragged in here."

"I want to know where you've been for the last three days."

"Is that all?" With a final twitch of his fingers, Richard released his hold. The man, flushed red with anger, recovered his balance, but kept his distance.

Richard turned once more to Demarest. "Where I've been, Chief Inspector, is none of your damned business."

"It is where the Prime Minister's safety is concerned."

So, someone upstairs had obviously been breathing down Demarest's neck for results on the investigation and now Demarest was trying to breathe down another's. Not because it would do any good, but simply because he could do it. Oh, dear, but wasn't that a familiar pattern? Richard almost winced. "My absence was a personal matter and had nothing to do with the case."

"I've got no reason to believe anything you say, not after you tried to mislead me from the very beginning. That Niagara killing still isn't settled to my satisfaction. There's more to it, I know."

The schooling and practice of centuries prevented Richard from heaving a sigh of vast relief just then. The man had suspicions, but nothing more. "Everything I could say was in my report," he stated, quite truthfully.

"You left things out, everyone leaves out things they don't want the official reports to carry."

Richard looked him up and down, smiled, and shook his head pityingly. "Don't try to measure me by your own standards, Demarest," he drawled. "You'll come up short every time."

Somewhere by the door the RCMP made a muffled choking sound, quickly suppressed. Demarest threw a murderous glance at him, then refocused on Richard. "In a situation as grave as this, where the life of the Prime Minister is under threat, it is my duty to ensure everyone involved in the investigation is above suspicion. In my book, you are not."

"Indeed?"

"I've had you thoroughly checked out, Dun."

"So?"

"What I've found is just too good to be true."

"You have a problem with me being competent at my job?"

"I have a problem with a record that has holes in it so big you could fly a 747 through them. When I try to fill them in they just get bigger, then I come up against a brick wall. There is too much missing information."

"It's not missing, only classified—my other work for the government."

"So I've discovered, but I have a double A clearance and—"

"The file on me requires a triple A clearance. Sorry."

It looked to be a hard struggle, but Demarest managed to keep his voice from rising beyond conversational level. "I am trying to conduct an investigation and to prevent a possible national emergency. To do that I need to see your file, all of it. I demand you allow me access."

"The triple A designation is there for very good reasons of national security. It's not for me to decide who has access. If you think it's really that necessary, then I suggest you talk to the PM about it. And give him a damn good reason why."

"My reason is that you are hindering an official investigation and have done so from the start. You go haring off after a so-called minor lead without any kind of support or backup to a man who, according to you, might have been our only connection to the assassin. The man winds up extremely dead with you being the only witness to tell how he might have gotten that way. Then, when you should be continuing with your duties here, you hop a plane and disappear to God knows where—"

"I did not disappear, and I had leave to go. I was on the west coast visiting my sick mother, if it's any of your bloody business, which it is not. If that's all you really wanted to know, you could have just asked politely instead of pawing the ground to show me how much dust you can kick up."

Demarest looked him, as best he could from his lesser height, directly in the eyes. "I don't like you, Dun, and I don't trust you. If it were left to me, you'd be in a cell this minute being interrogated by the Sureté de Quebec. And believe me, you would answer them."

Richard smiled at the thought. "Demarest, you are a fool. And trust me on this, it could kill you."

Demarest paled. "Is that a threat?"

"A warning." He loomed close over Demarest and whispered, "Against . . . hypertension."

Demarest's mouth twitched. Color now darkened his face.

Dear me, not amused, are you? "You really should relax more. You'd have a lot fewer headaches and greatly lower your risk of heart disease."

"You son of a bitch."

Richard gave a short laugh, shaking his head once. "If you were worth the effort, I'd be tempted to rip your heart out, but I'm tired, so today's your lucky day." Demarest started to speak, but Richard raised one hand, palm out, to cut him off. "No more. I've had quite enough of this. If there's any threat to the PM around here, it's you. Don't you think it would be a change for the better if you investigated the criminals rather than the investigators?"

He crossed to the door, and this time the constable hurriedly moved out of his way.

✧   ✧   ✧

Once more in the comfortable confines of the Jaguar, Richard eased the car into gear and pulled out of the parking lot into the light of a mercifully cloudy day. He cruised along the clear highway, smiling at the long lines of vehicles headed in the other direction stopped by the construction that had so irritated him earlier. Still no sign of the source of the obstruction, either. Winter and rehabilitation. Demarest could definitely use some of the latter, for if anyone in this business was obstructive . . .

Patience, patience. He's just a fool and you've dealt with his sort before. No need to let him get to you.

Demarest was a fool, but persistent. The chance certainly existed that he could somehow find access, authorized or not, to Richard's triple A file. Richard had paid a fortune to a computer expert to get that high of a security rating, and another fortune for what false data it covered, but one could do anything with computers if one knew how, and Demarest might have an expert who could also hack into the system. If Demarest dug deeply enough, he could find out Richard's birth certificate was false, or that he'd not attended this university or served in that military branch. For such an inquiry on so basic a level no computer was needed, a few phone calls and he'd discover no teacher, no trainer, no officer at any of the named institutions with a recollection of a person named Richard Dun. All hell would break loose then.

Damn, but modern life was getting much too complicated. He would have to find some sort of distraction to throw Demarest off the track, otherwise Richard would have to move on yet again, and one more thing he'd come to hate over the centuries was moving. Especially when it was hurried and entailed

changing not only his city, but in these days of better
communication, country—not to mention having a full
identity alteration. Easy enough to do, he had several
of those set up, ready, and waiting for just such an
emergency, but what a nuisance. Yet another matter
to deal with, along with Sabra and Charon. That, and
the brown Buick that was following him. It had been
on his tail since he left the airport.

The CN Tower and Skydome slid past, and soon he
was on the Gardner extension, nearing the Beaches. The
Buick stuck with him, even through the line-ups of
parents retrieving their kids at the primary school.
Richard could feel sorry for the other driver. If he was
trying to do a covert surveillance, this was hardly the
best neighborhood for it. If he was trying to make
Richard nervous, he was in for a disappointment.

The school line delayed him only a little, and a
scant thirty minutes after having left the airport, he
was pulling into the double driveway of his house.
The garage doors opened silently, mysteriously before
him from his remote signal, and he eased the E-Type
to a gentle stop next to its sibling, a Land Rover.
Checking the mirror, he saw the Buick cruise slowly
past.

Richard got out, retrieved his bag, and hit the
inside button that would close the doors, ducking
under them to go around to the front entry. Sure
enough, the Buick had turned somewhere down the
street and was coming back. It stopped on the other
side of the road and parked in front of Mrs. Simstead's
house. Oh, dear. She wouldn't like that at all. He'd
just blocked off her front view of the neighborhood
and the goings on of local life were better than
television to her.

Richard could just see her through her spotless
picture window, scowling mightily. In another minute

she'd work herself up into a fine righteous temper and be out to chase the car off with either a broom or a garden hoe, depending on her mood. No RCMP identification badge would faze her, she knew her rights, and he'd just better move along or she'd call the police on him.

Assuming he *was* RCMP. Richard waited on the shady step. Watching. There. She was coming down her walk now, carrying a *shovel* this time and wearing a nicely disgruntled expression. The man in the car noticed her. Richard relaxed as the fellow flashed his badge in her face. Good, he wasn't IRA, not that they would faze her, either. Mrs. Simstead began arguing with him, pointing down the street with the business end of her shovel, her body language broadcasting the unmistakable message of *clear off*. Rather than continue a futile skirmish with her, he finally rolled his window up, started the motor, and moved the car. As he passed, Richard waved a cheery greeting his way, then unlocked the front door and went inside.

He punched the code in to neutralize, then reset, his alarm system. It was a much more sophisticated version of the standard ones available to homeowners, but he didn't mind the extra trouble and expense. He had his personal treasures—like that Botticelli in the office—and God help anyone trying to take them away.

Richard loved his house. It was his nest. He had realized many years before the psychological importance of having a real home. Wherever he happened to be living, he made sure to indulge himself with a comfortable sanctuary, a place to recharge his batteries when he was drained, a place where he felt safe. He'd been happily living in this particular domicile for several years now and had no desire to leave. Not for the likes of Demarest, anyway. It was everything Richard could want, those wants being the result of centuries of consideration and testing. The inside was dark and comfortable and the outside shaded by tall evergreens. It was quiet and secluded, near enough to the lake so he could hear the gentle surf on the shingle as he fell asleep. The sound comforted him, ever reminded him of his lady. Even though parted from Sabra as he'd been for the last few years he never felt alone here.

He stretched lazily. The long flight and the events of the last couple of days were catching up with him. All he wanted was to strip and dive into his own bed. He'd be no good to Sabra unless he got some real rest. He opened the blinds in the front living room just enough to look along the street, and caught sight of the brown Buick parked a little way down. The driver had angled the rearview mirror so he could watch the front of Richard's house. The poor fellow would get a neck ache before his shift change thanks to Mrs. Simstead's interference. Richard made a mental note to gift his neighbor with a box of gourmet chocolates in the near future. As for the driver, he could wait. After all, that's what he was paid to do.

Richard went upstairs to bed.

The phone buzzed insistently, like an angry wasp. Many things had improved through the ages, but not the relentless sound of a phone whether it beeped, buzzed, whooped, wailed or rang; all were equally annoying. It reached into Richard's dreamless slumber and pulled at him like an impatient lover. And, like a lover, he was unable to resist. He fumbled for the receiver on the night stand.

"Yes? What?" he muttered.

"Good, you're back. We wondered where you'd gone." Philip Bourland.

"Personal. I had clearance to go."

"Yes, of course, you don't have to explain to me, but Demarest has been screaming blue murder."

"I know." Richard sat up, pushing away bedclothes, and blinked at the clock. Hell, he'd only been asleep for a few hours. "He met me at Pearson this afternoon. Tried to throw his weight around."

"Must have been very pleasant. You know he's having you tailed?"

"Yes. Not very good work. Not meant to be. Demarest just wants me to know I'm on his shit list."

"Well, I'm sure if you have to you'll be able to get rid of a shadow without too much trouble. Now . . ." Richard could see Bourland in his mind's eye, feet up on his desk, gazing out at the traffic inching its way past his office in the Parliament Building. His lazy attitude and seeming laxness had fooled many another, but Richard knew him better. He was like a snake sunning itself, seeing all, ready to move in the blink of an eye. " . . . now, about the other matter."

He'd want a private report. Unfortunately there was nothing Richard could tell Bourland that he hadn't heard already or was otherwise available through regular channels. "Do you want this on an open line?"

"Of course not. Go to seven."

Richard rang off, swung his feet around, shedding tangled sheets, and slipped on his bathrobe. Old, raggedy, faded blue, it wrapped around him like a warm puppy as he trudged downstairs to his office. The phone on his desk began ringing. He pressed the number seven extension out of the nine he had and picked up the receiver. From habit, he checked the little tap detector next to the phone. Green light for a clear line. There was a series of buzzes and Bour-land's voice came to him once more.

"What happened in Niagara?"

This was getting entirely too repetitive. "It's all in my report. Really. You've read it. You've had enough time to memorize the damned thing."

"Except that it's all in official language, which is very dry and tends to leave out uncomfortable details that would alarm those with a more squeamish nature. Did you question the subject closely?"

Richard loved the euphemism. Bourland's way of asking if Richard had gotten physical with the interrogation. He had indeed questioned Arlie Webb closely, would have continued but for . . . never mind. It would suffice that in his last moments the terrified man would have sacrificed mother, sister, and grand-mother to get out of that stinking motel room and away from him.

"Yes, I did." His voice betrayed nothing of his inner feelings, of the frisson of fear his loss of control raised in him, fear for Sabra and what she had become, of what he would soon become himself. "But I was interrupted before I got anything useful out of him. Someone cracked me solid from behind and the next thing I know the room's on fire."

"Pity . . . pity." Richard could clearly hear the sound of Bourland flicking his pencil against his front teeth, as he always did when he was thinking. "So the only name you got was somebody named Sean."

Yes, when the murdering sod was phoning for help to get rid of my body, but you don't need to know that, my friend. "Philip, I still have other sources I can try for information, but as long as Demarest is being a pain it's going to put a crimp in my progress. Today he demanded access to my secure file. None of that stuff is any of his business, nor does it have a bearing on this case. It's a hell of a distraction to have him nipping my heels. I'd hate to have the PM brought down just because some insecure twit has an ego problem with me."

"I'm not sure I can help you on that."

"Yeah, I know, he's got his head up your ass, but if that's how he works, then there's bound to be someone with their head up *his* ass. Find them and get them to convince Demarest I'm not Jack the Ripper so I can get on with my job."

Bourland made grumbling noises. "I can make no promises, but I'll see what I can do to shift him. Remember, time is probably short. Let me know when you have anything in the line of progress. If you have something positive to report it might help to take Demarest off the boil." And the phone went dead.

Richard hung up, strolled to the window, and looked out at the gathering gloom of early night. The brown Buick was still there, parked in exactly the same place. He couldn't tell if it was the same driver, but no matter.

Easy, he thought, going back upstairs. Getting around this one would be easy.

Showered, shaved, and feeling one hundred percent better in fresh clothes, Richard checked his window once more and saw to his deep pleasure that the Buick was still there. How he loved to see government employees earning their salary.

He opened one of his concealed safes to draw out a little extra cash, carefully noting the amount on the running account he always kept when working for the government. It would take forever, but he'd eventually get it back again, though they might complain of the cost. Well, a visit to the Judge was a necessary expense for this investigation, but his services didn't really cost all that much, not when one compared the price to a very expensive state funeral.

The Judge. If anyone knew of any strange goings on in the sad underbelly of Toronto it was he. Richard picked up the phone—he still had a green light on his tap detector—and punched in the numbers. The answer was almost immediate if lacking in gentility.

"Yeah, what?"

"Gimme the Judge."

The line was quiet for a moment, and a breathless voice, a voice Richard knew well from many a past interview, came on.

"What?"

"Dun. I'll meet you at Tim's. Seven o'clock." He hung up without waiting for an answer.

Tim's sounded far more innocent than it actually was. Positioned at the junction of Dundas and Sherbourne, the most dangerous intersection in the whole of Toronto, Tim's Bar saw more of the dark half of Toronto than any other. And yet it remained something of a neutral territory between law and disorder, for Tim was a solid man for both sides, and strangely honest. He tolerated no criminal activity in his house and was tough enough to enforce his rules. Consequently, the bar was safe and known to be safe, and thus a very good meeting place for those who would otherwise not take unnecessary risks. Richard had been there often.

He checked once more, almost out of habit, that the watcher was still watching, and having satisfied himself, left by the back door. Once in the alley behind his house, a cursory glance assured him that they'd failed to cover the rear entrance, and he went on his way. On Queen Street he hailed a cab and was at Tim's in no time, safe, unknown, and unencumbered.

Tim's was a great bar. The people who went there were interesting, the food, had it appealed to Richard in the slightest, was excellent, but above all, the music defied description. On those nights when a live band played it was a mixture of jazz and blues and modern that Richard loved. He had also discovered his own special kind of dinner here on more than one occasion, and more than a few of those ladies wanted to repeat the experience—or what they remembered of it—with him.

It was his kind of place, and he loved it.

At five to the hour, Richard took a stool at the bar and ordered his usual. It was from his private reserve. Tim, once he had realized how very grateful Richard would be in a financial sense, had not hesitated to stock it and keep it totally apart from the rest of his inventory. A good thing, too, for the cold mixture of red wine, human blood, and preservatives in the opaque bottles would have sent most clients scampering away into the night, rich with complaints. Tim brought forth a bottle, opened it, and poured a sampling in a wineglass as was his custom, and left both bottle and Richard alone.

Sparse pickings tonight anyway, he noted automatically. Two couples off in booths near the front, another lone man, one of the regulars, at a table reading a paper while eating fettucine with the special house sauce. Despite the distractions of the printed page, his tie was still clean. Good trick, that.

No single women, or groups of women. It was just as well for Richard was not on the hunt tonight. At least not for dinner.

He sat for maybe five minutes, savoring his special reserve before a slight breeze signified someone new coming in, and a warm voice with a West Indies accent husked into his ear.

"The Judge is here, mon, what you want?"

The voice belonged to Eugene Mantalessa, a large, gentle-looking man with blue-black skin, soft brown eyes, and the cold, guileless conscience of a pimp, drug-pusher and killer, which, after all, he was. Sell his mother for a song? Hell, he would kill his mother for a song, if only he could find her.

"You want a drink?" Richard offered.

"What you got's fine for me, mon."

"No, it's not. Have a beer." Tim arrived, beer bottle open and glass ready, and disappeared as quickly. The two men quit the bar for a small table far from the entrance.

The Judge disdained the glass and swigged straight from the bottle. He emptied half of it before favoring Richard with his full attention. "So, what's happenin'? Why you call on the Judge?"

"I need information. I hear that someone has been arranging a set-up for a very important man. I hear that someone's planning to kill that man. What do you know about it?"

"I know a lot of talk on killin's. One's just like 'nother."

"This is special. Some of the boys are bringing in hired help for it."

The Judge was very quiet for a moment. "The boys, huh? Shit, mon, I don' wanna stir stuff up with the Irish, they be crazy, mon. Least when I kill I do it for a reason, they do it just for the hell of it. An' they do an awful lot of it."

Richard sipped his drink, waiting him out.

The Judge finished his beer. He let his gaze wander around the room and made facial contortions meant to be interpreted as deep and serious thought. "What

I know," he finally said, "on a particular killin' depend on what you pay."

"What I pay depends on what you know." Richard knew this bargaining from long experience. He slid an envelope across the table. As the Judge picked it up, out spilled hundred dollar bills.

He eyed the money with vivid pleasure. "Mon, ya want him bad."

"Yes, Eugene, I want him bad."

The Judge looked at him suddenly, fear leaping into his eyes. Richard had only ever used his Christian name once before, and that had led to three men dying in the gutter, three of the Judge's best men, men he could not afford to lose. None of them weighed heavily on Richard's conscience, and the Judge was well aware of that hard fact. He began to rise. "I don't know nothin' you want t—"

But Richard's arm instantly snaked across the table and his hand wrapped around the man's throat, tight enough to make him gasp for breath. Tim looked over, mildly curious. His gaze met Richard's, and he turned away to increase the volume of the heady jazz playing on the sound system. Richard half stood, pushing until the Judge was well back into his seat, eyes reddening, sweat trickling down the side of his nose. Richard could smell the fear. Delicious.

"There is a very great deal of money in the envelope, Eugene, and—provided you give me the information that I'm looking for—it is all yours. Do you understand me?" The Judge nodded as best he could, and Richard let him go. Gasping in the smoky air of the bar, the Judge nearly slithered from his seat.

"I need the bathroom," he whined.

Richard nodded permission. "Don't fuck with me, Eugene. I don't like it when people fuck with me."

Eugene was a good source of information, but he always needed to be reminded who was in charge.

"Ya, mon." And the Judge skittered across the near-empty bar and down the stairs to the washroom below. Richard looked around. Only Tim had noticed the exchange, and he would say nothing.

Richard got up, envelope in hand, and sauntered to the top of the stairs, waiting there until the Judge finally plodded back up again. He stopped short and stared at the fat envelope, licking his lips once.

"I'll need to make some calls, contacts. It's gonna cost, mon."

He was smooth, confident again, and Richard knew exactly why. Caught on a hair in his right nostril was a telltale white crystal. Eugene sniffed and wiped his nose on his sleeve. His eyes shone. It must have been one big line, to have given him so much courage so quickly. Richard took five crisp hundred-dollar bills from the envelope and passed them over.

"The person you are looking for is called Charon. I want anything you get on him or the people who hired him. Absolutely anything, the faster the better. You call me, day or night, and tell me what you find out. If I like what you tell me, there's the rest of this waiting for you. If you're lying, I *will* know."

The Judge nodded, pocketed the money, and headed for the door.

"And Eugene . . ."

He stopped on a dime.

"Don't put it all up your nose. I want to be able to understand what you're saying."

The Judge left, and Richard turned back toward the table where Tim was now clearing things away. Richard crossed over and gave him a hundred. "That should cover everything. Recork the wine will you? I'll take it with me, there's no point in wasting it."

"No problem." Tim stuffed the bill into his shirt pocket and went back to work with hardly a blink of an eye.

Richard phoned for a cab. He would enjoy the look on the watcher's face at his return home, but he would enjoy his special reserve even more.

"He must have used the back door," the unhappy RCMP officer said into his radio. He'd been sharply awakened from his gentle doze by Richard's loud whistling as he strolled past the Buick and up to his front walk. He could have returned unseen by the back entry, but it was so much more fun twisting Demarest's nose.

"We need more operatives," the young man insisted to whoever was on the other end.

The night and neighborhood were quiet enough that Richard could hear every word through the car's half-open window. He grinned as he listened and watched, hidden from view in his darkened living room. He pulled the cork from the bottle and drank deeply, letting the fullness of the blood shudder though him. Not the same as taking it hot and pulsing from a vein, but a pleasure, nonetheless. He had been right about this in the bar: he was enjoying it and the show outside immensely.

The officer's radio report ended most unsatisfactorily, though, at least for Richard. Another car was to be assigned. Apparently Bourland's influence on the issue was yet to be felt. Richard shrugged. No matter. He had other work to attend for the moment.

Hours later, he finished off the last precious drop in the bottle and congratulated himself on a smart bit of trash clearing, the trash being three days worth of piled-up mail that had to be answered or tossed. Like it or not, he had to deal with the practical aspects of his now mundane-seeming business. He shifted his calendar dates around, clearing things for the next month and faxing detailed instructions to his part-time secretary. The modern world had its complications, but he liked some pieces of it, such as the electronic links that allowed him to run an international business from his home. His secretary, a busy mother of four, also liked the convenience for the same reason. Because of it, he'd only ever laid eyes on her once, during her interview some years ago, though from the phone he knew her voice as well as his own.

No word from the Judge in all that time, but it was early yet. Some of the places he'd check for contacts didn't even open until after midnight.

Working off the energy the blood imparted to him, Richard found himself pacing in the dim room, the only light coming from the gentle glow of his computer screen.

He hated waiting. It gave him too much time to think.

Sabra would not leave his mind, but he also had to protect the Prime Minister. That was his job, had ever been his job, from the very beginning in Arthur's court, and everyone who had met him over the centuries knew that Richard d'Orleans always fulfilled his responsibilities. Yet he also had to find a way to save Sabra, and himself. He had to find the Grail.

Well, the Prime Minister could wait while the Judge dug around. Richard would spend the remains of this night at the other—and to his heart much more important—task.

He logged on to the Internet, intent to mine it for fresh information on the Grail. He'd not paid much attention to current archeological studies on the topic. He knew there'd been some excavations at Glastonbury in the past, of course, but they'd found nothing significant. Sabra had seen to that, but she'd not been in England for several years now. Things could have changed. They always did if one lived long enough.

A red light on a detector attached to his Internet link came on, warning him that he was now being monitored. What the hell . . . ?

Demarest, the son of a bitch. Probably pissed off by Richard's earlier jaunt outside. God knows how many arms he twisted to get this tap accomplished.

Richard's first reaction was to log off and let them all stew, but decided against it. It didn't matter if anyone looked over his shoulder on this search, for what connection did it have to the case at hand? None. They'd take it for a bit of hobby work by a natural insomniac. Probably bore them silly. Good.

He continued, doggedly pointing and clicking to anything that might be directly or remotely connected to the Grail. Pickings were slim to none. He tried Camelot, and again came up with nothing but a schedule of performances of the stage musical. Finally, almost in desperation, he searched for any reference to the Arthurian legends, and lo and behold a single return flickered up onto the screen.

UNIVERSITY OF TORONTO . . . STOP PRESS.
The Faculty of History of the University of Toronto is pleased to announce that Professor Neal Rivers, world renowned expert on King Arthur and other myths of the Celtic world and author of Arthurian Legends: A Round View *will be a guest lecturer at the faculty for the rest of this semester.*

Richard read an impressive line of credits attached to the professor's capsule biography. Perhaps the term "world renowned" was not an exaggeration after all.

Here on a research sabbatical from the University of Southern California, he will be giving a series of talks on his latest work. These talks are open to the public. Please book in advance. Demand is expected to be great, and seats are limited.

Richard smiled. If he knew anything about talks on Arthurian legends, demand would not be great at all. Someone in the faculty was clearly trying to drum up support. Nothing worse than having a prize guest lecturer and no one to lecture to.

Perhaps the man would have some useful current data on Glastonbury Richard could use. He took down the details of how to book for the talks and, on a whim, decided to call the listed number there and then to see if he could get any further information. They'd have a machine on at this hour, but at the very least he could leave a voicemail message. He used line seven, which was still showing a green light.

He was quite surprised when someone actually answered his call.

"Hello. Yes? Who is it, and what do you want?" The man's wide-awake voice was firm and energetic, with a pronounced American accent, possibly Midwestern.

"My name is Richard Dun. I know it's late, but I was wondering if there was anyone there who could talk to me about Professor Neal Rivers and his work. I read about his lectures on the Internet, and—"

"Couldn't sleep either, eh? Same here, buddy. Damn jet lag'll drive you crazy if you're not careful. My body doesn't know what day it is, let alone what time."

"Tuesday," offered Richard. "For another twenty minutes, anyway."

"You're kidding. You're *not* kidding? Jeez, I gotta look at my watch more often. Well, how can I help you, Mr.—ah—Dun?"

"I'm looking for Professor Neal Rivers," said Richard, wondering who on earth this strange person was.

"Yeah. You got him. That's me. Guilty as charged. What'd'ya want to know?"

Richard could not believe his good fortune. The Goddess must be smiling down on him this night. His stomach tightened in anticipation of what he might discover from this man, and he plunged right in.

"The Grail."

"What about it?"

Richard hesitated. He would have to be careful how much he gave away. He was, after all, talking to a world expert. He could not let it be known that he knew more about the thing than anyone else alive with the exception of Sabra. He feigned innocence.

"Everything, really. Where did it come from, what does it look like, and are there any digs going on to find it?"

"You believe it exists, then?"

Richard wanted to say that he knew damned well that it did, but restrained himself. "So much has been written about it, why shouldn't it exist?"

"People write a lot a crap about a lot of things, but that doesn't always make it real. Check out the papers in the grocery lines if you think I'm wrong."

"I think the Grail is in rather a different area than Elvis sightings or crop circles."

"Don't be too certain of that. Here's a thought: what if crop circles are really gang signs from UFOs? Wouldn't that be a bummer?"

"I'm sure, but—"

The voice interrupted him once more, this time with an edge that Richard could not define. "Yeah, does the Grail exist or not. I happen to know it still exists.

It is real. In fact, I'm doing a new book on the subject."

Richard frowned. "Indeed? I'd like to hear more about it."

"Oh, yeah? You're letting yourself in for it, asking a writer about his work, I'll talk your ear off."

"I have the time and stamina."

"Wow, okay. Are you in the city? Great. Come on over then. I could use a break. I'll leave a message with security to let you in."

He gave Richard specific directions to his building and rang off. Richard sat quite still for a while, the telephone in his hand. This man clearly did know something, or at least he thought he did. And whatever he knew, Richard, too, would know before the night was gone. He replaced the phone on its cradle and looked out the window once again. The brown Buick was still there, a figure slumped in the front seat, just visible in the orange wash of a street light. It would have to be the back door once again. He logged off the Net and set the house alarm system.

This time, however, escape wasn't so simple. As Richard eased open the door leading to the alleyway, it became clear that the plea made by the other operative for more men had been answered. There was second car, yet another brown Buick. The man inside was far more vigilant than the other, and he wore night-vision goggles.

Of all the bloody cheek.

Take it as a challenge, Richard.

The man had come alert the moment Richard opened the door. There was no going back, so he closed the door behind him and walked north toward Queen Street. The operative spoke into his radio, pulled off the goggles, and emerged from his car. He kept a careful distance. Richard led him no more than a few dozen yards before turning and rushing back faster than a human eye could follow.

"I don't like being watched," he said casually.

The man turned, choking with shock to find Richard was now looming behind him, ghostly in the light of the waning moon.

The operative was just quick enough to work out that something uncanny had taken place—Richard recognized that kind of look very well—and was starting to back away, choosing flight over fight, but Richard fixed him firmly in place. No need for touch—with the power of the Goddess rushing through him a stare was more than enough. Red eyes, glowing in the darkness, glowing with the power of the hellhounds of Annwyn, irresistible, enveloping, Richard spoke softly, but knew his words would shriek right through all barriers of conscious thought to the man's very soul.

"Go back to your car. I haven't left the house. You were mistaken. When you report in the morning, you will say that I was at home all night. Do you understand?"

The operative nodded, walked slowly past, and returned to his car. He opened the door, a glazed, vacant look fixed on his face as he settled in.

Richard observed this with a certain amount of pleasure and pride. Another aspect of his condition that had yet to pall. Impressive. No doubt about it, he still had the knack when he needed it. He disappeared into the bustle of Queen Street.

The University of Toronto was a cluster of fine buildings on and around, of all places, University Avenue, near the downtown core. Richard found the Faculty of History nestled in an imposing Victorian edifice, the result of the munificence of a former student and Prime Minister. Richard had often been struck by the sense of peace that existed within the confines of these centers of higher learning. Even during the turbulent sixties, when students over the world had rediscovered their voice and political strength, he still felt a sense of detachment from the world, of safety within the walls of learning. *We care for our children even when they do not want it.*

He passed through the heavy oak doors, ornately carved and propped permanently and inexplicably open, and found his way blocked by modern glass and an intercom button. He pressed it and waited. Nothing happened. He pressed again and peered through into the dimly lit interior. He could see a large security desk with a pair of proportionately large feet propped up on it. He pressed the button again, and the feet still did not move. Whoever was there was clearly fast asleep. Richard banged on the glass and called out and there was still no response. He was about to give up and leave when he caught sight of movement in the corridor beyond and saw a man's figure heading for the desk. He leaned over the sleeping guard and the lock release buzzed. Richard pushed on the door and it opened, admitting him to the slightly too warm interior. As the door closed behind him all the sounds of the city disappeared.

"Security! I'm glad they're not looking after my bank account," said the man. "You must be Richard Dun."

Richard recognized the flat accent from the phone immediately and shook the firm hand that was proffered him. "And you must be Professor Rivers."

"Just call me Neal. I save the title to impress the students. I called down to arrange for you to get in, but there was no reply. Thought I'd better check. Good thing too. He'll be out until doomsday, or the end of his shift, whichever's nearer. Come on."

Richard followed. They wound their way through a seeming labyrinth of darkened corridors until light spilling from an open doorway beckoned and they entered Neal's office. "Make yourself comfortable, if you can. Though comfort is not a high point here. They like visiting professors to concentrate solely on their work, I guess. Reminds me of my dorm days when it was my turn to learn."

Richard looked around the cramped space and had to agree. A desk, two chairs, a computer terminal, not new, with books and papers crammed and stacked into and on every foot of shelf space. The wastebasket was overstuffed, with the shredded remains of some fast food wrappings balanced precariously on top, the scent of the food still strong in the air. Though it was distinctly lacking in any of the creature comforts, it was obvious that Neal had added some personal touches. There were white carnations in a vase on the desk, and a print thumbtacked to the wall opposite, an Aubrey Beardsley, the one of Salome gloating over the head of John the Baptist.

"Inspiration," said Neal.

"Sorry?"

"She gives me inspiration. The Beardsley. I see you looking at her."

"Forgive me," said Richard, "I didn't mean to stare."

"No problem. If you're wondering what sort of inspiration, it has to do with the political in-fighting around here. Doesn't matter what school you go to, there's always some vicious little fracas going on in the faculty and they want the newcomer for their side, whatever side that is. I really don't give a damn and just want to get on with my work, but if one of 'em gets my goat I just picture his head up there instead of old Johnnie B's. It's great therapy."

"I should imagine."

The professor went over to a small coffee maker. "Want some not-so-fresh caffeine?" he asked, pouring a cup, then stirred in half a dozen sugar cubes. "I got some instant amaretto creamer to take the bite off the acid." He held up a small jar, giving it a tempting shake.

"No thanks."

"Very wise, you'll probably outlast me, then. I practically have to live on this stuff when I'm pulling all-nighters." Neal pawed through a box of petrified doughnuts on the same table.

"Aren't all-nighters for students, not teachers?"

"Teachers do 'em, too, they just never admit it. This late it's easier to wrangle computer time for research with no annoying interruptions. Oh, jeez, I didn't mean that like it sounds." Embarrassed, he let a jelly-stuffed doughnut thud back in the box.

Richard smiled deprecatingly. "Not at all, it's very kind of you to see me."

Neal grinned, then sucked a sugar-smeared thumb. "Yeah, I guess it is. I'm truly a wonderful person. Now, how can I help you?"

Richard looked him over, seeing an ordinary man in his early forties, of medium height, slightly more than medium weight, a humorous, but otherwise bland face topped by thinning dark hair. His sharp brown eyes were his most remarkable feature, sparkling with cheerful energy. He was immaculately dressed in a dark brown suit of the finest wool, a crisp white shirt in which the newness almost crackled, and a tie of muted red perfectly knotted at his throat. A white carnation sat on his lapel, securely held there by a gold pin at the end of which was a tiny, exquisite diamond. Strange habiliment for such a late hour, but as a visiting lecturer, perhaps he had to try harder to make a positive impression on his peers.

As Richard looked, Neal passed a hand self-consciously through his hair, and absently touched the knot in his tie. "Well, do I pass inspection?"

"I didn't mean to be rude."

"That's okay, I can gawk right back if you like." Neal widened his eyes into a brief, pop-eyed stare, then broke off with a grin, and gestured at the visitor's chair. He fell into the one behind his desk, tilting it back as Richard seated himself.

"So you're into the Grail thing, huh? Get inspired by that Spielberg movie?"

Richard chuckled, liking his attitude. "Hardly. I'm just beginning research myself on the subject, for a book."

"Whoa, you think I'm gonna share what I know with the competition?"

Richard's initial lie came out with a smoothness born of hundreds of years of practice. "It's for a fictional book, nothing remotely scholarly, I promise."

"You're a writer?"

"I hope to be. I do know that to get good fiction one has to base it on good fact, and I want the full story on whatever facts presently exist on the Grail. Newspaper tabloids aside, there is a tremendous amount of text about it—"

"And you think it's real, too?"

"I know that everyone says it's only a legend, but I just don't believe that. Anyway, I'm stuck. I've read everything that I can find, in fictional works and in poetry, and am just now starting the factual investigation for archeological evidence."

"You should go to England, then, if you're really serious about it."

"I plan to, as soon as I can get vacation time from my day job.

"And the conclusion you've reached is . . . ?"

"That it certainly exists, and is probably hidden somewhere at Ynis Witrin." Richard had used the ancient name for Glastonbury without even thinking.

"That's the place, the Isle of Glass." Neal looked at Richard over his steepled fingers with a smiling expression of benign patience, rather like a parent watching its child's first faltering steps. Richard found it intensely irritating, but then he'd asked for it with such a cover story, so he would bear it out.

"I've read all that folklore has to offer, but factual data is a bit thin. I must confess that I've not had the chance to read any of your works—"

"Not surprising. Most of them are papers in academic publications, which are not known for their wide distribution to the general public. My first real book on Arthur and the rest has only just come out. That's why I'm here in this godforsaken place, to push the book and do research for the next opus in between lectures. I give a fascinating talk, then sell the book while everyone's all worked up and curious. But it's mostly about the legends, and you're interested in the actualities. Well, you lucked out, since the new one I'm working on has just that angle. I'm planning to go to Glastonbury soon to complete my research."

"Really? There's to be a dig, then?"

"Nah, couldn't get anyone to put up the money. Anyway, I'm not so great with a shovel, but just turn me loose in the old church archives and see what happens."

That was a relief.

"You do know why it was called Ynis Witrin, don't you?" asked Neal.

"Aaaah . . ."

And the professor was off, first sitting and waving his arms, then pacing around the cramped room, in full flight on what was clearly his favorite subject. Richard simply listened and nodded intelligently as Neal told him a number of things he already knew, imparting them with all the solemnity of the rarest of insights. He trailed off into myth again and again, which was both annoying and fortunate, annoying in that Richard wanted current hard fact, and the man knew no more than he did; fortunate, for it meant he was just another semicharlatan, making a dollar from historical inaccuracy.

"But it's all in my book, y'know."

Richard's frustrating but well-hidden boredom was broken by this last sentence. Perhaps the end of the dissertation was in sight.

Neal dug into the depths of a cardboard box. "Here, I'll give you a copy. I'm sure it'll help you in your research. I've got a helluva bibliography in the back." He presented it to Richard. Heavy slick paper, numerous full color illustrations and photos, the leather cover looked to be hand-tooled. "Lemme autograph it so it'll become a collector's item."

Nonplused, Richard said, "I couldn't accept this. It's far too valuable an edition for you to be giving away copies to walk-in strangers."

Neal dismissed the objection with another arm wave. "I gotta box of freebies from the publisher just for that purpose. And then you let me bend your ear for God knows how long and looked interested the whole time. When I find a good listener I cultivate 'em like crazy." He took the book back, opened it to the title page, and signed it with a flourish.

"Thank you," said Richard. "This is extremely kind of you."

"Just mention me in *your* book's acknowledgments page and we'll call it even."

"I will," he replied with a very slight twinge of guilt.

"I'll bag it up for you. Don't want to mark that lovely cover before it hits your coffee table." Neal scrounged again, this time coming up with a large white sack bearing the logo of a chain of taco restaurants. "No grease stains, great." He put the book in the bag, double-folded the top, and gave it to Richard. "You're gonna come to my lectures now, I hope?"

"I shall do my best to try."

"Great." He clapped his hands together, rubbing them. "Now, I don't mean to hustle you outta here— it's been real—but I still got work to do and . . ."

They then launched into one of the present culture's parting rituals, punctuated by mutual professions of gratitude and enjoyment, and before he knew it, Richard was once more escorted past the sleeping security man and going through the heavy glass doors. The sound of night time traffic was a relief to his ears after the forceful rush of Neal's voice and enthusiasm. His high energy compressed into so small a room was something of an assault to the senses, and the relative silence and cool air were a very welcome respite indeed.

He breathed it in deeply, relishing the break. The meeting was something of a disappointment, but then whims sometimes turned out like that. At least he'd gotten a book out of it, and a rather expensive one to judge by its weight and trappings. He wondered if the professor had gone to a vanity house to have all those extras. A leather cover, indeed. Hardly anyone went in for that sort of thing anymore.

He glanced back and saw Neal still standing behind the glass doors, looking out. The man sketched a breezy farewell wave, then turned away into the darkened corridors of the building. An interesting fellow, if exhausting, and Richard decided to add him to his ever growing list of useful contacts. *You never know when you might again need an expert on Celtic legends.* He made a mental note to send a thank you card for the book. It might make up a bit for the lie he'd told about his own fiction project.

Bag in hand, Richard headed north on University and found a cab easily enough on Bloor. But settling into the vinyl clad backseat he became aware of yet another car idling at the curb a few yards behind. A blue Dodge, one occupant. As his cab pulled away and into what traffic there was at this time of night, the Dodge confirmed Richard's fears by slipping into the stream two cars back and tailing them. Indeed, it stuck with them all the way back to the Beaches.

The computer tap. Was Demarest so obsessed he'd actually sent someone to check out the professor? Evidently. Enough was enough. Demarest's antics had gone too far. It was one thing to be a nuisance about the assassin hunt, quite another to poke into his private business about Sabra. Richard told the cab to stop on Queen several blocks from his home, paid the driver off, and quickly stepped into the sheltered doorway of a closed store. The Dodge stopped a little way back along the curb, idling its fumes into the night air. Richard glanced around and saw that true to form, this part of Queen was deserted at this time of night. Safe. His body was a blur as he ran to the car and wrenched the door open.

"I want you to tell Demarest . . ." he began, and got no further. The driver's seat was empty. His surprise turned rapidly to dismay as he felt the sudden cold press of a gun muzzle hard against the back of his neck. He froze.

"If I knew who Demarest was, I might be able to oblige. Now why don't you step away and keep your hands out where I can see them?" The voice was low, female, and the tone deadly. With an Irish accent.

He cautiously turned his head just enough to get a look at her.

Well, well, the leggy redhead from Niagara. He smiled. The Goddess at work again?

"I need to talk to you—" he began, slowly straightening and turning to face her.

"No," she interrupted, backing off a step and centering her aim exactly between his eyes. "I need to talk to *you*."

Chapter Five

Richard decided to be very, very cooperative. He could survive a bullet in the head even at this close a range, but it would take time to heal again—and hurt like hell. Definitely something to avoid. Besides, after what had happened when he'd been shot in Niagara . . . the young woman's presence brought the nightmare forcefully back to him, as if he needed such reminding. He would not risk losing control like that ever again if he could help it.

She was casually dressed now as she'd been then: dark shirt, denim jacket, snug designer jeans tucked into serviceable combat-style ankle boots, flat heels. Not that she needed any boost in height with those legs. A trim girl, and tall, nearly eye-level with him. He wasn't used to that, but liked the effect. Despite her grim expression, she had a nice face, more than nice, quite beautiful in fact. Fashion model bones, but with enough healthy skin over them so as not to look anorexic, and a cascade of deep red hair falling about her shoulders. Very striking, very tempting—but for the 9mm Glock semi-auto she held so easily in her hand.

Had she seen his rush across the street? There was no expression in her sharp green eyes to indicate she'd observed anything odd. In her place he would have slipped out the passenger's side and kept the car body between them until ready to pounce. He glanced within and was gratified to see the door opposite had been pulled shut, but not all the way, so his guess was right. She'd just missed his swift crossing. How fortunate for them both.

"Now keep still and tell me who you are," she ordered.

"My name is Dun, Richard Dun," he said, seeing no reason to lie. He could always edit her memory later if necessary. "And you are . . . ?"

"Never you mind. Just hand that package over."

He still held the bag in one outstretched hand. "You want this?"

"You'd better believe it."

"Introductions followed by armed robbery. Charming."

"Put it on the bonnet. Now."

He assumed she meant the bag and did so, setting it gently on the car. She side-stepped once so the vehicle's front corner was between them. One-handed—the other still held the muzzle's aim solidly in place—she seized the bag and upended it. The book inside slid out and kept sliding down the hood, landing on the street with the kind of dense thud reserved for massive tomes on serious subjects. She glared down at it.

"Oh, shit!"

Her Irish accent became more pronounced as she launched into a series of expletives, mainly aimed at "that bastard Rivers." Finally she kicked the book, sending it a few feet into the road, and turned her full attention back to Richard.

"That's it? That's all he gave you?"

"The professor? Yes."

"Holy Mary, mother of Jesus—" she began, but cut off before the air got too blasphemous. "Who are you to Rivers?"

"A somewhat less than perfect stranger."

"What d'ye mean by that?"

"I only just met him tonight. If you've a quarrel with him, I suggest—"

"Why did you go see him?"

"Private business. I'm doing research for a book on King Arthur—"

Her eyes sparked with an unholy joy. "Oh, are you now?" She spared the street a quick, apprehensive look. Empty as it was, as late as it was, their privacy could not last forever. She gestured with the gun. "Come around the front, then get into the passenger side. No fast moves."

"Or you'll kill me?"

"Believe it." She sounded chillingly sincere.

"May I pick up my book first?"

"Finger and thumb only, and take your time."

Richard did as instructed, retrieving the book from the gritty pavement, then walked slowly around the car to stand by the front passenger side. Stepping backwards, she circled before him, keeping pace with him like a dance partner while carefully maintaining her distance and aim. She had him open his door as she opened the rear door. They got in at the same time, shutting doors at the same time.

"Face forward and put your hands on the dash, and don't forget I can shoot right through the seat. If you don't want a half dozen bullets in your spine—"

"Yes, yes, you've covered that point already. I will behave myself. Who the hell are you and why are you holding up honest citizens in the middle of the night?"

"It's in a good cause, so never you mind, Mr. Dun."

"Who are you with?" He was fairly certain she was IRA. Whether she was with the main body or the splinter group that had hired Charon was what he wanted to know next.

"You for the moment. Answer a few questions and you'll be free to go."

Richard had a brief thought having to do with hell freezing over, but kept it to himself. "All right."

He heard her take a deep breath. "Good. Now tell me where the manuscript is."

"What manuscript?" he asked, honestly puzzled.

"The one you boys pinched from the museum."

He shook his head. "I think we're at cross purposes here, miss. I haven't the least idea what you're talking about."

She jabbed the muzzle hard against his skull. "Then start thinking before you lose an ear, and don't be forgettin' I can move on to other body parts."

"No doubt, but I still don't—"

"You were with Rivers and you were with Webb at Niagara. I saw you, so don't be denying it."

Oh, shit, he thought, echoing her. His heart rate shot up painfully. Had she returned and witnessed what had happened? The cabin curtains had been drawn, but he'd been thoroughly out of his mind during the killing. She could have seen or heard some or all of it. Damn, but he wanted to turn and *look* at her, freeze and question her. Not now, though, not just yet. He had to play by her rules until he got his chance.

The gun tapped his skull again. "Well?"

"Yes, I saw Webb. I saw you with him, too." That shut her up a moment. He pressed his lead. "I watched him throw you out of his cabin. Very noisy it was. What did you want from him? This manuscript?"

A long wait. Then a change in her tone. "Yes. I'll pay good money for its safe return. Cash."

She'd offered Webb money as well. "How do you know he had it?"

"I have my sources."

"It would have burned up in the fire."

"No, it didn't. He passed it to someone else. Maybe to you before you set him on fire and got away."

He held to a bland face. "You're sure about that?"

"I went over every inch of that cabin after the coppers left. Burned or not, I'd have found some trace."

"Unless the police took away the ashes as evidence."

"They didn't, or I'd have heard. However, they did take *you* away. Why'd they let you go?"

"I have connections."

"I'm sure. Perhaps you can use them to get the book back. For that favor I can put an easy five thousand in your pocket."

"Your top offer to Webb was ten thousand."

She hissed. "Right, but only if it's in good condition."

The view out the front window was really boring. Time to get creative. He paused long enough to give her the impression he was thinking things over. Then, "All right. But I'll need to make some calls."

"I'll wager you do. Just tell me where it is, and we'll go there and fetch it."

"Oh? And you've got that ten grand in your pocket ready to hand over? I didn't think so. For each of us to obtain what we want one of us is going to have to compromise a bit, and since you're the one with the gun . . ."

"All right, but nothing fancy or—"

"I've gotten the idea. Where's the nearest phone?"

"You tell me."

"There's a petrol station ahead." He nodded at a bank of garish lights a short block away.

"Too bright."

"All the better to see me by. They'll only be to your advantage. It's either there or we can cruise around and hope to get lucky."

She snarled a reluctant affirmative, warned him once more against doing anything he'd regret, then got out of the back. He emerged from the front and was instructed to walk ahead. With his hands in his pockets.

"Where did you train?" he asked, obeying both directives.

"'Tis common sense. You'd look daft holdin' 'em atop your head, not to mention noticeable."

He set an easy pace and heard her keeping up. How close was she? He glimpsed their forms reflected in the shop windows they passed. Seven feet, perhaps more. Too wide a gap for a normal man to risk, but then being normal was not something Richard had had to bother about for a very, very, long time.

Well, now or never. All he'd really wanted was a little elbow room.

Between heartbeats, he yanked his hands free, whirled, and got behind her. He smothered her gasp of surprise with one hand and seized the gun with the other while pulling her backwards and off balance. It worked, sort of, but instead of struggling forward to get away, she seemed to relax and fell heavily against him, pushing hard. His own balance went awry. She pushed again and down they went with her on top, the force of her weight driving the breath from him. He felt a sharp jab under his ribs, her teeth sank into one of his fingers, and she was twisting and snarling like a scalded cat.

She shifted to roll toward her gun hand. He released his grip on her face and caught at her other arm, pulling it back and wide, trying to hold her spread-eagled on top of him. He'd have found such a wrestling game to be rather arousing exercise except for the various painful jabs and kicks he was collecting.

She snapped her head back, slamming her skull against his face. He'd turned slightly; most of the impact caught him on the jaw, stalling, but not stunning him. She took what advantage she had, lifted, and shoved a sharp elbow into his ribs. That tore it; he'd been trying not to hurt her, but all bets were off now. He pulled the gun from her grip and sent it skittering along the walk, then folded her arm in across the front of her body. His turn to roll, and he did, hauling her over until she was facedown on the cement with all his weight on top. He brought her other arm around to the small of her back and pulled it up. She spat some choice curses at him, but stopped struggling.

"There," he puffed. "My turn to ask questions."

She began to shriek bloody murder and more. He clamped a palm over her mouth, risking another bite, and put pressure on her arm. Her vocalizations abruptly stopped, replaced by a grunt of pain.

He leaned forward to whisper in her ear. "Now here's *my* deal. You'll answer a few for me and I won't dislocate your shoulder."

He wasn't sure of the nasal growl she emitted was meant as acquiescence or not, but thought to give her the benefit of a doubt. Just in case, though, he raised her up enough to pull her other arm free and held them both in place behind her. It made things awkward while trying to stand, but they managed.

"I'll cut your fucking heart out, I will," she promised breathlessly as he propelled her back to the car. Along the way he picked up the Glock and held it hard on the back of her neck, but kept his finger parallel to the trigger guard. He didn't want her to see him putting the safety on just yet.

This time they both got into the rear seat. No need to have her within reach of the car's horn. It was a bit close, both of them taking up a lot of space. She tried to go out the opposite door, but a nudge in the belly from the Glock changed her mind. Oh, but what a potent glare she had. You could sear anything with that kind of heat.

"What's your name?" he asked, smiling.

It took another nudge before she spoke. "Geary."

"A good Irish name, to be sure," he said, imitating her accent. "Now where are the rest of the boys to be found? Surely they don't let a lass like yourself loose on the world without a bit of backup."

Another glare.

Nowhere fast with this one, but he had an excellent shortcut. He found the domelight and flicked it on. Yes, that was fine, more than enough to work by. The silence stretched for a long moment as he concentrated on her. Perhaps he lacked the gift for hearing thoughts, but this made up for it. The heat in her green eyes gradually faded; the tension in her face and the rest of her body began to ease.

"That's very good, Ms. Geary," he told her in an approving tone. "You just calm yourself. Everything's fine now."

Her breathing evened out, her eyelids flickered. He heard her heartbeat slowing as his influence took full hold of her, body and mind.

"I'm your friend, and we're going to have a nice chat."

"Friend," she repeated in a soft whisper like a sigh of love.

Her tone, though unconsciously induced, was not lost on Richard.

This was every man's dream, being able to get a beautiful woman to do his bidding, but Richard had ever been above that, having always found pursuit, capture, and mutual seduction to be far more rewarding than base coercion. However, he wasn't above enjoying the temptation of the moment and gave himself time to look at her from head to toe and all the lush places in between. Dear lord, but she was a lot of woman. Too bad about her politics.

Back to business, old lad, he told himself firmly. "Yes, we're friends, and you were just telling me who you work for."

"Lloyds."

"Who is he and where is he?"

"London. Other branches, too."

Richard blinked as all his mental works squealed to a jolting halt and abruptly shifted over. *"You work for Lloyds of London?"*

"That I do."

Oh, shit.

The change in her was remarkable. "I'm sorry about the misunderstanding, Mr. Dun, but when—"

"Quite all right. Could have happened to anyone. Look, here are my credentials."

"My God," she said, obviously impressed without any hypnotic help from him. Apparently a triple A clearance from the government of Canada, signed by the Prime Minister himself carried a lot of weight with her.

"And you?" he asked.

She unhesitatingly hauled out a credit card-sized piece of plastic from her jeans pocket. It stated she was Sharon Geary, Head of Recovery Investigations at Lloyds of London. It also added that she was twenty-six years old, along with a few other vital statistics.

"You're rather young to be head of Investigations, aren't you?"

"And you're rather easily taken to be with the Prime Minister's Special Security, but I won't tell if you won't."

"Fair enough. What do you want a gun for? You know how restricted they are."

"I'm sure *that* will be news to the IRA. Why don't you tell 'em about it?"

Point to her. "Another time, perhaps." He put the safety on the gun, ejected the magazine, yanked the slide back to remove the chamber round, then returned the weapon to her. He kept the bullets. Any law enforcement officer would have confiscated the lot, but he could be a bit more flexible on things. Besides, he didn't want to have to deal with getting rid of it himself. She could still attempt to use the gun as a club of some sort on him, but her present state of mind made that a very small possibility.

"You going to turn me in on this?" she asked, hefting it slightly, then tucking it into the waistband of her jeans.

"No need. Just don't go waving it about; it makes the police nervous."

It had taken no small effort, but once Richard had recovered from the surprise and sorted out his mistaken impressions, he was also able to sort out Ms. Geary's as well. He turned a few things around in her recent memory—like leaving in their scuffle to account for their mutual bruises and dishevelment—but he'd told her to look favorably upon him as a fellow professional in the business. By the time he'd finished she was fully awake and cooperating beautifully. They'd quit the cramped backseat of the Dodge and now stood on the sidewalk next to it.

"What are you doing here?" he asked. "What's this manuscript business, and why don't you like Rivers?"

"I came here trying to trace down an item stolen from the Irish Museum of Antiquities in Dublin. It disappeared about two weeks ago and looked to be an inside job. One of the museum employees who had access to it quit his job and vanished at the same time. The police later discovered he had IRA contacts."

"This item being a manuscript?"

"A very old one, one of the very rarest of antiquities, absolutely genuine seventh century. Unique and priceless, but insured with Lloyds for five million English pounds."

Richard whistled. "Go on."

"Through our contacts I traced it to that smuggler Webb in Niagara."

"And offered him a mere ten thousand for it?"

"It was as much as I had at the time. You saw how he lived; ten was a fortune to him."

"Not if he had another buyer waiting. So after he threw you out—"

"I came back on the quiet and kept watch. That's when I saw you after the fire started . . ." Her brows came down. "Wait a minute, you were in the—"

He fastened another hard stare on her, then told her the story he'd told all the others. Her face smoothed out as she—with no choice in the matter—accepted every word of it.

"Well," she continued, "I saw you outside with the fire brigade and the coppers, then they took you away. I got to thinking you were in custody for what had happened."

"No, I'm one of them. They wanted to get hold of you, too, you know. Why didn't you come forward?"

"Because it would have been a bloody inconvenience to my job. As it is, I had to dump the car and get scarce myself. With Webb dead and the manuscript missing, the only other lead I had was either trying my luck with the IRA and hoping they wouldn't kill me, or keeping an eye on Professor Rivers. He's an expert on the area the manuscript deals with, is a rabid collector, and not above cutting corners to get something he wants."

"Like receiving stolen property? Where's a professor get the money for something so valuable?"

"His family in California is posh as hell. They've covered up for him more than a few times, I'm sure, for past deals." She leaned back against the car, crossing her arms.

"And his area of expertise . . ." Oh, damn. "The manuscript is . . ." Oh, damn, damn, damn.

"The Abbey Book is what they call it, though which abbey they're not sure, but tradition holds that it was originally written in Glastonbury and taken away before the fire in 1184. It's probably the very earliest surviving account of the Arthurian legend."

Damn, damn, damn *damn*, DAMN!

"The closest artistic and historical equivalent is the *Book of Kells*. The few experts who have looked at it think the text is a transcription form of the bardic songs that were popular back then. Beautiful stuff, lots of illuminated letters and such. Actually, Arthur's not even mentioned much; it's mostly mystical gibberish about the Grail . . ."

Sabra's book.

" . . . with lots of symbolism thrown in. Some of the more rarefied academic circles are still trying to puzzle out the meanings of certain passages."

It's all in the old tongue, of course—and in verse. I was never very good with verse, but was mad for it for a time, so please forgive my faltering efforts at poetry.

"Something wrong?" she asked, pushing away from the car.

He shook his head, trying to hide the fact that the bottom had fallen out of his stomach.

"You're lookin' peaky."

"It's been a long night." *Pick up the threads, Richard.* "So you think Rivers is interested in this book?"

"If the chance came up for him to buy it, he would and no questions asked. When I saw you coming away from his building, and you had that bag, I thought—"

"That I'd gotten it from Webb and was trying to sell it to Rivers?"

"Something like that. Of course, it was a mighty puzzle seein' as how you went in with empty hands, then come out with 'em full when it should have been the other way 'round. I had to know what was goin' on and followed you."

Probably thinking he was IRA himself. She didn't lack for guts.

"My bad luck, though," she complained. "While I'm here with you, Rivers could have gotten the manuscript and hidden it by now, if he hasn't already."

"Is he the only buyer you're checking out?"

"There's a few other collectors, but not in Toronto."

"What about the IRA? Why are they involved with this?"

"Like as not they stole it to sell to someone like Rivers to raise money for the boys."

"Seems a roundabout method to do things." But a fast way to get major funds. Enough to pay for a top assassin? Perhaps. Even if Rivers paid a fraction of what the book was insured for, it would be a hell of a sum to play with. A thorough background check on the professor was called for to see how much he was worth, along with another talk with him about the manuscript. Perhaps this time to "question him closely," as Philip Bourland might have said.

"And why were you seein' Rivers?" she demanded.

"I told you, I'm doing research for a book on Arthur."

She favored him with a highly skeptical face. "Y' can do better than that. I don't believe in coincidence, Mr. Dun."

Neither did he. A smuggler like Webb—a known associate of Charon— bringing in a book about the Grail? Either the Goddess was working in a mysterious way, or there was more to things than he was aware of yet. He fixed Sharon with another look. "You do now. And call me Richard."

She winced, eyes closing briefly. "Oh, but I think I've been up too long as well, Richard. I'm feeling the lateness."

"Yes, time to pack it in."

"Are y' going to be wanting me to talk to the coppers about Niagara?"

"Not just yet."

"Why were you there, anyway?"

"Webb was a lead in another case I'm working on. Quite separate from yours." Maybe.

"Well, he had a wide range of business, from art treasures to weapons. Lots of people were interested in him."

"What do you know about Webb's gun operation?"

"Nothing, just that he dabbled in it." Sharon Geary stretched, groaning. "It'll be a hot bath for me tonight. I hope I didn't bruise you too much."

"I'll live. I need to know where you're staying."

"Just follow Professor Rivers and you'll find me right behind you."

"No, I mean it. There are some things going on you don't know about, and it could get very dangerous." He resigned himself to the necessity of imposing more hypnosis on her. He didn't need any loose cannons rolling about the city, especially now.

"I think I've an idea of the danger. That's why I got this." She drew the Glock out again. "I'm no amateur, Mr. Dun, but you need some more practice I'm thinkin'." Quick as thought, she pulled out a second magazine of rounds from her jacket pocket, slammed it into the gun butt, and racked back the slide to chamber a round. The safety was off, and she had the damned thing in his face again.

"You're not with Lloyds," he observed with considerable disgust.

"Not exactly, no, but I've work to do and won't be havin' you muckin' it all up for me." She backed away and around until the car was between them and fumbled for the door handle. "I've had a lovely time, though. I'd walk you to your door an' all, but—"

"No, thanks," he said dryly. "I'm a big boy."

She grinned at him. Her gaze traveled suggestively up and down his form.

"Don't even think about saying it," he warned, trying not to smile.

She laughed once, nimbly slipped into the car, and gunned the motor to life. He thought about rushing around and stopping her, but dismissed the idea. It was just too much work and risk. Besides, if he kept an eye on Rivers, the redoubtable Ms. Geary would not be far away. Richard could deal with her again, and not be so trusting of her apparent credentials.

She pulled out and made a U-turn with the car, cruising slowly past him, her eyes alight as she waved. "By the way," she called in parting, "*nice* ass!"

He suddenly found himself grinning back at her.

Absolutely, he thought, returning the compliment. *Absolutely*.

✧　　　✧　　　✧

The remainder of the night was rather more tranquil. Richard treasured it, for he was tired and wanted the rest. He walked home—it wasn't that far—slipped past the oblivious RCMP man on watch, and in through his own back door with no one the wiser. He trudged upstairs, pausing only long enough to strip to the skin.

Bruises. Lots of them. He noted their presence and forgot them. By his next waking they'd be gone. The blood he'd had tonight would speed the healing. He dropped, sprawling across the tangled bedclothes with a thankful groan, and surrendered to sweet forgetfulness for a time.

His answering machine was off, a necessary evil since he was expecting a call from the Judge. The damned phone's annoying buzz dragged him out of his voluntary coma far too soon to suit.

" . . . m'lo?"

"Catch you napping, old boy?" Bourland. "Thought you'd be at work by now."

Richard squinted at the glowing clock face on his night stand. It was past the midday meal for most people. He'd had a full eight hours and a bit more, but didn't feel like it. "What's up?"

"Did a little pest control. Your fleas are gone. Don't know for how long, though."

Richard went to the window and cautiously peered past the lightproof curtains. The sunny glare blinded him a moment, then he could see the street below. No extra cars parked where they shouldn't be. Good. "Thank you. I've had some wiring problems as well, you know."

"Shall I get an electrician for you?"

"I'd consider it a great favor if you would."

"Mind you don't squawk when I call it in." He rang off.

Richard set his shower head to firehose pressure in an effort to wake up. His system was better suited to sleeping the daylight away, and when possible it was his preference to do so. Now was not one of those times. He could certainly sympathize with Neal Rivers about jet lag; another eight to ten hours in the sack would be very nice, indeed.

With Ms. Geary, perhaps?

He smiled at that idea and woke up a bit more. She would be something of a challenge, but what a reward if he succeeded.

If. Circumstances were hardly favorable at the moment, and would become even less so after his next phone call.

A short time later, shaved and in comfortable clothes, he plunged into his office work for five highly focused minutes. His secretary had E-mailed him confirmation of the schedule changes he'd made. Excellent. He checked the computer line. The tap was still in place. Not so excellent, but he could wait a little longer before booking a first-class ticket to London. He had to wait anyway, until the Judge reported in.

Speaking of reports . . .

He punched in Demarest's number, identified himself, and was shot straight through to the man himself.

"Yes, what is it?" Demarest's manner had gained no shred of charm since their last meeting.

"I saw the Geary woman last night. We had a chat, sorted out our credentials."

"Who is she? Why didn't you bring her in?"

"She's not involved with the assassination plot."

"Oh, really?" Demarest was good with a sarcastic tone. Very good. "It's not for you to judge. You should have brought her in for questioning."

"I might have tried, but for her gun."

"Explain."

Richard summarized his encounter, skimming some points, such as exactly how he and Geary had come to meet, altogether leaving out certain items of information that were none of Demarest's business, such as the talk with Rivers. True, someone might connect the expert on Celtic studies now lecturing at the university with Richard's Internet mining, but they wouldn't find out from him. Let them do the work. "Apparently Webb smuggled in some sort of old manuscript and Geary was trying to buy it back from him. Claimed she worked for Lloyd's of London, but I've an idea she's working for herself, perhaps to return the thing for a finder's fee off the insurance."

"Or keep to sell it herself."

"It's worth checking on. I think an all-points would be a good idea—if you still want to find her."

"Of course we do!"

Richard gave a complete description of Sharon Geary, her current car and its plates, and added in a minor request. "If you check the car, you may find a large book in it, a new one. It's mine and I'll want it back." Demarest grumbled something noncommittal, apparently busy writing things down. Richard decided not to press; recovering the book wasn't that important to him.

"Where exactly did you go last night?" Demarest demanded after a moment.

"Just out for a drink," he said truthfully. "I'd have invited your man, but he was on duty."

"Planning to go out again tonight as well?"

"I haven't checked my social calendar yet."

"Don't push too hard, Dun, or I *will* find a cell for you."

"I'll keep that in mind." He hung up before Demarest got annoying. At least the fellow had taken him seriously about the woman. There had to be a degree of competence hidden somewhere under the insecurity and bluster, or he'd not have risen so high in rank. That, or he knew how to delegate to abler assistants.

Ah, well, Richard had fulfilled his duty. Nothing to do now but wait for the Judge to come through.

He hated this sort of waiting. It blew hell out of his concentration for most tasks, knowing that at any second he'd have to drop what he was doing and answer the expected interruption. In all his centuries of survival he'd never been able to cure himself of this particular type of impatience.

The longer the wait, of course, the worse it got. He paced about his house, occasionally putting an out-of-place item in its proper spot, and doing other small, unimportant chores, but little more than that. He did trouble to repack his travel kit and suitcase to have it ready for his trip to England. Once this irksome business with Charon was out of the way, or in some kind of a holding pattern, Richard would be on the next flight out. He wanted to make the necessary arrangements now, but the tap on his computer prevented that. Demarest would really go 'round the twist if he knew Richard was shortly planning to leave the country.

One hour passed, then three. Richard was glad he'd slept the bulk of the day away. Through it all he very determinedly did not call the Judge's number. Eugene Mantalessa worked better when no one was looking over his shoulder.

Phone.

Richard picked it up, the wretched thought flashing through his head that it wouldn't be the Judge but someone trying to sell aluminum siding.

"The Judge is back and has your sentence ready," announced the voice on the other end.

Richard kept the relief out of his voice. "Let's hear it." He checked his tap detector. The light showed green for clear. Thank God for Bourland.

"Uh-uh. This one cost me big. I need to get that back again."

"You know I'm good for it."

"Uh-huh, but if you get killed before I collect, then where would the Judge be?"

"Eugene . . ."

But the Judge had a smile in his tone. The distance between them and probably another line of snow must have given him the courage. "You meet me by McGill's Pub and settle out, then you're on your own."

"I'm leaving now. Be there."

Richard had been ready to leave for far too long. His coat, hat, and gloves were laid out and ready; he swiftly donned them, checked that he had enough money for the Judge's expenses and more, then used the inside door leading to the garage.

This time he chose to leave the Jaguar in and take his other vehicle, a late-model Land Rover. It was lower profile. He usually drove it during the winter months when the streets were icy, rather than risk the more valuable Jag to the scrapes and bruising of accidents. He started the Rover, thumbed the remote button to open and then shut the garage, and was off to McGill's.

The sun was a painful nuisance. He had to head into it, and its light blasted against him like a fury. No amount of sunscreen would protect him for long. Hurriedly, he yanked a heavy woolen scarf from a pocket and wrapped it around his face, covering the lower part right up to his eyes, which were already shielded by very dark, wrap-around sunglasses. The glass was polarized with UV blockers. They helped, but he still had to squint.

The evening traffic jam was off to an early start, compounding his discomfort, but he got far enough along Gardner to turn north, and things eased a bit. His hat and turned up collar kept him from burning, though he could still feel the heat beating on the side of his head and neck.

McGill's was not one of his favorite recreational spots. They supposedly had decent food and drink, the music was excellent if you liked it Irish, but the watchful atmosphere always put his teeth on edge. Too many eyes, too much suspicion for outsiders, certainly it was no place for him to hunt down his own kind of food. The owner was more than a little sympathetic to the IRA and made no secret of it. Most of his customers were of a like mind, and if not, then they were better off staying away.

Richard found a parking space down the street and walked up slowly in the safe shade of the buildings, getting a look at things. The neighborhood had been new about a hundred years ago, but was now more than ready for retirement. Usually he wasn't in favor of tearing down old edifices for modern replacements, he'd seen too much beauty and history destroyed, but in this instance he'd make an exception. The street was lined with mean little one- and two-story structures, stuffy and hopelessly plain, huddling under the tall high-rises that overlooked them. Even when the first coat of paint had been fresh these affronts to architecture had been ugly, and time had not improved them one whit. Windows were caged over by wire mesh, doors were obscured behind protective bars, or boarded up and covered with gang graffiti. The exception was McGill's Pub. No gang in the area was foolish enough to spray their signs on its walls.

He'd nearly reached McGill's when someone hissed at him from the gap between two buildings. The

Judge. Looking nervous. Richard cast a cautious glimpse around, saw things were clear, then went to join him.

"Thought you'd be in the pub," he said.

The Judge shook his head firmly. "Mon, nobody there ever mistake me f' bein' Irish. An' one thing I don't need is for the boys to know I even breathe; they might want to change it. What's with the getup? I almost din' know you. You cold or somethin'?"

"Or something. What have you got?" He moved deeper into shadow to avoid the slice of a last stray sunbeam.

"That depend on what you got."

Richard pulled out the envelope with the remaining cash and let the Judge see it. "Only if what you have is good."

"It's good, you can trust me."

"Get real, Eugene," he said with a smile.

The Judge gave a half-hearted laugh, but couldn't keep the sudden alarm from showing in his eyes. "Okay, there's a mon, IRA, call himself Sean, who deals with th' guns, any guns. He collects 'em, buys, no questions asked, 'n' ships 'em out to you-know-where."

Sean. The same one Webb had called? "His last name, location?"

"Don' got a last name, mon, but he got a place you can check out. What I heard was he got a special customer wantin' a special gun. It coulda come in by now, I couldn't find that out for sure, but him and his boys are freaked up bad an' it ain't because of the cops."

"Who, then?"

"A friend of a friend tol' me that one of their boys got snuffed, he check out so hard and nasty his own mama wouldn't know him. Happen a couple days back in Niagara—"

Richard held to a stony face and was glad he still wore his concealing glasses. "What about it?"

"Well, this dead mon is the one who brought the gun over the border. He deliver to Sean, then someone got to him. Now Sean 'n' his boys're lookin' over they shoulder so much they gonna get the whiplash."

"Give me a description of Sean."

"Big hairy bastard with a busted nose. They say he used t' fight heavyweight till he kill a mon."

"In the ring?"

"In a bar. He cut someone up with a bottle, then hada run, get a new name. The boys took care of 'im till he got set up again."

"Where can I find him?"

"It's real close, just across 'n' down. Used to be a store, but they shut it up and use it to hold stuff for shippin'."

"Which one?"

"Number 118, jus' short of the corner. It locked up good, though, mon. You ain't gettin' in easy."

"I'll manage."

"Gettin' out be harder. You wanna pay up before you start?"

Richard handed him the envelope with the other portion of his payment, but didn't release it. "I'll come for a refund if this turns out to be a waste of time." He was smiling again.

The Judge swallowed, blinking hard. "I know, mon. But this is th' straight stuff. Cost me big."

"Cost you more if it isn't." He let go and the Judge swiftly crumpled the envelope into a pocket, not bothering to count the contents. "I'll see you, mon. Maybe." He took off toward the alley's other entrance, not looking back. Richard lingered in the shadows, listening, finally hearing the nearby thrum of a car motor coming to life. It could be the Judge's, or not. No matter.

Damned sun. He checked the time. A few minutes to go before it was fully safe for him to move. Not long. He leaned against a dingy brick wall and watched the light fading, retreating. The sky was still very bright, but soon now.

People passed by the alley, some looked in and moved on, most didn't even notice his presence. Not very good urban survival skills on their part, especially for this neighborhood. Had he been more like his bloodthirsty cinematic cousins, he could have had his pick of them to drag in and feed upon. How lucky for them all he knew the meaning of caution, restraint, common sense . . . and good manners.

The darkness got thicker, more comfortable. Some of the skin on his face stung a bit from too much exposure, but not for long. Like last night's bruises, it would heal. He briefly returned to the Rover to stash his outer garments to allow himself greater freedom of movement, then went back along the twilight-washed street.

Artificial lights sprang up. No threat from them; they only made the shadows that much darker. The sign over McGill's flashed on. He passed under it, catching the sound of voices and music. No live band tonight. A pity. It would have improved the place.

Like a good citizen he crossed the street at the corner and kept going around the block, finding his way through the maze of walls to the delivery entrance of number 118. The trashy flotsam in the alley was old: crushed and tarnished beer cans, dusty, broken glass. No oil stains from standing vehicles, indicating it was not much used. He tried the featureless metal door. Locked, of course. Several deadbolts. He thought of picking them, but that would take too long.

The low window next to the door looked more promising. A sturdy iron grill had been bolted into the brick as a deterrent. Discouraging to a casual intruder, but not to him. Richard took strong hold of the lower part, braced his feet, and pulled.

A century of Toronto winters had had their way with the bricks. He heard a crack, then a grinding sound, then the whole grill suddenly came away in a puff of dust. He recovered his balance, set the thing aside, and tried the window. One of the panes was broken and someone had covered it with duct tape. He tore it away, put a hand in to unlatch the thing, then slowly raised the sash.

It protested noisily, but lifted enough for him to slip inside to a small, bare chamber. His eyes quickly adjusted to the gloom. He smelled chilled damp concrete, moldy wood, and something sharper: metal, oil, and sawdust. At his feet lay crushed curls of excelsior. He left the window up and quiet as a ghost moved toward an open door that led further into the building.

No lights on, but he didn't need them. He saw a number of crates in all shapes and sizes, some open, others nailed shut. The aged labels declared some items to be machine parts, others were supposedly toys, the boxes bearing the logo of several legitimate companies. In one partly packed crate declaring itself full of fragile glass ashtrays he found a goodly quantity of hand grenades nestled in curls of wood shavings.

Sound.

He froze, listening.

Yes . . . someone else was here. He could hear their breathing. Faint, but . . . Richard followed the sound, his senses stretched as he eased closer to its source.

Now he could hear a heartbeat drumming away strong and fast. The other person knew he was here all right, only fear worked that kind of a strain on a human heart.

Richard softly changed course, gliding past a tall stack of boxes. His quarry was behind them somewhere. It was hard to keep silent; the floor was filthy and the grit crunched between his shoe soles and the concrete. He reached the last corner and cautiously peered around.

There he was. Richard could just see him standing a few yards off, back pressed against the crates, holding to a tense listening posture. A big fellow, bearded, dark hair down past his thick, bunched shoulders. Sean? Oh, yes, very likely. Gripped in his right hand was a short-barreled revolver, aimed at the ceiling. Finger on the trigger. Nothing unexpected.

Very slowly, Richard stepped clear of his own concealment, intent on rushing in fast to take the other man down. Unfortunately, the unswept floor betrayed him. His shoe audibly scraped over something; Sean whirled and fired. No time to duck, but the shot went wild. Before he could get out another round, Richard surged forward, grabbing the gun, first pushing it wide, then plucking it free. Sean didn't waste time trying to get it back, and instead brought a strong left hook in under Richard's ribcage, knocking the breath quite out of him. He staggered, got his arm up in time to block another punch, but the next one caught him square in the belly, doubling him over. A knee shot up to crack Richard's chin. He reeled to one side just in time to avoid it, caught Sean's leg and pulled. The man grunted, lost his balance, and clutched Richard's shoulders as he fell, dragging them both to the floor.

Sean twisted, landing on top, using his greater

weight like a wrestler to pin his opponent. His hands went around Richard's neck, thumbs locked hard over his windpipe and gouging deep. Richard heard the sudden snap of his own cartilage giving way and gagged against the heavy pain. *Forty pounds of pressure, that's all it takes*, he thought dimly. He still had the gun in his left hand, but the wrong way around. He used it like a club on the side of Sean's head. That helped. The agonizing pressure abruptly lessened, but didn't stop. The breakage was still with him, choking him. He retched and gasped, tasting blood in the back of his throat.

Sean recovered rapidly. He rolled off, clawing for the gun; Richard stubbornly held on to it. Sean caught his arm in both hands and slammed his wrist against the unforgiving corner of a crate, hard enough to fracture the bones. The gun went flying. He heard it strike the concrete with a dull clank. Sean pushed away. Richard turned over in time to see the other man pounce on the gun, turn, then the business end of the thing was in his face.

He shut his eyes, expecting, dreading the shot, but nothing happened. When he opened them a second later Sean was still there, catching his own breath. Reaction from the choking hit Richard, and he began to cough, trying to force air in and out. God, it hurt. He tore at his collar and still the pain clung to him. Healing would come, but never fast enough.

"Right," said Sean. "Now who the devil are you?"

Too soon for questions. Richard was in no shape to reply. He gagged again, air wheezing in and out of his throat like a rip saw. An ordinary man would have been dying or dead from the damage. Richard wasn't so sure he was much better off.

When no immediate answer was forthcoming, Sean walked over to a cardboard-covered window, peeled back a flap, and looked out. He grunted once, then returned to stand over Richard.

"Who are you? Why'd y' come here?"

Richard could only manage shallow breathing. Damn, but next time he'd carry a gun himself. This bastard had been entirely too fast and strong. He fitted the Judge's general description; add in thickened ears and facial scarring and a well-broken in nose to clinch things. Definitely a former boxer and still very solidly in shape.

"Come on, or I'll blow your head off. Why're y'here?"

Things were a shade less agonizing. He pointed to himself and coughed out a single word. "Buyer."

"You're saying you're a buyer?"

Richard nodded.

Sean had a singularly unpleasant smile. "No way in hell. I know 'em all an' the ones I don't always set up a proper meeting. You're a cop is what I'm thinkin'. A dead un'." He cocked the gun, the muzzle touching lightly right between Richard's eyes.

He struggled, dragging in more air. "Charon. Sent. Me."

"Did he now? That'll be news to him, I'm sure. How is it you even know his name? Eh?"

Richard held his hand up, palm out, a gesture to ask for more time. The man was smart enough to be curious; he held off shooting and eased the hammer back into place. Richard rallied to the point where he noticed his injured hand. He gingerly felt things. No broken bones, he could thank his changed nature for that, but hellishly bruised. He looked forward to some payback time with Sean.

"Right, now tell me a story or two," Sean ordered.

"I'm looking for a special gun. Heard you could get it for me." His vocal cords felt like sandpaper.

"From Charon?"

"We're in the same business. You're the one to see, he said."

"Very flatterin', but I don't believe you."

"Then believe this." Richard—very slowly and with great consideration for his hand—fished out his wallet. It was fat with hundred dollar bills. He drew out the lot and placed them on the closest crate. "Downpayment. I've more where that came from."

Sean's expression remained the same, except for his eyes—something was different there. The glint of greed. Excellent. Miraculous stuff, money. It could almost always be relied upon to produce instant and universal understanding between opposing viewpoints when conditions were right. And if not that, then it made for a marvelous way to stall for time.

"Thank you very kindly, I'm sure, but—"

"You don't want to kill me and take the cash," Richard advised him.

"I don't? An' why not?"

"Because you are a business man, and you're not stupid. This is a chance to turn a hell of a deal."

Sean worked through that one, taking a lot of time. Good. Richard felt his strength reviving and with it his full concentration. The big fighter was now in a fairly receptive state for suggestion. Sean something-or-other, probably the man Arlie Webb had called for help, and certainly a dealer for special weapons. Demarest would be delighted, but Richard had him first and could question him first. Closely.

"You need to listen to me on this," Richard said, locking his gaze hard onto the other man's eyes. "*You really must listen to me.*"

Sean's determined expression wavered. His eyes clouded slightly. He wasn't too deeply under, but enough to be able to work with. "I'm . . . listenin'."

"I'm here to make you very rich."

Sean nodded in dull agreement.

"I'm here to help you. But you have to help me as well."

"Yeah."

"Now, I very much need to talk to Charon first. You must tell me where he is before—"

Sean shook his head; his big frame shuddered from top to toe. Resisting. A tough will to go with the tough body.

"Charon wants to contact me—it's important that—"

"No . . . I can't . . ."

"You can, Sean. You will." Richard stepped up the pressure.

Sean flinched, blinking fast, continuing to shake his head.

Something was wrong. The man should have been babbling his head off by now. "Easy, Sean, you can relax, you're perfectly safe. Just tell me where Charon—"

Sean moaned as though in pain and brought the gun up to fire. Richard barely knocked it away in time. The roar this close buffeted hard against his chest and deafened him for an instant. With his uninjured fist Richard struck the man a solid one in the jaw, sending him right over. He instantly and soundlessly collapsed.

Damn.

Richard pushed away from the body, indulging in a few more soft curses of reproach. Now he'd have to try and revive the bastard and God knows how long that would take. There hadn't been time to pull the punch. What had gone wrong, anyway? He'd never had anyone react quite that way before.

Standing and dusting himself off, Richard retrieved his stack of money, then went to the cardboard-covered window and looked out as Sean had done a few moments ago. The sky was much darker, the artificial lights more intense. The view was of the street that faced McGill's Pub. One or two hard-looking men were filing in, intent on an after-work drink and certainly to talk a little treason. If anyone noticed the last shot, no one appeared to be interested in investigating it. The neighborhood was not the sort to encourage such curiosity.

Wait a moment, one person standing outside was looking this way.

Sharon Geary. What the hell was she doing here? Maybe Rivers had proved to be a dead end. She'd said she might have to try her luck talking to the IRA. Her accent would carry her a bit with them, far enough to get killed if she wasn't careful.

He glanced back at Sean, who hadn't moved a fraction and wasn't likely to for awhile. Richard sighed, thought, *why not?* and checked the front door of the place. Lots of deadbolts and an iron bar across the middle to keep out intruders, but nothing to keep anyone from leaving. He undid the bolts, lifted the bar away, and slipped outside, pulling the door shut behind him.

Sharon was no longer to be seen. Inside the pub, then. He crossed the street and pushed through the entry. It was early yet, and few people were inside. He was invited to pay a cover charge and gave the man behind the counter a fiver.

"An' something for the boys," he told Richard, indicating a foot-high glass jar with a slot cut into the plastic lid. A hand-lettered sign taped on it had some nonsense about the proceeds going to a charity Richard had never heard of; without argument he put another five into it. Anything less would draw attention, and if he chose not to "contribute" he'd be followed out of the pub when he left. Not that he couldn't have taken care of them, but he had more important things to do than get into alley fights with Republican sympathizers.

Sharon was toward the back, leaning over a table, talking with a couple of uncooperative-looking men. They were shaking their heads to whatever she was saying. The other men in the room were openly staring at her, their thoughts clearly on their faces. Richard would have been worried for her but for the knowledge she was probably still packing that Glock and a hell of an attitude.

Richard got close behind her. The men at the table looked up, triggering a reaction from Sharon, who straightened and turned, her eyes going wide.

"You—!"

He put on a brogue again, talking loudly. "Why if it isn't Sister Mary Margaret collectin' for the parish! The Mother Superior's been lookin' all over for you. Come along, Sister, or you'll miss the evening mass." He got a firm grip on her near arm, caught her other hand to keep it out of mischief, and steered her inarguably toward the exit. Laughter trailed after them.

"You son of a—"

"Now, now, you'll have to do penance for that thought."

She gave up struggling until they were outside near the curb, then made a decided effort to shake him off. He backed away half a step, hands out to show how harmless he was and collected a glare for his trouble.

"Lose interest in Rivers?" he asked.

"He's doing one of his lectures now; it was safe to talk to them."

"You've got a strange idea of what is safe, Ms. Geary."

"I've no need for you to be tellin' me how to run my business."

"And what might that be?"

She scowled.

"My guess is you're trying to recover the manuscript to claim the finder's fee off the insurance. Am I right?"

She gave a short laugh, then a short nod. "A quarter million pounds—an' I've no plans to be sharin' it with anyone."

"I wouldn't think of interfering."

"You just *did*, you daft loon! I was almost—"

The interruption was a loud one, almost too loud to hear. Richard hadn't heard or felt anything like it since the last time he'd been under cannon fire. Instinct cut in far faster than thought; he grabbed Sharon and dragged her to the ground.

Too late. If you can hear it, it's already too late.

Chapter Six

His ears rang; one side of his face stung. The dust spray and mortar flinders were yet to settle from the head-sized hole that had magically exploded into the brick wall of the pub on his left. He brushed at the grit clinging to his skin, staring.

Sharon pushed him off and started to rise, then froze as her impossibly wide eyes followed his gaze. She mouthed the word *shit* and scrabbled quickly backwards on hands and knees to questionable shelter behind a parked car. Richard followed her. As his hearing recovered, he caught the sound of screams and shouts coming from within the pub. Some fool poked his head out the front door; Richard bawled at him to get back inside. He spotted others standing confused on the street and yelled for them to run. They finally got the idea and removed themselves from the area. Not fast enough to suit, but he couldn't help that.

After a few moments, he raised up a bit to peer over the car, scanning the rooftops on the opposite side of the street. Clear. He looked at the hole in the wall. God. Whoever fired a round like that could have been on one of the more distant high-rises. There was no way to tell.

"What the hell was that?" Sharon asked, rather loudly. Apparently her hearing had also been affected.

"Long gun. Sniper." *Charon*, he thought. He

196

remembered the other men who had made a special project of hunting for Charon and the fate of three of them. All taken out by a rifle, the last catching it in the neck. Richard didn't think even he could possibly survive such a massive wound. His heart skipped once and shuddered against his ribcage.

"Sniper?" She shrank farther behind the car. Not that it would have helped. Whatever had gone through the pub wall could just as easily go through the vehicle. "Against the IRA?"

"Against me."

Her face was set, in control, but she trembled. Flight or fight, but with nowhere to go and no one to hit. He understood the feeling. "What lovely friends you have. And lucky for you he missed."

Richard shook his head. "Not luck. He missed on purpose." The bullet had gone right between them, or so his impression of the instant told him. A warning. But why? Why would Charon even bother? "Stay here, I have to check on things."

"Don't worry," she said with great sincerity.

He kept to human normal speed, but darted quickly from his cover to the entry of the pub. There was no second shot. Inside, people were still on the floor or under tables, for all the good it would do them.

The exit hole of the bullet was a full foot across. Brick dust, plaster, splinters of wood lay everywhere. He smelled blood.

"Anybody call nine-one-one yet?" he asked no one in particular. He had to speak up, not for his ringing ears, but to be heard over the the pub's sound system. Irish folk music blared insanely from the speakers.

"I'm on the phone now," a woman in the back replied, her own voice tight with the sudden stress.

"Tell them it's a sniper."

He got an affirmative snarl in return.

The smell of blood came from several people who had been caught by shards of flying brick. The stuff had shot out from the bullet's passage like shrapnel, creating the same devastating effect. He spotted one man clutching his bleeding scalp and helped lift another with blood streaming from a gash in his leg. He guided both toward the far wall where the others were moving. Without exception, they were pale-faced and shaking with fear, but trying to aid their cursing and groaning fellows. Someone found a cache of bar towels and began using them as makeshift bandages on the wounded.

His corner teeth began to bud. *Damn, not now!* The beast inside, having scented food, was scratching to be let out. It was too soon for him to feed again; this wasn't hunger so much as gluttony. Control. He could control it. *Had* to control it. Richard held still a moment, and briefly succeeded in shutting down the chaos both without and within. It was very much like praying. When he was ready, he allowed the outer noise to flood back again. His teeth were normal, and he was able to deal with mundane realities.

He began by herding the strays through the back hall and delivery area and out the rear door, telling them to stay low in the alley until the police came. A few muttered unanswerable questions, but no one argued with him. Probably glad someone had taken charge for the moment. He went back in. The pub area was clear except for the mess: overturned chairs and tables, broken and scattered bottles and other minor debris. No bodies, thank God. He was quite sincere in his gratitude; it had been a miracle no one had been directly hit by the bullet. They'd have gotten cut right in two.

He did find a sizable hole in the floor. There'd be

hellish damage in the basement for sure. He bent low, lining his gaze up to peer through the hole in the outside wall to do a rough calculation of the angle. Yes. He could see the roof of the building opposite. The sniper had set himself up there. Probably gone by now. At least Richard hoped he was gone.

Only one way to find out.

Sharon was in the same spot when he emerged and joined her, crouching again by the car.

"What's—?" She indicated the pub.

"A few people cut up, no one killed."

"Thank heaven."

"Absolutely." He heard sirens. Hell. He didn't want to hang about the rest of the night trying not to talk to the law. "I think you should leave."

"It had crossed my mind, but is it safe?"

"Haven't the faintest. Where's your car?"

"Turned it in on the chance you got the plate numbers. I cabbed over."

Damn. "I have to do something first, but I still need to talk to you. My truck's just down the road." He described the Land Rover to her. "Will you wait there for me? I'm not after the finder's fee for your manuscript, so you needn't worry about that. I just want to *talk* with you, and that's all."

"Talk about what?" she demanded, all suspicion.

Damn again. "About my nice ass," he improvised.

She puffed out with a single mirthless laugh, but nodded. Keeping her head down and her body bent and close to the parked cars, she hurried away.

Nice ass, indeed, he thought with brief appreciation as she retreated, then rose as well for a rush across the street to get to number 118.

He paused next to the door and gingerly pushed on it. It swung heavily open into darkness and silence. Good. No gun fire. He slipped inside. Fast.

Another pause, to listen and so his eyes could adjust.

Stillness and more silence. The wrong kind of silence. He should have been able to hear Sean's breathing.

Then he smelled blood again, lots of it, as pervasive as petrol at a filling station. He licked his lips—from nerves, not hunger. There was something else mixed in with the blood, fouling it: the sting of digestive acid, the reek of bowel. He'd experienced both stenches in the past on battlefields . . . and much more recently in Niagara.

His breath came short and shallow as he moved forward.

Sean's body sprawled where he'd left it by the crates. Richard could see immediately the man was dead, quite thoroughly dead.

Blood everywhere. Lots of it. Footprints in the blood. The departing trail led off toward the back entry. A man's shoe size, he noted absently.

The voice of his newly born daughter came back to him: *Where it walks it leaves a trail of blood* .

She-Who-Walks had gotten that right enough.

Richard forced himself to study what was left of the body. He'd seen death before, countless variations of it, but this particular one turned his belly differently, more profoundly than all the others.

Sean's exposed skin was torn, clawed, ripped . . . and bitten.

Oh, dear God.

Richard reached his Land Rover just as the first of the emergency vehicles arrived on the scene: police, ambulances, even a SWAT team; they were gathering like flies to a corpse. God, if they only knew.

They'll find him soon enough.

Within the hour they'd be all over that building.

Another horrific murder like the one in Niagara and himself, Richard, close on the scene again. Demarest would have a perfect seizure; he'd—

But Richard could not complete the thought as the vision of what he'd just seen crashed upon his mind's eye again, scattering all other worries to the sky. He knew exactly what had made the mess in 118, the mess that was all that remained of Sean the boxer. He recognized the tearing and the wanton spilling of blood and bile.

Another vampire.

A vampire at just about the same stage of degeneration as himself.

His hands were leaden as he fumbled to unlock the door and hoist his suddenly chilled body inside the cab of the truck. The familiar smell of leather and plastic weren't enough to dispel what now permeated his clothes, clung to his skin. He'd taken great care not to touch anything, but the stench of the warehouse was very much with him. He glanced apprehensively at his shoes. They were clean—at least of visible crimson evidence—but he knew he'd throw everything away at the first opportunity. As before with Arlie Webb, he felt an overwhelming urge to wash it all off. He'd see to it as soon as he was in the sweet sanctuary of his home.

He started the engine, gunning it to angry life, a reflection of his inner tension, then protective instinct cut in and he eased off to let the truck merely idle. There were quite enough police around, no need to attract their attention.

He didn't half jump out of his skin when Sharon suddenly appeared at the driver's door and pounded on the window.

"Here! I thought you were wantin' to talk with me!" she shouted through the darkened glass.

He stared, having utterly forgotten her.

"Well, come on, then! Your place or mine?"

It occurred to him that for her own good he should just drive away. Safer for her, and he'd have time to himself to think this one through. She pounded again, impatiently, her face projecting annoyance, but her eyes showing fear as she threw a nervous glance over her shoulder at the growing commotion down the street.

He undid the lock for the passenger side and motioned for her to come around. She did so with alacrity, hauling herself inside even as he shifted into first. The door slammed shut from their abrupt charge forward, and she was thrust hard into the seat. She squawked once, clutching her shoulder bag to keep it from flying, then scrabbled for the seat belt.

In silence Richard flung the vehicle around corners and through stop signs, heading for the expressway. Sharon stared at him with a mix of undisguised alarm and amusement. He ignored her and simply drove hard, as if the hounds of hell were on his tail, and dear Lord, it felt to him that they were.

The Hounds of Annwyn, perhaps? His forebears, according to Sabra.

And who was this other vampire? A relation, perhaps, some cousin he'd never heard of? It wasn't as though he'd met many of their kind over the span of centuries. He racked his long memory, but no one suitable emerged from the mists of his past. They either had no quarrel with him or were dead.

"Is this your idea of an encore, or some strange male ritual designed to thrill and impress?" Sharon asked.

"What?" He dragged his thoughts reluctantly to the present. He'd barely been aware of her next to him.

"This wonderful Stirling Moss impersonation that you're giving."

Embarrassed, he immediately slowed, trying out a thin smile. "Sorry. I needed to get away from there."

"That much is obvious. What happened?"

"Nothing."

"I doubt it. You were cool enough when I went off, then you turn up peaky as a rabbit in a dog kennel, so something happened."

"I had a shock."

"Did you, indeed? When you went across the street?"

She'd seen enough to both annoy and alarm him, but he saw no reason to lie to her. "Yes. Found a body."

Her demeanor sobered. "Someone you knew?"

"Not exactly, but it was bad. Like . . . like Arlie Webb." *Careful, Richard.*

"Sweet Mary." She watched him a moment, made an uneasy gesture, and said, "Can't stand the sight of blood? No one will be blamin' you for that."

Wrong, wrong, wrong. It's death. This kind of death. That kind of killing. "I suppose so. Yes." She started to speak again, but he raised one hand in a quelling motion. "Please, if you don't mind, I need a few minutes." He swung the truck just a little too wildly off the expressway ramp and down onto Lakeshore, tires protesting. "We're nearly there."

She clamped her jaw shut and held on tight for the rest of the ride.

He was not in so much of a hurry as to forget to check the rearview mirror. It remained reassuringly clear. Just as well. He could deal with any such problem, but Sharon's presence might limit his choice of action.

He hit the remote to open the garage doors and slipped the Rover in neatly next to the Jaguar. Sharon got out, pausing an instant to gape once at the car, then hurrying to catch up as he unlocked the utility entry. He made sure she did not see the code he punched in to deactivate the house's security system. He was taking her into his home, true, but there were degrees of trust, after all.

He ushered her in, reset the system, and firmly closed the door behind them, feeling an illogical sense of relief for what was essentially a sham of protection. If Charon was outside somewhere and wanted to he could level the whole place.

Maybe he doesn't want to. Not yet.

But why?

He guided his guest through the kitchen, across the hall, and into his office. It was the center of his web, the place he felt safest. Illusion only, he knew, but for the moment illusion was enough.

Sharon took in the room with its combination of expensive, high-tech toys and old-fashioned comfortable furnishings, turning to look carefully at everything, perhaps trying to get a few clues about him, about who he was. He liked that; it was something he did with other people. She dropped her purse on a table, then lingered for a long time before the Botticelli, peering at it closely, too closely.

"Is this what I think it is?" she asked, finally breaking the silence he'd requested during their hasty drive.

"What would that be?"

"It looks to be very old and impossibly valuable."

As he'd done a few times before with sharp-eyed clients, he allowed a glint of mischief to show in his expression. "You think so?"

"Tell me this is not an undiscovered Botticelli." Such an item hanging in a mostly ordinary home in Toronto would blast through the art world with the force of an atom bomb.

"All right, it's not."

"Then what is it?"

"I had business some years back in Florence and met a charming young forger who made her living doing this sort of work. She could imitate all the greats from Giotto to Surat. I commissioned it from her."

"Really?" Sharon looked even closer at the work. "She did a bloody marvelous job, right down to the cracks in the varnish. It even *smells* right."

Not many would catch that detail. His regard for Sharon went up another notch. "Her specialty."

"Quite the skilled charlatan, then. Who's the subject?"

"A lady I know."

She glanced over, interested. "You're attached?"

"Nothing formal." His ties to Sabra were far stronger than any signatures on a bit of parchment, certainly stronger than any temporary dalliance, and with ephemeral human women all dalliances could only ever be temporary.

"How 'nothing formal'?"

He chose to ignore the question. "Would you like a drink?"

Sharon's eyes flashed once. Too bad, but she was on a strictly need to know basis for the time being. "Jamesons, if you have it."

Though he drank nothing but his special stock, his bar was well-supplied with a variety of brands for the benefit of all visitors. He poked through the bottles until he found the right label, pouring a generous double for her. From the built-in fridge he selected one of the dark bottles from the front, checking the hand-lettered date he'd taped on. Yes, it was still good. He filled a black-tinted wineglass close to the brim for himself.

The scent of the blood tugged at him. Strongly. His inner beast had been overwhelmed earlier, crowded from his thoughts by the sheer horror of Sean's body and all the implications that went with it, but now seemed more than ready to emerge again. Richard held it hard in check as he gave Sharon her whiskey, then, with social duty out of the way, downed most of his glass in one shuddering draught.

The stuff flailed through him, fire and ice together. Sometimes it was like that. Almost as good as sex. Almost. He looked at Sharon, then looked away and returned to the bar for a second glass. He might have to empty the bottle to keep himself in control.

I should have left her behind.

Sharon appreciatively inhaled the whiskey in her hand, then sank a healthy mouthful. "Mother of God, that's good." She sat back in an overstuffed armchair near the painting, stretching out her long, jeans-clad legs, crossing them at the ankles. She wore boots again and a dark green blouse that was open almost to her bra. Her long red hair cascaded down over one shoulder, ending in a bunch at her breast.

She was much too beautiful for his own good. He became conscious of decided stirrings in his groin. He shifted his gaze to Botticelli's portrait of Sabra. Her smile gently mocked him. He could almost hear her amiable teasing about his fondness of fleshy pleasures. Though the acquisition of human blood did not absolutely require lengthy intimate contact, he enjoyed a successful seduction as much as any man. Happily, she'd never had a problem over his indulgence in his various appetites in that area, so long as he returned to her in the end. And he always did.

But now is not the time. Sabra was dying, slipping away forever even as he stood staring at her portrait.

"So," said Sharon, diverting him from the darkness.

She fastened her gaze hard on him. Amazing green eyes. "What the hell was it that nearly took our heads off?"

He gave an inward shrug. She had a right to a few answers. "I believe it's what's known in the trade as a BFG."

"And what is that? Some kind of bazooka?"

"It's a special sniper's gun, very rare, only used by experts. If it's what I think it to be, then we're dealing with something that can fire a fifty-caliber anti-tank round, about that big." He held his thumb and forefinger some seven inches apart.

Her mouth sagged open. "That's the *bullet*? My God, is that what went through the wall?"

"The wall, the floor beyond, and on into the cellar. For all I know, it's probably still tunneling to Java." He finished his second glass and debated over having a third. There was a fine balance to strike between having enough blood so as not to sucumb to temptation and taking in too much alcohol as to negate his self-control.

"Rare, is it? Then can you trace it from the BFG company?"

He blanked a moment, then understood her and smiled. "There is no company. The initials stand for 'Big Fucking Gun,' a term of endearment the soldiers coined for it. And excuse the French."

"Oh." She smiled back. Absolutely amazing eyes. Like green crystals catching the light.

"One could probably trace it to the arms specialist who constructed it, there aren't that many around, but my job is to find the man who has it now."

"Your job?"

He'd thought of lying to her as he'd done about the Botticelli, but something about her and the way she looked at him, a strange mix of innocence and

toughness, changed his mind. He didn't want to lie.
Didn't want to lie to *her*. He had no logical basis
for the desire, this was all instinct. He'd learned to
rely on it, for it seldom, if ever, betrayed him.

"I'm a security specialist, call it my day job. Now
and then I get a contract for the government. This
is one of those times. Can I trust you not to talk
about it?" He had ways of insuring she would not,
but thought they wouldn't be necessary.

"So long as you give me another of these." Her
glass was empty, and she held it at arm's length. As
he took it, his fingers brushed hers and something
akin to pure electricity crackled between them. She
was still smiling. "Hurry back."

He did exactly as he was told.

She curled up in the armchair now, glass in hand,
head tilted to one side, green eyes locked on him.
"So who is this man you're looking for? Is he an arms
dealer? Or the shootist?"

"Not a dealer as far as I know, but certainly a very
skilled sniper."

"Who missed? No, you said he missed on purpose.
Why?"

"I'm still working that one out." He had an idea
now, but it went contrary to his instincts.

"Who is he?"

Richard shook his head.

"You don't know or you won't answer? Or perhaps
you want to play twenty questions all night?"

"Hardly. I'm just not sure how much to tell you.
What you know of this could get you killed."

"I'm flattered that you care, but if this lad's any
good, then I'm likely to be on his list of errands
already. What I *don't* know could get me killed."

An excellent point.

"I need to know who I'm fighting," she added.

"Very well, but I'll warn you that others have tried to go after him and died. Two possibles and three for certain. That doesn't count all the people he's dropped for pay."

"A hired assassin? After you?"

"I'm a side issue. We're fairly certain he's after the Canadian Prime Minister."

"Huh." She shook her head. "Silly target, why doesn't he go after Revenue Canada instead?"

"Because the people who hired him have their hearts set on the PM, not the taxman."

"Is it the IRA? Is that why you were at McGill's?" She was too quick by half.

"Probably not *the* IRA. A splinter group of theirs—we think—since they hired an outside man for the job. I was in the neighborhood of the pub, saw you going in, and thought I'd check up on you."

"An' why were you in the neighborhood?"

"I had a lead."

"Like Arlie Webb was a lead?"

His lips thinned. She was far too quick. "Yes. He smuggled the gun into the country and probably passed it to the man whose body I later found, an arms dealer."

"All your leads dyin' on you, hardly seems fair. Should I really be worried for m'self?" She gave him a dark look.

"Worried, yes, but not where I'm concerned." *Liar.* "Which brings me back to the point where we were interrupted . . ."

Her eyes narrowed. "I said I'd not be sharin' the recovery fee with anyone."

"I don't want any part of that. In fact, it is my own fondest wish to see that you safely rescue the *Abbey Book* and deliver it back to the museum."

"What would you be gettin' out of it?"

"An altruistic gesture is its own reward," he said

in a pious tone, collecting a hearty laugh from her for his trouble. "All right, what I could get from it is a new lead to the assassin. You said the professor was the most likely buyer for the manuscript."

"If he's not gotten it already. He could have it by now."

"Let's make a worst-case assumption that he does and has already paid off the sellers, who turn the money over to Charon for services to be shortly rendered. In order to stop him I need a few undisturbed minutes with the professor."

"Durin' which you'll convince him to part with the book and—?"

"Perhaps the name and location of the thief or thieves who sold it to him. I'll go after that person in turn to find the assassin, and you can hop a flight back to Lloyd's with the book to claim the finder's fee."

"Which you say you want none of?"

He indicated the house around them with a lift of his chin. "I don't need it. The living I make is more than sufficient for my needs."

"Then you're a man to be envied, Richard Dun. Very well, I'm willin' to try."

"Then let's go."

She glanced at her watch. "Too early yet. He'll still be giving one of his famous lectures right now, and I think you'll not want to draw attention to yourself by interrupting it. In a couple of hours he *might* be finished. Sweet Mary, but how the man can prattle on forever once he gets started, and even when he's through that's not the end of it. He hangs about to sell his books, then gathers some of the more masochistic students around him for drinks afterwards. I think he feeds on their worship."

"You *have* followed him closely."

"More than enough for one lifetime. If we're lucky he could be free around eleven or so. He's seen you, and there's a chance he might be recognizing me from my sittin' in the lecture hall every night. If he spots us both together it might strike him strange."

"No, we don't need to put him on the alert. I've other means to cover that."

A call to the Judge was in order and Bourland, too, but not Demarest. Not yet. Better to put him off for a bit, or he'd haul them both in along with the professor just to be aggravating.

"Was this dead man you found the one who shot at us?" she asked.

"No. That would be the assassin. He probably picked up the gun from the dealer. . . ." The bastard had probably been in the building the whole time, watching and listening to the business with Sean. He'd taken his opportunity, firing a warning round, then killing and feasting upon Sean for good measure on the way out. Fast. At least it had been fast, and Sean unconscious for it. Not so for Webb. He'd *known* what was happening to him.

Scowling, because another particularly nasty idea occurred to him, Richard went to his desk, opening the drawer where he'd left the case file Bourland had given him. He pulled it out and flipped over pages to the crime scene photos of the murdered undercover man, McQuin. It was as bad as he remembered, but now he looked more closely at the damage to the man's body. Yes, he'd been torn up badly, but could the trauma have been inflicted by an out-of-control vampire? He studied the images, but could not be certain. Nor could he discount the possibility . . .

"The dealer?" Sharon prompted.

Richard snapped back to the present. Damn, but

he'd have to unwind soon, before he got careless. He shut the report away in the drawer again. "Yes, he then shot at us and murdered the dealer to keep him quiet. Charon doesn't like witnesses."

"That's the assassin's name?"

He glanced once at his wineglass and decided against a third one for now. Down to business. He stared hard at her. "Yes. After the Styx ferryman."

"I knew tha—" Then her face changed and she put the whisky aside, swinging her long legs around to sit upright. "Half a minute—you're not . . . you can't be thinkin' that *I'm*—"

"Well, the names *are* close, Ms. *Sharon* Geary." He set his empty glass on the desk, waiting, watching her.

She glared a long moment, then relaxed slightly. "If you really thought I was this Charon, you'd have taken me into custody, not home for a drink."

"Unless I wanted to get the shootist, too. Your partner or whatever could still be out there, waiting for a chance at me. This time to kill." And if the round didn't take his head off they'd both be in for a hell of a surprise shortly afterward.

"Then why not kill you earlier in the street? It'd have been easier."

"Absolutely, but this way you get the opportunity to find out how much I know before you take me out permanently. You could have either arranged the whole thing, or your partner just took advantage of the situation when it dropped in your laps."

Her face flushed red. "Then you're a bloody idiot! I have no partner! And do you think I'd have gone within a mile of McGill's if I'd known *you* were in the neighborhood? All I'm tryin' to do is find the blessed manuscript, collect my money, and—" She bit off the last, eyes going to slits. "You misbegotten son of a—you're just hauling my lead, aren't you?"

"The correct American phrase is, I believe, 'yanking your chain.' I wasn't sure before, but I am now." *Perhaps.* "But just to be certain, I'd like some credentials to verify. *Real* ones, if you don't mind. We can start with your passport."

"I don't need this," she grumbled.

"I'll put it this way, you can deal with me here, or I can take you to meet a singularly unpleasant RCMP officer named Demarest who would delight to throw you into a metal-lined room with a very efficient sink and toilet combination and the sort of flat mates who—"

"All right! Here—" She pulled a wallet from her purse and sorted through the items there. Soon he had enough official paper and plastic to work with and took the lot over to his computer. He checked for a green light on his tap detector. Good. Demarest was no longer eavesdropping.

Sharon looked over his shoulder as he played with the keyboard, calling up programs and entering in strings of data from her credentials. It took about twenty minutes before he hit the last command and sat back.

"What have you done?" she asked.

"Begun the most thorough background check you'll ever have in your life, Ms. Geary."

"You've got software and the accesses for that sort of thing?"

"I have connections in the most surprising places. This is only to confirm things for the likes of Demarest. I've already made up my mind."

"Indeed? And what have you decided?"

He stood. "That it's past time for you to sup. You are hungry, aren't you?"

"Yes, now that you mention it."

He knew she must be starving. He'd heard her stomach rumbling as he'd worked and was only trying to be polite about it. Leading the way to the kitchen, he opened the freezer, gesturing at the stacks of frozen items within. "You should find something edible here. I never keep fresh food around; I'm a miserable cook, so I don't bother."

"What'll you be having?" she asked, frowning at all the choices. With no recent experience in consuming solid foods, he had a variety of the more expensive brands, operating on the hopeful assumption that you got what you paid for.

He grimaced. "Sorry, I've not much of an appetite after what's happened. You go ahead, the microwave's over there and you'll find soft drinks in the refrigerator, teas and coffee in that cupboard, or help yourself to anything in the bar. Take what you like and take your time. It'll be a couple hours before the last of the information filters back. There's a spare bed and bath at the top of the stairs on the left if you want a lie-down. Make yourself comfortable and at home for the duration."

"You sound like you're leaving."

"No, nothing like that. I—I just want to clean up a bit."

Then he left her, quickly, before she could say anything else to delay him, and headed for the back of the house. He needed immediate solitude to deal with the night's stresses, to calm his beast and keep it contained. Sharon was far too distracting. And tempting. He detoured to get the rest of the bottle of his stock, partly to prevent the risk of her sampling it, and partly to finish it off. A bit of time to himself, a bit of nourishing blood mixed with soothing wine, then he could keep his beast safe and sated in its cage without danger to her.

He poured out a last glass and made two calls, one to Bourland's voicemail to say that he was making progress, and the other to the Judge.

"You alive," he brilliantly observed once Richard got through to him.

"For the sole purpose of providing you gainful employment."

"Hah."

"I want you to go to the university, to this lecture hall." He gave detailed directions on where to go and hoped the Judge was listening. "Are you sober?"

"Mon, I'm clean as a saint," the Judge assured him.

Richard had known a few saints in his time. Not all of them had been particularly spotless prior to their canonization. "Cleaner than that, or I'll know the reason why. You're to find a Professor Neal Rivers." Richard provided a physical description. "He'll be giving a talk about King Arthur there—"

"Wow, the bad mon with the cool sword, like Sean Connery?" The Judge actually sounded interested.

Richard raised an eyebrow, but suppressed all comment. "Something like that. Go there and keep an eye on him and follow him home without being seen. See who he speaks to and where they go. I'm not talking about his students, but the big lads, the nasty ones, you know the type. Bring along whatever help you need and tell them to be completely invisible so they don't get into trouble. I'll pay for it."

"You got it, mon, th' Judge is on th' case." He sounded entirely too happy about the work.

"Eugene?"

Brief silence. Then a cautious, "Yeah?"

"Keep your head focused on the business or I'll know the reason why." He rang off. Irritating man. Useful at times, but irritating.

Richard took a deep swallow from his glass and let the red heat work on him from the inside out. Good. But it could be better.

He wanted to wash the memory of finding Sean's body out of his mind.

Fat chance.

He had to try, anyway.

Though it meant the risk of interruption, he was technically on call, so he took the phone with him so as not to miss anything important coming in. He pushed through a last door into the tropic mugginess of his own private rest and recovery zone. Shielded from the sun as well as triple-insulated against the worst of Canadian winters, he could revel year-round in heated comfort. To the left was the large redwood-lined box of the dry sauna, to the right was the always-ready hot tub. It was huge, large enough for half a dozen or more, and fitted with every conceivable convenience for those with a hedonistic turn of mind. The hot, clear water beckoned to him, as compelling as a lover.

Richard had long ago developed a near-ceremony for relaxation once he'd installed the thing. It was simple enough: the lighting of a number of fat candles already in place and a few sticks of incense. Sandalwood and patchouli tonight. The aromatic smoke began to rise in threads and drift over the room. He shut off the now harsh electric lights, stripped, throwing every stitch of his tainted clothes in a corner, and slipped into the steaming water with a grateful sigh.

He finished his glass, put it in one of the built-in holders, and hit the switch for the pump. The water bubbled and jetted around his body. Since it was not the free-running stuff of nature, he had no difficulty enduring it. Quite the contrary. He rested his head on the padded niche designed just for that purpose and shut his eyes. Sweet Goddess, but he needed this. He stopped fighting and let the buoyancy take his body, arms and legs spreading just under the roiling surface. The hum of the pump, the rush of the water, the heat, all had their way with him, lulling him into a kind of half-doze. He was safe from the immediate cares of the world, though not unaware of their threat.

Cats must feel like this, seeming to nap, but still alert to all that's around them. He liked cats, though they were often less than pleased with him. Perhaps they sensed the part of him descended from the Hounds of Annwyn. He had the same trouble with some dogs.

The door opened and shut. He felt the change in the air. He made no move, not even to crack an eyelid. He knew it was Sharon. Damn. He thought his abrupt and graceless departure would have given her a clue that he wanted to be alone.

Yes, alone. Then. What about now?

Good question. Why had she come, anyway? Curiosity about the house? A little harmless exploring, or something more sinister? His instincts had said to trust her. They were rarely off. It would be a sore disappointment if she attempted to take advantage of his seeming vulnerability. He hadn't searched her purse to relieve her of that Glock. If she betrayed him, tried to shoot him . . . he'd deal with it then and not before.

He dismissed the vile thought.

She was being damned quiet, though. He could hear little over the noise of the pump and the bubbling water. He continued to float, letting the water gently buffet him this way and that, continued, until something disrupted the rhythm created by the flow. He opened his eyes in time to glimpse Sharon, quite wonderfully naked, quickly easing into the tub with him.

Well, well.

She'd pinned her glorious hair up, but a few russett tendrils had escaped and now floated on the water. She lay chin deep in it, eyes closed and arms behind her head, her back arched enough so her hard nipples were just breaking the surface.

Goddess, but she is beautiful.

The water lapped against her, both hiding and magnifying her nakedness. He drank her in with his gaze, the hardness again growing in his groin.

"I hope you don't mind the intrusion," she said.

He looked up from her body to see her eyes, open now, regarding him softly.

She smiled. "Of course, you don't have to answer. I can see for myself."

There didn't seem to be any reason to remark on that. Richard went back to admiring the view. Sharon returned the favor, studying him as closely as the Botticelli.

"What's that?" She indicated his shoulder.

Many women had asked about that scar over the centuries. Like the one about his ring finger, the reminder of an ancient sword thrust that had nearly cost him an arm was still with him along with others he'd collected before Sabra had changed him. "Knife fight, years ago."

"Must have been some fight. May I?" She drifted closer. She didn't touch the long healed wound, only looked before lifting her gaze to meet his. The candlelight cast a golden sheen upon her skin and glinted off her hair like fire. He shifted, reclining no longer, to face her.

"Indeed you may," he whispered.

"Ah," she said. Then her mouth was suddenly on his, her lips wet, her tongue probing, gently at first, but then ever more fiercely. Her arms slipped around him, her body pressing close, fighting the water. Her hand was on him, touching, stroking his hardness. She pulled away and looked him up and down. "Oh, yes . . . oh, yes."

My thoughts exactly.

Water sloshed over onto the floor as she moved up his body and clamped her mouth once more onto his. Locked together, they slid ever so slowly beneath the surface.

It seemed an eternity before she wanted air and lifted away. Their heads broke free at the same time, each gasping, water cascading from their faces and into their open mouths. She brushed at her wet hair, which was coming down, which he found utterly tantalizing. Her breasts shone gilded in the candlelight, and oh, so gently, he drew her close and took a firm, pink nipple into his mouth, sucking, teasing, delicately rolling its hardness with his tongue, nipping, biting. Sharon held his head against her, her breath stilled. Despite the noise of the water, he could sense the silence within her, the concentration.

Then she pulled away again, smiling, to look him in the eye. "Ah, Richard, what a comfortable man you are."

He found himself laughing and wondered at it, but not for long, for she smothered it with another in a seemingly endless procession of kisses, each one better, more passionate, more loving than the last. Their tongues intertwined helplessly, deliciously, in total surrender. She licked the water from his face, from his ears, from the small hairs at the back of his neck. And all the time her hands were on him, exploring, holding, moving, as his were on her, caressing her breasts and her belly, sliding down to the slickness between her legs.

And when she seemed more than ready he lifted

her effortlessly so as to enter her, but she held back, grinning at him, full of mischief.

"Say please."

He looked deep in her eyes. "Please." Never had he said it like this before. The need and the feeling had never been so strong, so raw upon his soul.

Perhaps she saw it. Suddenly she was grinning no more. Her body slid down onto him, her legs wrapping tight. He felt his hardness pushing against her, sticking on the water on her outer lips until he encountered her own sweet moisture and slipped easily inside.

She moaned at this, holding still, then leaning forward to rest her head on his shoulder. His hands soothed over the length of her back, down to the taut muscles of her cheeks. He pressed on them, pushing her more firmly onto him. She lifted her head and sat upright. They started to drift in the water; he grabbed the sides of the sauna to hold them in place.

"Look at me, Richard," she said, and cupping her breasts in her hands, she began to move on him.

He did as he was bid, more than willingly, and it seemed to him that all his world was contained in those bright green eyes reflecting the flickering light. Not able to touch her for the moment, she did it for him. Her tongue licked around her lips, and a groan escaped her as she pinched her nipples, rubbed them, squeezed them harder than he would have ever dared.

He felt his heart beating faster and faster as she rode him. Her body heaved and bucked, and he felt harder than he'd ever been . . . then another sensation. His corner teeth began to bud, and a low growl escaped him.

No! Not this, not now!

Fighting to keep control, he stopped his own echoing movements and tried to pull out of her.

"What the hell . . . ?" she began, her rhythm disrupted.

"I can't, I mustn't."

"It's all right, I'm safe, and my cycle is—"

"No, you don't understand."

"I understand a lot more than you think."

And she grabbed him roughly by the ears, kissing him, thrusting her tongue into his mouth, all the while her hips moving, pumping up and down on him. He tried to think of something else to keep the beast fettered, to keep it from killing. He turned his head away, shutting his eyes so she wouldn't see the change in them, wouldn't see the flush of red flames within. She-Who-Walks had assured him he'd be safe with her, but with other women? He couldn't gamble Sharon's life on that.

But his control was breaking down, crumbling, even as his body neared its climax. Try as he might, he couldn't fight both it and the beast at the same time.

Sharon held tight to him, pressing his head against her breasts, pushing her hips, gasping from her mounting passion. Goddess, but she was so beautiful.

He clamped his teeth together and concentrated on that beauty, forcing his thoughts away from scarlet visions of death and killing. He dwelt on the feel of being inside her, on her youth and strength, on the anticipation of his approaching release, not the infliction of pain, the glutting of appetite.

Head thrown back, her body shaking into a scream, Sharon burst onto him and unbidden, unstoppable, his seed pumped forth, his own guttural cry adding to hers. He could feel the dark creature claw at his soul, snarling, in thwarted rage or in carnal triumph, he could not tell, nor did he care as the

ecstasy seized him, tore through him, utterly consumed him. For a few precious moments in the
dance of the universe he was nothing and everything,
joined to the woman, yet separate, giver and taker,
feeder and fed, creator and creation. A fierce cry of
joy, of bright defiance, burst straight from that
wounded soul, searing his inner darkness like a sun.
It freed him from all fear, succored and sustained
him, healed him.

Sharon's last moans slowly dwindled, and she
slumped forward, her head again on his shoulder,
spent. Panting, he put one protective arm around her,
the other still holding fast to a grab bar to steady
them against the churning water.

And then came the *petite morte*, the little death
as, inevitably, the light inside paled and faded to
nothing. The darkness swelled once more.

He waited. Waited for some sign that things were
settling within him. His muscles ached from it as he
held still, held his breath till it hurt.

Then he noticed his corner teeth start to recede.

Immediate and intense relief overwhelmed him. She
was safe. The beast had spared her. Spared them
both. *Goddess and the blood wine be praised.*

"Thank you," he murmured, resting his head far
back on the padded niche.

"You're entirely welcome, I'm sure," Sharon sleepily
responded, unknowingly answering for the Goddess.
But then was She not in all women as God was in
all men?

Richard smiled, unseen by Sharon at least, and
closed his eyes.

Chapter Seven

"I've heard of afterglow, but this is elephant," Sharon said, sitting up from him some time later. Her movement nudged him to alertness. "I want to be lying with you, but I'm noticin' the heat too much now." She drifted away, used one of the built-in seats as a step, and hoisted herself up to sit on the edge of the spa. Water streamed from her fever-red skin and tangled hair.

"Why?" he asked, looking at her, marveling at her.

"Why what?"

"This." He gestured to indicate themselves.

"Because I wanted to."

"No more than that?"

"It's more than enough where I'm concerned. If you're worried, I don't pass my favors to just anyone. I had a feelin' about you. A right one, I'm happy to say."

A *feeling*. He rolled that one around in his mind. Could it mean she had a touch of the Sight as well? Possibly. Many people possessed it unawares, especially women.

"Then there's the other thing," she added. "There's nothing like nearly getting killed for driving a person into bed . . . or whatever." She nodded at the spa. "I'm told that's how my mum was conceived, with Gram and Gramp going for all they were worth in their basement shelter during the Blitz when he wrangled some leave time."

Richard recalled a similar incident in his own past . . . well . . . *lots* of similar incidents, actually. She had that facet of human behavior down right enough.

"They moved back to Ireland not long after. Probably wantin' a quieter place to shag. An' you'll be wantin' to get out of that cauldron yourself before you turn into a giant pink prune."

"But I like it here," he protested mildly. Extremes of heat never bothered him much, no more than extremes of cold.

"Ah, but I'm not in there with you now."

Excellent point. He heaved up and she put a hand out to take his, which had indeed become rather prunelike. Despite this and the shed of water from him, she drew close, body-to-body, and kissed him, making it last. It was more than enough to inspire him to a second celebration, but . . .

Not a good idea. He'd escaped—*they'd* escaped—the threat of the beast once; he was reluctant to tempt it again so soon. Perhaps later, after he'd fed deeply on undiluted blood, they could—that is, if she *wanted* to—

"Tell me what that was all about earlier," she said. "All that 'I can't' stuff? It was a bit of a surprise y'know."

Oh, yeah, I'd love to do that, to tell you the truth, that I was this far from tearing out your throat and drinking you down, then I could watch you run for your life from this lunatic.

"It's . . . difficult for me," he lied, and was about to continue when her gentle fingers on his lips stopped him.

"I know, I know, my darling lover."

"You do?" His eyebrows shot upward. *The Sight again?*

"I've seen it before. You forget I'm from Ireland."

He tried to work that one out and what it had to do with anything when Sharon kissed him on the cheek, whispering close in his ear.

"I can tell a Catholic boy when I see one."

His jaw dropped. *A Catholic!* Well, yes, she was right again for so had he been raised, though by now he was a severely lapsed one.

"It'll be easier next time, I promise."

His heart gave an unexpectedly strong leap. "Next time? There's to be a next time?"

She smiled in the dim light. "Oh, yes. If you want it."

"Oh, absolutely." A next time sounded good. It sounded very good, making him feel more complete than he had in many a day. Inner resolves of caution to the contrary, he began nuzzling her neck. He was in control now, so the prospect of biting into it and sucking at the nectar within . . . then after he'd fed, he'd waken her fully and they could . . .

But the phone trilled. Insistently.

"Damn."

Sharon stifled a laugh. "Go ahead."

"I wish." He punched the "on" button. "Richard Dun."

"I'm so glad you're home, Mr. Dun." Demarest. The bloody fool. With fairly rotten timing. At least he hadn't called earlier.

"Yes, what do you want?"

"I'm sure you already know what that is."

"No games, Chief Inspector. We're both busy men."

"And you've been busier than most this evening."

Richard glanced around the room, suspicious. Ye gods, had the little weasel put in a surveillance camera?

"That incident at the pub?" Demarest reminded him.

"What pub?"

"Don't lie, Mr. Dun. We got a description from the bartender and she identified you from your file photo. You and that redhead made quite a show just before all hell broke loose."

"Yes, the sniper—our sniper, Charon—sending me a warning I should think. It's a miracle no one was seriously injured—"

"Charon. Charon takes a pot shot at you and you neglected to report in about it."

"I got involved with other threads of the investigation that couldn't wait. Until my chance came to break away I thought your people would be competent enough to deal with things."

Demarest made a familiar choking sound.

How—if he was so easily baited—in seven hells had the man risen this high in the ranks? He couldn't have his head up *that* many asses, no one could. *Or maybe it's just dealing with me that sets him off.* Richard decided against giving him another friendly reminder about the dangers of high blood pressure. "So did they find the body across the street?" It seemed best to get that detail on the table first, before Demarest could work 'round to it.

"You know damned well they did. Two men torn to shreds and you in the same neighborhoods at the same time."

"Don't get your hopes up, Chief Inspector. It's only because I've been on Charon's trail. He left a very messy spoor. Be glad he didn't set the place on fire like the last time."

"*Charon* did that? Killed both of them?" Demarest's voice was high and strained.

"I believe so." Might as well shift the blame for Webb onto another, more deserving fellow. Hardly honorable, but certainly practical. "He may have also

killed the undercover man, McQuin. He wasn't as
badly damaged as the others, but perhaps Charon
hadn't quite gotten the hang of things yet. You might
have your medical examiner check for any similarities."
The vision of Sean's ravaged body floated over his
mind's eye, blending with that of Arlie Webb's. Richard
shivered, tried to suppress the image. Unsuccessfully.
"What's your forensics team found on the new one?"

"They're still picking up the pieces. Literally. The
bastard who did this is certifiable."

"Agreed. He's also more than extraordinarily dangerous. . . ." Damn, again. Another vision rose up to
replace the first, but it was no less horrific. If he hadn't
been so distracted, he'd have thought of it before. He
shouldn't have sent the Judge to keep an eye on the
professor; he should have gone himself. Now both men
could be dead.

"Are you listening, Dun?" Demarest. Annoyed,
more so than usual.

"What?"

"I want a full report on—"

"Right, first thing in the morning. I'll fax it."

"Morning, hell. You'll come right down to the—"

Richard cut the connection, found his watch, and
put it back on. A quarter to eleven. He'd have to
hurry, but was heartsinkingly sure he was already too
late.

Sharon was nearly dancing with curiosity, having
heard but half of the conversation. "Well? What's
going on? Who was that?"

"The singularly unpleasant RCMP man I mentioned
to you. I have to get to your precious professor."
He strode into the hall.

"Why?" she demanded, following.

"He's a loose end, and we already know that Charon
hates those."

"Mother of mercy." She ducked back toward the spa, presumably to grab up her clothes. Richard took the stairs to his room three at a time and hastily threw on whatever was handy. He was still damp as he dressed, an uncomfortable reminder of the aftermath of Webb's death.

Never mind that, just keep moving.

Sharon was ready when he came down again. She scrubbed at her wet hair with a towel.

"You'll stay here," he stated.

"The hell I will. If the professor is a loose end, then so are we both. 'Tis no safer here than anyplace else, an' I'd rather be a moving target, thank you very much."

He bit back any argument. In light of their situation, hers was a very sensible viewpoint, one he wholly shared himself. Instead, he went to his work area and checked the fax machine. Several responses to his queries on her had come in while they'd been otherwise involved. A glance of each was enough to confirm that the credentials she'd given this time were authentic.

"What's the verdict?" She dropped the towel over a doorknob.

"That you're on the side of the angels."

"I'm sure they'll be very relieved to hear it." She picked up and shouldered her purse, which swung rather heavily for its size, banging against her hip.

"How many rounds in your shooter?" he asked casually.

"The clip's full—" She glared at him and pulled the purse closer. "I've no mind for loaning it out, either."

"Keep it, just don't let the cops see the thing."

"I thought you were in a hurry to leave."

"Right." He headed for the garage.

✧   ✧   ✧

The Rover had a mobile phone; Richard made use of it as he negotiated the streets on the way to the university. The operator connected him to what he hoped was the right rat hole in the academic maze.

"Medieval Studies." The answering voice was blank and uninterested to the point where even its owner's gender was in question.

"I'm trying to locate Professor Neal Rivers, the one giving the lectures on King Arthur."

"Sorry, can't help you." Its tone was an obvious prelude to hanging up.

"Wait, this is an emergency! He is there, isn't he?"

"Well, he *was* here." The crack of chewing gum garbled the line. "But he seems to have gone."

"Gone?"

"Didn't turn up for his lecture tonight and no one knows where he is. If you ask me—"

Richard had not asked and so he rang off. The dreadful feeling of knowing exactly what had happened to the hapless collector rose up like a storm. And what about the Judge? Richard punched numbers into the keypad, waiting with growing anger and fear as the phone rang and rang.

I should have gone myself!

Then it stopped ringing and the Judge's voice slurred at him over the line.

"Yeah, mon. Ya know what th' fucking time is? What ya want?"

"It's Dun. Why the hell didn't you call and tell me?"

The voice faded and came back, definitely less slurred, with an edge of panic. "Shit, mon, I watched like ya told me. I di'n' see nothin'." Silence a moment, then the sound of sniffing. "That place was empty, nobody talkin' King Arthur there, but I went in and waited till they threw me out—"

"Then you should have called to tell me. What the hell were you thinking? Forget it, you weren't."

"Chill, mon, don't you worry, I gonna put my best mon on it. I gonna kick th' ass for you . . ."

Richard listened, impatience growing as the litany of excuses came over the air with ever more confidence as the coke kicked in. Then he interrupted, his tone all Arctic ice. "I told you, *Eugene*, I don't *like* it when people fuck with me. It makes me very irritated, and when I get irritated I can sometimes be quite irrational."

Silence at the other end.

"Eugene. Leave."

The line went dead before Richard could cut it first. Good. The Judge had the sense to get out of the way for the time being, sparing him not only from Richard's wrath, but from being noticed by Charon.

"Who's Eugene?" asked Sharon. She was in the process of combing out her damp locks and pinning them up again.

"An associate—ex-associate—of mine. He screwed up."

"Badly?"

"More than badly. He was supposed to be watching Rivers tonight, couldn't find him, and then managed not to inform me of that little detail. Rivers is missing—at least from the university."

Sharon was all attention now. "What about the manuscript?"

"Probably missing, too—if he had it."

"Perhaps he took delivery and ran out while he could."

"We'll see. Have you his home address?"

"I should hope I do." She gave him directions, and he altered course accordingly. They were only minutes away, but Richard's instinct told him they were likely to be far too late to help.

A scarcity of spaces forced them to park a little distance off. They could have gone to the building's visitor lot, but Richard preferred a more discreet profile until he knew what lay ahead. Still, it seemed a much longer walk than it should, mostly because he kept scanning the nearby rooftops for the least sign of a gun barrel. A futile, irrational gesture. If Charon was out there watching, he'd not let himself be seen.

Neal Rivers resided in a large, modern condominium block. A very expensive one for the neighborhood, it was all glass and steel, and "every apartment with its own balcony and sun room," or so declared a self-consciously tasteful promotional sign on display in the landscaped grounds. They hurried past and entered a darkened foyer with a bank of elevators. A uniformed security man looked up at them from behind a reception desk festooned with surveillance monitors. *Damned things*, Richard thought sourly. Well, if it came to it, he knew how to bugger the whole system so as to leave no record of their presence, though at the moment he couldn't imagine the necessity. If something untoward had happened to Rivers, then Demarest would have to be informed.

"May I help you?" asked the young guard. A small rectangle on his uniform's pocket declared his surname to be Adams.

Sharon smiled dazzlingly and moved in. "We're here to see Professor Neal Rivers, apartment 1004. He's not expecting us—we want to surprise him."

"I'm sorry, but our policy is to always call ahead."

"Oh, but you can't. This is Neal's brother, and he's not seen him for twelve years. We *have* to surprise him. He'll be so excited."

Adams, however, was not. He looked at Richard, and Richard smiled winningly. Deadpan, Adams looked back at Sharon. "I'm very sorry, but there are no exceptions. I'll have to call ahead and get permission for a guest entrance. It's a security thing."

There was no arguing with that, at least as far as Adams was apparently concerned. He turned his attention to the monitors, clearly dismissing Sharon and Richard until they decided to come around to his point of view. They backed off out of earshot.

"What now?" she asked.

"Wait outside a moment."

"Outside?"

"I'm going to reason with him. It's a guy thing."

She smiled. "Well, try not to make too much of a mess." She waved once at the guard and strolled away.

Once he was sure she was well out of sight and hearing range, Richard went back to the desk, wearing what he hoped was a polite but earnest expression. Adams's face was wariness mixed with thinning patience as he looked up and . . .

An instant was all it took.

Richard popped his head out the main door and called Sharon back in.

Young Mr. Adams smiled glassily at them as they passed, looking a bit too happy with the world, the only sign of Richard's unnatural influence on his mind. "Please go on up. I'm sure there will be no problem bending the rules just this once," he said cheerfully.

"Very impressive," Sharon muttered. "How much did it cost?"

"Nothing. I reasoned with him."

Her eyebrows bounced. "Ah, sweet reason."

The elevator arrived and they stepped into its

mirrored confines. Richard, unlike his cousins of legend and film, was fully reflected in the shining surfaces surrounding them. Sharon took the opportunity to better secure her hair into a knot on top of her head.

"You're lovely with your hair up," he remarked, putting his hands behind him for the duration of the ride.

She paused, shooting him an intense look. "Thank you."

They were still looking at each another when the door hummed open on the tenth floor.

"Back to business," she said.

"More's the pity. I'll go first, if you don't mind."

"Not at all."

Richard in the lead, they crept silently into a plushly carpeted hall toward 1004 at the far end. He paused and listened a long time, his senses straining, but all he heard were their own heartbeats. When he shook his head, Sharon reached gently into her purse, removing a credit card and her Glock. With the gun ready in one hand, she inserted the card quietly between the door and the jamb, trying to slip the latch. From the strained expression on her face it wasn't working.

"Deadbolt," she whispered. "I'll have to pick it open."

But Richard put a hand out, motioning for her to stand back, lifting a finger to his lips. As soon as she was well clear, he stepped forward and in one smooth movement kicked the door in. Wood splintered and cracked, the noise deafening in the morguelike silence of the hallway. He went into the apartment. Sharon hastily followed, pushing the ruined door shut behind them.

"That was subtle!" she sputtered, all outrage.

Richard ignored the comment as he surveyed the entry and living room. "He's not here."

"How can you tell without the lights?"

He flicked the switch, bathing the room in artificial brightness from an overhead. It was empty of all furnishings except for the drawn draperies and a phone abandoned in the middle of the floor. "Sure this is the right address?"

"On my life," she said. "I don't undertand this. I've been following him all week—when could he have moved out?"

"Perhaps he never really moved in." Then Richard caught his first solid whiff of it. The hair stood up along the nape of his neck and on his arms. Once again, and to his very great alarm, his corner teeth began to bud.

"Richard?"

He shook his head, fighting for control. *It's getting worse.*

"What's the matter?"

The least stimulus and I begin to go.

Control. A few steadying breaths. Yes, there was the smell of blood everywhere, but it need not effect him. It *could* not effect him.

"You're makin' me worried. What is it?"

"I—I think something's very wrong here," he said thickly. He swallowed hard.

She renewed her grip on her gun, staring around. "I'm listenin'."

But this was no time for words. He brushed past her, trying to locate the source of the blood. The first passage he tried led to an empty kitchen. On impulse, he opened the refrigerator. It was clean of all food except for a greasy bag bearing the logo of the Mexican fast food restaurant Rivers favored. Inside it were several paper-wrapped bundles.

Leftovers from a last meal? He tapped the bundles. Petrified, or nearly so. He slammed the fridge door shut and moved along.

The next room showed the remnants of occupancy. No furnishings except for a thick futon, sheets all tangled, that lay on the floor in one corner, along with drifts of discarded clothing. Pants, underwear, shirts . . . Richard picked up one of the latter. It was new, had never been washed, but was wrinkled enough to indicate it'd been worn at least once before being tossed aside. Piled in another corner were crumpled package wrappings, and nearby were four identical white shirts still crisply folded and pinned around their thin cardboard backing. The closet was empty except for some wire hangers.

"Did he do a lot of shopping for clothes?" Richard asked, mystified at the find.

She shrugged. "I don't know, but then I didn't catch up with him right away. He must have bought out a whole store. What a mess. Maybe this posh place doesn't have a laundry."

Or he couldn't be bothered with such mundanities. Richard looked past the heaps of clothes and noted the drapes were drawn shut here as well. The scent of blood was stronger, but . . .

"Naught left but the lav," Sharon whispered; she'd obviously picked up on his unease.

"I'll look. If it's what I think, you won't want to see."

He pushed the last door slowly open with one knuckle, futilely trying to brace himself for the worst. It was dark like the other rooms, to the point where even he needed help. He felt for the switch and flicked it on.

Yes, this was the source. The air was heavy and very damp, as though someone had taken a long

shower with the exhaust fan off. Broad red streaks and
drips smeared the floor and shower curtain of the
bathtub, its walls, and the sink. Soaked towels were
strewn about the floor, stained red. Lying next to the
tub were yet more cast off clothes, sodden from their
bright gore.

But no body.

What the hell . . . ?

Then he saw another bathroom in his memory—
just as blood-streaked—only in that one the discarded
clothes were his own.

Richard hissed and abruptly backed from the room
as though it burned him. Sharon stepped forward,
all concern, but he waved her off with an impatient
gesture.

Damnation!

She moved past him for a look and froze a
moment to take it all in. "What the hell is this about?
Where is he? If he's not . . ."

"Oh, but he is."

"What d'ye—?"

"*He's* Charon. The thrice-damned bastard's *Charon!*"

"My God." The dawn burst upon her.

"Devil more like," he rumbled. "He killed the gun
dealer, then came here to clean up." Then Richard
had to work very hard to keep from smashing a wall
in as the anger welled and flooded inside.

Anger . . . no, this was *far* beyond that, beyond
anything he'd felt in a very long time. Rage, humiliation, and self-scorn seethed freely in him, craving
expression. He wanted more than to smash a wall, he
wanted to flatten the whole fucking building.

Sharon got one glance of his face and put space
between them, alarmed.

Oddly enough, that helped steady him until the
worst of his reaction passed. He had no desire to

distress her in any way, but it still took him no little time to calm down enough to be able to speak, and then his voice didn't sound quite right from the internal strain of holding things in. "I should have seen this when I first met him," he finally said.

"Indeed?" she asked, all caution.

"I was right there in his office. I should have—" *What?* Known him for what he was? Instinctively recognized one of his own kind? That was one trick none of them could do except for Sabra, and she only because of the Sight. "The name alone should have tipped me off. Charon—ferryman—Rivers. He was laughing at me the whole time."

"Better than killin' you, but why should he hold back from that?"

"I think he likes to play games, to see how much he can get away with before anyone tumbles to the truth." Yes, all the food leavings in the university office, that alone had been enough camouflage to suit. Add to it the false background Sharon had discovered on him—what a pretty penny that must have cost to set up. He must have laughed himself sick after Richard's trusting departure, and *that's* what stung so.

Pride and overconfidence had always been his weak points, the only ones Sabra had ever really chided him on. Well, they'd once more worked against him, even more so now than on that last day in the old Roman arena when he'd faced that damned boy. Back then he'd not had centuries of experience to draw upon, now he had no such excuse.

"He knows we're on to him since he shot at us," she said. "More game playin'?"

And what was that shot if not Charon throwing down the glove? "He knew I'd go back to see his dealer afterwards. He knew I'd find the body, that you and

I would talk, and I'd make the connection to Rivers, that I'd come here to find this. The son of a bitch is still laughing." More anger washed over him, but he had a better hold on things; this was a cooler, more calculating kind, allowing him to think more clearly. And to fear. He looked at her. "I'm wondering how much he knows about you."

"I've been careful enough to stay low."

"He would keep links open to the people that stole the book you're after, and *they* know you from your poking about. He's been wary of hunters coming after him in the past, and I doubt if things have changed. Sooner or later he'll come for you."

She snorted and didn't look as worried as she should have been. The threat either wasn't real enough to her yet, or she was refusing to see it.

"Sharon, he could drop you the next time you walk outside. Or worse." Like tear her to bits, as he'd done with Sean.

No.

"Or I could get hit by a drunk driver," she said. "What would you have me do, skulk in a basement until he keels over from old age? And what about yourself? You're marked as well."

"I've had more experience at this than you."

"Fine, then I'll rely on it to keep us both safe until we can catch him up."

"Sharon—"

"Don't be wastin' time with argument, man. I'll tell you now you won't be winnin' with me on this. Our best hope to live is to find the misbegotten son of a bachelor before he can do for us."

He started to speak, but turned it into a sigh and a shake of his head. "All right."

"Good. We'll start again. We know he's disappeared to God knows where, manuscript, monster gun, and all. We'll have to backtrack a bit. Some of that gun dealer's mates might know something we can use. If we find this splinter group you mentioned we can find where he's—"

No, that wasn't it. Charon was a vampire, and starting to lose control of his beast, starting to die, and apparently knew the Grail might help him even as Sabra knew. That's why he wanted Sabra's book, to research it for clues to the Grail's location. If he had it, he'd be on the first plane to Heathrow.

Because that's what I'd do.

There was still a chance to salvage things. He shook his head, waving to interrupt her flow of ideas. "I've another course to take."

"What might that be?"

Richard went to the front room and tried the phone. It was still hooked up. He called his 24-hour travel service. The news was not good. The next flight for the U.K. was at dawn the next day. He looked into the possibility of chartering a private flight, but none were to be had any sooner. They could not ascertain if other transatlantic flights had been chartered. That was something Bourland or Demarest's people could check out, but asking for their help at this point would require more explanations than Richard was willing to provide. Best to keep this quiet for as long as could be got away with.

"Right," he said to the travel agent. "See what you can book for me on the next flight, a first class if you can manage, but just get me aboard."

Sharon's eyes blazed. "And me as well!"

"What?"

"You know something I don't, or you'd not be haring off like this. I'm comin' too, if I have to strap mesel' to the wing."

His inner debate took all of two seconds to resolve.

Yes, she might be safer here, and yes, he could hypnotize her into forgetting the whole business and send her on her way, but no, he couldn't take the chance. If he was wrong, and Charon was still in Toronto, she'd be his next practice target, only then he'd not deign to miss. Either choice and she could die. *Would* die. Charon would see to that no matter what. At least if she came along Richard could better look out for her.

"Make that two tickets, whatever you've got, but it must be on that first flight." He gave a credit card number and rang off.

"Now what's this about?" she demanded. "Why do you suddenly think he's going to England?"

"Specifically, to Glastonbury."

"Glaston—why the hell would he go there?"

"He's an Arthurian scholar and that place is solidly connected with the legends."

"Oh, now, you can't be serious."

"Rivers is, or rather Charon. I think he's taken the Abbey Book as his payment for the hit he's to do. He needs it."

"Needs it? Whatever for?"

How much to tell her? "That book is absolutely unique with scholars debating on the meaning of some of its passages, right? Suppose it has information Charon needs to find something? Something very precious and important to him."

"What? Merlin's hat?"

He looked at her hard. "The Grail."

That stopped her cold. "The Grail. *The* Holy Grail?" She gave a short derisive laugh, shaking her head. "Surely you don't believe in that rubbish, do you? You'll be tellin' me about leprechaun hunts next."

"What *I* believe in is beside the point. *He* does believe in it and that's what matters."

"It's too daft for words. He's got his book—he's only gone to ground until the time's right for him to go to work. 'Tis as simple as that."

"You've heard his lectures, heard how he talks on."

"Well, yes—"

"I heard some of it, too, that night in his office. He's truly obsessed with the subject."

"Enough to run out on the IRA before doin' his job for them?"

"Yes." *If he's as desperate as I am to find it. And he is.*

"Then he's right 'round the twist. The boys are not the forgivin' type."

"I doubt that they matter much to—" He stopped, listening. The elevator. He signed her to silence, hoping it only meant another tenent on the floor was on the way home. But just in case, he swept her along with him toward the bath. She still held the Glock and now grasped it expertly in both hands, left cupping the right, elbows slightly bent to absorb the recoil. It would be nearly useless against Charon, though, and likely only send him into a killing frenzy. On the other hand if she pumped enough bullets into his heart it would slow him quite a lot and give Richard a few moment's edge over him. There was nothing left in the apartment that could be employed as a stake, but Richard was unnaturally strong. If he had to he could twist Charon's head right off his neck. Messy, but effective, and he'd worry about explaining things later.

Richard shut the bathroom light out and put one eye around the corner. He was just able to hear footsteps whispering over the carpet in the outer hall.

At least two people. They paused at the broken-in front door. A few heartbeats later and the door slowly swung inward, but no one came through.

Then: "Come out, come out, wherever you are."

Demarest? Richard slumped, relief mixed with irritation, and Sharon stared at him quizzically.

"Who is it?" she whispered.

"It's all right, I know him. You'd better put that away. He's supposed to be one of the good guys, but he'll object to that little item." He indicated the gun, and Sharon obligingly tucked it back in her bag.

They stepped out of the bathroom to be confronted by a large armed man—his gun drawn and squarely aimed at them—standing next to Demarest.

Richard paused, uncertain. "How the hell did you—?"

Demarest bore an expression that was miles beyond mere smugness. "After the pub shooting I sent Doyle here to watch your house and he followed you." The officer next to him nodded politely. Obviously he was somewhat more careful at tailing than the previous two efforts.

"Who is he?" Sharon asked Richard in a stage whisper.

Demarest smiled and gave a slight mocking nod of the head. "Forgive me, mademoiselle, I am Chief Inspector Etienne Demarest of the Royal Canadian Mounted Police."

"Where's your red jacket, big hat, and horse?" she inquired, obviously underwhelmed by his manner.

Before Demarest could frame an appropriate reply, Richard stepped in. "What's this about, Chief Inspector?"

"It's about the great specialist falling flat on his face, Mr. Dun, though I can hardly blame you for allowing *her* to divert your attention from the job. Your description hardly does her justice." He looked her up and down, all but licking his lips.

"Descrip— What the hell is this?" Sharon asked, turning to Richard.

"There's been an all-points out on you since the business in Niagara," he explained. "You can call off the dogs, Demarest, I've checked her credentials. She's clean and has been helping me on the case."

"No doubt she's been very helpful, more than helpful. Please put your purse down, Mademoiselle Geary, and step well away from Mr. Dun with your hands on your head." Under the threat of the gun Sharon did exactly as she was told, even though her searing look would have melted steel.

Richard glared at the man. "What are you—"

Demarest smiled. "I'm placing you both under arrest, so let's be civilized about this and the two of you come quietly."

"You've nothing to charge me with, you great fool, you're just trying to harass me."

"Oh, but I've a very solid charge against you. What about the willing collusion of yourself with this terrorist in the assassination threat to our prime minister?"

Richard gave him a blank look. "What?"

"Dun, you are so short-sighted you cannot see what's directly before you. This woman. *She* is the threat to the PM, the one we've all been searching for, and you, unless you can prove otherwise, have been helping her. *This* is Charon. Didn't you notice the similarity of names?"

"Sweet Mary," said Sharon, shaking her head. "I'd not have believed it, but he's as stupid as he looks!"

Demarest bristled. "I'm glad that you find a degree of amusement in this situation. I hope that you will continue to do so after your trial. You'll need it."

Richard started to speak, but Demarest cut him off. "I suggest you save any objections for later, Mr. Dun, and you'd better acquire some legal representation very soon. I believe you know the part about anything you say being taken down and used in evidence against you. You're both up to your necks in this so don't make things harder than they are. Doyle, take her out to the car; be sure to caution her." Demarest drew out his own gun to cover Richard.

Officer Doyle produced some handcuffs. With a minimum of fuss, he pulled Sharon's hands behind her and locked the restraints into place. "This way, miss, if you please," he said. He retrieved her purse, tucking it under one arm, and guided her toward the door.

Sharon looked wildly back at Richard, who shrugged. "Do what he says, I'll sort it out for us in just a few minutes."

"I think not," said Demarest. "Place your hands against that wall, lean on them, and spread your feet."

Richard stalled long enough until Sharon and Doyle were out of the room and he heard the elevator opening. "All right, have it your way. But there's just one thing you need to know . . ."

"Really?" Demarest was very sure of himself, and that was a big help. It meant his guard was down.

Richard went utterly still and focused his complete attention upon the man. For the briefest moment he felt no connection, then . . . yes, there it was. Demarest's chronically bad-tempered expression went slack. His gun arm sagged. Richard stepped forward to catch the weapon before it struck the floor.

Eye-to-eye with him now. "Demarest, you are a fool. A monumental fool."

"I am a monumental fool," he echoed in a faint monotone.

Well, *that* was satisfying. "Sharon Geary is not the one you need. You will cancel the all-points out for her. The real Charon is Professor Neal Rivers. Do you understand?"

"Professor Neal Rivers."

"In fact, you never saw either of us. You were following up an anonymous tip and came here. When you arrived, Rivers surprised you and locked you in a closet. This one will do." He took Demarest to a coat closet by the front entry.

"Rivers surprised me . . ."

"Yes, yes, now get inside and have yourself a nice long nap. You're very tired and need the rest."

Demarest did exactly as he was told, slumping down on the floor and breathing deeply, gone to the world. Richard shut the door, wishing he had a chair to prop under the knob, though it hardly mattered. Demarest wouldn't wake up until tomorrow. To prevent any disturbances, Richard thoughtfully relieved the man of his radio and cell phone, putting them in the refrigerator next to the bag of petrified tacos.

Then he shot out the door for the elevator. He debated on taking the stairs, but dropped the idea. Sharon and Doyle would have reached the ground floor by this time, too late now to head them off. He'd just have to catch them up at their car. He pressed the down button and noted from the pointer above that the car was already ascending. More police? He pressed his back to the wall, partially concealing himself behind a potted plant.

The doors parted . . . and nothing happened.

Then the barrel of a 9mm Glock peeped out, swiftly followed by Sharon. She whirled, aiming at him in one fluid movement, and he crashed to the floor. But there was no gun shot, only a half-stifled giggle.

"At last, a man on his knees to me!" She was quite unencumbered by handcuffs and looked to be well in control of things.

Richard gave her a dark look, stood, and dusted

off his trousers. "Very funny. What if Demarest had been here instead with his gun?"

She stuffed the Glock back in her purse. "Then I'd have gone to Plan B."

"Which is?"

"I'll let you know when I think it up. Where is the little git, anyway?"

"Busy. What about your man?"

"Havin' a lie-down." She gestured at the elevator. Doyle was crumpled on the floor, quite boneless, with his arms behind him and handcuffs neatly locked on his wrists.

Richard stared. "What the hell did you do to him?"

"Just a friendly Glasgow handshake is all. Not my fault he's got a tender skull and surprises easy. We can't leave him there, so—"

"I'll take care of it, you go fetch the car; I'll be down directly." He gave her the keys to the Rover, then bent to lift and drag Doyle out. He hoped he could revive the lad enough to hypnotize him so his memories would match Demarest's.

"Are we still off to the airport?" she asked.

"Yes, but I'll have to stop home first for my passport and some cash. We can pick up your things as well for the trip. There's plenty of time before our flight."

"What about the law here?"

"Not to worry. I've gotten it all straight with Demarest for the time being."

"Maybe you'll tell me how you managed that. Reasoned with him, did you?"

Richard grunted an affirmative as he pulled Doyle along the floor. Doyle moaned, consciousness returning. Good.

"And are you sure about this Glastonbury thing?"

"Absolutely."

"If you're wrong we could all be in for a state funeral."

"I know."

"So we're really searching for the Grail? Honest to God?"

"Yes." *Honest to Goddess as well*, he thought, smiling inside.

She *tsked*, shaking her head as she slipped into the elevator. "I'll believe it when I see it. Well, if we're on such a daft quest, can I be Guinevere and you be Lancelot?"

He paused, looking at her with startled bemusement. "The story of my life," he wryly murmured as the doors shut.

Chapter Eight

"God, but I'm ready for bed," said Sharon as she resettled the shoulder strap of her flight bag.

"I'm delighted to hear it."

"To sleep," she added, a smile twisting the corner of her mouth.

"You slept on the plane," Richard pointed out as they, along with the rest of the weary, flight-stoned crowd, filed along toward Heathrow's version of customs.

"You've a strange definition for it, then."

"What are you complaining about? It was first class." And what a stroke of luck it had been to get those seats. A last-minute cancellation had worked in their favor. Richard didn't care if it was mere coincidence or divine intervention that changed their status from standby to boarding, but made a mental note to offer formal thanks at the first chance. Of course, no matter the comfort, he still hated the flying itself. He'd been very glad of Sharon's company to keep him distracted from the horrors of too much thought on the topic.

"Sorry. Just havin' a touch of nerves," she said, keeping pace with the herd.

He shot her a quick, sharp look. "You're not carrying anything you shouldn't?"

"Don't be daft. I left the shooter at your place. They'd have turned it up when we went through Pearson's security, anyway." Despite popular claims to the contrary, Sharon's plastic-handled Glock would have given the airport X-ray machines and their operators seven different kinds of fits. He didn't have to ask her twice to leave it behind. "It's Demarest. If he wants to put a call out on us . . ."

So, she was worried the authorities on this side of the pond would be looking for them. "It won't happen. I made sure of that, I told you."

Demarest had been of great help there, thanks to his scrambled memories on just how he spent the night and much of the next morning ignominiously stuffed in a coat closet with Officer Doyle. The hapless chief inspector had been predictably livid about the incident—once he regained consciousness—and was now rabid to find the man he thought responsible. Now everyone in Canada was looking for Professor Neal Rivers, a.k.a. Charon.

And Demarest had met with some minor success according to the progress checks Richard made with Bourland during the long flight. The tapes from the surveillance cameras at the condominium block had proved fruitful. The ones in the parking garage caught Rivers emerging from his car, his clothes covered with gore. He'd not bothered to obscure his face. About an hour later the entry cameras recorded him leaving with a bag in hand and all cleaned up, presumably to go to ground.

Or the airport.

So far no cab or bus driver admitted to picking up Rivers as a fare, but then none would be able to if the memory had been hypnotized out of their brains. The same held true for any airline employees.

They'd searched his lease car; the blood inside matched Sean's. There was no sign of a sniper's gun. He'd had plenty of time to stash it, though, prior to coming home, and that worrried Richard.

If I'm wrong, if he's still back there and this is a goose chase . . .

No, that didn't matter. Even if Charon was still in Toronto, Richard had to get to Glastonbury.

"And just what tale did you spin to put us in the clear?" Sharon asked.

"A damned good one. We're all comrades in arms again, the flowers are blooming, the skies are clear, God's in His heaven, and all's right with the stock market."

"Sounds like you've a touch of nerves yourself. An' I thought you didn't have any."

"Impatience, not nerves. I want to get going. Do you really need to sleep? I can put you up in a hotel while I—"

"Not a chance. If Rivers has that manuscript, I'm going to be there to pry it from his grasping fingers."

Good trick, he thought, *considering what Rivers is.* Having Sharon along for the hunt was a hellish risk for her, but Richard preferred her with him rather than crashing about on her own. At least while they were together he had the chance of protecting her from Rivers. *If I let him get that close.*

Despite Sharon's misgivings and his impatience they passed through customs without incident, and Richard led the way to one of the exits. The sun was still up and lethally bright. But this was England in the summer—of all the rotten times for it *not* to be raining. Richard called for Sharon to pause while he wrapped up against the dazzling weather: coat, gloves, hat . . .

"'Tis hardly a cunning disguise," she observed as he popped on his sunglasses. "You'll be drawing attention in that stuff."

"I told you I had an allergy to sunlight."

"Damnedest thing I've ever heard. What are you, a vampire?"

He pretended shocked surprise. "My God—my secret's discovered! How ever did you guess?"

She rolled her eyes. "Get on with you."

He hefted his now much lighter carry-on and quickly led the way straight to his waiting Jaguar, unlocking the doors, then slipping inside with a sigh of relief at the shade. The darkened windows weren't complete protection from the sun, but much better than nothing.

"Didn't we leave one just like this in your garage in Toronto?" she inquired, fiddling with her seat belt.

"It's part of my company fleet."

"An antique like this that gets twenty miles to the tank? You've a very understanding crew of stockholders."

"Oh, they are. And by the way, a thing is only an antique when it's been around longer than you've been alive."

"Then this qualifies for me, if not for you."

"*I'm* an antique, then?" he asked, removing his sunglasses to give her an arch look.

She put her hand firmly on his thigh, squeezing. "Ah, but I like a man with some experience." Then she moved her hand first north, then east, making him squirm when it reached its final destination.

Nothing to do for that but kiss her, which Richard did. Thoroughly.

"You can put me up in a hotel providin' you come yourself," she told him some minutes later. She was beautifully breathless.

"I'll hold you to that when we have the time."

"You can hold me any way you damn well please," she said, getting comfortable in her seat and patting her hair back into place.

Despite the diversions of the moment, Richard remembered something he had to check, got out again, and went around to open the boot. His part-time secretary on this side of the Atlantic had followed his telephoned orders exactly. Not only was his London car serviced and ready to roll, but she'd seen to the other, special equipment as well. It was all there, innocuous-looking stuff, very much like gardening tools: picks, shovels, a large, mallet-style hammer, then there were ropes, chisels, crowbars, several sharpened staves of yew wood in varying lengths . . . everything he might need for this expedition. Even the batteries in the torches were fresh. He slammed the lid shut with a grimace of satisfaction, piled back in behind the wheel, and started the engine.

"Fancy a trip to Glastonbury?" he asked as he negotiated the intricate tangle of traffic and roads to escape the airport. He put his sunglasses back on.

"If it goes past a take-away. I could use some fresh fuel."

"Right. Just point one out and we'll stop."

"But not for long. D'ye think Rivers will still even be there? He's had a hell of a start on us."

"Perhaps only a few hours." Then there was all this sun. The brilliant weather might have worked in their favor to delay Rivers. He would have loathed getting out in the stuff. "If we miss him there's an alert on should he try to leave the country." Philip Bourland had seen to that, acting on Richard's suggestion—for all the good it would probably do. If Rivers had any kind of experience, he could slip free to anywhere in the world as easily as going through a door. Richard had done so himself countless times.

"Perhaps when we get there he'll still be digging for the Grail. After readin' all the stuff he put in his book on it, I see now that he really believes it's there." She'd brought along Richard's signed copy and had read it off and on during the flight.

"Learn anything else?"

"Quite a lot. He made it interesting, I'll give him that."

"Tell me about it."

With a few prompting questions, he got a full report from her about the book, concentrating on information connected with the Grail, rather than the literary works about Arthur. Richard compared his own memories of the time with Sharon's gleanings. Its inaccuracies amused him, but there were enough facts mixed in to cause him worry. The legend Rivers believed in was that the Grail was buried somewhere beneath Glastonbury Tor. Close enough to the truth for discomfort.

Originally the Grail had been kept in that sacred spot under the guardianship of the sisterhood of the Goddess. The duty was gradually passed to the monks when the Christians arrived and built their monastery on the same holy ground. The monks did not know the real import of what they guarded, only that it was a sacred relic entrusted to their care. Those were simpler times, when faith was truly all consuming and blind. If you asked someone to do something, it was accomplished without question and they thanked you for the honor.

But tradition can break down and be forgotten in the span of a few lives. He had seen that happen again and again. Sabra, her sisters, their followers, and their descendants had ever kept a watchful eye on things, but sometimes even their power wasn't strong enough to stand against the irresistible force of violent change. Sabra and Richard had had a lively time of it just trying to survive when that bloody usurper William took it into his head to wrest the throne from Harold and crossed the channel with his band of freebooting Normans. It was enough to make

Richard ashamed of being one himself. What a century
that had been.

"If the Grail's still there, why haven't they dug it
up by now?" Sharon asked, dragging his mind back
to the present. Now she was flipping through a
guidebook she'd found in the glovebox. His secretary
had thought of everything.

"Not enough grant money, I suppose. Archeology's
an expensive sport even with volunteers doing the
grunt work."

Or perhaps because the Goddess, with her servants
dead or scattered, had been actively protecting it
Herself for all those lost ages—that or the scholars
believed the whole business to be a troubadour's
dream and chose not to bother. Either way, it worked;
the Grail had been kept safe. Until now.

"What I want to know is how Rivers expects to
accomplish what centuries of pilgrims, historians, and
archeologists haven't been able to do," said Sharon.

"Maybe he got a lead from that stolen manuscript
of yours." Privately, he was sure of it. Sabra would
have disguised things in a web of words and verse,
but not to the point where Richard couldn't have
made sense of it, and if he could work out the
meanings, then so could another.

"Must have been a strong one for him to be running
out on the IRA after they paid him for a job he's not
done. Why is he taking such a risk with them?"

"Who knows?" But if Rivers was a very old vampire, beginning to lose control, beginning to die, he'd
be desperate to find a cure. God knows how he found
out about the Grail's possible power to save him in
that regard, but there it was. Maybe he was only
following a dream and a hope, like countless pilgrims
before him. If the Grail proved to be a disappointment,
then maybe he'd try the waters at Lourdes next.

"If he's not cooperative, how will *we* find the thing?"

Richard shrugged. He'd just have to trust his memory and the Goddess on that one. It wouldn't be the first time. "I'm sure we'll work something out."

She gave him a long sideways look. "You know more than you're telling. Are you planning to short me on this?"

"We're both on the same side, Sharon. You want the museum manuscript back, and I'll help you on that, no question."

"But the Grail?"

He made no reply.

"You want it for yourself, don't you?"

"I want to keep it safe from Rivers, which is quite different."

"And not an answer to my question. If you turned up with the honest-to-God article, you could write your own ticket for life. Everyone from the *National Geographic* to the *Tattler* will want a piece of you and be ready with the cash in hand for the privilege."

"That's one path I don't plan to take."

"What then? Turn it over to the British Museum, or perhaps to the queen so she can put it in the Tower with the rest of the Crown Jewels? Or will you be takin' it directly to the Pope himself?"

"Sharon . . ."

"Tell me, then."

He scowled against the road glare. An opening presented itself in the lines of vehicles, and he seized it. The Jaguar responded as smoothly as its sibling in Toronto and surged effortlessly forward.

"Well?" she asked when the speedometer needle steadied again.

"There's no point in telling, because you wouldn't believe me."

"Takin' a lot on yourself, aren't you? Deciding what I'll think before I've heard anything."

He could have pointed out that she'd been making some broad judgments on him as well, but chose to let it pass.

"So what is it I wouldn't be believin'?"

"That I need the Grail for someone else."

"Who?"

"My . . . my mother."

"Your—whatever for?"

"She's dying." There. The absolute and pitiless truth. And he couldn't hide his feelings about it. They rushed up, choking him with their unexpected strength.

Sharon's tone was softer, more subdued. Apparently she'd picked up a lot from the husky tremor in his voice. "I'm sorry."

For a second he couldn't see the road and fought to blink his eyes clear. "No doctor can help her."

"And you believe the Grail can?"

Again, he made no reply.

"You really believe in it—just like Charon?"

"My belief is beside the point, I can only try. It's the only hope she has left. I have to get it to her and soon. I've given my word on it. That's why I went to see Rivers in the first place—trying to do research. I'd no idea he was also on the hunt for it, or that he was the assassin." *Or that he was a vampire.* "Not until you involved yourself."

"An' here I'm thinkin' I was a spanner in the works for you by interruptin' things."

He spared a glance at her. "You're no interruption. I'm glad of your being here no matter what."

Silence, then: "'Tis a flatterin' man you are and no mistake, Richard Dun." She said it lightly, but another glance at her face proved to him that he'd really touched her. Perhaps more deeply than he anticipated. For either of them. He suddenly wanted her, wanted to pull over and take her right then and there on the side of the road.

Be careful, Richard. How many women can a man be in love with at one time?

Blessed night finally eased over the land. When they paused at a British rendition of an American fast-food franchise, Richard took the opportunity to divest his long coat, trading it for a lighter zippered jacket. He quietly excused himself from ordering anything to eat, but bought a container of coffee for show, pretending to sip, and then "forgetting" about it until it was too cold to drink. By that time they were miles along their way again, with the Jaguar's headlamps cutting swiftly through the growing darkness. He kept a heavy foot on the pedal, hoping to make up for lost time. It was hell on the petrol consumption, and he was risking police notice, but too bad. This was an emergency.

Time passed in comfortable silence. Sharon had tucked into her food like a starving chipmunk, then dozed, sometimes sleepily opening her eyes when there was a shift in the car's momentum. Richard was very wide awake himself. As the distance between him and his goal closed with agonizing slowness, he felt more and more tension for the task to come building inside, demanding release. If he wasn't careful he'd be overstrung on arrival, and that would be entirely too dangerous. Better to be calm and receptive, ready to respond to whatever awaited, rather than nerved up and jumping at every shadow. He tried breathing deeply and concentrating on the act of driving. It helped, a little, though more than once his thoughts would stray into useless speculation on what to do if Rivers had been and gone with the Grail by the time they got there. If that proved true . . .

The road. Focus on the road, *not on things you've no control over.*

Another mile slipped away beneath them. Then another, until sufficient numbers of them accumulated to the point of meaning something.

He turned off the main highway to negotiate the meandering turns of narrow country roads, and then suddenly he *felt* it and had to stop. He pulled the car over onto the grass verge, doused the lights, and stepped out. A brisk wind was up, sending clouds scurrying over the face of the waning moon like frantic ghosts. He crossed to a gap in the hedge and stood facing west, tasting the uncanny vibration in the air. Through the blackness of the English night, his sensitive eyes could see the Tor as clearly as his other senses perceived the presence of things beyond mere sight.

Sweet Goddess, but there's magic afoot. Strong stuff, too, for him to feel it from here.

A hand unexpectedly touched his shoulder and he flinched. Sharon stood next to him in the darkness, rubbing sleep from her eyes.

"We're almost there," he told her.

She checked her watch in the fitful moonlight. "What'd you do, fly when I wasn't looking?"

"Just about. You can see the Tor." He pointed.

She squinted, then shook her head. "I'll take your word for it." And she stumbled back to the warmth of the car.

Richard's hopes had risen at the mere sight of the great hill. It was *the* landmark for miles around, always had been. Glastonbury, in legend and in language called the Glass Place because of the waters that once went right up to its base. When the light was right and the day calm, they'd perfectly reflected the Tor like a mirror. Ynis Witrin, the Island of Glass, the Island of Apples, Avalon . . . His heart began to beat fast and hard at the prospect of walking there again, and he didn't try to quell this feeling of excitement. It was a sacred place to him, and he had every right to revel in the joy it inspired, no matter the circumstances that brought him back.

But I've been away for so long. So much has changed.

The waters had receded, either by shifts in the climate or from man-made draining. Only a faint memory of their presence lingered in the low places in the land, collecting in wide sheets upon the rain-soaked earth. The Tor appeared to be the same as ever, though, rising from the otherwise flat plain like a woman's breast, the tower on top jutting up like a nipple. The comparison had once amused Sabra, and she'd playfully chided him for having his mind ever on fleshy pleasures. He recalled more than once taking action against her teasing on that particular topic, much to their mutual delight.

Then the thought of losing her stabbed through him, killing his joy.

Mouth dry, he joined Sharon back in the car and fed it more petrol, hurrying forward.

The village of Glastonbury, like many in this part of the world, nearly ceased to exist once night had fallen. The shops were all closed, their owners and patrons home, probably parked before their television sets or asleep. Excellent, there'd be no inconvenient witnesses blundering about.

They entered the village from the east, passing a couple of silent farms before a National Trust sign announced the abbey ruins to the left, and the Tor to the right. The main body of the village—stores, hotels, and ugly modern housing—lay further ahead. Richard took the left turn and pulled quietly into the parking lot of the abbey ruins. He switched off the engine and coasted down a slight slope to come to rest silently in the deep shadow of some windswept trees. They climbed out, both stiff from the long ride, and Sharon stretched mightily, loosening her long immobile muscles.

"How do we get in?" she asked, nodding toward the ruins.

"We don't need to. We go to the Tor. Around and from the far side."

"It's a bit of a walk."

"If he's here I don't want him to know we are as well."

The wind was high, running over the grass, turning it into a restless sea; it whipped through the trees, gifting them with thready-voiced speech. Richard recalled once meeting a woman who could understand their language. Interesting sort, claimed she always felt like an eavesdropper.

Sharon shivered, pulled a dark jacket from her flight bag, and slipped it on. "Creepy place," she commented, tying a scarf firmly over her wind-blown hair.

"I suppose it is if you're not used to it." As changed as it was, this was still like another home to him. He could no more fear it than the more prosaic one he'd created in Toronto. He opened the boot and handed Sharon a torch, putting another in his coat pocket. "Don't use it just yet, not until we find him," he cautioned. "And if you should see him, duck and run. Don't forget how he's killed before. Stay absolutely out of his way and let me handle him, I've had the training for it."

"Not to worry, you're welcome to him. I know the

difference between an off-guard RCMP officer and a homicidal maniac, thank you very much. What's all this other stuff you've got?"

"Prospecting equipment. We might have to do a bit of excavation." He gave her the crowbar and pick, then shouldered a coil of rope, hung the mallet and a folding grappling hook from his belt, and hefted the shovel and a couple of the sharpened yew staves. She shut the boot, and he led off along the line of the ancient stone wall away from the abbey entrance and deeper into the darkness.

Richard strode quickly and quietly, with Sharon struggling to keep up. He was barely aware of her as the memories of the place flooded back to him, the past becoming more real than the present with every step he took. The very stones at his feet seemed to smile up in welcome. Many was the night that he had trod this same path rushing to meet Sabra at the base of the Tor, ready to be led along the mystic way to Avalon.

And yet, how much it had changed. The glorious abbey was in ruins now. A break in the clouds gave him a moonlit glimpse of the great arch of the nave, still standing, still reaching upward in its futile attempt to reach heaven. Little else remained, save bare stone walls, crumbling in their inevitable return to the earth whence they had been torn, and empty shadowed windows staring malevolently like skeletal eye sockets.

The ruins were sad enough for anyone, but especially so for him as he remembered them in their original splendor. And, ah, the times *before* the abbey had even been built, when the sacred ground had been dedicated solely to the Goddess. Over the years the Christians had gradually made a place for themselves on the same spot, coming to the festivals of the

Goddess to speak of their Savior to others, making converts, and finally building, ever building. But the Goddess had not minded sharing the land or the people.

Her followers had been forced to accept the changed way of things in order to survive, but still managed to keep the old worship alive simply by integrating it into the new. Certainly they had much in common: lighting candles, burning incense, saying prayers, chanting, celebrating with feasts and serving penance with fasts, but there had ever been conflict from both sides. It usually resulted from insecure faith and basic greed. Richard had often noted the ones most shrill about defending their religion at any cost were either plagued with inner doubts, or wanted power over others, or both. The people at peace with themselves and their deity he never had to worry about.

The abbey took the place of the original church when the latter burned down in a devastating fire that had consumed the priceless books in its keeping. It was mere chance that he and Sabra had gone to Ireland that year, and she'd taken her own book with her, thus sparing it. He'd asked if that had been her Gift of Sight at work, but she'd only shrugged. "It serves me well for people, but not so well for events," she told him.

Although she'd not been able to predict the time the monks of the abbey "discovered" the graves of Arthur and Guinevere. That had taken Sabra completely by surprise.

"Perhaps I should have tithed more," was her rueful comment.

For centuries afterwards the abbey benefited from the monetary offerings of countless pilgrims who came to pay their respects to the long vanished king and his queen. The sham angered Richard, for he knew their resting places to be very much elsewhere than the plot of ground summarily chosen for them. Certainly Sabra didn't approve, but she advised him to do nothing about the business, eventually leaving an offering herself before they went on their way.

Unrest was the rule of the land just then and, forced to see to their own safety, they had to move on, leaving the hidden Grail behind with its unknowing guardians. For a time Richard worried that it might be discovered, but Sabra told him to have faith.

"The Goddess will look after things," she said with serene certainty.

And so it had proved for the last eight hundred years. Even Henry Tudor's ravagings—which had destroyed the beautiful abbey, reducing it to the present ruin—had failed to find the sacred cup. He'd have likely denounced it as papist and destroyed it, the hell-bound butcher. Talk about a prime example of greed and insecurity . . .

The Tor stood a little way off and above the abbey, across the road they'd just driven along. The tower of the Church of St. Michael had been built on the very summit in some last mad attempt to drive out the old ways, only to become itself a victim of the swift progress of violent times. It also stood in ruins, in defiance of the elements for many centuries, but wearing away nonetheless.

Stealthily, he moved out from the shelter of the abbey wall and, pulling Sharon along with him, sprinted across the road and once more into the welcoming darkness of the other side. A little way along the road in the direction of the town, and they would be at the yew groves with their twin springs, one red, one white, their sacred waters colored by the earth itself.

It's so good to be back.

They came to a narrow laneway, emptying out onto

the main road, and he stopped. Richard's heart plummeted.

Oh, Goddess, what have they done now?

It had been many years since he had been at Glastonbury, and he'd expected some change, but he'd underestimated the capacity of modern man for destruction. The beautiful yew trees were gone and of the White Spring and the Chalice Well there was no sign. Where once the Druids had walked barefoot in this holiest of places, now there ran a road, winding gently along the side of the Tor, with large buildings at this end, and farmer's fields further along.

Sharon sensed his hesitation. "What's the matter?"

How could he ever explain? "It's . . . different from what I expected. There should be a well here, and a spring. At least, according to my research."

"This is the White Spring, here." She indicated a building standing empty and in darkness at the junction of the lane and the main road. "The Water Board capped it and built a reservoir long ago, but it's not used anymore. It got clogged up or something. And the Chalice Well is further along the lane, on the left. I read it in the guide."

"Oh, yes. Yes, of course . . ." He trailed off, unable to conceal his disappointment and sorrow for that which was lost.

There was a moment of awkward silence, then Sharon touched his arm. "Well, I'd love to stand here in the moonlight with you, but isn't there something that we should be doing?"

He shook himself out of it. Time to grieve later. "Yes, there is, come on."

Richard led the way along Well House Lane to the site of the Chalice Well. It, too, was capped. The rough stone surrounds were surmounted by a metal grill secured with a formidable looking padlock and chains, and standing almost incongruously next to it was a modern drinking fountain.

"The water's reputed to have curative powers since the Grail's supposed to be linked to it somehow," she said. "Maybe we should have brought diving equipment." She descended the few steps down to the well, pulled out her torch and, cupping her hands around the light so as to shade it from anyone else's view, inspected the stout metal grating. "Is it deep? What's this for? To keep people from stealing the Grail?"

"More likely to keep fools from falling in and drowning themselves."

"But the Grail could be down there."

"That's only a story, no one really believes it or they'd have found it by now."

"Rivers might. I'm going to have a better look." She put down the pick and swung the crowbar, bringing it to bear.

He was about to point out that if it were true, Rivers would already be trying to break in, then stopped himself. "Good idea. You work on that, while I check the rest of the area. I'm going to make a circle of the Tor, so it may be a while. Try not to make too much noise."

"You think he could hear anything with all this wind in his ears?" She shone the light again in the well, then energetically set about destroying National Trust property.

Richard left behind the rope and the other things he carried, keeping only the torch in his pocket and one of the sharpened yew tree staves. He walked unhurriedly away, taking a roundabout route toward the Tor and using what cover was available.

While Sharon was focused on the well he'd glimpsed a shadow moving there, moving against the wind—and at vampire-fast speed.

There was no way of knowing if Rivers was aware of their presence, so Richard assumed the worst, moving cautiously and keeping his eyes wide open. Hearing was next to useless with the row from the wind, but he crept along silently, just in case. Looking back, he checked on Sharon. He grimaced, unhappy at leaving her alone, but he'd been aware of that risk from the start. Better to have her busy and out of the way while he looked things over, than smack in the middle of things. He didn't know what to expect from Rivers, but again, assumed the worst, remembering the man's other name was Charon.

He crossed Well House Lane, and started up the gentle slope toward the base of the Tor. The wind was fairly howling now, growing stronger by the second, and the moon dipped and sailed between the flying clouds. Most of the way to the Tor was open field, littered with a few sheep, yet there were low trees and bushes enough to give him cover, and in a few minutes he reached it.

You must use the True Way.

The voice of She-Who-Walks came unbidden to his mind, as clear and real as if she stood next to him. It was more than enough to make him freeze in his tracks, glancing to one side, then the other, chilled to the bone. He *knew* she was not there. Not physically. Very well, then she was close by in another sense, either from thinking of him or as part of his unconscious mind's own protective instinct. Past experience with Sabra had taught him to always pay attention to such occurrences. He did so now, crouching in the thick turf behind a shattered wall and surveying the area very carefully.

He knew well what was meant by the True Way. It was the way that Sabra had always led him, blindfolded, to the wonders of Avalon. He had asked her often why he was not allowed to see it for himself, but she only said that it was part of the mystery and the power of the place and must always be respected.

"There's a reason for following the old rituals. We must honor them even if we don't understand why," she told him time and again.

All she allowed for him was that it began at the Living Rock, as she called it, and he knew where that was— if the ravagers of the present century had left it alone.

Keeping low, he scrambled along the base of the Tor in the direction of the road that he and Sharon had driven along earlier until he could see the rock gleaming in the moonlight. It was smaller than before, or so it seemed when compared to his memory and for a second, he was unsure, but then like a scent on the wind, the feeling came to him, the old power that had slumbered for so long in the land turned in its doze and reached out to him, and he *knew*.

The true magic of the Goddess had ever been Sabra's domain, but he wasn't entirely immune to it, sensing it as a deaf man senses the beat of a drum in the air about him. For all the despoilments visited upon the place for good or ill, nothing could change the basic forces that lived here unseen and unmarked by any but the most attuned. He was hardly in that number, but centuries of time with Sabra had taught him much, including being able to recognize such presences.

There is something in the path ahead of you.

She-Who-Walks's voice came to him once more, and in obedience to its warning, Richard flattened himself against the damp grass in the lee side of the rock. Slowly, he lifted his head and looked around.

The darkness keeps me from seeing anything but where its shadow has been.

The place was full of shadows in the fitful light of the waning moon. A shadow had drawn him this way in the first place. They all seemed alive because of the wind. Its voice rushed between the broken stones, whispered over the grass; tree branches creaked, adding faint laughter to the night.

There.

His roving gaze fastened on a single moving patch of darkness in the trees.

It drifted, halted, then pressed on. Richard spared a short curse for the wind that masked whatever sound the thing might have made, but took it back as he comprehended it could work in his favor as well. So long as he kept out of sight he had the initial advantage.

The shadow took on more definition, but was still far enough away that he could only determine it was a man. His sturdy figure strode purposefully along, pausing now and then to stare at some object along his path, looking for all the world like a tourist determined to see the sights.

And he was coming in Richard's direction.

Chapter Nine

Closer . . . close enough. It was Neal Rivers all right, and if Richard had entertained any doubts of him being a vampire, they vanished now. The man had a small, flat, square object in one hand and often stopped to look at it, holding it like a book, reading from it. The moonlight was fair, but not nearly enough to read by, not if one were a normal human.

Rivers passed Richard's hiding place, working his way up the hill toward the tower at its peak. He carried something in a sack slung over one shoulder. It was clearly heavy, even for him, and he paused, put down the book, and hefted the thing across to the other shoulder. Picking up the book again, he checked it again, and moved on upward in a straight line along the spine of the Tor.

Sabra's book? Most certainly. It was about the right size. Sharon would be pleased.

As soon as he felt it was safe, Richard stood and watched Rivers disappearing up the hill. He had to quickly get to the summit as well, yet hesitated. True, he could go around to the other side, racing at preternatural speed and easily reach the top first, but the—warning?—from She-Who-Walks made him pause. The True Way was not short or easy, but anything else would dishonor the holiness of the place, and with the restless energies flowing about him like the wind, he'd be a fool to ignore the ancient tradition.

But Sabra had ever been the one to lead him, only she knew the path.

He had no idea. He stood next to the Living Rock and faced up along the spine, full of inner doubts. And as ever, when they consumed him, he turned to her in his heart.

I am in your hands, my dearest love. If you have ever helped me, help me now, and if not you, then let she who is my daughter be my guide in your stead.

Richard closed his eyes. He became very much more aware of the wind, of how it roared in his ears, nipped at his clothes. He waited, hoping to hear a voice as before, but no one spoke into his mind. Perhaps instead he would receive some sort of unmistakable revelation that would carry him along.

Nothing. Only the wind. Wind that tugged insistently at him until an errant gust sent him staggering forward a few stumbling paces. His eyes popped open and he started back to the rock, but another strong gust pressed him forward again. Its force culled tears from his eyes. He turned away, rubbing them, for it felt like a spray of dust had struck him blind.

The True Way . . .

He stopped, frozen with the realization. Of *course* he would have guidance, but in a manner best suited for him and his limitations. He grinned at the simplicity of it all, stopped fighting, and let the wind push him forward this way and that. It was not as smooth a walk as it might have been had Sabra been there to take his arm, but it worked, and that was all that mattered. He stumbled more than a few times, but the yew stave helped him keep his feet for the most part.

He spared a brief thought that Rivers might spot him out in the open, mark his progress, and take action, but that threat did not seem so great against what was happening. This was magic, the old kind he'd lived with for so very long; Richard trusted it, and in his heart knew all would be well regardless of whether he was seen or not.

After a few yards he veered off to the left, picking up speed as he got used to things, threading along the age old labyrinth, through the maze that lay all around the Tor, overlooked by most. Faster he went until he was running, actually *running* at his best speed. He almost laughed from the sheer, joyous exhilaration of it. He spiraled upward and upward, eyes closed, never faltering, safe in the care of his Sabra, along the path that they had trod so often together on the way to Avalon.

Then abruptly the land became level under his feet, and he came to a swift stop, opening his eyes. Though still rocked by the screaming wind, he was at the top of the Tor and facing the open entry of Saint Michael's tower. It was also in ruins, the same as the abbey, but not so far gone, its broken stones glimmering faint in the moonlight.

In past visits Richard had been content to wait outside while Sabra had entered, such was the compelling power of the place. His comparing the Tor to a woman's breast wasn't so far off after all, for the feeling around him, from the living earth under his feet, to the wide sky overhead, and the lands stretching below was that of overwhelming femininity, powerful and sacred. It had always been so, sometimes making him, the man, feel superfluous. His duty and privilege was to be guardian and protector to Sabra and her sisters, and that had ever been more than enough for him. But tonight, though . . . that might have to change. He hoped the Goddess would understand the necessity of it.

There. Only a little way ahead was Rivers, for the moment completely unaware of Richard's presence. Once more he lay flat in the grass and watched.

Rivers looked up at the niches in the face of the tower above the vanished door. There were seven altogether, three on the right, three on the left, and one in the center above the doorway. One of the three on the right still held its statue of Saint Dunstan. The lowest on the left contained the lower half of a statue of Saint Michael, left foot pinning down his dragon for all eternity, but the rest were empty. Rivers had put aside the sack he'd been carrying and now took from it a statue, laying on the turf next to him. In what was left of the moonlight, Richard could plainly see that it was a statue of Saint Bridget. Rivers must have found it in the abbey ruins below.

Like a body left forgotten on a battlefield, Richard thought. Memory tugged at him. Saint Bridget. But before that she'd been Brigid, the goddess of fire, and very important to Sabra and the others. How they would dance around the flames in the early spring to celebrate the change of the season; Richard could almost hear the music again, the pipes and drums.

Gone now. Perhaps never to return.

Rivers produced a small plastic bag and slipped the book inside it, drawing his finger and thumb across the top to seal it shut before tucking all into a pocket. Unencumbered, he now closely regarded the statue, slowly circling, then suddenly bent and lifted it and began walking toward the tower.

More of Richard's memories flooded in. Yes, the goddess-saint needed to be returned to her place. He recalled Sabra reading that bit aloud to him to see how it sounded: "When Brigid is home and thrice to widdershins turns . . . something, something . . . she looks now to the mystery below, holy and secret . . ." He forgot the rest, but Rivers had the book and would take it from there.

He was climbing now, using the carvings as footholds, clinging precariously to the remains of the wall with one hand, while trying to push the statue back into place with the other. Clearly he had understood Sabra's instructions well enough, for he had headed straight for the center niche, and Richard recalled that that was where Brigid always stood. A short ladder would have helped, or a tall assistant, but Richard patiently waited to see what happened. Even over the wind, he could hear Rivers's grunts of effort. Good, let him do all the work.

He finally got it settled. A moment's rest to get his breath . . . now he was turning the statue, turning . . . damnation, that was the wrong direction. He held his peace until Rivers figured it out and corrected things. One turn, two, three—but the statue stopped and would not go any further. Rivers tried to force it, then gave up, and dropped to the ground.

Taking stock, Richard thought.

Rivers paced back and forth a few times, then climbed up to try another turning. It didn't work. Brigid was stuck fast now, not quite on center and angled so she faced inward toward the wall of the niche.

The mystery below, holy and secret . . .

Richard grinned to himself, and blessed Sabra's early efforts at verse. The reference could only be for the Grail, which he'd always known to be hidden under the Tor even if he didn't know precisely where or how to get to it. Brigid now pointed the way—at least to those who understood the clue. Rivers was now closely examining the area over Brigid's head, probably wondering where the mystery below came into things—until he gave up in disgust and dropped down again.

He paced completely around the structure, checking every inch of the area, going out of sight for a few moments. Richard took the opportunity to rise and scurry inside the tower. He leapt lightly up onto a stone ledge that ran the length of one wall, pressing himself into the inky blackness of one corner. He held his breath, waiting. Sure enough, Rivers, too, came inside.

After all the noise of the wind, the relative quiet within the sheltering walls was a soothing respite. It was also quite dark, so much so that Rivers needed the aid of a pocket torch to look around. Richard heard him muttering aloud to himself as he played the light over the floor. How strange it was to hear the old tongue spoken again, though his pronunciation was atrocious. Obviously, it was not the professor's native language. He sounded as though he'd learned it by memorizing an inaccurate dictionary.

"The accent's on the second syllable," Richard said loudly.

Rivers gave a satisfying yell of surprise, turning fast, mouth and eyes comically wide. He frantically threw the torchlight around until it picked out Richard's form crouching on the ledge like some latter-day gargoyle. Rivers gaped for a long moment in undisguised shock with one hand to his heart. "Jeez! You scared the shit out of me!"

"Mind your language, if you please, this is a church."

"What the hell are you doing here?" he demanded, disregarding Richard's request.

"I think we both know the answer to that one, Neal. Is that your real first name? Your last one is certainly a fake."

His surprise had been genuine, but Rivers recovered fast and grinned up with unpleasant humor. "Took you long enough to figure it out. I was wondering if I was that good or if you were just too thick in the brains department."

I'll ignore that. "Having much success?" he inquired innocently.

Rivers snorted and waved the torchlight around. "I followed the goddamned manuscript, turned the statue and all—nothing. Another fucking fake—unless you know something I don't. You must or you wouldn't be here."

"And you accuse me of being thick." Richard clapped his hands together once, rubbing them. "So . . . what shall we do now?"

"How the hell should I know?"

Just to be irritating, Richard was about to admonish Rivers yet again about his lack of reverence, but events took their own course. The wind outside abruptly stopped howling, and an eerie silence descended upon the tower, as solid and final as the shutting of a door.

Rivers hurriedly put his back to the far wall, staring every which way and holding the torch out like a weapon. "What the—"

Richard did much the same thing, instinctively grabbing the yew stave, holding it tightly in one fist. The hair on the back of his neck stood on end, and he had to fight an almost irresistible urge to run away. There was vast energy surging here, basic and primal—and no one around to control it.

"What is it?" Rivers demanded, his voice rising. "What's out there?"

"The power of the Goddess, I'd say," Richard whispered.

Rivers face flashed uncertainty for a moment, then

he shook his head with a nervous laugh. "I don't think so. You're not spooking me with that scam. This is just a break in the windstorm—like the eye of a hurricane. A coincidence."

"Are you so sure?" Why shouldn't the Goddess use the elements—Her servants—to Her best advantage? Richard pressed hard against the cold stone wall, all eyes and ears and drumming heart.

Then the sound began, and he flinched from it. It was as if the Earth herself was groaning aloud, finally reacting to the outrages worked upon her by generations of presumptuous humans—a long, low, rumbling moan that shook the whole of the Tor, hollow and lonely beyond comprehension.

Richard could hardly breathe for the heaviness of the restive Power stirring about him. His limbs went thick and sluggish just when he most wanted to run, and denial of that instinct only made his growing fear blossom all the faster. His panicked beast threw itself against the gates of his self-control, bursting through them like a paper screen. His teeth began to bud, and he knew his eyes shone red as hellfire.

And I'm only on the edge of it!

He looked down at Rivers, who was much closer to the source of the sound, and saw that he was completely changed: his hair now dulled and coarse, nails turned to rending claws, his sturdy form gone even thicker with blood-flushed muscle, and his face . . . dear God. Were there nothing human left in it, that might make it easier to bear, but vestiges of the man remained, twisted and corrupted, and unfortunately not beyond recognition. This was no longer Neal Rivers, though, that illusion was quite gone. This was a killer; this was *Charon*.

The revelation gave Richard no joy, for it was just like looking into a mirror. He felt the changes coursing through him, his shaking hands also going rigid and clawlike as he tried to fight it.

This is my present, my future, and finally my death. Sweet Goddess, preserve me!

She made no reply, but the earth continued to tremble. Pieces of the wall flaked off, raining upon him. Then suddenly the grinding of stone upon stone drew his gaze to the center of the floor. Cracks appeared around a single great slab there, growing wider with each passing second. With a rush of centuries-old pent-up air, the slab split down the middle, and its two pieces fell inward, crashing noisily into the darkness below. From his higher vantage, Richard glimpsed the top of worn stone stairs leading down to the very heart of the Tor itself.

Silence closed upon them once more. A very dreadful silence, the kind that exists only in the tiny spaces between eternities.

Then as abruptly as it had stopped, the wind began again, with more force than ever, screeching and howling around the tower. Echoes reverberated up from the opening in the floor. It was the voice of the Hounds of Annwyn, Richard's own dread progenitors, awakened out of turn, before the proper time of the Wild Hunt of winter. Though of their blood, he was not immune to their cold terror, and hid his face from their furious storming passage. The gale shrieked for uncounted seconds about him, the force of it first slamming him against the wall like a leaf, then dragging him away. Helpless, he spun and fell, arms flailing, before he landed with a breath-stealing jolt upon the hard stones.

Then the Hounds were gone, tearing madly through the skies at one with the flying clouds, their wild cries merging with the wind.

Richard lay still, panting, trying to master his fear, and only marginally succeeding.

Someone will die this night, he thought.

He shivered and renewed his grip on the stave that had come with him, startled to see his hand was normal again. Perhaps his own beast had been cowed by the presence of energies so much greater than itself and retreated. No matter the reason, he was grateful; he needed to be thinking and acting, not mindlessly reacting to whatever was to come.

A few yards away he could see Charon lying half-curled on the floor. He seemed to be in pain, his marred features slick with sweat as his body shivered and twitched. His talons slashed at the floor, leaving scratches in the stone flags.

He's fighting his own beast.

And having far more difficulty. He was farther along in his degeneration than Richard, but not so far as Sabra. Richard watched, fascinated as Charon struggled with the demon, until slowly, ever so slowly, he came back. His hair smoothed, his nails receded, his very body seemed to shrink. The effort left him pale and gasping for breath for minutes afterward. Unsteady, but determined, he managed to sit up and looked at Richard with a ghastly grin, eyes gone black with fear.

"Well, now you know, buddy." He swiped at his brow with one arm and made a sound that was halfway between a laugh and a sob. "This is what's in store for us both, sooner or later."

Richard found his feet and edged around the gaping entrance to the nether world until he was opposite the other man. "I knew already."

"You did, eh? Yeah, you had to. That old lady of yours, Sabra, she must be in about the same state or even worse, huh? Tell me I'm wrong."

Richard's surprise must have shown, for Charon smiled up at him and continued. "Yeah, I know all about her. And you, too, d'Orleans or Lancelot or whatever the hell your name is now. I've been watching you for centuries, old buddy."

"You couldn't have. I would have known."

Charon smiled again as he slowly stood, dusting his hands, an unnerving smile, too close to a snarl for comfort. "Well, maybe you were just too busy having a good time to notice. And I wouldn't say we shared the same circle of friends. Soldiers and academics don't exactly mix, y'know. Could have knocked me over with a feather when you called my office that night."

"You covered it well."

"I've had lots of practice. But you? You need to work on your act more, be better prepared when you're trying to feed a load of crap to somebody like you tried with me. I mean, researching a *book*? I almost choked when you gave me that one. I'm surprised you can even read a book. I'd always figured you for a jumped-up jock who'd struck it lucky, and I've never had much time for jocks."

Richard wanted to say that he'd never had much time for self-satisfied intellectuals either, particularly cocky ones, but let it lie. The man was afraid, and all his babbling was his way of dealing with it. Richard was also afraid, but his fear had shrunk in the last few minutes, encompassed in a cold glass ball hiding deep in his belly. He knew the feeling well, was quite comfortable about it even, because of its familiarity. He'd known his portion of fear in the past, but could spare no time or effort for it at the present. It would just have to wait until later.

He gestured at the stairs. "Do you want to throw insults all night or go exploring? This could take a lot of time and dawn isn't all that long away."

"Exploring?" Charon shook his head in incredulity. "You mean you don't *know* where it is?"

"I'm a guardian. It is enough. I've never needed to know."

"Holy shit, I don't believe this! All these years and you never—?"

Richard gave a small shake of his head, smiling at the other man's reaction.

Charon slapped his hands on his sides. "Of all the blind, bone-headed—oh, Jeez, you take the cake."

"The frosting, too," Richard politely added.

"And proud of it, yet. That's the difference between us, I've never gotten much satisfaction out of being ignorant on anything."

Not ignorance, faith. Faith that's always been proven out and fulfilled.

"Are you behind the times. Didn't you ever get tired of being pushed around by a lot of skirts spouting mumbo-jumbo and calling it religion?"

"Now who's behind the times?" Richard said evenly. "You felt the power of this place, heard it. I know you did. I saw you fighting it."

"Oh, don't start on me. That was no more than a freaking gust of wind and bad nerves. Save the fairy stories for someone else, I'm immune, Blackstone."

"Apparently not to the point of discounting the power of the Grail, though, or else you'd not be so keen to get it."

Charon's mouth popped wide.

Gotcha. Richard showed his teeth, enjoying the moment, then pointed at the opening. "Shall we get on with things?" He stepped down onto the first of the stone flags, but with incredible speed, Charon was before him and growling into his face.

"*We?* I don't think so, buddy boy. Since you don't know where it is, *we* doesn't come into this. *I* will go and get the Grail."

Richard, determined to be civilized, mastered his

developing anger. Negative emotions would not serve
him well in this of all places; besides, he didn't much
relish the prospect of crawling around in the unknown
that lay below. "Whatever you want. I'll take it after
you've finished, if you don't mind."

Charon stepped closer, forcing Richard back onto
level ground. "Oh, but I do, very much. If you think
I've done all this work just so you can waltz in and
take the prize—"

"You'll have no reason to keep it once you're done."

"Man, you are a *dinosaur!* You think I'd let anyone
else use it?"

"Why not? What harm would it do you?"

"Competition, Elwood—competition! Something I
don't need."

"The world is big enough for us."

Charon laughed. "Are you really this dumb or just
being irritating?"

"I'm trying to give you a chance to live—call it
an honor thing."

"To live? Oh, I see, if I don't share then you'll
kill me because you're the guardian of the brass ring?"

"Absolutely." He spun the yew stave once like a
baton. "And you accused me of being thick."

Charon looked at the sharpened wood, eyes glit-
tering. "Golly gee, I'm wetting my pants."

"Your choice."

"Yeah, that thing will do the job just fine. A bull's-
eye in my heart and it's bye-bye birdie. The truth
is that so many have already tried, both humans and
our kind, but none—and I mean *none* of them—even
came close."

Now it was Richard's turn to smile. "You forget
who I am—a trained fighter with over a thousand
years of experience—the jock who got lucky. There's
a reason for that luck."

"Oh, yeah, but the problem for you is you don't know who *I* am. I've been killing people for a *long* time—I've made a regular art form of it, I'm a goddamned Rembrandt when it comes to death. If you think you're facing some puffball academic, think again, Lance-baby."

Richard did, but not for long. Bragging was one way to throw an opponent off, one way of winning a fight before it ever started. He shifted his weight, dropping forward slightly for balance, bringing the stave to bear.

"Oh, I'd hoped you'd go dumb on me." Charon shifted as well, stepping up onto level ground. "I could use a workout. But since I'm such a sweetheart of a guy, I'll give you one more warning to take a hike."

"Really?"

Charon mimicked his disdainful tone. "Really? Yeah, you know anything about the original assassin's cult of the East? They'd get high as kites on the best pot in the world then cut loose for fun and games. Nasty bunch of boys, and I taught 'em everything there was to learn."

"So?"

"So don't tell me you've never heard of 'The Old Man of the Mountain.'"

Richard had indeed heard of the legendary founder of the assassins, and his smile faded. *Perhaps this won't be as easy as I thought.*

Charon spread his arms wide, wearing a madman's grin. "Come to papa!"

And why not? thought Richard, but as he'd done many times before held off a moment to take the full measure of the man he faced. Charon was stocky, but fast on his feet for his build, and certainly miles faster than any normal human. He was unarmed, but that didn't mean a damned thing. He'd be strong as a bull, could take an otherwise killing blow, and still get up for more. His eyes were alight with unfeigned pleasure. Not good. He'd likely be unpredictable and that much more dangerous.

Richard held the yew stave firmly with both hands. It had been some years since he'd wielded a spear or quarterstaff in combat, but his body still remembered the old drills. Without warning he tried a lightning quick thrust at Charon's midsection for starters, just to see which way he'd jump. He didn't, but parried it out of the way with one swift arm block, bringing his other hand around to grab the end. Richard pulled back just in time.

"That the best you can do, kid?" Charon asked, still grinning.

Only testing the waters. Then Richard twisted and launched a head kick, which was dodged, followed by a swing with the stave, which connected. Not hard, just enough to glance along Charon's skull and break the skin near his receding hairline. He hissed, but didn't slow down and tried again to grab the stave away. Richard ducked, brought the sharp end up, and struck once more, but this time got only empty air. Charon's thick body blurred as he went full speed for a second.

Something caught Richard hard on his right side, sending him staggering, as if he'd been hit by a bus. He felt a strong tug on the stave, but froze his hands solid to it and pulled. Charon came with it, using his onrush and weight to push Richard back toward the opening. He knew it was somewhere behind them, just waiting for him to stumble in.

He pivoted hard, lifting his arms and bringing up one knee where it would do the most good. Charon anticipated that and broke off, releasing the stave. He missed falling in himself only by some very last-minute foot work.

"That the best *you* can do, 'old man'?" Richard found himself laughing. All those centuries past and gone and nothing had changed: it was ever youth against age. Though in this case the overall difference of years was bound to be only marginal. If so, then this was also a matter of skill. And he had him there. For all his boasting Charon was not the best of fighters. His assassin's talents were obviously better suited for more subtle employments.

Unless he wants me to underestimate him.

Nasty thought, that, then he had to concentrate on the task of staying just far enough from Charon's reach to keep out of trouble, but close enough to stab out with the stave when opportunity presented. Not easy, since Charon frequently put on speed, moving almost too fast even for Richard to follow. If not for his own quick reflexes he'd have come to grief several times.

"We could be at this all night," he remarked. "Why not be sensible and—"

"Share the goodies?" Charon paused. "No thanks."

"Why not? You'll have no further need of it."

"Yeah, like you're really going to let me ride off into the sunrise? I don't think so, not with the job I've got."

True. Richard had rather purposely overlooked that point.

"Square one, Lance-baby. You're not about to let me go finish the gig in Canada, are you?"

"I will if you forget it and find other things to do with your time."

"No way. I keep my commitments. I gotta reputation to hold up. Besides, I like the work. Always have. Killing people isn't what I do, it's who I am."

He blurred again, but Richard saw what was coming and jabbed hard backwards with the rounded end of the stave.

And connected. When he turned, Charon was staggering away, clutching his stomach. Richard flowed through with another stab, but Charon got his left arm up and took the blow in the flesh above his wrist. The scent of blood swept past on the wind. Charon hissed, clutching his bleeding arm as he retreated. Richard pressed forward, taking his advantage and struck again, this time in the shoulder. Charon blocked the fourth strike and lashed out with his right hand, catching Richard with his claws on the side of his head. Pain and blood. He ignored them for something more important.

Claws. Charon's eyes were flushed red; his corner teeth were extended and bared. He was giving in to his beast.

The change was appallingly rapid: from one second to the next, from man to monstrosity. Then the thing launched itself at Richard. He barely got out of the way in time, and his tardiness worked in Charon's favor. As he whipped past he caught hold of the sharp end of the stave and with shocking strength, snapped off a foot long length for himself.

Richard went for him before he could turn, ramming the blunt end of the broken stave into Charon's moving legs. He was going too fast to dance clear, and down he went, but only for a heartbeat. He rolled as he hit the flags, just before Richard could plunge the stave into his chest. Wood struck rock with a hollow thud. He raised it for another try, but Charon surged up and was on him. His weight threw Richard off balance, and then they were both down and tumbling crazily over the stones, each trying to stab the other. It lasted until Charon landed a sledgehammer force blow of his fist to Richard's kidneys. The world lurched and suddenly Charon was behind him, the arm with the stake around his throat, his other clawed hand scrabbling at Richard's head, tearing hair out by the roots and carving deep bloody gashes into his scalp.

"Going to kill *me?* You fucking amateur." Charon's breath stank as he hissed the words into Richard's ear, then hauled his head back even more.

Richard rightly guessed what was coming and frantically fought to get free. His struggles were enough to throw off Charon's aim. His teeth clamped down just as Richard pulled sideways. Instead of his throat, Charon's fangs tore into and clean through Richard's ear, severing it halfway down. Richard stifled his roar of pain and blindly thrust the stave backward into Charon's face.

It hit. He felt the bones crack satisfyingly under the impact, heard the yell of outrage. More blood. The stuff from his own wounds streamed into his eyes, turning the night world red. He scrabbled clear, blinking. A jolt of pain lanced through him. The side of his head was on fire, and there was something wrong with his ankle, wrenched or something. *Why do the little things always hurt the most?*

He made out Charon's form. He was hunched over, kneeling, one hand to his face, the other still holding his part of the wooden stake. Charon's hand dropped, revealing a mask of blood; white bone jutted through what was left of his nose.

The stave—where? Discarded a few yards away. Too far. Better to take Charon's, now, while he was trying to recover, but even as he started forward Charon was suddenly on his feet and rushing him at unnatural speed.

Richard threw himself to one side just as fast, kicking his leg out—the injured one, damn—and caught Charon, neatly tripping him while clubbing him hard across the back with one arm as he passed.

The extra push of momentum sent him crashing brutally into the wall behind. Charon hit the unyielding stone with a massive thump and grunt, bounced away, and dropped.

"Yield, old man," Richard panted out. The words echoed back to him through the centuries, and despite his pains he laughed, reveling in the irony. For once he was the younger man outlasting the older champion.

He tried to stand, but could only manage a half-crouch. Charon wasn't moving, though, and in truth, did not look like he was about to in the near future. Blood pooled on the ground from his shattered nose and open mouth, and from the odd angle of his head Richard thought his neck might be broken. He wouldn't be truly dead, but the damage would force him out of things long enough for Richard to finish the job.

Weary, he limped over. Now that he had a respite, all his hurts were clamoring for immediate notice. His ear was the worst. Blood streamed freely from the burning wound, and lay cold on his skin where the air struck it. He would need time to heal before returning to the Chalice Well, and though fast, the experience would hardly be pleasant.

But first, Charon.

Richard had lived far too long and seen too much to be at all troubled in conscience about killing when and where it was required, and this particular death was certainly long overdue. He had the stomach for it, but to do so here, in this holy place . . . it hardly seemed right.

Just do it. The Goddess will understand.

He reached down for the broken stake. As he did so, Charon opened his eyes and grinned maniacally through the blood sheeting his face.

"Ain't life a bitch?"

Then Charon's near hand—still firmly clutching the yew stake like a sword—made a strong, convulsive move upward.

The pain, the utter blinding agony of impact was all enveloping. Richard felt his breast and rib bones snapping before the sharpened wood like brittle twigs, and the tissue of his body tearing apart like so much paper. His blood spurted out in a great rushing flood onto the flagstones of the floor. Charon pushed the yew stake deeper and deeper, gouging and twisting it as he did. Richard's hoarse shriek ripped across the landscape and was caught up and lost in the lonely wind.

He fell back and looked down in horror at the end of the thing jutting from his chest. The strength instantly went from his legs; his knees buckled. He choked, tasting his own blood as it filled his throat and mouth. He started to tumble forward and threw his arms out at the last second, turning to land on his side to prevent the stake from driving itself further into his body. Another scream wanted to cut its way clear, but there was no air left in him. A convulsion took him instead; it struck from the inside out, coiling down his body like an electric shock. He rolled face-up, his spine arching until only his head and heels touched the ground, until he thought he would break in two from the spasm. Then it abruptly subsided. He collapsed completely.

He tried to lift his hand, to get the *thing* out of him before—

Another seizure. A bad one.

His limbs jerked uncontrollably; he was helpless as his arms and legs hammered against the stones with bone-cracking force.

It finally released him, an infinity later, leaving him

stunned, exhausted, and unable to breathe. He desperately sucked at air, trying to force it in, then out, and could only manage short, inadequate gasps. He heard the stuff wheeze and bubble sickeningly past the stake. With each breath more precious blood trickled and pulsed from him.

And he could *not* move.

Control was gone. He was well and truly paralyzed, and *that*, not the rending pain, not the inevitability of dying, was what sent the panic rushing through him. Panic that could find no expression, that lashed him like a whip. He frantically tried to move his arms, to lift them enough to grasp the stake, to pull it out, but it was as if the threads of all his muscles were snapped clean through. He could breathe, barely, and move his eyes, and that was all.

Sabra, help me!

But his cry was silent, unheard. Only more blood came out, a thin rivulet from the corner of his sagging mouth that trickled down to stain the stones under him.

His whole being was compressed under the weight of the stake, his body leaden, utterly inert. What waning strength he had became focused on taking one short, choppy handful of air after another. He could spare concentration for nothing else. To do so was to die.

Putting off the inevitable. Charon stood over him.

His beast had retreated, and his face was starting to heal. He'd forced the skin back over the bone and it was already knitting itself up into something recognizable again. He was actually smiling, smiling down at Richard.

"What a mess. You should see yourself." He reached out and experimentally tapped the end of the stake.

Richard's body flinched. He made a gagging mewl of pain. What rhythm he'd achieved to breathe was disrupted, and he frantically struggled to reestablish it.

"Hoo, boy, this is soooo tempting," said Charon. "It's been awhile since I've had one of us like this. I'd love to stay and see how long you last, maybe play a little, but you know how it is. So much to do, so little time. Too bad for you I left my pen knife at home," he drew a finger lightly over Richard's vulnerable throat, "or I could have put you out of your misery, but them's the breaks."

He moved off a few paces, and when he came back had his discarded torch in hand.

"Well, it's been real, Lance-baby, but all good things and so on. Wish me luck, I'm off to see the wizard." He leaned close. "Word of advice—don't try fighting, it just makes the whole process worse. Just give in and let it happen." He patted Richard's shoulder. "Thus endeth the lesson. Hasta la Winnebago."

And he disappeared down the stone steps.

Richard could not move, speak, or even groan. The struggle to take in air was overwhelming; giving in and giving up seemed quite perfectly reasonable. He had to resist the temptation on an instant-to-instant basis.

But his blood still dripped away. He could hear the last throes of his pierced heart beating in his ears, weakening, fluttering like a bird's wing.

One more breath, one more minute, one more second . . .

Time enough to experience a universe of regret.

He'd failed Sabra.

Tears lay cold in the corners of his eyes. He could weep an ocean and still change nothing. And the worst was she'd never know. She'd wait and wait and hope and look for him in vain until her own beast finally consumed her.

Failed.

The ending of his life was nothing. His death was swift and sweet compared to hers.

Sweat covered him. His flesh prickled against the chill night air. More blood seeped away into the earth. His shattered heart beat all the faster, trying to work despite the terrible damage. Were he a normal man he'd have been dead in the first few seconds, but this was the price for his difference from others. His body wasn't yet ready to give up. Only he could do that in his mind, and it still wouldn't speed things.

Goddess have mercy. Release me.

But he had no right to ask anything of her. A moment's misjudgment and all was lost. His damned overconfidence had betrayed him once again. This was his punishment.

Very well, punish me, but have mercy on your servant Sabra. Don't let my failure hurt her.

No one answered. No other sound but the wind, which was on the rise. How it moaned and howled between the stones. Howled like . . .

The Hounds of Annwyn.

They were coming for him.

In between gasps he fancied them running toward him, their clawed feet slapping swiftly against the grass and stones. But no, that was his heart shuddering away, palpitating fit to burst. In a last effort to pump the dregs of his blood, it beat faster and still faster, or so it seemed for a few awful moments, until he realized that it was another heartbeat he heard. It was far from him and out of sync, but coming closer, closer. Its rhythm gradually blending and finally merged with his own, became one with his.

Light. He blinked. It was strong, like the dawning sun, but it came from the north, not east. An utterly beautiful silver light, coming toward him, coming for him. He wanted to rush up to meet it, it was so lovely, but could not quite escape the restraints of his flesh.

His breathing faltered.

Not long now. If it meant he could go into that light . . .

"Richard."

His heart continued to beat, as if supported by the other, stronger one. But he wanted it to stop so he could—

"Richard!"

What? Who?

"Stay with me, my love."

No mistake. He heard Sabra's voice, his lady's voice, ringing clear in his ears, coming from the light which was very close to him now. It was like looking into a moonlit stream, the water ever shifting, moving too fast for the eye to fix upon. Then its motion began to slow, coalesce, take on form. The beginnings of a face, the shape of an arm, a reaching hand.

Sabra? He was beyond speech and his thought was hardly more than a whisper.

"Yes, my Richard."

And she was suddenly there, standing above him, as serene and glorious, as noble as she'd been on that day of his first defeat. As he had then he forgot his own wretchedness in the presence of something greater than himself. He tried to speak, but a cough came out instead, spewing more blood over the earth. Sabra only smiled her angel's smile and put one finger to her lips to still his efforts.

"I can hear you. I've always heard you."

I failed you, my lady. I'm sorry.

"Not you. Never."

I love you.

"And I you, my Richard." Her gaze dropped to the stake and still she gently smiled. "Is it a bad hurt?"

The centuries shifted. He was standing in her tent again by the west wall of his father's castle, for so she had spoken to him then about his wounded hand. He remembered his reply.

Indeed it is.

She caressed him along his face. He felt and yet could not feel it, for this time her hand was made of moonlight, not flesh.

All his hurts, great and small, melted away from her shimmering fingers. He wanted to sigh out his relief, but it was too much for him. His next breath would not come, nor did he try to take it. It was time to let go and leave with his lady.

"Not yet. Stay a little longer," she told him, her tone urgent. Her hand closed hard around the source of all his torment. As easily as if it had been a feather, she plucked the stake from his chest and sent it spinning through the night air.

But not even her sweet touch could block out that kind of pain.

He hissed in reaction, felt and heard the air rush down his windpipe and out his chest with a spray of crimson drops. Sabra's hands were on his gaping wound now as if to hold the blood into him, but it was too late for that.

He closed his eyes. Couldn't help but close them. It was all too much to bear.

Too . . .

Much . . .

And Richard slept.

Chapter Ten

The absence of sound brought him back to awareness; the absence of pain persuaded him to remain there.

Just for a little while.

He had the strong feeling he was supposed to be very much elsewhere. The exact where and why would come to him shortly, he was sure. For the moment he wanted only to collect himself, and when he was ready he would move on to . . . someplace.

His present location was the cause of a certain mild confusion for him as he was viewing the surrounding lands from a considerable height.

I must be atop the tower.

But the ruin of St. Michael's was gone. No trace of it remained except for a few slabs of stone in the same spot. As for the rest, there was only a vast dark landscape far below him. He tried to work out how he could be so high above ground without benefit of support. It was strange, but not especially frightening. He had no sense of danger, no feeling of falling. He seemed to simply float on . . . what?

No matter.

He accepted the peculiar situation. He was safe and free from pain, far removed from the turmoil that had delivered him to this odd sanctuary. He did try looking about, but saw only the bulk of the Tor and the gleam of the fading moon on the shallow marsh waters around its base.

That's not right.

His recent memory of the place was that of the nearby town with its streetlights, paved roads, and scatter of houses. Now he saw only wandering tracks and thin paths leading far away into the immense country darkness. The only light remaining was a wan silvery glow by the stones on the peak of the Tor. A thin, near-invisible thread of it extended up toward him, puzzling him until he understood it was actually connected to him in some manner. Its anchor point he couldn't quite determine, though it was somewhere in his midsection. The thread moved with him, seemed to keep him from drifting, yet it flexed, stretching if he went farther away.

He wanted to go lower to find the other anchor point and was gratified when he could do just that merely by thinking about it. The thread did not slacken, but grew marginally thicker the nearer he came to its source. He was a little surprised to see its origin attached to a solitary man lying sprawled on the virgin grass. His forlorn body was quite broken. A savage hole pierced his chest, one ear was torn away, and he was drenched with blood from those and other terrible injuries. His blue eyes were wide open, but fixed and unblinking. He looked dead.

It's me, Richard thought, without the least flicker of alarm. In this silent place he was beyond such mundane worries. He observed the pathetic remains with only detached curiosity and an unwillingness to go any closer. There was no obvious need to do so, and his inner instinct told him it would only bring a return of pain. He'd had quite enough of that.

With some of the mystery explained he vaguely wondered if others were present. He saw no one, high or low, though he did become conscious of a bright light somewhere behind him. Each time he turned to face it, it seemed to turn along with him. He glimpsed only its edges, but never the center. Frustrating, that. And, again, strange, for the light cast no shadow below him, nor did it really illuminate anything there. Perhaps if he rose higher he could finally turn and go toward it.

Then he saw movement below.

Not from the mangled body, but from the flanks of the Tor. Lights, fainter than the glow of the smallest candle were coming up the ancient maze path. They hugged the earth, yet moved smoothly as though skimming over it. He remembered walking that path himself, recently and in times long past. Very long past, before they built the tower. Sabra had led him . . .

Pain. Emotional pain lanced through him. He was not immune to that here. He wanted to leave. The closer he stayed to his body, the stronger became the feeling of . . . of . . . loss. That he'd left something very vital unfinished.

I failed you, my lady.

Though not fully understanding why, he wanted to weep from the hollow grief of it but found he could not, and that made him all the sadder. He didn't want to feel this way any longer. Better he leave now and let matters of the earth take care of themselves without him.

But the little lights were growing as he watched. They held his interest, distracted him from his burst of sorrow.

They were nearly to the top and had taken on definition and form if not distinct features. Women, nine of them, nine ghosts in long white robes that covered their flesh, yet revealed their lithe shapes as they walked. Their serene faces shone the purest white he'd ever seen.

The Nine Sisters of Avalon. Cerridwen's priestesses.

They formed a circle around his body, facing outward. Each held a sword in one hand and a cup in the other. He recalled other ceremonies done here, but could not place this one. They walked in an earthwise circle around him, neither fast nor slow. Their bare feet hardly seemed to touch the ground.

Their lips moved, either in a chant or a song; he could not hear, not at first. If time passed in this reality, then it was some few minutes before he began to pick up the faintest of sounds. He thought it was the wind starting to rise until he looked around and saw *them* floating like clouds against the moon.

Hounds. The Hounds of Annwyn.

Panting and snarling, their massive bodies danced effortlessly on the moonlight as they milled impatiently about one another. Some paused to look at him, but nothing more. He had no fear of them now; in fact, he thought of them as friends who would guide him to wherever it was he was supposed to be. He turned and started toward them.

A thin, piercing cry from below stayed his movement. One of the sisters broke away from the circle and threw herself onto his mangled body. She obscured his view of the connecting thread, but as she did some of her own glow merged and rushed up it. He felt something tugging strongly, insistently at him. It was the first real physical reaction he'd had in this place.

She looked up—right up at him as though she alone of the nine could see him—and formed his name with her lips. He thought he could almost hear her. She stretched her arms toward him, beckoning, begging him to come closer.

He temporized, glancing at the waiting Hounds.

I should go with them.

But the woman below called to him again, and this time he heard her voice.

Sabra?

Now did he tardily recognize her. How had she come here? He'd left her in a land very far away, setting out to do something very important for her.

And failed. His failure costing them both their lives.

His inner pain returned. *No, I don't want this.*

But memory began to return as well, and with it, growing understanding. Memory of his fight with Charon, his wounding, and ultimately his shameful failure washed swiftly over his mind. But despite that failure Sabra had still come to him as if in a dream, appearing in a dying man's vision to comfort him at the last.

"You are my champion, Richard d'Orleans, and I will not let you die!" she shouted up at him.

But he was not dead, only the shell that once held him was gone beyond recovery. No matter what she wanted, it was ended. How could he make her accept it? He pointed at the Hounds, not knowing if she could see them.

"It is not your time, Richard!" she insisted, her voice shrill with desperation.

Never in all their years together had he ever purposefully tried to hurt her, but now he had no choice. The Hounds had come for him, and they would not be denied.

"Not. Your. Time!"

A trepidatious look at the Hounds. They couldn't, wouldn't let him return, but this was *Sabra* calling, pleading with him, and he could not deny her, either. He had to try even if the Hounds tore his essence in this reality to shreds.

He began to descend along the silver thread, it becoming shorter the lower he got, thickening to a string, then a cord, then a fat twist of rope. The closer he got the more horrific his own discarded body became to him. He didn't want to touch its base clay.

The Hounds began howling their hunter's song, their voices wild. He paused.

"All will be well," Sabra promised him. "Just come!"

But he did not see how that could be possible.

Then the Hounds broke off their howling—

"Hurry!" she screamed.

—and flew toward him like a storm.

"Now, Richard!"

He heard their growls, the click of their snapping teeth; he dove desperately toward the cooling lump of flesh below.

Dizziness as he spun into the thing.

Blackness for an instant, then shrieking cold.

But his first breath was fire.

His next almost would not come as the pain of life overtook him.

He could dimly see Sabra above him now, her sword at the ready, her sisters also. As the Hounds approached the women lashed out with their blades to hold them at bay. Richard wanted to rise and help them, but his body was unable to move. Once more he had to lie helpless and waiting for death to deliver him away from the travail of living.

"Not yet, my Richard." Sabra knelt by him, putting down the cup she carried. She held her hand over it, then quickly ran the edge of the sword over her inner wrist. Her blood, pale as her glowing face, dripped into the cup until it was full to the brim. She raised it high, a salute to her goddess, then slipped an arm around his shoulders, lifting him that he might drink.

Her blood was earth and honey, birdsong and

firelight, mountain flowers and winter dusk. He'd never tasted its like before. How it rushed through him, filled him, sustained him.

But there wasn't enough. As soon as it was gone, his head lolled to one side. He hadn't the strength to even look at her one last time.

"Not yet," she whispered.

One of her sisters broke off fighting and backed toward them, turning at the last second and kneeling. She, too, cut her wrist and let her blood fill the cup she carried. She put its edge to his lips and he drank.

More life. Such a tiny portion of it, though. Not nearly enough.

But another sister came as the first rose up to return to her place, and she also gave of her blood to Richard. Then another and another, turn on turn. He lost count, concentrating on the slow, the so very slow return of life to his battered form. Life and healing. His breathing ceased to be so labored, the hurts great and small began to ease, until they ceased altogether. He heard the sounds of the earth once more, the whisper of the wind rather than the baffled snarling of the Hounds.

The women expanded their circle around him. As Sabra protectively held him close, he watched as her sisters gradually herded and finally surrounded the Hounds. The beasts had become smaller, as if their power were being taken from them. In turn, the light around the sisters grew stronger, brighter for their efforts.

Richard saw there was an opening in the face of the Tor, a hole with sharply cut steps leading down, and the women urged the Hounds toward it. With a last grumbling bark, they scuttled inside.

He looked again at Sabra. He'd never seen her so beautiful, like an angel she was, but infinitely greater.

Now could he reach up and touch her. His fingers, silhouetted black against her white skin, brushed upon her cheek. She smiled down at him, brown eyes clear and alight and loving. She said nothing, but simply bent and kissed him, her lips soft and tasting of the stars. She lay him back flat upon the turf and caressed her hands over his eyes, forcing him to shut them.

When he opened them again she was gone. Only the tingling aftermath of her touch remained.

He sat up cautiously.

The Tor was as it had been when he'd fallen asleep: St. Michael's Tower very solidly back in place along with the unforgiving stones under him. The only changes now were in himself.

Though still covered in drying blood, his chest wound was quite vanished, the skin firmly knitted up and restored, the broken bones beneath sound and solid. His ear was whole, and all his other hurts were healed as well. He felt curiously heavy, though. So odd it was to have a body again. He'd rather liked floating about.

Of course, breathing without agony was nice, too.

How had Sabra managed it? Or was that a foolish question? Probably so. Here he was in the seat of her power, her goddess's stronghold, strange it would be if she could not do something to help him in this of all places. How she had reached halfway around the planet to touch him he did not know, nor, he supposed, did it matter much, so long as he had been touched. Few of the mysteries of Avalon had ever been revealed to him; if this was part of it, then so let it be. Sabra and her sisters were more than welcome to their secrets.

He stood and carefully checked himself over, stretching a bit. Everything seemed to be working to specs, so to speak, but instinct told him he shouldn't push himself. He was back together again, but low on reserves. Best to get started and get on with it while he was able. Sabra had gifted him with a second chance; he would not receive another.

He found the yew stake some yards from where he'd lain and gingerly picked it up. Coated with his blood, of course, but in the middle he saw the clear outline of her handprint where she'd grasped it. Somehow that made it easier for him to hold the damned thing.

Richard went back to the opening where the Hounds had gone. The steps, no longer sharp and newly cut, were worn again and slippery from the damp. Taking his time, he slowly descended, feeling his way until the entry was well over his head. He listened hard. To him there was no other silence quite like that of the deep earth, and it was very thick here, much thicker than the darkness. For that, at least, he had a small remedy. His torch was still tucked away in his jacket pocket. He drew it out and switched it on.

No sign of the Hounds. Something of a relief, that.

Though he'd never been here before, it was very much as he expected: a naturally formed cave, not large, not small, stalactites and stalagmites vying to meet each other in the middle and some having succeeded. The surrounding countryside was riddled with similar places, many of them sacred spots and many others nothing in particular. The only sign of human intrusion in this one were the stairs, which now took a turning to the right, and appeared to spiral down into the heart of the Tor. He stepped around the fragments of the flagstone that had fallen in earlier and followed them. In the dust coating the steps was the imprint of Charon's footsteps.

This shouldn't be too terribly hard.

He hoped.

It was more than dark here. It was absolutely black, as solid as lead and just as dense to his seeking soul. The blackness seemed to eat up the faint sky glow coming from the opening and gave nothing back, and did much the same for his torch light. He felt very out of place here, the back of his neck prickling in anticipation of some alien touch. His feeble twentieth-century illumination would not have much effect upon or last long against this sort of power. He hoped the Goddess wouldn't mind his invasion; he thought it likely else he'd not be here now. It seemed certain she'd rather have him than Charon barging about in her holy of holies.

At least I'm not a thief, he thought virtuously as he made his way down. Every few turnings he paused to cut his light and listen, hearing no other sounds but those he made himself, which could be both good and bad. What if Charon had already left? It hardly seemed possible, for not that much time had passed according to both Richard's watch and the position of the moon, but he was well into a worrying mood by now. This cave was a decided inspiration for galloping anxiety.

Natural formations gave way to artificial tunneling, very old and somehow more unsettling to his imagination. How many years, how many lifetimes had gone into the making of this place? He could almost sense the presence of the ancient people who had determinedly executed the work using only the meager light of small oil lamps and the most basic of tools. Blistered hands and aching backs, constant dust, sweat, and certainly blood, generations of it, all for the glory of their deity. Their only reward on this side of the veil was whatever fulfillment came from serving that deity in such a manner. Richard felt quite humbled by it all.

The stone walls narrowed, pressing close on either side, clearly showing the marks of carving. Several times he saw where an enterprising cutter had left behind an intricate knotwork motif in the rock. He recognized the patterns from long past, having seen Sabra's careful copies of them in her book. From the ones on the wall, if from nothing else that had happened, Charon would know he'd come to the right spot.

As best he could, Richard increased his pace, though he risked losing the element of surprise. Charon's hearing was every bit as good as his own. But one important particular was in Richard's favor: he was absolutely, positively the *last* person Charon would expect to see down here.

Twice the spiraling tunnel widened to natural caves leading along to deeper chambers within the Tor. Part of him wanted to explore, while another part wanted only to leave as quickly as possible. If he didn't find Charon fairly soon, he'd give serious thought to making a fast exit and simply wait for the bastard to emerge again above. Somewhere down here the Hounds slept and only the Goddess knew what else hovered in the dark just out of the reach of his torch beam.

You're getting a fine case of the creeps, old lad, he chided himself. But being aware of his weakness didn't make it any easier to endure. That, and the knowledge the Hounds were entirely real. What terrible creatures they were. He remembered their eyes the most vividly, the ghastly way they flashed green sparks while reflecting the moonlight.

And Richard gave himself quite a start when his torch plucked out a similar flash of green at the next turn of the passage. His recently pierced heart frantically leapt halfway up his throat, settling only when tardy reason told him the flash did *not*, after all, belong to a supernatural hound, but to something rather more prosaic.

Sabra's book. One of the gems embedded in its leather cover had caught the light just right and glinted through the plastic bag. Richard stopped cold in his tracks and listened.

No sound came to him, and he was sure that if Charon was nearby he'd be able to hear him breathing. Hell, in this silent place he could hear the blink of a flea's eyelid.

Had Charon left the book behind as bait for some sort of trap? But why should he bother if he thought Richard to be dying or dead? Then Richard saw a freshly broken away portion from the next step down and scuff marks in the dust. So the stone had cracked underfoot, Charon had slipped or staggered, and the book had fallen unnoticed from his pocket.

Not good. Might he miss it soon and retrace his path to find it again? He could have already started to do so and be waiting just out of sight and sound at the next turning. Richard zipped the book safely away in his own jacket pocket and debated on the wisdom of switching off his light and making the rest of the way by touch. His blunderings would be noisy though, and alert Charon to his presence just as well as the torch glow, and if there should be other broken steps ahead . . .

Scowling, Richard kept the light on and moved forward. He wryly thought how convenient it would be if he could turn into a bat and thus navigate in total darkness and stealth like his literary cousins. Those buggers had all the advantages.

Sound.

So very faint, but constant. After a moment he

identified it as the gurgle and rush of water. He knew
two streams ran under the Tor, the White and the
Red. The Red, rich with the iron that gave it color,
eventually ran to the Chalice Well . . . and to Sharon
Geary—if she was still there. He hoped so, for her
sake.

Very slowly, Richard continued, covering his light
with his fingers until he had barely enough to see
by. He thought he was very close to the base of the
Tor by now, if not below it, his conclusion coming
from intuition rather than logic because of the
invisible thrum of power surrounding him. The
presence of the Goddess? Or something else?

The Grail?

The air, which should have been quite still, to him
fairly quivered with *some* form of energy. He wished
Sabra could be with him for this. She'd know what
it was and what to do if anything needed to be done.
Again, he wanted to simply leave. He was superfluous
here. The place itself didn't welcome his intrusion,
he was quite certain. Well, if so, then such went
double for the likes of Charon. How was he faring?
Was he aware of what was around him, or being
purposely obtuse as before?

Another few steps. The water sound grew proportionately. Heart beating faster and faster, he sensed
a large chamber looming ahead.

Light. And not from Richard's torch. He shut the
thing off completely and let his eyes adjust to the
change.

There. The faintest glimmer bouncing off the curve
of the wall. One more turning and it was stronger
still, as was the sound of water. The latter was easily
loud enough to cover any noise Richard made as he
moved.

The passage ran straight now, became slightly wider,

and the dank tang in the cool air more pronounced. The ceiling also came down much lower, forcing him into a half-crouch. The walls shone from the damp until cut stone gave way to a sizable section of earth shored up by timbers. He didn't like that. The wood had to be utterly ancient by now. He carefully touched a supporting beam. Damnation, but it was as soft as a sponge. The only thing holding up the whole weight of the Tor at this point was force of habit. He passed under it with much caution, scrupulously avoiding all contact with the walls.

An archway, made of stone, thank goodness. The passage suddenly opened into an unexpectedly huge natural cave. He picked out brilliant colors hidden for eons, released for the time being by the harsh light of another torch. It lay on its side, the beam reflecting a thousand subtle shades, mineral rainbows frozen forever in the rock. They fairly danced about the chamber, dazzling him. He thought about Merlin's crystal cave and wondered if this was it or a close relation.

The light also played brightly off the shifting patterns of a cascade of water emerging from the chamber's far wall. From its red tint he knew it to be the Chalice stream. It poured out of a substantial crevice, splashed down about three feet to hurry along another twenty or so before vanishing again into a second opening on its underground journey. He was surprised at the strength and swiftness of the flow. It was nearly two yards across. He wondered if that was natural or had also been carved out by ancient worshipers.

No matter.

He'd found his quarry.

Unlike Richard, Charon hadn't had the benefit of a miraculous healing, so he still looked much the worse for wear from their fight. Clothes torn and covered with muck and blood, his movements were slow, but determined. Half turned away from the entry, he knelt by the foot of the falls, staring intently at the roiling water, wearing a grimace of distaste mixed with naked fear.

As before, Richard opted to quietly watch and wait and let someone else do the hard work for the present. He tucked his torch away and brought the yew stake around to an up-and-ready position, and felt a cold, hard smile creeping over his own features. He was very much looking forward to payback time.

Charon braced one hand on the stream bank for balance; after taking a deep breath, he thrust his other arm into the running water.

That's going to hurt.

Indeed. Charon held back his reaction for several long moments, then could take it no longer. He yanked his arm clear and screamed, the noise shockingly loud in the confined space. It struck the earthen walls with enough force to make them quiver, and Richard fancied he heard the echoes traveling right up the spiral stairs behind him.

Charon's initial vocal expression gave way to unrestrained cursing before he finally wound down. He rubbed and shook his injured arm, hissing and flexing his fingers. It would have felt cold, unbearably cold, Richard knew, for he was quite familiar with their shared vulnerability to free-flowing water. That was one point the legends had gotten right about their kind. When Charon recovered, he glared at the stream a bit longer, then scowled and tried again.

It took less time for him to break. Screaming, he fell back, but now there was something large and square in his hand that clanged when it fell heavily to the cave floor.

Richard couldn't make it out at first for all the flurry of movement and distracting noise. Then his impressions sorted themselves, and he saw the thing was some kind of metal cage about a foot square with a heavy chain attached leading back into the stream. The cage bars were thick strips of metal riveted together like a lattice. From the design and workmanship he could tell it was old even by his standards.

Charon was going through the same motions as before about his injured arm, but it didn't last. He quickly came upright and with his left hand began tearing and scrabbling at some object on the cage. A simple latch it proved to be, for as soon as he worked it loose he was prying back the thing's lid. The stiffened hinges gave a brief, metallic squawk and the cage was open.

He stopped, grabbed up his torch, and shone the light inside.

A long stare, then his unrestrained whoop, laughter, and triumphant grin gave Richard all the answer he needed concerning the nature of the contents.

Charon reached in and pulled it out. It was not very big, being all but engulfed in his grip. There was a glint of metal, gold or brass in color, between his fingers.

The thrum Richard picked up from his better attuned senses increased in intensity and then suddenly ceased. He watched Charon, but the man seemed utterly unaware of it.

Bloody Philistine. The damned interloper was positively gloating over his treasure. Not for long. It was payback time; however, Richard wouldn't leave the body here to defile this holy spot; he was more than willing to drag it every inch of the way up the stairs and get rid of it someplace else.

Pushing the cage out of the way, Charon, still on his knees, went over to the stream and dipped his hand into the water. He lifted his arm high, revealing the Grail as he balanced it on his fingertips, admiring it. He brought it down, brought it down to his lips to drink.

But Richard was already moving, silent, swift.

The idea of Charon merely touching the Grail was more than enough to set him off—but to *drink* from it—

He was at full speed when he slammed into Charon's very solid body.

Their collision made a quite satisfying *thump*. Also a thud, grunt, and other sounds of pain and effort as they tumbled over and over the cavern floor. Richard knew he wasn't precisely in control of himself, but not doing too badly as he pummeled with one hand and stabbed with the stake in the other in those first few decisive seconds. Charon got the worst of it; his moves were for defense, not attack, and hampered by his own complete surprise. Richard was dimly conscious of someone cursing, but not sure if it was himself or Charon.

Then he was violently pushed away. He curled and rolled, tucking his chin down and came up on his feet like a cat. Charon was doing much the same, though not as fast. For the second time that night he gaped at Richard.

"How in hell—?" he gasped.

"Not hell," Richard assured him.

Charon pointed at Richard's healed chest. "You son of a bitch, you had help."

"Oh, yes, I've friends in high places."

"Who?"

He pointed straight up, grinning. "*Very* high places."

"No way." But there was that same mix of disbelief and near hope on Charon's features as before. Perhaps he wanted to buy into it, but was afraid to try, afraid of the consequences to himself. "No fucking way."

The Hounds will feast tonight after all. "As you wish." Richard rushed him again. Full speed.

Charon's panicked dodge was barely adequate. As it was he caught the glancing blow of Richard's passage in the back and went flying as though struck by a train. His body slammed against the opposite wall and dropped, but he still had some strength left in him. He was up and scrambling toward the entry and the stairs. Richard intercepted him, throwing one arm around his neck and lifting him back. His free hand, gripping the stake, came firmly down, connecting hard with flesh and bone. Charon bucked and screamed in reaction—and continued to do so. Richard knew he'd missed his heart.

He felt the impact of an elbow dig into his belly, caught the smell of fresh blood and stale sweat tainting the air, and heard another outraged scream as Charon ripped the stake from his chest. Bleeding, he staggered, fell against the wall, but kept going, still trying to reach the stairs. When Richard caught up to him, Charon whirled, striking out blindly with the point of the stake while backing away. He made it to the arch, ducking low.

Richard darted forward into the dimness. Something struck his arm; he noted the blow and ignored it, reaching. He grasped sodden cloth, a sleeve, perhaps. It ripped free. He clawed and got an arm this time, but a bruising fist came out of nowhere and sent him reeling.

The wall, damp and soft, gave under the impact as he hit it, as if it were made of living flesh. He felt rather than heard something around him shifting mightily.

Oh, shit!

He threw himself out of the way as a torrent of mud, earth, and rotted wood collapsed into the space he'd been an instant ago. More rolling as he desperately tried to get clear. Darkness, then light. Instinct drove him toward the light, scrambling on hands and knees. The force of the sound of the fall itself seemed to physically push him forward—that, and pure terror.

Dust, rocks, the stench of old decay overtook him, choked him. The universe shook and moaned. The sound was really too loud to hear, but how he *felt* it thundering over every inch of his body. He pressed his face into his crossed arms and braced for the rest of the collapsing cosmos to pulverize him.

Which, after many strained heartbeats, he slowly realized was not going to happen. Not just yet, anyway.

When he dared open his eyes, he saw through a cloud of settling dust that the earthen section beyond the entry had thoroughly fallen in. A giant, with his giant's shovel, had dropped what looked to be several lorry loads of rock and dirt into the opening. It was blocked right up to the top of the stone arch, and fanned out over a wide area of the cavern floor and even into the stream. Richard lay on the edge of it.

For a moment all he could do was stare, making no attempt to take it in, to think it out. There was no need, really. All the ghastly factors galloped through his stunned mind in the first instant.

He was well and truly a dead man, now.

Still breathing, still aware, but dead nonetheless.

Buried alive.

Gradually, the first cycle of alarm and horror gave way to a small degree of calm and reason, neither having one whit of favorable influence on the overall situation.

Appalling, he decided. It was all quite terribly appalling.

Cautiously, as though his least move would bring the rest of the ceiling down, he cast about and picked up Charon's torch. The batteries were still strong, but would give out long before he was—

Let's not think about that just yet, old lad. His hands were shaking and not like to stop anytime soon. Best to keep busy then.

He brushed dirt from his hair, checked himself for damage. There was blood, not his own for a change, though he was bashed around a bit. Nothing that wouldn't mend itself.

Next he looked for the cup that had been knocked from Charon's hands. That's what the whole fuss was about, wasn't it? Find the Holy Grail and save Sabra, save himself, save—

Shutup.

The place was littered with rubble and polluting dust. The glorious colors in the rocks were muted or obscured completely. Gone was the magic, gone like so many other things, forever. Soon he would be gone as well.

Had to face that. No way to escape the fact—in more ways than one.

Yes, he had air, water—for all the good it would do him—but nothing that could be remotely considered food. He had no hunger now, but over the course of the next few days it would awaken and impatiently start making demands that could not be met. And then what? His beast finally emerging, ravenous, needy, with naught to feed upon except that which he carried in his veins. Would he then mindlessly rip into his own flesh, or be too weak to try?

Damn that bastard to hell, to worse than hell. Damn him to this kind of death, to this kind of . . .

Richard stopped and had to force himself not to think about anything until he got his breathing and racing fears under control. He closed his eyes tight, but only for a few seconds. The world was too dark that way, and before long he'd have more dark on top of it, the kind that wouldn't be dispelled with the blink of an eyelid.

Yes, I'm scared. I'm scared shitless, but that won't help me.

Help of a kind—to his spirit at least—came when he saw the cup lying near the stream bank. It had nearly fallen in.

On his knees, he inched toward it as quietly as he could, almost afraid it would take fright and skitter from his reach like a bird. He was being foolish, he knew, but given the circumstances he allowed himself the indulgence. He needed it.

He got quite close, playing the light over the little shining prize, and froze, staring in abrupt wonder.

Despite the dust and a smear of mud, it was utterly beautiful. Beautiful beyond petty fears for his own ephemeral hide, for compared to this he was no more than a candle burning itself away to nothing. This thing, this extraordinary treasure, had been around longer than memory and would continue to be long after memory itself was gone.

It wasn't a cup so much as deep bowl, like a sphere cut in half with a flattened base so it would not roll when set down. Not large, no more than five or six inches across and made of brass rather than gold. A wise choice by the ancient crafter who had shaped it. Gold was too easily coveted, melted down, and made into something else. Brass was much better, though it would corrode away with age.

Except there was no sign of it on this precious piece. It looked new, shimmering through the grime as though it had just gotten a final polish from skilled fingers. Magic again? Some supernatural gift to preserve it? No doubt.

With a humble mental apology to the Goddess, he gently picked it up and brushed it clean. It was unexpectedly heavy. Inside, the finish was even brighter, smoother, though at the bottom he saw evidence of what looked to be a very old staining, like undrunk wine left to dry in a glass.

Or blood?

He shivered at the thought of his own Savior's connection to the relic, and for the first time in more than century, reverently crossed himself in the old way, the way he'd been taught in his youth.

So long ago. So terribly long . . .

He felt tears sting his eyes and swiped at them with the back of his trembling hand.

Around the upper edge of the cup was a band of knotwork, fluid, intricate, in an unending circle of truly amazing artistry. Just beneath, a row of rounded nubs stood out from the surface, five in a line, then a cluster of three forming a triangle, then five again, three, five three. Sacred numbers. The three groups of three he could guess to stand for the nine sisters of Avalon. The rest he wasn't sure about, but Sabra would—

Well, actually Sabra wouldn't. Not unless he could dig his way clear sometime in the next week or before he starved to death. Sharon would miss him right away, though it was a thin hope. Perhaps she'd find the entrance hole at the top of the Tor, guess what had happened, and send a rescue party down to find him.

Unless Charon discovered her first.

If he got out himself.

Richard found himself grinning at the utterly delightful idea of Charon trapped and smothering under a few tons of mud. It cheered him greatly. A good end for a bad soul. How dare he have deigned to touch—

"Hey! Lancelot? You still kicking?"

Hell, damnation and all the fiery stops in between.

Charon's voice was very muffled, though he must have been shouting at the top of his lungs to be heard through the barrier between them.

"Hello! Earth to Lancelot, come in, come in, over and under!"

The great twit risked bringing down more of the roof with all that row.

"'Allo-'allo!"

Though his legs were barely up to it, Richard stood, getting well away from the arch, and yelled back, "I'm here, now shut the hell up!"

A pause, then: "Well, well, you can't beat that with a stick. You all right?"

"Why should you care?"

"Good point, Elwood. I should have asked is the Grail all right. Is it?"

Richard's heart leaped. *This could be my ticket out.* "Yes, it's fine. I have it in my hand now."

"Whoa, that's just peachy. I'm *so* glad to hear it. Now what I want is for you to hang onto it like a good little guardian until I can come back and dig you out."

"Uh-huh. What's the catch?"

"You wound me, Lance-baby. Twice now, as a matter of counting. But I'm feeling better by the minute. I'm down a quart but should be able to top things off before sun-up, which is more than what you can say."

Too true.

"Yeah, you may have the magic whatsis, but I have an exit sign. I wouldn't advise you to try digging free from that side, you'll just make it worse."

"You can't know that, you've no light."

"I got ears, and it don't sound good. Mommy Nature is royally pissed about this one and no mistake. I'm going to boogie in a minute, but I'll be back, don't you worry."

"And the catch?"

Laughter, faint and unpleasant. "Weeeeell, I've got a *really* busy schedule lined up. There's an important job I have to do in a couple days, and you know how I love my work. I'm gonna have fun with it, too. I'm gonna do something special and dedicate this one to you, good buddy."

"What do you mean?"

"I always cover my tracks, but I think I'll leave a few for that asshole Demarest to find. Before I'm done messing with their heads, the Kennedy Conspiracy's going to look like amateur's night. The cool part is that all the pointers are going to lead straight to you. I'm in the clear, and you're branded suspect number one—Charon—who has conveniently disappeared. I can't thank you enough."

Richard licked his lips. They tasted of the earth. "The Grail, Charon. You need it. You'll die without it."

"You'll go before I do. You know, that's one thing I never researched—how long one of our kind can last without feeding before we go nuts or croak. Your contribution to science will not be forgotten, my son. The way things are, I can afford to wait. I'll come back in a month—make it two months, I can last that long—with proper equipment, do a little excavation and find out then if there's enough left of you to autopsy. Oh, and I'll look after the magic dingus real good, no fear of that."

"I'll destroy it first."

Silence. Then, "No you won't."

Dear God and sweet Goddess, but the son of a bitch was right.

"Vista la hasta, O Great Guardian of the Coconut. I'll see you in the bye and bye, so bye-bye!"

"Charon!"

But no answer came. The bastard was probably feeling his unsteady way up the long spiral stair. A nasty trip in total darkness—and Richard would have given absolutely anything to be on it.

Anything but the Grail. And Charon would have that eventually.

Richard thought of hiding it somewhere, of burying it in the cave-in debris, but knew the attempt to be futile in the end. Charon would bring metal detectors and who knows what else on his next trip in anticipation of just such a ploy.

Throw it into the Chalice Stream? He'd think of that, too, and would have divers along to recover it for him.

The stream . . .

That eventually led to the Chalice Well.

Richard's heart began to pound rather too heavily and hard at the awful idea that came to him. He had to sit down and did so right in his tracks as the physical reaction seized him and his legs gave way. He clutched the Grail to his breast, hands shaking more than ever, his whole body shaking at the prospect.

It'll kill me.

But he'd die here anyway.

It was a diabolic choice: a slow, painful death or fast, painful death. Pick one, no returns, no refunds. Starvation and madness or . . . .

He looked up, half-laughed.

Oh, Goddess, why me?

To which the old response of "why not you?" popped into his mind.

He laughed again, forcing himself to stop when it began to turn into sobbing.

It took him ten minutes to work up to the task. Not too terribly long, considering.

During that time he let his mind wander over many different paths, nearly all of them leading to Sabra. A few went to other aspects of his life, the things he'd done, the people he'd known. He thought wistfully of She-Who-Walks, the lover and daughter in blood that he barely knew, of Sharon Geary, a woman he wanted to know better but would not now have the chance. If she survived this night, she'd never find out what really happened to him. Any rescue party would discover the cave-in and be met with silence to their shouted questions about his well-being, for he would be gone.

Toward the end he gave himself over to a bout of prayer, one to the deity to which he was born, another to the one he worked for, asking both for the blessing of success to his endeavor and the strength to accomplish it, but nothing more for the preservation of his soul. He was content to leave such judgments in wiser hands. Having glimpsed the light on the other side of the veil he had no real fear of death, only in his manner of conveyance to that state, and this one promised to be a very bad journey, indeed.

Once more he crossed himself in the old way, stood, and paced the few steps over to the edge of the Chalice Stream. He held the Grail close in one hand. It seemed lighter, now.

He left Charon's torch on the cavern floor and took

out his smaller model. Into the same pocket he slipped
the Grail, firmly zipping it in. Then he began breathing
deeply, striving to flood his body tissues with oxygen.
He stretched this way and that to make sure everything
was warmed up and working. He was no skilled
swimmer, not since he'd met Sabra, but physically
strong, and that's what would count most here.

When he was ready, he took the deepest breath he
could manage and stepped off the edge, dropping into
the racing stream.

The sheer agonizing shock of it drove the air right
out of him again in a potent scream.

He staggered and writhed, from both the burning
force of the water and his every instinct shrieking
for him to get out, get out, getoutgetout*getout!*

Panting, he fought it off until the initial trauma
passed.

Yes, I can live with this, I have to.

But not for very damned long.

The water was just up to his chest and threatening
to throw him off his feet to drag him downstream.
It was what he wanted, but it had to be controlled.

He got his breath back again, took another, this
time to hold, and dove headfirst into the swift flow.

God, but it was cold. Worse than icy, worse than
anything he'd ever experienced in all his life. It was
like swimming in freezing acid. He wanted to scream
again, but that was an unaffordable luxury. He needed
to hang onto what air he had for as long as he could.

Beneath the flow, the water was absolutely clear.
The torch beam briefly revealed the rust-colored sides
and bottom of the stream. He saw smooth rock and
ahead glimpsed a black opening, like a huge greedy
mouth. The current pushed him toward it at a
frantically fast pace.

Then the beam went out. Blackness closed over

him. The mouth engulfed him completely and on he rushed, blind.

He dropped the torch and spent all of his limited energy and concentration trying to keep from being smashed against the endless walls of the tunnel. And all the while it felt like his skin was being unendingly peeled away, layer by layer in the frigid water.

His questing hands unexpectedly broke the surface once, and he rose hastily, cracking his head on low rock. The air in this little pocket of heaven wasn't that good, but sufficient to use. He gasped and wheezed for a moment, recovering until the pain of the water became too much, took in another breath, then hurriedly moved on.

Unrelieved blackness met his wide open eyes the whole time, a minor thing compared to the fire crawling over every inch of his being.

How far had he come? A hundred feet? Two hundred? Or less? Not nearly enough. He must achieve as much distance as possible. His body and the precious burden he carried must be lost so deep in the course as to never be found—at least by Charon. Hopefully the son of a bitch would be dead and gone to earth himself before he could ever reach the Grail. After that it was out of Richard's ken. The Goddess could look after it Herself.

Hand-over-hand, half-swimming, half-tumbling in the rush, the air in his lungs swelled beyond tolerance. He wanted immediate release and replenishment for them. But there was none to be had. His hands, reaching upward, found only rock, not air—if it was indeed up. He couldn't tell. He pushed the panic away and kicked with the flow, driving himself another few yards further along.

His chest ached, then burned, then felt ready to explode.

Just a bit more, a few yards, a dozen . . . just a bit more.

But the burning, biting agony was overwhelming. Bubbles leaked from his nose and mouth. Regardless of his will, the trapped air finally burst forth, and the insidious water clubbed at him, trying to take its place. He tried not to breathe in, but some of it had got in anyway and that triggered a cough, which allowed more water to pound into his lungs. He bucked against it until it numbed him. His movements faltered.

A bit more . . .

His arms were so heavy. Hard to lift. He had to give up on his legs. They dragged at his progress. The iron numbness spread out from his chest. The cold wasn't so bad as before . . . neither was breathing water. After the first choking rush, after the first protesting struggle, it was almost soothing.

He drifted now, mind and body, the two starting to separate again. He dreamed of floating and idly wondered if he could float away through the rock to find the sky, or if he had to continue on until the water finally surfaced above ground level.

A bump, then a startlingly painful knock on his shin, then a terrible jolting plunge. Only partly drawn from his stupor, he flailed out, and felt the slap of spraying water on his face. Instinct told him this was very important, and this time he listened, or tried to—his limbs weren't cooperating too well.

He gagged and sputtered, vomiting water. It felt like his lungs were being torn inside out.

His body spun in the current. His face submerged again.

No, raise up. Swim, dammit!

Air. Lovely, glorious air. And with it, reviving life. The next few minutes—as his sluggish brain labored

hard to deal with necessities for survival—were
anything but pleasant. The terrific cold, the fire in
his chest, the feeling that someone had rammed an
ice pick into the front of his skull, all blended into
a singularly awful dose of wretchedness. And he'd
thought that his death would be fairly quick.

His fingers brushed rock. Clumsily, he grabbed at
its slick surface. His body drifted, still going with the
stream, but he made this point an anchor. By random
touch he determined that it was some kind of low
ledge, perhaps a foot or so wide and only a few
inches clear of the water. More than sufficient.

He let his body come up parallel and with much
splashing and effort got an arm and a leg onto the
ledge. God, he was so weak. It seemed to take hours
before he finally heaved clear of the deadly water
and rolled panting onto his back.

And then he just could *not* move.

He coughed and choked, ridding himself of the
stuff, wheezing one minute, retching the next.
Gradually, breathing became more common than
coughing and he dimly took stock of himself.

His skin tingled, burning the same as when he got
too much sun. Perhaps it would heal and pass in a
like manner now that he was free of the water. His
chest hurt, but not as badly as before. Then there
was the growing nausea, but that was also familiar.
It was the kind he got when forced by social require-
ment to partake of normal food and drink—in other
words, he'd swallowed some water. Sweet Goddess, but
it felt like he'd taken in the whole bloody stream.

I should be dead.

Not that he was complaining. Had he been a
normal human he would have certainly met with his
mortality much farther back in this mad place. This
was like any other wounding, he supposed, take the

damage and wait through the misery until he healed
again.

He trembled from head to foot, teeth chattering.
Reaction, he told himself, and let it happen. He'd just
had a reprieve from dying; it was perfectly under-
standable.

Temporary reprieve, old lad.

He'd have to go back in again.

But that wasn't worth thinking about for the time
being. It could wait.

This chamber wasn't nearly as large as the other one,
if his judgment of the sound quality was accurate. He
listened to the noise of the waterfall, rested, and now
and then touched his pocket to make sure the Grail
was still there. He found Sabra's book again, having
quite forgotten it. As far as he could tell the seal on
its plastic bag was unbroken. Damn, he really should
have left it behind for Sharon Geary to someday
recover. Charon might have gotten it, though. Oh, well,
it hardly mattered.

Not to me, anyway.

When the latest wave of nausea passed Richard
slowly sat up, his hands out to determine what was
around him. Not very damn much. Stone and more
stone, damp and smooth. He faced upstream, but
corrected that, turning round. Ready or not, he started
to crawl. He had no idea how far the ledge ran, or
how long he could physically continue, but had to play
both out while he could.

Impossible to keep track of the distance. He tried
counting, each number to approximate one foot of
progress, but lost things somewhere around thirty.
Or was it forty? If only he could see. He imagined
the comfort of light and with the imagining saw
ghostly flashes of color, creations of his mind, nothing
more, his eyes starving for input.

The ledge slanted a bit toward the water. He expected it would continue to do so, forcing him back into the flow. Then the question would be of how far he could get before it finally consumed him.

His movements were mechanical now, his concentration focused on pushing himself forward. Damn, but his bruised shin ached. Palms and knees, too.

The passage narrowed, the ceiling getting lower. Not long now. The water flow was considerably slower here. The passage had widened and the depth must have increased, that or the stream had divided, the major part of it going elsewhere. He wouldn't have to fight the current so much, but then he'd have to put more effort into forward motion to compensate.

The ceiling reached a point where he couldn't push through without the danger of getting stuck. Here he paused to collect himself again, to brace up for the last bout. He knew it to be the last from his waning endurance.

One more sick-making pang of nausea delayed him. He curled into a ball, hugging himself. More reaction from his body to the abuse he'd put it through, and there was naught to do but shudder in his own sweat until it subsided.

As he waited it out and listened to the water he came to be aware of another faint but regular sound, like a dripping tap. No, that wasn't quite it. What, then? The heartbeat of the Goddess of the Underworld? He could believe it in this place. Perhaps they were the footfalls of the real Charon, not his murderous namesake, coming for him at last.

Richard shook his head, trying to clear it. The air was so stale here. He listened more carefully, realizing there was a metallic quality to the sound, and at that point his heart gave such a jump in his chest that he went dizzy for a moment.

Waiting suddenly cut short, he half-slipped, half-fell into the water and slogged forward. As before, it was so cold it seared, but he ignored the pain.

The ceiling got much lower, no matter, he still had air. He pressed on with the current, and the stuff gradually became shallow enough for him to push his feet against the bottom to send him on. He made too much noise to hear beyond it, nor could he stop to listen.

The stream bed widened, got much more shallow. Soon the level dropped to his hips, his knees, then he stumbled over another ledge of some sort and was nearly free of the water. He still had to crouch low, but it was a place to rest.

Clink-clink-clink. Steady, like a hammer on metal, and getting louder.

He felt his way along, sometimes splashing, sometimes clear.

The air freshened.

Then he saw light. So pale, so ill-defined as to be nonexistent, and nearly blinding to his straining eyes.

"Sharon!"

The sound stopped. He kept going and called out again. It had to be her. Had to be. She was still working away at the Chalice Well, God bless her stubborn heart.

He now saw signs of past intrusion by the Water Board, their reshaping of the stream's path, bits of trash dropped in by boorish tourists. He hurried on, encountering an artificial barrier meant to slow the stream. He squirmed over it, dropping into deeper water. The stuff was hardly moving, though, he barely noticed it.

"Sharon!"

A long pause, then: *"Richard?"*

He bawled up a joyous affirmative, hurrying until he breathlessly made it to the base of the well. He squeezed through a small opening and shouted upward when he saw her head and shoulders silhouetted against the sky. So near, so far. The actinic beam of a torch light blasted at his eyes and was whipped to one side as he raised a protective hand against it.

"Mother of God, man, what the hell are you doing down there?" she demanded with near-palpable astonishment.

A reasonable question, that. "I'll explain later, just get me out!"

It took time, of course, but they worked through it. In his absence she'd broken the grating free and had been methodically hammering anchor spikes into the stone and concrete base to hold the ropes she would use to descend into the well.

"Never mind," he yelled. "Use the grappling hook!"

"There's naught for it to hold to, or I'd have done it by now. Wait! I've just thought of a brilliant improvisation." She bobbed from sight a moment. More metal sounds, then the opening above was obscured by the grating. She'd put it back in place, but not quite on center. Next, she started feeding one end of a knotted rope through the slats until it reached him, tied the other to the grappling hook and jammed it onto the grate.

"Are you able to climb?" she asked.

"I'll manage." Anything to escape. He'd levitate up the damn thing if need be.

The knots helped, but the rope was rough on his sore and unprotected hands. His feet occasionally found purchase on the uneven sides, and he made progress, but God, he was so *tired*.

Then he was within reach of the lip of the well. He hooked first a hand, then an arm. Sharon dragged the grating off to give him more room and pulled at his shoulders as he emerged with many a grunt of effort and pain, until, miraculously he was sitting on the ground, back to the well, blinking and befuddled. He'd been in hell for centuries it seemed. This sudden normalcy would take getting used to.

She knelt by him with her torch and checked him over. His long immersion had cleaned him up, washing the blood and muck away, leaving behind only torn clothing and violently reddened skin.

"You look all right," she announced tentatively, but sounding relieved. "How do you feel?"

"I feel incredibly fragile," he confessed, staring at the ground and not really seeing it. "Everything hurts."

"Well, if you're in pain, it means you're alive."

"Oh, God," he groaned, slumping bonelessly to one side, "then am I ever alive."

Chapter Eleven

"That is the daftest, most idiotic thing I've ever heard," said Sharon, torn between anger and wonderment. "You could have been killed and no one the wiser for months."

"Better than letting Charon win. Besides, I made it through," *By the grace of at least two deities and the devil's own luck*, Richard added to himself.

He had—in his sketchy explanation to her of just how he gotten to the bottom of the Chalice Well—omitted the little detail that he'd honestly not expected to survive at all. He was himself still taking it in.

"It was a bloody miracle," she pronounced sternly, then her anger melted and she pressed her head against his shoulder, one arm going around his chest. Because of his recent bashings it hurt a bit, but he endured, feebly patting her thigh with a free hand.

"I know it was. Now would you mind very much bringing the car round as close as you can? I don't fancy a long walk just now."

She straightened and shifted back to practicalities. "Keys?"

He tried one pocket, then another, before finding them zipped away in his jacket.

"There's another miracle," she said, accepting them. "It would have been a shame to have to break in and wire it. Back in five, darlin'."

"Just a minute, I've something else for you." From another pocket he drew out the plastic-sealed Abbey Book and placed it carefully in her hands. "It may have gotten a dent or two, but I think it's—"

Sharon let forth a wild crow of delight and threw herself enthusiastically upon his bruises in demonstration of her appreciation.

"Careful, woman! You'll kill me for sure!" he cried out in weak protest.

Her verbal response was rather unintelligible, but she did ease off her more violent expressions of joy and settled for simply kissing him. Quite a lot.

Much better, he thought, sighing with inner contentment. How nice it would be to stop everything right here and stay awhile.

But she eventually broke off and all but danced away for the car. When she drove back he was almost asleep and reluctant to stir again.

"You're too big to carry, so shift yourself," she urged, helping him up and guiding him to the open back door of the Jaguar. "And let's get you out of those wet rags."

Richard let her fuss and meekly followed orders. It was rather nice having someone else in charge. He'd expended so much energy—mental, physical, and emotional—that he had none left to spare for such mundane matters. He badly needed some down time. He did manage to keep track of the jacket with its precious burden still safe in a sealed pocket while she got him stripped and into a change of clothes from his flight bag, wrapping his long coat about him.

"Right, that should hold you until I can find a hospital," she said.

Now his eyes opened wide, fully alert. "I'm *not* going to a hospital."

"The hell you're not. After what you've been through?"

Instinct told him this could be a long discussion unless he offered a logical counter-argument. Happily, he had one. "I only need a bit of rest, which I can get on the road, but we can't afford to waste time with any doctors because Charon's on his way back to Toronto."

"So we'll make a few phone calls and have the police lookin' out for him. You've done more than your share for one night."

"If it was anyone else but Charon I'd agree, but he's an expert at disappearing. If he gets past the authorities here, then *I* absolutely have to—"

She raised both hands to stop him. "All right, no lectures. I had enough of those from *him*. Let's be off, then."

He paused. This was too easy. "Just like that?"

"Not really. You made me remember something. When I went for the car I saw a little sports job tear by and race up the main road like a bat from hell. I didn't see the driver, but wouldn't it be just the thing for us if he was the professor? So let's see if we can catch the bastard."

Sharon quickly tossed the remains of their gear into the trunk, dropped into the driver's seat and got them moving at top speed, but it soon became evident that Charon had had too great a head start or taken another route. After the first hour of peering ahead and seeing nothing but more road, Richard gave up, stretched his long frame as best he could on the backseat and went to sleep again, hugging the jacket with the Grail close to his chest. It only seemed like a few dreamless minutes passed before Sharon was shaking him and loudly calling his name.

"We're at Heathrow," she said. "What d'ye want to do with the car?"

Phone calls and paperwork: prosaic details requiring his personal attention—not one of his favorite activities. *Welcome back to the twentieth century, old lad.*

He rallied and emerged to deal with things, noting with regret that the night was almost gone. The rest had done him good, though. He could move more easily, so his stiffening muscles were healing. Even in the unflattering artificial lights of the terminal Sharon told him he looked better than before.

"'Tis mostly in the eyes, but the rest of you is white as a toad's belly," she said.

He refrained from comment over her honesty and made some calls. The first was to Bourland, waking him up. Richard gave him a brief report containing the essentials: he'd followed a lead on Rivers, now definitely Charon, found and lost him again.

"He said he was going to go through with the assassination—and see to it that I got blamed for the job," Richard concluded.

"That sounds a good trick. Wonder what he's planned for you?"

"I'd just as soon not find out. Look, I have to get back as soon as possible, what can you do to cut the red tape for me and my associate?"

"Your associate?"

"She's been of tremendous help to me."

"Ohhh, *that* associate. The one Demarest was looking for."

"The same. We've sorted our credentials. I hope Demarest hasn't gone back on—"

"No, no, he's all right where your Ms. Geary is concerned, but he's still hopping mad about Charon. That closet business was something of an embarrassment to him—it's inspired no end of bad jokes around here."

Richard all but smirked. "I can imagine. If he wants something constructive to do, you can have him checking for Neal Rivers on all incoming flights originating from Europe today—*all* of them. Go by his physical description, not name. I'll start things at this end, but I need some of your clout to help do it, so would you mind very much waking up a few other people? Oh—and I need a diplomatic pouch and the papers to go with it."

"Good God, whatever for?"

"It's to carry through a weapon against Charon."

"A weapon? You're not smuggling another one of those fifty-caliber jobs are you?"

"Sorry, poor choice of words on my part. What I have is a small article that Charon would very much like to get his hands on. I may be able to use it as bait to draw him out in the open, but the customs authorities on both sides might take a dim view of my borrowing it. I need across-the-board clearances from as high up as you can manage and as quickly as possible."

Bourland sighed. "I hope you'll provide me with a full explanation once you're here."

"Oh, absolutely," Richard assured him, while mentally crossing his fingers against the lie. "But about the next flight back—"

"I'll take care of it, not to worry. Now be a good lad and just stand by so I can start things on this end. Of course, if Charon *should* happen to turn up in front of you in the boarding line you'll save us a bit of bother and head him off, won't you?"

"More like take his head off." A risk making that statement, but it was entirely true. Bourland only chuckled.

Richard's second call was to the head of Heathrow's security and that took much longer. Once he actually got through to the person on duty he then had to convince him that the gravity of a budding situation required an immediate conference. A meeting was arranged and someone would be by shortly. Richard hung up, having gotten the distinct impression the fellow on the other end of the line thought him a perfectly insane nuisance. *Ah, well, I'll set him straight when he's here.* Nothing like a face-to-face encounter for a little persuasive hypnosis.

Sharon had not been idle, either, having made use of another phone. She dropped the receiver into place just as Richard came up. "I'm all fixed with the book," she announced, her face glowing.

God, she was beautiful. He wanted to kiss her, saw not a single reason not to and proceeded to do so, wrapping his arms around her.

"Talking with Lloyd's?" he inquired a moment or two later.

"That I was. They're sending someone over to take charge of it. Once the paperwork's sorted I'll be finding my bank account in a healthier state than it's ever known before. I'd love to thank you for it." She pressed close, sliding her arms about him and down, resting her palms on his backside and squeezing gently.

He squirmed against her in response to the pleasantry and grinned. "I'll look forward to it. I've arranged for our return to Toronto—that is, if you want to come back. Now that you've got the book—"

"Oh, I'm coming back all right, to pick up my gear and settle some details, then I have to get back to London. But I can spare a day or two, if for naught else to satisfy my curiosity."

"Curiosity?"

"Well, I've an idea of how much fun you are in a spa, now I've a mind to see how you do in a proper bed with sheets and pillows." Another squeeze. Lovely.

"Nothing less than my best, I assure you."

"Ah, Richard, you do fill me with confidence."

Before he could offer a highly suggestive rejoinder he spotted several grim-faced men marching purposefully toward them. The one in the lead wore a conservative dark suit with an airport ID badge clipped to the front pocket; the others were in security uniforms complete with radios. Richard gave Sharon a quick kiss. "There, that's on account. Time to go back to work."

The red tape cutting took a little more than two hours, much faster than Richard expected, but Bourland had obviously woken up some very important people, indeed. A few more phone calls—this time made from the now highly cooperative security man's office—settled things. Richard and Sharon were escorted to a private waiting area and generally coddled and cosseted until it was time to board the day's first transatlantic flight, a direct to Toronto.

No sign of Charon, though, but then Richard didn't really expect to see him. The man was too careful by half.

"First class again," Sharon commented as she belted herself in. "How do you manage?"

"It helps to have some very good friends." Excellent friends to be sure, to get these seats the airline had quietly bumped a million-a-year fashion model and her budding film star boyfriend to a later flight. Richard hoped the paparazzi lying in wait for the couple's arrival at Pearson would not be overly disappointed by the substitutions. Then the plane began moving, and the long, bouncing lurch as it taxied along had him grabbing reflexively for the chair arms. The leather bag in his lap began to slip away. Sharon caught it before it fell.

"Steady on, we're not even airborne yet," she cautioned.

"Tell me something I don't know, why don't you?"

"What is this, anyway? I saw that office man give it to you before—" She read the discreet notices printed on it and felt the outside of the thing, where it bulged slightly from the object within. Her eyes went wide. "Richard, is this what I think it is?"

He managed a brief show of teeth, more of a wince than a smile. The plane paused, as if trying to make up its mind whether to proceed or not. "And what might that be?"

Her fingers went white around the bag, and she glanced uneasily about. "*Why* didn't you *tell* me?" she whispered.

"Well, you know now, don't you?"

She thumped his shoulder.

"Ow! Are you going to be like this for the rest of the flight? If so, I'll take my chances in coach." Another lurch, the engines started to howl as they powered up, and the plane began moving forward, faster and faster.

"You bloody beast! Open it up, I want a look."

The howl changed in pitch, and they were suddenly off the ground.

"All right, but give me a minute." *One, two, three . . .*

"Why—?" She took in his face. "Oh. That."

"Yes, that." *Seven, eight, nine . . .*

"Honestly, there's nothing to worry about, the chances of our crashing are—"

"Sharon, darling, my own dear love, please and for God's sake—shut the hell up." *Seventeen, eighteen . . .*

She snorted, but kept quiet until he reached the magic count of *sixty* and opened his eyes again. "All better?"

"Only when we're on land again. Safely on land."

"Then take your mind off the flying and show me."

He hesitated, thinking perhaps it might be unwise to display it so openly; after all, the Grail had been guarded, then kept utterly secret for all those centuries, and not without good reason. On the other hand, if anyone deserved a peek, it was Sharon. And, he admitted to himself, he wanted another look as well. He didn't think the Goddess would mind. Not too terribly much.

Turning halfway in his seat to block the view of others in their section, he fished out the key for the pouch and opened the lock, then carefully pulled free its contents.

"What's that?" she demanded. "Surely not one of your spare shirts?"

"Sorry, but I didn't have any red samite on me, and I had to wrap it in something. Don't worry, I put the buttons on the outside so they wouldn't scratch it."

Then he peeled back the fabric, and Sharon caught her breath. Transfixed, she stared in silence for many long moments.

He understood perfectly. His own heart seemed to catch upon itself, recovered and went on, but just a bit faster than before. After a time, he lightly touched Sharon's cheek, startling her. "Well? What do you think?"

"Sweet Mary, 'tis not for me to judge."

"Want to hold it?"

She shook her head, once, very quickly. "No. This is enough. More than enough." She continued to stare and made not the slightest move to touch it.

"Sharon?"

But the cup held her rapt attention. When she finally spoke, her voice was thick with emotion. "'Tis not what you'd expect, not from the legends, nor the art, nor the films, but it's perfect. The most perfect thing I've ever seen in my life." She sucked in a fast breath and it shivered out again. Her green eyes glittered with sudden tears and she blinked, swiping at them. "Ah, man, you'll be thinking me a fool."

He leaned over, brushing his lips against her temple. "Never. I feel it, too."

She looked around. "Can no one else sense it?"

"I don't know. Perhaps those with the Sight—" He bit off the rest.

Now she looked at him, looked for a very long time, her face solemn, but otherwise quite unreadable.

"What?" he asked, genuinely puzzled.

"Nothing." She folded the shirt gently back over the little brass cup. "Only that I see why you did so daft a thing as swimming the Chalice Stream to keep this away from that damned Charon. Seein' it here, seein' what it is, *feelin'* what it is—I'd have risked all and done the same thing myself."

"You would?"

"In a heartbeat. So wrap it up, sweet Richard, and keep it safe from the Philistines of this sad world."

Someone shook his shoulder and called his name. *But we've left Heathrow.*

The blanket he'd pulled well over his head to shield him from the brutal daylight seeping through the many windows slipped down. He came sluggishly awake, groaning in protest.

"Whazit?" he rumbled. He peered blearily up, first into the pleasant and apologetic face of a hovering flight attendant, then over to Sharon.

"Ye've skipped breakfast for all your sleepin'," she

told him. "I'll not have you be missin' the noontime meal as well."

Long practice kept him from registering automatic disgust at the suggestion of solid food. He rubbed his grit-clogged eyes instead. "All right, I'll have whatever you're having."

Sharon decided on the steak instead of chicken, tucking into it with evident gusto. Richard regarded his own meal with well-suppressed revulsion and listlessly pushed the food around with his fork. He *was* hungry, for much of the blood the Nine Sisters had given to him had been used up by now in healing. Hungry, yes, but certainly not for this exanimate garbage.

"What's wrong?" Sharon asked. "You're not a vegetarian, are you?"

"Hardly. This just doesn't appeal to me."

"Your taste buds are still asleep. Just try some and you'll come round." She lifted a sauce-drenched forkful to his lips.

He grimaced, drawing back. "Um, thank you, but no. All the schedule disruption, the physical stress, this damned light's playing hell with my allergy—it's really thrown me."

"But you have to have something."

"I will, just not this." He handed the food tray to her and lifted his seat-back tray so he could stand. "Here, you eat it. I'll—ah—go see if the attendant can help me." He released his seat belt and got unsteadily to his feet, experiencing an instant of lightheadedness. He recognized the symptoms. Yes, his body had recovered quite a lot in the last few hours and was in very sore need of replenishment. The problem was, even on a plane this size, hunting opportunities were bound to be extremely limited and dangerous. He'd have to improvise, but with caution.

He made his way forward to flight attendants'

territory: a small, curtained alcove. It looked promising. The young woman who had served them a few moments ago was there, busy with a coffee machine. No one else was about. Very promising.

"Excuse me?" he said, stepping in. It was a restrictive space and put him in closer quarters with her than what was considered socially acceptable between strangers in this day and age. That registered quite strongly on her features as she turned toward him, but she smoothed over her surprise with the professional veneer of her training.

"Yes, sir? Mr. Dun, isn't it?" Of course she'd have heard his name from someone because of the sudden passenger change.

"That's right, Ms.—uh—Ms. Patterson," he said, reading her badge. Doubtless her next response would have been to inform him about this area being off limits to passengers, but he'd already fixed his gaze hard upon her, coupling it with his best, most winning smile.

Full force.

She froze for one instant, then returned a dazzling, if rather blank, smile of her own. The poor woman never had a chance.

Richard prudently whisked the curtain shut behind him and moved in.

The devil of it was he didn't know how much time he had. She could be called away at any moment, or another attendant could interrupt them, otherwise he would have drawn out the enjoyment for them both. As it was, he rushed through the preliminaries more quickly than was normal. Like anyone else, he preferred to take time with his meals, but he dared not chance it here. He left nothing out, though, as he soothingly, compellingly whispered for her to shut her eyes, relax, and stand perfectly still, which she did, even as he swiftly unbuttoned the cuff of her blouse and pushed the sleeve up her arm.

"There, now, you won't feel a thing," he assured her, trailing his fingertips lightly over her forehead. His hands trembled a bit, and his heartbeat was high, thundering hard from excitement and anticipation.

But she must have felt something, for he heard her sharp intake of breath as he buried his extended corner teeth in the taut skin on the inside of her elbow. She remained still and quiet, however, as he fed—except for an occasional long sigh of pleasure.

It was like that for a few of them. They were dimly aware of an unusual activity taking place but of little else, save that it was extremely pleasant. He ever and always made sure to plant that suggestion with them, for why should he not share the intense delight he felt himself?

God, but it tasted good. When had he last really fed from a living woman? Not since She-Who-Walks, but that had been different, and he'd been fearful of losing control of his beast with her. This time was . . . was like it had always been for him with its hot, sweet sharing, with the headiness of another's life flowing into and enriching his own. He shuddered, head to toe, as the latest wave of it washed over him. There was nothing, absolutely *nothing* else quite like it.

When he'd finished, he gently kissed away the last seepage from the small holes in her arm and inspected the damage narrowly. No bruising, no obvious capillary damage; he'd done it just exactly right.

"Thank you, Ms. Patterson, you've been of great help," he whispered, and he was sincere about it. He felt much better now.

Digging in his back pocket, he drew forth two small adhesive bandages, such as he always carried for these occasions, breaking their seals and placing them carefully on the wounds. "There, you needn't give these a second thought. You happened to see a blood donation center on your way to work and surrendered to an impulse to contribute. Very generous of you, to be sure. Now I'm going to slip out so you can get on with your job, and you're going to forget all about me, aren't you?" He pulled her sleeve down, rebuttoned the cuff, and was gone before she could wake to answer.

He paid a brief visit to the toilet for a quick check in the mirror to make sure no traces of blood smeared his face. It was all part of his usual feeding routine, honed by over a thousand years of practice, but as he washed his hands and peered thoughtfully at his unshaven reflection he came to understand that there was something distinctly different about this one.

Well, he told himself, *I suppose I have finally joined the Mile-High Club—albeit with a new twist.*

Certainly for him the taking of a woman's blood was sensually comparable to making love, but there was something else, something less obvious nagging at the edge of his mind. He knew the signs; whatever it was would come in its own time, so he let it go and went back to his seat.

Sharon had finished her lunch and was nearly through with his. "You were a time. Didn't she have anything?"

"Yes, she turned up a little something to tide me over, and then we got to talking."

"Did you now? Why doesn't that surprise me?"

He shot her a quizzical look.

"You're a handsome, charmin' man, Richard Dun,

an' most women would have to be dead not to notice. I'll wager you spend most of your free time being chatted up by them."

"Not anymore."

"Eh?"

"Only because I'll make a point of spending all my free time with you."

That pleased her. He gave her knee a friendly squeeze, then glanced down to check on the leather pouch at his feet. Still there and quite safe. He reclined back in his seat, content for the moment with his portion of the universe. His beast was well sated, all he wanted now was to resume his nap and . . .

His beast.

Oh, my dear God . . . and dear Goddess, for that matter.

The elusive thought teasing on the edge of consciousness abruptly came square to the front and center.

He'd fed as he normally did, without the cold dread that had haunted him since his madness at Niagara. His beast had behaved itself. He'd not had the least sense of it escaping from his control; it was as obedient as it had ever been to his will.

And he did not have to wonder why that was so.

Richard picked up the pouch, felt the solidity of the precious object within. And more. A whisper of its power thrummed up through his fingers.

All that fiery immersion in the Chalice Stream— with the Grail. The water he'd swallowed, nearly drowned in. It *had* to have affected him, reversed the degeneration for him in some manner, perhaps even cured it.

He suppressed his laugh of astonished joy, not wanting to catch Sharon's attention and have to answer questions. It was hard going to hold such stuff inside; he wanted to jump up and shout about it. Talk about miracles . . .

Drastic cure, though. Not unlike chemotherapy, in that it was almost worse than the ailment.

If it would—oh, but it must—do the same miracle for Sabra.

He hugged the pouch to his chest, eyes shut as he silently offered up thanks again and again until sleep took him once more.

A bright, sunny day in Toronto.

Miserable weather.

And jet lag. Richard preferred sleeping late when he could, it was part and parcel of what he was, but unavoidable intrusions often made it impossible. They'd gained some time over the Atlantic as well; this was turning into one of the longest days he'd endured in recent memory.

Sharon had finally given in to the toils of travel, and for a change he had to wake her when they landed. Gathering their carry-ons, they marched slowly forward with the other exiting passengers.

"Thank you for flying with us, Mr. Dun. I hope you enjoyed your trip."

Startled, he glanced up, right into the smiling face of the flight attendant, Ms. Patterson. She was positively beaming with warmth for him. Sweet heavens, how much did she remember?

"Do come again, and have a nice day," she said with unusual sincerity. It was rather beyond what was required by the airline.

"Ahh—thank you . . . yes . . . and you, too."

Sharon did not miss this exchange and flashed him an arch look, probably thinking he'd done a bit of "chatting up" himself. At some point he'd have to find a quiet moment and persuade her not to worry about such things.

A varied crowd clustered around the arrival gate outside of customs: several hungry-looking newspaper types clutching cameras and peering hard at each passenger, ordinary folk come to greet friends and relatives, and a trio of men not unlike the fellows at Heathrow, one in a conservative suit and the others in airport security uniforms. They spotted Richard right away. They must have been told what to look out for: his unseasonably heavy clothing, extra-dark sunglasses—and the diplomatic pouch.

The Suit approached, made rapid, and to Richard's daylight-befuddled mind, largely meaningless introductions, then led the way past customs to one of the exits. Bourland had sent a car and driver for them, along with a message to call him immediately. Richard used the vehicle's built-in phone as the driver guided them smoothly out of Pearson's maze and onto the Macdonald-Cartier Freeway.

"We're back," he said when he got through to Bourland.

"Glad to hear it. We'll want your help tonight."

"Is this a secure line?"

"Quite secure. We may talk freely."

"What's tonight, the trade conference?"

"At the Royal York Hotel. We'll have people all over the place, but—"

"I know, I'm still on retainer. I'll be there, if you think this is the right event for Charon to show. There may be other opportunities for him to take, don't forget."

"It's attracted world-wide press and TV, what better place for the splinter group to make a point?"

"What are you doing to cut down the PM's vulnerability?"

"All we can, but he insists on making a front door entrance along with the rest of the VIP's. Says it won't reflect well on the country or his faith in our security if he's smuggled in through the kitchens."

"Is he aware of the danger?"

"Thoroughly. I even showed him photos of that wall from that pub shooting, but he will have his way. Won't be budged."

"One can admire his idiotic courage, but at least put him in a bullet-proof vest or he'll get a lot more than fifteen seconds of coverage on CNN."

"I think we can do that much."

Not nearly enough, Richard thought. A vest was no more than a gesture. Charon always went for head shots. It was standard procedure for snipers: go for the head, then if the bullet dropped over the distance it could still kill by hitting the neck or chest. Of course, with a .50 armor-piercing round able to punch a large hole into anything up to and including most tanks the question of anyone, with or without a vest, surviving such a hit was hardly worth considering.

"Has Demarest any news on flight arrivals?" Richard asked.

"Actually, yes. He went up to Newfoundland."

"What the devil's he doing there?"

"Beating the bush for Charon. We're fairly sure he originally chartered a jet to the Bahamas, then hijacked it to Gander Field instead, since one made a very unscheduled landing there earlier today. From there we think he had other transport standing by, but Demarest is having a lot of trouble getting people to talk. Says even the pilot is pretending not to remember anything about the business."

Not surprising, that, if Charon was any good at hypnosis. Its coercive effect on a vulnerable human mind was far more profound than any commonplace loyalty, bribery or fear.

"He and the crew may have been drugged," said Richard. "There are some tailor-made exotics on the market that could have such an effect. Assume Charon's an expert and see if you can turn up a hypnotherapist who's got some deprogramming experience. Demarest might have better luck that way."

"That will take time."

"Yes, we're shutting the barn after the horse is gone, but we can at least be thorough about it for the investigation later."

A long silence, then, "You don't expect to get him, do you, Richard?"

"To be perfectly honest, I don't, not here. He's had too long to prepare and there are too many variables. He's been successfully doing this sort of thing for a very long time. He takes a positive pride in his work. And you can be sure it will be nearly impossible to track him afterward. A long gun means he'll be a safe distance from the scene and have a well-prepared getaway. If you want any clues to finding him later, then you must work with what you have at hand this moment. But if you really want to prevent a kill this time, then persuade the PM to do a bit of handshaking with the hotel's kitchen staff. Have them cleared first. Just because Charon's been hired, doesn't mean he's the only assassin on the job. He could be a high-profile distraction, y'know."

Bourland made grumbling noises, indicating he was not at all happy with what he was hearing. "I'll have another go at it. After all, we're paying you to be professionally paranoid."

"Absolutely."

"What about that 'weapon' you brought in? Bait, you said?"

"It's the sort of thing that will be more useful later when the hunt is on. It requires a bit of preparation, unfortunately." Richard glanced at his watch. Damn, it was still on English time. He looked over the seat at the dashboard clock and reset things. "When does all this start tonight?"

"Delegates will be filtering in between eight and nine for the banquet. The PM is scheduled to arrive at eight twenty-five."

The sun would still be up. Damnation.

"We'd like you at the York as soon as possible, though."

"I'm going home to get presentable first. Is this a black tie thing?"

"Afraid so, old boy. That is, if you want to blend in and not look too very much like a security man."

"Right. See you shortly." He rang off and gave the driver fresh directions.

"That sounded intense," Sharon commented. "Your half of it, anyway."

"It's a terrific nuisance. Waste of effort for everyone except Charon."

"You said something about variables. Those apply to him as well."

"Not when he's planned for them."

"He'll not have planned for this one."

"Oh? Which is?"

She tapped a light finger on his chest. "He thinks *you're* safely rotting under Glastonbury Tor."

Richard allowed himself a short laugh. "Yes, there's that." *For what it's worth.* But he still thought the whole business a waste of precious time that was not his own, and it would likely consume even more in what looked to be a vile aftermath, time he would much rather use getting the Grail to Sabra.

✧   ✧   ✧

The Royal York Hotel—which had much experience in such events—had outdone itself for the evening reception: a perfectly turned out staff, red carpets, live music, special decor, almost enough to distract from the dozens of uniformed and plainclothes security people moving among the well-dressed delegates who had already arrived. Important-looking men and women, dressed to the teeth and then some, drifted about, some shaking hands and talking, others eyeing the doors as newcomers were ushered in.

"This place is a bloody zoo," said Sharon, scowling at the splendors. She was quite splendid herself, having in the space of a few hours piled her red hair up high and kitted out in a sort of shiny black stretchy thing that covered her from wrists to ankles. It might have been meant for gymnastic use, but she'd hung a near-transparent black lace skirt from her naturally nipped-in waist and trimmed the lot with flashes of cut onyx jewelry. Chic, but still practical, right down to her flat-heeled shoes. If she had to move fast, she was ready. The only real sign setting her apart from the other visitors was the security ID badge she'd clipped to one shoulder.

Richard, attempting to complement her elegance in his custom-tailored tuxedo, very much regretted that he could not pay more attention to her, though many of the other men were trying their best to make up for it. One of them had actually tripped and fallen into a potted plant when Sharon glided past.

"Why such a huge fuss?" she asked. "It's only a trade conference."

"It's the largest one to be held in this hemisphere in the last twenty years. There's also a touchy ecological issue on the table and that's attracted some civic-minded film stars. Don't think all this is for a few politicians and business types."

"But so much attention, even for some actors?"

"Perhaps someone let slip to the media about the free buffet in the lobby."

She shot him a crooked look. "Sometimes I can't tell if you're shaking my crate or not."

"Rattling your cage," he corrected.

"As I said: this is a zoo."

"Agreed. But which are the animals and which the keepers?"

"Oh, we're the keepers, leastwise all the ones with badges . . . and headsets." She nodded at the one Richard sported.

It was about as discreet as a foghorn, but a necessary evil so he could keep track of what was going on. He tended to miss Sharon's frequent observations as he listened to broadcast exchanges from the rest of the security team. One incident proved to be rather interesting when several zealous female fans of an expected film star were discovered lurking in a freight elevator and summarily taken into custody. For some mysterious reason they'd each been carrying pink plastic garden flamingos and cans of Macadamia nuts, all of which had been confiscated as being a possible bomb threat. Closer inspection indicated the things were exactly what they seemed to be; now the guards were having a lengthy debate on what to do with the items and their disappointed T-shirt-clad owners.

Richard impatiently pressed the Send button on his set. "Hallo, this is Control Three. Do their IDs check out?"

"Yes, sir. They're just tourists in from the States."

"Is there any immediate and obvious threat from those damned flamingos?"

"Uh . . . no, sir," someone answered after a moment.

"Or the Macadamia nuts?"

"No, sir," chimed in another sheepish voice.

"Then I suggest you pitch the lot out of them out the back door and get on to something more important; you're cluttering up this channel."

"Yes, sir!"

"Flamingos and Macadamia nuts?" asked Sharon, baffled from hearing only one side of the conversation.

Richard shrugged, shaking his head. "I'm terrified to ask."

That distraction out of the way, he and Sharon made a circuit of the area, occasionally pausing as he dealt with one thing or another filtering into his headset.

"It's like you're telepathic and I'm not," Sharon complained mildly. "Your eyes go strange an' then I know you've phased out."

He laughed once. It was comparable to all those years of dealing with Sabra's Sight. Certainly this was as close as he'd ever get to achieving the Gift for himself. "Come on, let's get some elevation."

He found a back stairs and they went up to a hotel office that had been taken over as a command center for the security team. More uniforms here, which he thought ridiculous; they were needed elsewhere for crowd control. Instead they were standing around and gossiping, the tightest knot gathered around a table piled high with doughnut and pizza boxes.

"What's the hold up?" he demanded of the harried-looking co-ordinator.

"We're short of radios, sir. There's a new batch coming in later."

"Then hand them out later, and get these people to posts that don't require radios."

"Yes, sir." Orders were barked and the ranks instantly thinned.

"You enjoyed that," said Sharon.

"I despise inefficiency."

She followed him to one of the windows where they had a grand view of the front entry, which was packed with members of the media press awaiting the coming of the more newsworthy delegates. The sun was still in the sky, but lowering. The bulk of the York and other buildings cast a vast shadow over this section of the street.

Thank God for small favors. "Hand me those field glasses, would you?"

Sharon plucked a set from a nearby desk and gave them over. He couldn't open the window, but was still able to focus beyond the glass to Union Station across the street. There were men on the roof, but they were supposed to be there, being part of the security team. He scanned everything within view that could be a potential hunting blind for Charon: from the needle-sharp CN Tower on his right to the twenty-five anvil-shaped stories of the Esplanade on his left, and all the area in between. There was far too much of it. Bourland had been unable to convince the Prime Minister to use more caution. Unless Charon chose another time and place, he would probably succeed tonight.

Richard watched a helicopter buzz past, sweeping the rooftops for anything suspicious. If Charon wanted to he could knock the thing right out of the sky with one well-placed shot. Hopefully, he would concentrate on his prime target rather than a high body count. A chopper crash in the downtown area did not bear thinking about.

"You're looking grim."

He glanced at Sharon. "I've every right to be."

"Well, I'll not try to buck you up with cheerful patter, 'tis a grim situation. I'm only sorry you have to be the one to deal with it."

He smiled, lifted the headset out of the way a moment, and placed a swift kiss right on her mouth. "I knew there was something about you I liked."

"Only the one thing? No, don't answer that."

"Mm. I could be here all night doing inventory."

"Back to work with you." Smiling, she broke away to inspect the pizza boxes and helped herself to some of their contents.

Richard crossed to one of the radio coordinators. "I want another post check before the PM's arrival. Make sure everyone reports in by name and number and tick them off against your list. Anyone who doesn't have the right password—"

"Yes, sir," she said briskly, picking up a clipboard.

He went back into the relative quiet by the front window to better listen to the check-through while watching the outside. Sharon joined him again and apparently recognized his distracted look, for she made no conversation. She did silently offer him pizza, which he turned down with a brief head shake.

Post Seven, Post Seven, report in, over.

Post Seven, over.

Check in.

Roger that. Clarkson reporting. The password is "zenith." All quiet here.

Richard looked to the right. Post Seven would be on the CN Tower. It was a highly public, therefore unlikely, place for a sniper, but he'd placed extra people there for just that reason and had had the tower's own security staff double-checked before putting his team inside. It took the coordinator some little time to work through them all, but apparently nothing was amiss.

She moved on to the next post and the next. There was a short false alarm when a man didn't respond right away, but one of his teammates located him a few minutes later being sick in a lavatory. Richard didn't bother to gather details and simply broke in on the exchange to order a replacement sent out.

All the rest were routine and happily boring. The different voices cluttering his ear almost started to drone together, and he had to fight to stay alert to each and to visualize as best he could their locations. Of course the coordinator had a map for all that, which Richard had pored over earlier when he'd observed the setting-up process, but he was striving to match the flat map with the three-dimensional reality outside his window. Not easy.

Post Fifty-eight responding, over.

Check in.

Roger that. Marquand on post, and the password is "globe."

Richard jerked as though from an electric shock.

Everything's right-a-rooney here.

No mistake.

Nothing's shaking. Over.

It was Charon's voice.

The coordinator blithely ticked him off her list and went on to the next. Dry-mouthed, Richard strode unhurriedly to her to look over her shoulder at the clipboard. He got the location code for fifty-eight and checked it against the map on one of the desks. Good God, Charon was on top of the Esplanade. A rough calculation of the distance put him within easy shooting range for one of his experience.

Time. How long until—the PM would arrive in less than a quarter hour.

Richard held a necessarily fast inner debate on what to do next. A radio message to the team assigned to the Esplanade could interrupt Charon. That was what the job was all about, stopping him before he could fire; that was all that was needed. On the other

hand, Charon—being what he was—could likely
overcome any such interruption and continue or
escape and go to ground for another try later. He'd
have allowed for such a variable. Who knows but he
may have not only substituted himself for the real
Marquand, but done the same for the rest of rooftop
security team. A little hypnosis to get the names and
passwords as he'd obviously done for himself—hell,
they could *all* be IRA.

With this in mind—assuming the worst—then
Richard could gather some people and weapons
together and go in. Large and distracting, but messy.
There would certainly be casualties. The lives of a
dozen of his team against the single life of the target.
Yes, he was the Prime Minister, but for one of
Richard's years all human lives were much the same
to him, being equally ephemeral. Who was he to
judge from a crowd of strangers whose was the more
valuable life?

Or he could handle it quietly himself. As Sharon
had noted earlier, he was the one variable that Charon
could not have possibly allowed for.

The debate was over and done in less than a
second.

Richard was out the door and heading for the street
in the next.

Alone.

Once away from the crush of the Royal York
Richard went to full speed, tearing past the Royal
Bank Plaza and the glass and steel needle of the
Canada Trust Tower. He slowed slightly crossing
Front Street, then blazed down Yonge to veer hard
left toward the Esplanade. He was seen, of course,
it couldn't be avoided, but he knew he was moving
too fast for anyone to get a clear look. He'd have

registered as a blur of black and white, nothing more. The sun caught him once or twice, but not enough to affect him.

He did have to cut back to normal as he approached the building's sheltering entry, and there was a check as he flashed his ID to the police on duty in the lobby. He said he was on a personal inspection round, and after giving the senior officer a slight hypnotic push got the full and unquestioned run of the place. It was primarily shops and other businesses on the lower floors, above that, condominiums.

More lives to worry about.

Richard went straight for the service elevators. He could negotiate twenty-five floors of stairs somewhat faster running, but even he would be left rather breathless at the end. Better to conserve until he knew what was ahead. He had the time. Barely.

When he emerged in the utility hall at the penthouse level, he found a man on post there who reported with a smile that all was quiet.

"Everything's right-a-rooney," he said cheerfully. "Nothing's shaking."

Oh, yes, Charon had gotten to *him* all right. He hadn't a clue. Richard had him shut off the automatic alarm and open the fire door to the stairs leading to the roof.

The lowering sun was the first thing to hit him as he stepped outside. He fumbled for his dark glasses before recalling they were in his coat at the York. Squinting, he raised an arm to shield his eyes, eased the door shut, and stepped quickly around to the merciful shade on the east side of the stair's kiosk.

The next thing he noticed was the wind. Not nearly as strong as it had been on the Tor, but still an environmental factor to consider.

The breadth of the sky made up his next impression. One could not see all that much of it in the man-made canyons below, here it just went on and on, interrupted only by the taller towers of the city.

The fourth point to register was the uniformed cop also standing in the shade, staring straight ahead like a Buckingham palace guard. He took absolutely no notice of Richard—another man turned into an obedient and oblivious robot by Charon.

Richard glanced warily about the roof's otherwise flat expanse, spotting two other officers at its north and easternmost points next to the low rampart wall of the building's perimeter. They also stood still, not even remotely marking his presence. The far west side was another story, he found, peering around the corner. At the small end of the building, the point of the anvil, a stocky figure knelt by the rampart, looking intently west. Just on his right, all set to bring to bear, was something that at first glimpse seemed to be a length of piping with other pipes attached. They soon resolved into the recognizable shapes of a long muzzle, telescopic sights, and shoulder stock. Instant and inarguable death in the hands of an expert.

Charon. With his back turned. As vulnerable as he'd ever be.

Pay-back time.

Richard focused a moment on the officer and spoke quietly. "Right, I want you to go on standing here, but I should like to borrow this and this, there's a good lad." Richard relieved him of his firearm and wooden baton. He checked the gun to make sure the safety was off and a round racked in the chamber. Good. Excellent, in fact. Not wanting any sudden distractions, he took off his headset and gave it to the officer to hold, which he did.

A quick check. The other men held their posts,

and Charon still faced west, but he was reaching for the rifle. Yes, the PM would be arriving just about now. Charon placed the barrel on the rampart and peered into the sight before pulling back for a another unaugmented look. He must have been satisfied, for he settled into place, making his body comfortable for a moment's total immobility. In that moment he would time himself to move his trigger finger only in the crucial instant between heartbeats, sending the bullet out to precisely smash into another man's brain, turning live, thinking matter into so much dead tissue.

Richard eased from cover into the crashing red heat of the sunset, his borrowed gun up and ready, and stepped slowly forward. His shoe soles crunched against the grit on the roof, but the wind carried the sound away. He was able to get quite close; he didn't need to worry much about shooting between the beats of his own heart. Good thing, too, for it was hammering away far too fast.

He paused. His peripheral vision briefly noted the other high buildings, the vast blue void of Lake Ontario on his left, the fading sky above, then everything slid away from his consciousness. His mind dismissed all the rest of the world, centering entirely upon Charon, not five paces away.

Now or never.

Richard double-tapped twice with his gun: two bullets into the base of Charon's spine, two more into his upper back for his heart.

The man's body bucked and twisted, and he let forth an ugly tearing scream, an animal's screech of pain and outrage. The sound lanced through Richard, right to the bone. Charon collapsed and rolled away from the rampart, sprawling on his back. He wore a full ski mask and dark glasses against the sun. Richard walked close, bent, and plucked the glasses away for his own use. He settled them in place, then peeled the mask from Charon's head. The smell of fresh blood tainted the wind.

The first burning jolt of pain from the shots would not be swift to leave, but it was obvious when it eased slightly, for Charon froze and stared up with undisguised shock. And despite his obvious agony, he tried to speak.

"You . . . you—"

Richard grinned. "So nice to see you again. Can't stay long, though, you won't, anyway."

"You . . . don't. Give up. Do. You."

"I've some good news: I still have the Grail."

"Gra—?"

"And it works, I'm happy to say. I'm ever so much better than I was."

"Glad to. Hear. It. You sonova . . . . I—" But a spasm took him. *"Oh, God!"* His strangled cry cut off as he arched backward.

The spinal wounds, Richard thought. Then the truth of it dawned: Charon was starting to change.

Time to end things. A few more bullets in his heart to slow, then ram the baton into the holes in his chest to finish him and worry about smuggling the body out for cremation later.

Richard brought the gun to bear, but it was already too late.

Charon's beast swiftly emerged, whipped on by the pain.

Lightning fast, the thing launched itself at Richard, claws out, fangs extended, slamming bodily into him. Richard got off one last futile shot and they were rolling across the roof.

No time to think or plan, this was on the level of pure instinctive reaction: be quick or die. Richard got his arm up just as Charon bit down trying to reach his throat. His teeth tore through the sleeve like paper and ground deep into the skin beneath. Richard snarled and pushed, trying to get on top, but Charon's greater weight, frenzied rage, and complete desperation gave him the advantage here. He was neither beast nor man, but with the qualities of both, and wholly focused on killing.

His jaws closed hard and he pulled his head back, intent on ripping the flesh right from Richard's arm. Richard had done the same himself in his frenzy with Webb. Charon needed—craved—the blood. Grunting, Richard went with the move, pushing hard. He lost the gun as it slipped from nerveless fingers, but it bought him a second.

He still clutched the night stick in his left hand. He slammed one blunt end hard against the side of Charon's head. A deathblow to anyone else, but little effect here. Another strike. There, the bastard felt *that*. His jaws loosened and Richard yanked his arm free. Bloody and it hurt like hell, but still fairly intact.

He struck again, now against Charon's temple. The force impelling him seemed to slacken, then recovered. His claws tore into Richard's shoulder, raked his neck, his face. More blood. Lots more pain.

Forget it. Fight!

He rolled to his knees, lashing out with the baton. Charon avoided the blow and dodged to one side, feinting to the right, driving in on the left. Richard lunged away, gained his feet, but staggered, vision blurring as his blood streamed into his eyes. Half-blind, he managed another strike, this one square in Charon's face, breaking bones and cartilage. *That* stopped him.

Nothing fancy, now, just beat him insensible and kill him. Richard raised the club again, but Charon reeled from him, running unsteadily. He turned once, got in a vicious swipe that connected, making thin, razorlike cuts along Richard's abdomen. He folded over, trying to keep the baton up to ward off the next strike, but it never came.

Through a veil of blood he saw Charon's sporadic but swift progress toward the eastern rampart.

No!

Richard pressed after him, staggering himself from his hurts and the brutal press of the dying sun.

Too late.

Charon was up and over the low wall. Richard reached the edge seconds later and saw the ropes, the pulleys. Some sort of rappelling gear, only Charon was in too much a hurry to do it properly. His distorted hands were wrapped around the rope, and he slipped dangerously fast down its length to a secondary roof some ten stories below.

Richard had no knife handy, had lost the gun, and undoing the knots would take too long. He grabbed the rope and hauled it back as hard as he could. It was no light load. His shoulders strained, his wounds burned. He grunted and kept pulling. He felt hard tugs from the other end, like a fish struggling against the hook.

Then the weight suddenly vanished and he fell flat on his back, banging his head hard enough to make lights flash behind his eyes.

Get up!

But the breath had been knocked right out of him. By the time he returned to the wall to look down Charon was quite gone.

But where? Inside the building?

Then Richard saw another piece of rope attached to a similar rampart below. It snaked over the edge, leading down to the narrow space between the Esplanade and its much shorter neighboring structure, the Novotel Hotel.

Oh, Damn. Damn, damn, damn!

Weary and sick from the sun and the fighting, Richard knew he'd have to follow. Somehow.

The descent was a nightmare. Horizontally, crossing a hundred feet was insignificant, vertically was something else again. Especially now. He tried hand-over-hand, bracing his feet against the wall. It reminded him uncomfortably of the Chalice Well. At least he wasn't fighting gravity in quite the same way this time.

The last five yards he skipped by simply letting go the rope and dropping. He was wasted enough to have to roll with the impact, but found his legs again and tottered to the second rope.

Fifteen stories below in the shadows of the alley he saw Charon's foreshortened figure lurching toward the curb and a waiting car. A frigging limousine no less. Because of the reception at the Royal York the streets were all but choked with the damned things, making one more in the area all but invisible. Its back door popped open at his approach; he half fell inside, and it immediately sped away.

Richard thought of several things he could do to get the alarm out and initiate what would likely prove to be a futile pursuit. None were remotely practical for him, though. Not in the shape he was in. What the hell. He'd stopped the assassination. It would have to serve.

But dear God, how he *hurt*.

The reaction swept over him, gave him the shakes, forced him to sit down. At least it was shaded here. His exposed skin was cherry-colored and itching madly. It was almost enough to distract him from the wretchedness of the other injuries he'd taken.

He'd have to feed soon to compensate for the healing.

As would Charon.

Richard groaned.

Chapter Twelve

God, what sad places airports are.

Richard sat in a plastic chair at Pearson looking morosely at his hands lying in his lap. He idly rubbed the white scar at the base of his left ring finger as the latest wave of it washed through him.

He felt empty, a feeling he knew rather too well. It was always like this after battle. Amid the fierce guilty joy of survival was the hollowness inside, the strange barren sadness overwhelming him, dragging him down to immobility of body and spirit. Centuries past when he still walked in the sun he used to numb it with drink and whoring and finally the blessed escape of sleep, but now . . . that kind of numbing was beyond him and had been so for a very long time.

But since then Sabra had ever shared with him the burden; her unwavering love keeping him from plummeting wholly into the darkness at the bottom of his soul. And when they'd been apart, he'd always heard her voice speaking in his mind soft words of comfort to ease the heaviness in his heart.

Not now, though.

Not a single murmur of her presence stole upon him, even when he slept and in dreams was more receptive to her thoughts.

The silence frightened him.

Had he taken too long? She'd said she would not

364

survive the next turning of the moon, but he was well ahead of that deadline. Her appearance to him on the Tor might have changed things, though. Her use of her Gift often drained her much the same as healing drained him. Could she have used herself up beyond recovery?

No, if something had happened to her I would feel it. I have not the Gift, but I would know.

He held fast to that thin piece of hope as he waited for Sharon and tried to push the doubts from his mind.

With indifferent success.

The aftermath of the assassination attempt had proved to be as complicated and exhausting as he'd expected. Thank God for his ability to hypnotize people or else he'd have been forced to abandon this particular life and move elsewhere.

His first subjects were the officers assigned to the Esplanade's roof. When his hurts had healed enough to allow it, he climbed back up the rope and begun a kind of detoxification process for them, determining the level of influence Charon had committed on each, then correcting things. By the time he was done he was ready to collapse for a month, but the four of them—including the man in the service hall—were convinced they'd been knocked out for the duration by someone with an ether-soaked rag. How Charon managed to get all the passwords from them was someone else's problem.

Richard then had to face the rest of officialdom.

Over the next few hours he had to tell over and over of how he'd recognized Charon's voice on the radio, gone to the Esplanade, and fought with him before he'd escaped. The blood on his clothes, he explained, was Charon's. That satisfied a few of them. However, others—the armchair generals—demanded to know why he had not followed procedure and taken along backup.

Bourland had been of their number.

"Suppose you'd failed and Charon made his shot?" he asked.

"The whole point is that I did not fail," Richard wearily answered.

"I'm glad for that, and I can understand you taking a personal interest in getting the bastard, but cowboy tactics are not the done thing in a case like this, y'know."

"Yeah, right. I'll remember that next time."

"God forbid there should be one."

"Just make sure someone pays my bill when I send it in."

"Of course, though you might expect a dinner invitation from the PM as well. He wants to thank you."

"A card will do nicely."

"Oh, remember you said Charon was going to frame you for this? The local office of *The Globe and Mail* got an anonymous parcel about an hour ago and they contacted us. Full of papers, had a lot of rot in it about you being behind the assassination along with some other stuff implicating a number of people in the government. Of course, it would have only worked in conjunction with your unexplained disappearance and had the PM actually been killed. We've asked the newspaper to hush it up as a security matter."

"Sending it in without confirmation of the hit— someone in the splinter group had crossed signals, then."

"Yes, nice to know that. One is better able to deal with things when one realizes that they're only human after all."

A fat lot you know about it, my friend.

One bright point in the whole business was that he managed to get out of the thick of it before Demarest's hasty return from his goose chase in Newfoundland. Richard, all too obviously battered and shaken, had had no trouble presenting his excuses to Bourland and demanding a few days off to recover in Vancouver.

"Not sure if it's a good idea for you to get that far from things," he drawled. "Demarest will—"

"The devil with him. My mother is seriously ill, and I need to be with her. There's absolutely nothing more important than that. If he tries throwing his weight around with me again, I'll put his head up his own ass."

Bourland suppressed a laugh and acquiesced.

Before anything else could intervene, Richard called his travel service and booked two flights. He would go to Vancouver, and Sharon was bound for London again to finish her business with the Abbey Book.

Her bright presence had helped to push back some of his fear, to fill the emptiness, but Richard took care to conceal from her just how deep and black it was. The night before he'd made love to her as though she was the last woman on earth. He'd been gentle, intense, giving, and gotten the same and more in return from her, but lain wakeful long after she'd dozed off in his arms. When morning came, he loved her again, slowly rousing her from drowsiness to laughing, gasping delight. It had been extraordinary, and far too brief, but then a decade of doing nothing but making love to Sharon would be too brief.

So it was on the drive to the airport a little later that morning that he asked her to come back when she was finished in London.

"Come back?" she asked. "And . . . ?"

"Anything you want." His throat was tight and hot, his face flushing like a boy's. He could hardly breathe.

"And what is it you want?"

"You. I love you."

There. He'd been quite unable not to say it. He had said it before, in the heat of passion, or using the word as an endearment, but this time it was something altogether serious. The declaration hung between them, naked and vulnerable, waiting in agony for a reply.

Her long silence told him straightaway her answer.

His heart sank to an even lower level as the seconds of that silence stretched out between them to an unbreakable length. He felt foolish and stupid and tried to hide his raw hurt by focusing on the drive. He parked in one of the underground lots, cut the Jaguar's motor, and started to get out, but Sharon put a hand on his.

Her eyes were filled with tears.

Yes, answer enough. No one weeps like that when the news is good.

"It's not you, Richard, it's me. You are a wonderful man, the best I've ever met, but I know me. It'd be the finest for a month or two, maybe even a few months, but then I'd have to be up an' goin' who knows where, an' I'd feel badly about leavin' you, an' that'd make me angry an' I'd start to resent you, an' that would turn to hatin' an' . . ."

He put one hand up and she trailed off, leaving the rest of the decline unsaid. "Sharon, it—it's all right."

"No, it's not, an' we're both smart enough to know it."

He brushed at a tear trail on her cheek and managed a smile. "Well, if we're so smart, then maybe we can get around all this."

"Oh?"

Richard looked at her, fixing her face in his mind.

He didn't need the Gift of Sight to tell him that suggesting anything remotely resembling a commitment would drive her away forever. Either it was not for her or she was simply not ready yet. He could force a change upon her, but had long ago learned the brutal futility of such a selfish ploy.

"I want you, Sharon, and I love you, that is the given fact of it for me. The given fact for you is that you are your own woman."

"That I am."

"It's the way it should be."

Her brow puckered. "What are ye leadin' to, Richard?"

"A suggestion, nothing more." He swallowed, hoping the right words would come. "If it pleases you, and *only* if it pleases you, would you share some of your time with me? When and how long is up to you, and when you choose to leave I won't make a fuss."

She was shaking her head before he'd finished. "No, I've done that before. It never works."

"With someone like me?"

That made her stop and think. "No," she admitted. "But when it comes to it, I don't know you all that well."

"I can say the same about you, Ms. Geary."

She thought again, staring out the windshield. "I— I just don't know."

Well, it was better than an outright refusal. "Then when you do, give me a call. Or just drop in. I promise you no demands, no obligations, no arguments. I swear it."

"I've had such promises before."

Another smile twitched across his face, and he suddenly reached into the backseat and brought forward a sturdy aluminum camera case.

"Oh, now ye' can't be thinkin'—" she began, eyes going wide.

"Oh, but I can," he said, popping the latches and lifting the lid. Nestled within the protective foam padding was a small, rounded object, carefully wrapped in white silk. His hand hovered over it, barely touching the fine fabric. "I'm serious enough to swear on this. Knowing what it means to each of us, believe in the Grail, if not in me."

She breathed out an *oh*, half-astonishment, half-alarm. Within the confines of the car he heard the fast thrum of her heart, and it was a minute or two before it settled to something like a normal pace.

He shut the case lid, having made his point and then some.

She shook her head, but now it was in wry admiration, not rejection. "You're a once in a lifetime man, Richard Dun. An' I will drop in for a visit. Not just now, though. I'm wantin' some time."

He nodded. "Then whenever."

She leaned forward and kissed him. Soft lips, a whisper of her scent, fingers warm on his face. Sweet and loving. But most importantly, it was not a good-bye kiss. Not yet, anyway. It would have to do.

They walked slowly to the entry, passing through the security check without incident. Sharon had again left her Glock at his place, saying she could get another if she had need. He didn't doubt it.

He had to open the case again for inspection, but it excited no comment from the people on duty. In addition to a story of transporting a valuable antique to a collector, Richard was more than prepared to use hypnosis on the lot of them to get through, but glad to find it unnecessary.

Another slow walk. They would have to part at customs. Sharon excused herself to the ladies' room, and he found an unoccupied and desperately uncomfortable chair to wait for her. At least it was in a sliver of shade.

He stared at his hands a lot, trying to ignore his inner darkness, and occasionally glancing at the shiny case at his feet. Strange, he could feel its power like the warmth of a winter's fire against his leg. He reached down and touched the case, fully expecting to encounter the heat, but all there was was the cold of its metallic exterior.

"I don't think it's going to go anywhere." Sharon, back now with fresh color on her lips, smiled down at him.

Maybe not. He wasn't going to take any chances.

"Y'know, Richard, at first, I didn't want you to have it. I was sure it should be in a museum somewhere, or at some university to be studied. Sweet Mary, it's a national treasure. It'd make us famous, to be sure. But I don't feel that now. Something tells me you're the one to keep it, and I'm heartened that you do. It feels right somehow, if I'm makin' myself understood."

Richard simply nodded and stood, taking her hand.

"I hope it helps with your mother. I truly do."

Sharon was silhouetted against the morning sun, and he blinked against its intensity, feeling the exposed skin of his face tingling in the first stages of burning. Absently, he thought that he should move, but he stayed where he was, looking at her. Dear Goddess, she was so special, so very rare.

They lapsed into a sweet, sad silence, holding hands like two children hearing a storm in the distance, waiting for its arrival. Giving each other strength, giving each other love in the face of things beyond their control. And so they stood until the storm arrived: the harsh reality that they were finally out of time.

He could not remember walking close with her to the customs entry, but suddenly they were there, and her face was pressed upon his neck, her breath hot and wet with tears.

"Expect me when you see me, Richard Dun."

Then she was gone, and he felt more alone than he ever had. He stood silent as the wetness on his neck turned cold and dried. Stood silent until the announcement of his own flight pierced his churning mind, and brought him roughly back to the world. Then he turned and hurried to his flight.

Goddess, what sad places airports are.

A letter from Bourland was waiting for him at the gate. Richard opened it only after he boarded. No official stationery, no salutation, not even a signature. Very discreet.

"Found abandoned escape car. Two bodies. Same condition as the others. IDs pending, but think they're in the same club. Likely our man again.

Watch your back."

He already knew to do that. He'd not seen the last of Charon. Not until the bastard was well and truly dead would Richard feel safe again.

The takeoff was slow and gut-wrenchingly turbulent. Sweat stood out on his forehead, and he gripped the arms of his seat, staring at the closed window shutter next to him. Deep inside fear scurried in the shadows like a rat, malevolent, gnawing at him.

He counted to sixty, and when he'd finished thought how nice it would be to take a train for the return trip. Perhaps, just perhaps, he could talk Sabra into coming with him. She wasn't fond of modern cities, not with their sprawls of concrete and filthy air, but he might tempt her away with the promise of a lengthy hunt through the bookstores. If she had a weakness for anything it was for the printed page.

He read Bourland's note again. Not one word of it had changed.

Foolish of him to make plans until he'd finally dealt with Charon. It would be soon, but that problem could wait until Sabra was better.

If she can get better, he thought, his heart going cold for an instant. He glanced down at the case where it rested between his leg and the wall panel of the plane. The sight reassured him.

After his usual instructions to the flight attendant he closed his eyes and willed sleep to come. Easy enough, since he was exhausted. Slowly, like an old lover, sleep took him in her arms and carried him sweetly, gently, into the all-enveloping darkness.

Until a heavy hand clapped hard on his shoulder, jolting him wide awake. His seat mate, a besuited businessman, stared up in abject terror at the sturdy figure looming over them both.

Charon, utterly immersed in his beast-form, grinned down at them. With a casual, effortless movement, he raked his claws savagely across the man's throat. He made a terrible coughing scream, hands coming up in a hopeless attempt to stop the blood, but it speared out regardless, its dark red scent filling the air. The man slumped.

"You're next, Lance-baby." Charon pulled the man's head up by the hair to display the seeping wounds. "But how about one last meal? No? Maybe you prefer something fresher." He let go the man and seized the white-faced flight attendant. She began to scream, but he slapped a fist against her temple and her eyes rolled up.

Frantic, Richard tore at his seat belt.

Too late. Charon bowed briefly over the young

woman's throat, worried at it, and pulled sharply away. He laughed as the blood sprayed out across Richard's chest.

"Shucky darn. I guess I owe you a new set of threads." Another laugh, then he shoved the woman's body at Richard. "Catch me if you can, Mr. Lusk!"

Charon darted through the curtains to the coach section. Richard untangled himself and sobbing with rage, followed.

It was dark on the other side. All the shutters were pulled closed. The only light came from the emergency strips running the length of the deck, but there were— things—covering them. He tripped over one of them. A man. Dead. Beyond him, another huddled shape in the narrow aisle. A little girl.

No! Please, God, no!

But Charon had gotten to them all. Row after row of them. Dead. Eyes open, eyes shut, some shamming peaceful sleep, others . . .

And blood. Everywhere. The deck was awash, the seats soaked, the overhead compartments painted with it.

Charon stood at the far end and spread his arms. They, too, were red. "I said I was a goddamned Rembrandt at this. Tell me I'm wrong!"

Richard rushed at him, stumbling over the bodies, sight clouded. All he could see was Charon's distorted face, mouth wide with laughter. He closed on him, was almost within reach, but Charon, using unnatural speed, turned into a blur of motion.

Richard whirled to meet . . . nothing. He turned again. Clear.

Where?

Charon came at him hard out of nowhere, knocking him flat. Richard didn't care, he was within reach now. He fought, frenzied madness taking him, heedless of his own injuries, heedless of everything but the need to kill. He felt bones break under his hands, tasted hot blood, but it wasn't enough. The damned thing still lived as it wrenched free of his grasp—still lived as it staggered to its feet, looked down at Richard, and laughed again.

A huge hole in Charon's chest gushed blood, and one arm hung useless by his side; one eye was swollen shut, the other shone red in the dim light.

"That was a nice warm up, but what-say we get serious? I'm gonna make you my own special magnum opus, buddy-boy. I'll stuff you full of sawdust and put you on display, then do the same for your old lady. You'll make a hell of a conversation piece."

Richard tried to get up, but something was wrong. He couldn't move. Pain shot up his spine like fire. Before he could work past it, Charon launched forward and was on top of him.

And Richard couldn't—absolutely could *not* move.

Charon's canines were fully extended, dripping scarlet. His breath stank of rotted meat. He pushed Richard's head to one side, exposing his neck, and sank down for the kill.

No!

With desperate effort, Richard twisted away. Or tried to. Something gripped his waist, kept him from—

"Sir! Mr. Dun! *Mr. Dun!*"

His eyes shot open, his first sight that of the shocked and fearful attendant. Standing next to her in the aisle was the businessman. Except for their anxious faces, both were perfectly all right. Richard glanced around. People stared, but everything was normal, intact. The air was the usual dry recycled stuff, untainted by the slaughterhouse.

He put his hands to his face and scrubbed away

the sleep. Looking down, he noticed the covers of his chair arms were ruptured, the stuffing blossoming out where his nails had torn through. Embarrassed, he mumbled an apology to the woman.

"Bad dream," he added.

"Are you all right? Would you like some water?"

"I'm fine. Please don't bother." He had to repeat himself a few times before she reluctantly moved on.

He rubbed his eyes again and realized he was soaked with sweat; he could smell the stale stink of his own fear rising from his damp clothes. Fingers trembling uncontrollably, he undid his seat belt, picked up the camera case, and made his way to the toilet. Once inside, he splashed his face clean and tried the airline's cheap cologne to cope with most of the smell.

He stared at himself in the mirror, for a moment unsure of who was looking back.

The face is familiar, but I forget the brain.

The dream had come out of himself, of course, based on his own anxieties; so how had the Richard he'd known for so many centuries come up with such a horror?

Damn Bourland for sending that note.

Richard made his way back to his seat. The businessman moved his legs to give him space.

"You can blame me for sending for the stew," he said in a low voice. "I thought you were having a cardiac."

"Thank you, but it's nothing, just a dream."

"Must have been a real bear. I get 'em sometimes. You in the war, too?"

Richard glanced sharply at him.

"Thought so. You've got the look." He nodded at the other people in first class, the ones who were keeping themselves carefully occupied as though nothing at all had happened. "Don't mind them.

There's no way anyone can understand unless they been through it themselves."

"Indeed."

Richard belted in and stowed the case under the seat in front of him just as the landing announcement came. He held tightly to the torn chair arms as the great bird dipped sickeningly. Then he closed his eyes and waited for it all to be over.

His seat mate spoke again, sounding sad and tired. "Guys like us, we might as well be from another world when the stuff kicks in."

Quite another world altogether, my young friend, he thought.

The man had not asked Richard which war. No need for it, since every generation had at least one to scar it, one to make instant brothers of strangers.

Until the boat taking him to Kingcome docked, Richard held the camera case safely between his feet. When the craft finally bumped against the buffer line of old tires tied to the small pier he picked up the case and, thanking the boat's captain, stepped out into a fine, all-drenching drizzle. The pilot behind the wheel did not even look at him, but was somehow able to determine that the boat's only passenger had safely disembarked. He gunned the motor and sped away into the gathering gloom. Richard stalked toward the shore, looking around, but seeing no one.

The place was as depressing as ever. Here and there smoke half-heartedly struggled up into the sodden air from the ramshackle buildings, but not a light shone from any of them. Not a sound could be heard above the dripping of the rain and the fading ripple of water from the boat's wake.

Odd that someone had not come to meet him . . . unless they were reluctant to present him with bad news.

"There is great power in rain."

Black Eagle's voice came from behind him, and Richard, heart in his mouth, spun to see. The old man stood at the end of the dock near the water's edge. How he had got to the end of the dock, Richard had no idea. Black Eagle had not passed him, and no other boat had come along, for Richard would have heard it. Both men stared at each other, silent for awhile, sharing the little mystery.

The ceremonial robes Black Eagle had worn to greet Richard previously were gone. Instead he was clad in faded blue jeans, a dirty red plaid shirt, and cheap, filthy sneakers, yet power still flowed effortlessly from him. He seemed not to mind the drizzle soaking him to the skin.

"It is the life-blood of the world," the old man continued, his ancient eyes looking up, "the purest gift that Wakan Tanka can give. At the end of the rain is the rainbow, the sacred bridge between here and the other place. You will accomplish much before the end of this rain, dark father."

"The dark mother, is she—" Richard hesitated. He didn't quite know what word to use. To ask if she was still alive risked the response that she was not. And he couldn't bear to think of that, especially not now when he was so close.

"I have not seen her since long before you first came. I do not see her. That is the task of She-Who-Walks. You ask her. She is at the dark mother's house. You go now."

Richard tucked the camera case under his arm, and headed off along the trail toward Sabra's cabin. Mud soon slimed his boots as he sped up the unpaved street and began to ascend the rise that would lead him into the forest.

"Dark father!"

Richard stopped and looked back.

Black Eagle yet stood at the end of the dock. The old man obviously wanted to say something, was struggling with it. He waved a hand in front of his face as if to brush away an annoying insect. Then his shoulders slumped, and he looked down, shaking his head. He made a dismissive gesture.

Fearful, Richard debated on going back and questioning him, but now that he was here a desperate hurry to find Sabra and give her the Grail overcame all other considerations. Whatever needed to be said could wait. He moved on, passing the lodge house and its guardian totems, going up the trail he had so recently taken with She-Who-Walks.

He'd just entered the first rank of trees when a swirl of icy mist wrapped thick around him, obscuring his view. A single word was hissed in his ear, making the hairs on his nape rise.

"Beware!"

When the mist cleared he turned back once more. Black Eagle was gone, and Kingcome lay below Richard as desolate and deserted looking as it had been on his arrival. The old man could not have possibly moved from sight that quickly. Perhaps he was very much elsewhere and the figure on the dock but an apparition of the reality. Richard had known stranger things to happen.

Thank you for your words, old man. I will beware. But nothing will stop me.

Richard continued up the trail, gathering speed until he was no more than a phantom threading through the trees. The rain was not so heavy under their shelter, but stray drops stung his face with his swift passage. It was full dark now, country darkness, unlit by either moon or stars, with none of the bright comforts of so-called civilization to leaven the gloom. His eyes were well used to it.

He hurtled forward until the yellow glimmer of a
lantern in Sabra's window came into sight. He slowed
to an abrupt standstill before the closed door of the
little cabin, quite drenched, heart pounding. Then
suddenly the door opened wide, spilling a soft golden
glow into the night, and a woman's shape cast a shadow
across him.

For a breath-stealing instant his heart tried to
mislead him into believing that it was Sabra standing
there, welcoming him home as she had so often in
the past in so many other places. But his head knew
better, and was right: the woman in the doorway was
She-Who-Walks.

She gave no greeting, only drew back so Richard
could step inside to the warmth and dryness. Like
her father, she was no longer in ceremonial dress.
Frayed shorts showed off her long brown legs, and
she wore a man's shirt, the front tails knotted around
her waist. Her feet were bare, one behind the other
like a nervous child's. Then she stood on tiptoe and
kissed him, once on each cheek, chaste as a virgin.

"Welcome, Father. Your journey has been long—sit
by the fire and warm yourself."

But Richard wanted none of this. "Where is Sabra?
I have the Grail, I must see her."

She-Who-Walks smiled gently. "When the time is
right, Father."

But Richard was not to be put off, and he grabbed
her roughly. "No, no more waiting, girl. Sabra has
no time. I must see her now to save her life.
Understand that!"

She-Who-Walks simply took his hands from her—
she had the strength to do so—and calmly eased onto
the rocking chair by the blazing fireplace. The cabin
smelled of herbs and apple wood.

"You cannot see her now. She is not to be seen

now. Even I do not see her now. This is the part of night when her affliction is at its worst. We must wait for the hour before dawn, when the beast finally leaves her and she is herself for a little while. When the rain ends, the door will be opened between the worlds to allow her through. That is the time when she will need this . . . Grail . . . you have brought. But for now, you must wait."

"It's not necessary, I've already tested—tried—it, and it saved me. There's no need to wait, she can—"

"*Not* when the beast has her. You of all people know what hold it has on the spirit."

And in his sinking heart, despite all his headlong worries, Richard knew she was right. He turned away a moment to master himself, then finally put the camera case on the table next to some books. They were the same ones as before, all about the legend of Arthur. His conscience twinged, for he'd forgotten to bring back the thick volume by Malory.

"How has she been?" he murmured.

"She feeds well, though not on any other than me. All the animals have gone, even the birds. Did you not notice the silence? None in the village can withstand her when the beast is in her. So, I feed on them, and she on me."

Pushing back the loose sleeves of her shirt, she held out her arms. Richard saw huge jagged scars on both, still red in their healing.

"It is this bad?" he asked, humbled.

"Ever since the Spirit Walk. She came to me a few days ago as clear and beautiful as she had ever been, and said she needed to go to you . . . to save you. I helped her, and she made the journey, but her hunger was very great when she returned. I almost didn't have enough for her."

"I'm sorry you had to suffer. It was my fault."

"It was the fault of the one who kills." She let her gaze wander to the fire for a time, then rose to stand by the table. "Show me the Grail."

Richard could not refuse, and carefully opened the case. He lifted the silk-wrapped object out onto the books, and the white material slithered away, revealing the cup in all its simple glory. She-Who-Walks stared at it for a long time as it glinted in the firelight, but made no effort to touch it. When she finally moved it was to wipe the back of her hand across her face to brush at the tears.

"This is worth the pain," she pronounced.

"It *will* help her," he said.

She nodded. "When the time comes. We must wait."

And wait Richard did. He stripped from his wet clothes to let them dry before the fire, and She-Who-Walks found a towel and then a blanket for him to wrap up in. She invited him to take the rocking chair, for which he was grateful. The bed would have been much too comfortable. He didn't want sleep, not if it held any more dreams like the one on the plane.

She piled more wood in the fireplace and sprinkled into it dried herbs and a quantity of sweet grass. The cabin filled anew with its wholesome green scent and he breathed deeply of it, watching the flames as they grew and faded to embers and ash through the whole of the long night.

He had held vigil once before when he'd taken his vows for knighthood, but it had not been like this. Then he had been young, excited by the wild game of life, invincible in his youth. Now the dying embers spoke to him of life passing, inevitably, finally into nothingness. Outside, the sound of the rain's steady pour made his very soul ache.

The minutes stretched into hours, and a deeper

silence than that of the deserted forest took hold
of Richard's body and mind. All the shrill voices of
the world that had nagged at him through the last
days one by one hushed with each breath he took.
His heartbeat slowed, and his eyelids drifted shut,
though not for sleep. He was aware of everything
around him, the quiet of the night, the heat of the
fire, and She-Who-Walks's steady breathing, and yet
there was something more. One last small insistent
voice remained.

A small child's voice, weeping.

In his mind he followed the sound down stone
passages, the voice growing clearer and louder until
Richard found himself in a great gray stone room.

It was cold and dark, the only illumination coming
from a window set too high in the wall to reach. No
shred of comfort eased the place, not a single
cushion, not the most threadbare blanket. This was
a prisoner's cell. He was afraid here, though the only
other presence was a small fair-haired boy. He lay
across a low wooden bench in the center of the
flagged floor, face hidden in the crook of one arm,
his little body racked with sobs.

Richard heard a man speak, and it was a moment
before he realized that it was his own voice, speaking
the old language of his long lost youth.

"What ails thee, boy?"

The child did not reply at first, only sobbed louder.

"Boy?" He knelt by the bench and reached out
with both hands to gently lift the child's face into
view. It was red and streaked with tears. Richard's
hair stood on end as recognition sparked; his breath
came short. Answering through the tears was a voice
he knew, oh so well; a voice that he'd stifled for so
many years.

"My mother left me. She hates me. They said so.

They all hate me." The tears flowed anew, and Richard held the frail little body close, so close, fighting his own tears and failing.

"Your mother has indeed gone, Dickon, yet she did love you."

"They said I killed her."

"Oh, no, never. 'Tis a cruel lie. She gave her life for you, that you might live. It was her willing gift."

"But I miss her," said the boy.

"I know, I know. Yet she is with you always, she sees you, she glories in you. Truly, she will never leave you."

The boy pulled his head away from Richard, and looked up to him, his eyes intent and piercingly blue. "Never?"

"Never." Richard held him by the shoulders to look at him squarely. He was so young, so terribly defenseless. He needed something to shield him from the harsh world. "No matter what happens, you are loved. You are always loved. Know that in your heart. I love you, Dickon."

Through the streaming tears the boy smiled. "And I love you, Richard."

Then the delicate little arms wrapped hard around his neck and man embraced his child, and both knew peace.

No matter what happens, you are loved, Richard.

Like a swimmer from a deep dive, Richard slowly came up from within himself back to the lowly, one-room cabin. He opened his eyes. The fire was dead; the last embers gone out. There was a change in the air. The sweetgrass smell was gone, replaced by the freshening unique to the dawn.

Why had he had *that* particular vision? He could work out its obvious meaning, but was there another one beneath the first? One he dared not consider?

She-Who-Walks stood by the open door looking out into a faint gray world. The rain still fell steadily.

"It is time," she said.

Richard rose, leaving the blanket in the chair, and hurriedly dressed. Tying the last lace of his boots, he straightened and picked up the Grail from where it had rested undisturbed in its silk nest all the long night. It felt cold and weighed heavy in his hand.

"There is one more thing," she added.

Something in her flat tone filled him with sudden dread.

"The mother would have your promise that should all else fail, you will ease her of her burden. She has ever trusted you in the past, and begs you to give her one last comfort." She-Who-Walks turned. She had a stake of sharpened yew in one hand and a sword in the other and held them out to Richard.

Panic and terror crashed against him. "I cannot!"

"You can, and you must. Promise her, Father."

"'Tis too much to ask. I *cannot*!" To drive the stake through her body, through her heart in one swift brutal blow, then to take the sword and cut off her head . . . and this to *Sabra*, his mother, his sister, friend, and lover, the woman he loved above all. He would surely go mad. His mind was already reeling with the hideous vision of what he was being asked to do.

She-Who-Walks's eyes glittered with tears. "I've lived with her pain for all this time. Her spirit cries and cries and cries without pause because of it. I'd have gladly done the task to ease her passage, but she has held off from asking it of me until your return. This is *only* if the Grail should not work."

"But it will!"

"Then you've no reason not to make the promise."

Richard choked off his next words. Logic and faith

together. *God and Goddess, what demands you make of your servants.* "Very well. I swear it," he whispered, all too aware that he was holding the Grail.

"Come, then." She-Who-Walks quickly wrapped the sword and stake in a piece of buckskin. He followed as she stepped out into the soaking darkness. She strode forward without hesitation, mud staining her bare feet, the splashes creeping up her strong legs. Within minutes they were both wet to the skin and he glumly wondered why he'd bothered to dry off in the first place.

They walked a quarter mile perhaps, until reaching a fern-lined clearing in the shape of a rough circle. Richard noticed four large flat stones at each compass point, but could not immediately determine if they were natural or had been placed there on purpose. On the other side of the circle ran a stream, pregnant with the night's rain, the flow bursting forcefully over the rocks in its course. The chill sound of it reminded him of the Chalice Stream under the Tor, and he had to suppress a shiver.

The smaller ferns nodded from the rain, but around them the inner forest was preternaturally still, holding its breath, waiting. Waiting. Then his ears picked up the faintest sound over the water flow. It came from the black under the trees and almost at the same time She-Who-Walks's hand clasped his arm.

"See!"

A small patch of shadow detached itself from the greater darkness around it and moved hesitantly across the open ground before them. It stopped in the middle of the clearing and waited, a tiny, distorted figure, loosely wrapped in a thin blanket, swaying.

"Sabra?" The figure lifted its head and looked toward him. Her voice came to him across the night, a voice filled with weariness, fear, and pain.

"Oh, my Richard . . ."

Unresisting, he entered the circle. He started forward to embrace her, but was brought up short by her imperious shout.

"No! Do not come near!" Now her voice possessed a hard edge that truly frightened him. There was madness and hunger here, both barely held in check. Her tone softened. "It is for your own sake. The beast is wild in me, and I may do you harm. I would not hurt you for all the world."

Richard nodded. "I know, my love, I know." What there was left of Sabra lingered most in her eyes, and he tried to look only at them, not the ravages her beast had committed on the rest of her body.

"The Grail." Hers was not a question, but a statement.

He held it out to her, arms shaking from the weight of it.

"Fill it from the stream."

Richard did so, dipping the brass cup deep into the water. It rushed over his hand, and the pain was exquisite. He gasped and nearly let it go.

"There is always pain," she murmured. "There is always pain. Bring it to me."

He steadied himself and crossed to her, holding the Grail well before him. Only now did he see clearly her face, twisted, scarred, racked by the beast.

"Oh, my love . . ."

"Say no more, Richard, I know what I am. I thank you for coming—you are and ever were a brave and noble soul, and my one greatest love. Now trust the Goddess and her ways."

Sabra took the Grail from him with trembling hands and raised it high, first to the north, then the lightening east, and on around, saluting each compass point in turn before bringing the cup to her lips. She drained it in one long draught, then knelt, placing the Grail in the thick grass before her in the center of the circle. For many seconds, she remained motionless, as if waiting, then her head snapped back and a scream more horrible than any Richard had ever heard escaped her. She fell convulsing to the ground.

He was by her in an instant, trying to hold her down, to keep her from hurting herself. She made terrible little mewling sounds, and the panic swelled in him to the bursting point. He held her, tried to hush her, shouted her name, and it seemed to work for she went suddenly still, so very, very still in his arms.

"Sabra? No . . . no, you mustn't—*Sabra!*"

Her head lolled away from him. She was utterly limp. He bent low, his mouth on hers, and he breathed into her, again and again.

Take me instead or us both together, he pleaded to the Goddess, *but not this!*

No answer came from the dull silence surrounding him.

No!

He pressed his ear to her breast, but heard no reassuring thump of her heart.

Nothing . . . nothing at all.

For an awful moment, he felt brush of cold things sweeping around them. The Hounds? Was Sabra already being led away by them to the light he'd seen? He looked up, straining to catch some glimmer of her or of the silvery cord such as had anchored him before to his body. All he saw was the rain streaming down out of the grayness. He shouted her name, hoping she might hear him and return as he had returned. He shouted, screamed, pleaded, sobbed.

Then he used his nails to tear open his right wrist, and let the flow from the wound run into her lax mouth. It welled full, then trickled out the side. When the tear began to heal, he opened it again.

Useless. All useless.

He combed the tangled hair from her face, kissed her forehead, her eyes, then held her close, rocking back and forth, moaning.

The rain fell and gently cleansed his blood from her, washing it into the earth.

The rain fell, washing them both clean.

She was gone. He held her, yet had no sense of her. Where her presence should have been in his soul there was now a vast empty space, rapidly, agonizingly, collapsing upon itself.

She was gone. He went numb with the awful realization of a world without her. Forever. Sabra, who had ever and always been there, who had given him new life and a reason for living, was gone. She was dead and all hope dead with her.

He raised his head and like the hound that was part of his soul, howled his grief and fury to the endless sky.

Then it was beyond such expression. Beyond tears. Beyond exhaustion. There was nothing left in him. Nothing—

"Well, howdy doody, good buddy." The alien voice sliced crudely across his anguish like a dull knife. "This really is a touching scene. Brings a tear to my old jaundiced eye."

Charon stood across the clearing, grinning like death.

He held She-Who-Walks tightly before him with the point of the yew stake pressed up under her breastbone. The tableau was too much like Richard's dream from the plane. He stood up. She struggled briefly and was rewarded with a jab that made a trail of blood down her belly. Her face and hair half obscured his form, but Richard could see Charon was in bond to his beast; that was how he managed to hold her with such ease. His crazed eyes glowed red in the gloom, and his corner teeth were fully extended.

"Listen, buddy, maybe you should tell little Pocahontas here some of the stuff you learned about me on top of that damned hill. You know? Like how mean and tough I am, and how much I know about anatomy, and how I really *hate being pissed off!*"

Richard held up one hand in a placatory gesture. The girl struggled regardless. Her own strength was formidable now, but no match against Charon's while he was in this state.

He drove the stake in enough to make her gasp, and she froze. "One more twitch, painted sister, and you'll be joining the old broad! You savvy?"

She made no reply, but there was a murderous gleam in her eyes to match his own.

Richard spoke to distract them both, voice thick with anger and grief. "You saw what happened to Sabra. It killed her. It didn't work."

"I saw, and it's only because your old lady screwed up. It's the water from the Chalice Well that you have to drink, dumbfuck! I didn't figure a mega-jock like you would catch on, but she was something else again. Really surprised me she missed that little trick. Guess she was too far gone to think straight. Too bad. Maybe if I'd thought you'd have asked nicely I'd have shared some of mine with her, but them's the breaks."

Richard felt the beginnings of a tremor just under his heart. He fought the fury back before it could seethe up beyond his control. Charon's baiting was meant to keep him off balance, to make him too enraged to think or plan.

"There's no need to hurt the girl. I'll give you the Grail," he said, stooping to pick it up. He carefully did not look at Sabra's body.

"Mighty white of you, Kemosabe, but I've got my hands full—just gimme a sec. . . ." He brought the stake around and slammed the blunt end against the side of the girl's head. Her body abruptly went slack, and he let it fall, dropping on one knee to center the point of the stake exactly over her heart. "There, one thing at a time, I always say. Now take three giant steps—don't forget to say 'mother, may I,' okay?"

Richard walked slowly forward until he stood just within arm's reach of Charon. A quick lunge and—

Charon's left hand blurred. "Well, well, old habits die hard, don't they, Lance? Were you figuring to celebrate her recovery with a party, maybe do an Errol Flynn impersonation?" He'd pulled the sword free of its buckskin wrapping, hefting it lightly. "Nice piece of work. I'm impressed." He swung the blade up, bringing its razor edge to Richard's neck. "Snicker-snack."

"You'd be doing me a favor."

"Hey, I'm a big-hearted guy, anything to please. Besides, I owe you for the screwing over in Toronto."

Smiling, Richard lifted his chin, leaning into the sharp pressure on his throat. "I know."

But Charon hesitated. "There's a catch here someplace. You're not the type to give in."

"Without Sabra I've nothing left to live for."

"Heartbreaking. What about Pocahantas?"

Richard glanced down at her, then shook his head. "You'll kill us both, anyway. You don't dare not kill us thinking we'd come after you later."

"You got that right, buddy boy."

"Just . . ." His face twisted as the grief tried to overwhelm him. He shuddered and pushed it back.

"Just let me be with her." Without waiting for an answer, Richard turned from Charon and went to Sabra.

"Wait a second!"

He ignored the man and still with his back to him, sank to his knees by her. He lifted one of her cold hands, then the other, bringing them together across her body. How thin and wasted she'd gotten. How had she endured it for so long?

Some distant small part of him that still gave half a damn for such details noted Charon's snort of disbelief and the sound of movement as he stood and walked over. He stopped a pace or two off. Plenty of room to allow for the swing of the sword.

Tenderly, Richard stroked Sabra's forehead and waited.

Not long, my love.

Not long at all. He heard Charon's intake of breath as he prepared to swing.

And also a soft, very soft whisper of sound, hardly audible above the rain, but then he'd been listening for it. Richard turned to smile beatifically up at Charon in time to see She-Who-Walks seize him from behind and rake her nails across his face.

He'd badly underestimated her ability to recover, perhaps from too many years of dealing with frail humans. Richard had seen her eyes flutter open, and for a tiny instant they'd locked gazes, wordlessly uniting to common purpose and plan.

Bloody flesh shredded from bone and Charon's right eye gushed fluid. His maddened shriek of agony cracked through the forest like a gunshot. He twisted to lash out at her with the sword, but Richard lunged up and dragged it away, breaking the man's arm in the process. Another cry and a louder curse. Richard's memory of the dream superimposed itself upon this reality. In both Charon had a damaged eye and a useless arm; only one thing remained—

As Charon staggered around to face him, Richard grabbed up the sword and thrust the point deep into his chest. The beast screamed and flailed and tried to slide off of the blade, but Richard drove forward until it stumbled and fell sprawling on its back by the stream. The metal was not as effective as yew wood, but good enough for the purpose. As in the dream blood gushed from Charon's chest. His limbs twitched, gouging the earth.

"Bring me the cup!" Richard ordered.

She-Who-Walks plucked it up and hurried to him. He jerked his head and she knelt by the stream filling the Grail with water.

He glared down at Charon's wrecked face. It had begun to heal. "You want the Grail, Charon? You really want the Grail?"

"You fucking, sonova—"

"Not exactly what you had in mind, but what the hey, I'm a big-hearted guy—anything to please."

"No! *Don't!*" He writhed against the sword pinning him down, frantic to escape.

She-Who-Walks seized him by his tangled hair and poured the water into his gaping mouth. He retched and coughed and spat, trying not to swallow, but some of it got into him. His cursing turned to unintelligible shrieks, and finally the terrible convulsions took him. Laughing, Richard wrenched the sword from Charon's body and stood back to watch the ugly spectacle with an unholy joy. Watched until the last spasms subsided, the last whimpering cries faded, and sweet silence again settled on the forest.

The thick clouds shielded them from the killing light of dawn, but not for long. High above the wind began to shred at their billowing forms. Soon they would be mere tatters and the sun would flood the land and make the forest steam with its heat.

They hurried back to the cabin, Richard carrying Sabra and She-Who-Walks bearing the Grail, sword, and stake. They'd left Charon by the stream for the present.

Richard held Sabra's small form easily, lightly, but his walk was that of an old man with too heavy a burden. *I shall always feel this moment,* he thought. It would never leave him. He had horrors beyond count imprinted forever in his long memory, but none like this, not with Sabra.

You asked me to trust the Goddess, but I trusted you instead. Always you. May you both forgive me.

He had loved her for so long. She had given him his life, shared all with him, filling him with joy and beauty, but without her, his continuance was an empty mocking thing. He knew that he could not live in such a world without her love.

No matter what happens, you are loved, Richard.

That was the true meaning of his vision. It was meant to prepare him to go on regardless. It was enough for a small boy, but not so for the man. Not after all this.

He knew exactly what he had to do.

The easternmost clouds suddenly broke apart, and hammerlike, the sun struck the land. Where the burning light pierced through the trees to heat the earth, patches of mist rose like ghosts. She-Who-Walks gasped and hurried faster. Richard stumbled as the glare blinded him.

They made it to the shade of the cabin, hobbled inside, weak and blinking in its dark shelter. He kicked the door shut, shuffled his way to the bed, and gently laid Sabra's body there, pulling a blanket up to her chin.

He would not cover her face. Distorted as it was, he could not bear to perform that finality just yet.

She-Who-Walks put her own burdens on the table, then sat right on the floor, breathing hard. Her exposed skin was red and blotched from the sun.

"It hurts," she said, staring at her hands, then gingerly touched her face.

"You'll be better in a few minutes. Next time wrap up." He bent low and kissed Sabra's lips. They were cold. The shell was empty; her soul was gone, truly gone.

He turned from her and went to the table, picking up the Grail. He dropped on one knee to be level with She-Who-Walks and held the cup between them.

"*Why?*" he demanded.

Her dark eyes were blank.

"It renewed me, tamed my beast, healed me. Why did it kill her? Why did I live? Why did she die?"

"Dark father, I do not *know*. She could not tell me everything."

He had to work to master his frustration, for she spoke the truth. How could Sabra with more than a thousand years of knowledge even begin to impart it to this young girl in the space of one short lifetime?

She-Who-Walks hesitantly reached out, caressing his face. "Perhaps it was because you were not so far along as she."

He caught her hand, turning his head enough to kiss her palm. "Perhaps. I drank of the water, but not from the cup itself. Maybe that was it."

They slumped toward one another, foreheads touching, sharing the grief for a long moment.

"Do you love me?" he asked.

"Yes."

"Then I am sorry."

"For what?"

"For what I shall ask of you." He stood and drew her to her feet. She looked hard at him, confused—until he put the Grail down and picked up the stake instead.

She shrank away. "No, I cannot!"

He held fast to one of her arms and forced it roughly into her grasp. "You will."

She broke from him and retreated to the shadows against the far wall, throwing the stake down. "I cannot. The mother made me promise!"

"The mother is dead!"

"But you—"

"I will not live without her."

"But how will I live without you?" Her eyes glittered with tears. "I am a child to this life; you are my maker, would you abandon me?"

"You have a family, a village full of friends to care for you and to be cared for in turn. They will teach you more of life than I can. Mine is over. All I had, all I ever had was Sabra. It's over now. If you won't release me I'll find someone who will, or I'll sit in the sun until it burns me to the bone and you have to kill me out of pity to take away the pain."

"*No!*" She turned to the wall, sobbing.

"Yes," he whispered, and went to the door. The porch and steps faced west. All he need do was go around to its east face, sit, and wait. It was a hellish thing he was asking of the girl, but when she got the worst of it out of her system and was too listless with exhaustion to think, he would persuade her. In a few hours, the burns would turn him into something she could more readily kill.

He opened the door, but She-Who-Walks sprang forward, leaning her weight on it. He snarled and pushed her back.

"*Richard.*"

He froze.

"I would not have thee do her harm."

Her voice. It stopped his heart.

"You have done well, as has your daughter. Do not quarrel about death."

He turned.

Sabra was by the table, holding the cup in her hands.

Hands. No longer twisted claws. Her body was straight again, unblemished, her long brown hair fell shining over her bare shoulders and down her back. Her face—restored, beautiful, glowing, eyes bright and clear and loving.

He went to her, fell on his knees before her. He pressed his head against her white belly, holding her while she stroked his hair.

"The Grail has indeed saved me, my lover, my son, my best of all friends."

Tears sheeted his eyes, clogged his throat. He held her the more tightly.

"Be gentle, my Richard. I am not as I was. The world has turned for me."

"My world is restored," he said, voice husky.

"Changed," she gently corrected.

He looked up, trying to understand her.

"You will see." She gradually pulled from his grasp and went to the door, opened it, and, still carrying the Grail, went outside.

He unsteadily followed and She-Who-Walks as well to stand next to him in the shade.

He watched in horror as Sabra stepped naked into the full force of the morning sun. He started after her, but she held one hand up to stay him, smiling that wonderful smile, so full of joy and love and life.

"My time in the darkness is over. The world has changed for us. A new one begins this day."

She-Who-Walks whispered in his ear, pointing. "The gateway, Father. From this world to the other."

A last pale curtain of rain still fell just to the west. The sunlight caught its veil and a rainbow, perfect in color and shape formed, arching from one side of the sky to the other. A second one appeared within it, then a third. They formed a vast frame for the roiling clouds behind them. Richard drew a sharp breath. Within their shifting forms he saw a face, a woman's face, beautiful, serene, smiling down. It was there clear and solid but a moment, then gone, and he was ready to doubt his eyes. He glanced at She-Who-Walks. Her expression was that of exultation and wonderment. She'd seen it, too.

Standing beneath the rainbows, Sabra raised up the Grail, offering it to the sky. Her head thrown back in joy, she began to sing one of the old songs in the old tongue. Sweet and swift, her strong voice rose to greet the day.

The shimmering fires above her dipped, engulfing her, and she laughed at their touch, spinning in a wide, earthwise circle. Arms high and head thrown back in wild elation, she danced before them in the light.

In the small clearing in the forest, the light also touched on the prone body of Charon. A small smile crept across his face as some memory of dozing in the sunshine came to him, and he rolled comfortably onto one side, content with his dream.

Then he was aware of pain, a great deal of it. His arm, his face, and a heavy ache in his chest. His one eye fluttered open, and he gasped from the effort of it.

The sun! Jesus palomino, get out of the sun, you jerk!

He staggered to his feet. There was running water at his back and the circle before him. He started to cross it, but an invisible *something* slammed him back, almost into the deadly stream.

What the hell? More of Lance's goddess crap?

Charon decided not to test it. He needed shade before the real frying started.

He edged around the circle and ran.

Tired. He was really, really tired. Puffing like a whale. Weak. That shit-for-brains jock and his new girlfriend had done one hell of a number on him. Charon's run changed to a weary, stumbling walk and finally stopped altogether when he reached the protective shade of the forest.

Leaning on a tree, trying to catch his breath, he took stock of himself. He'd healed a bit. Still couldn't see from one eye and it hurt like hell. His chest had recovered some, else his heart wouldn't be giving him such fits. His arm, well, he just wouldn't use it for a couple of hours. Be hell to pay trying to pilot the boat to get off the island again, but he'd manage. Maybe he could hypnotize one of the locals as he'd done the old shaman to keep him from spilling the beans to Lance . . .

Charon looked at his hands. They should have been cherry-red in reaction, itching so bad as to burn. He'd been out in the sun long enough to bring on a bad spell of it.

But his skin . . . his skin was not burning.

No, no, its just a fluke.

The longer he thought about it, the less he liked it. There might be something seriously wrong here. He had to be sure, and there was only one way to find out.

He stepped back into the full strong sunlight and waited.

Nothing. He shaded his eyes and squinted up at the golden life-giving orb. He could not look directly at it, no one could, but he should *not* have been able to get away with this.

He stared in wonder, then amazement, and finally horror at his unharmed skin.

Then, he *knew*.

"Oh, no. Oh, no. *NO-NO-NO-NO-NOOOOOOOO!*"